GRIM EXPECTATIONS

"This is the real thing – a mad inventor, curious coins, murky London alleys and windblown Scottish Isles... A wild and extravagant plot that turns up new mysteries with each succeeding page."
James P Blaylock, a ̄ ̄ ̄ ̄ ̄ ̄*unculus*
and Under Londo ̄ ̄

"A skillfully handl ̄ ̄ ̄ ̄ ̄ ̄ ̄ ̄ ̄ ̄ ̄nd agreeably witty adve ̄ ̄ ̄ ̄
Kirkus Reviews

"Jeter's sequel, too long delayed, proves well worth the wait, and sets a new high bar for that ever-evolving style of speculative fiction whose Frankensteinian form he first galvanically jolted into life."
Locus

"*Fiendish Schemes* is a darkly humored portrayal of Victorian London written in the style of the period and is not for the faint of heart."
Historical Novel Society

"*Infernal Devices* is a ripsnorting, grandly comical Victorian-era potboiler that is far more entertaining than the most recent Indiana Jones movie; indeed it is more exciting than any big budget Hollywood blockbuster that I have seen in the past five years. It's full of crazy, clockwork automatons, cliffhanger chapter endings, sinister conspiracies, and gloriously impossible super-science. It is a book which will transport you to another reality."
Tetsuo Broker

"Jeter's vision of a Victorian world transformed by steam power is fascinating and funny, populated by ambulatory lighthouses, grain-disdaining meatpunks, anarchist coalpunks, and depraved 'fex' addicts obsessed with 'valve girls'. He thoroughly entertains readers with brilliant speculation and a charmingly reluctant hero."
Publishers Weekly, starred review

K W JETER

GRIM
EXPECTATIONS

The George Dower Trilogy
Vol 3

ANGRY
ROBOT

ANGRY ROBOT
An imprint of Watkins Media Ltd

20 Fletcher Gate,
Nottingham,
NG1 2FZ
UK

angryrobotbooks.com
twitter.com/angryrobotbooks
Cogs and wheels

An Angry Robot paperback original 2017

Cover by John Coulthart
Set in Meridien and Modern No 20 by Epub Services

Distributed in the United States by Penguin Random House, Inc., New York.

ISBN 978 0 85766 691 8
Ebook ISBN 978 0 85766 692 5

Printed in the United States of America

9 8 7 6 5 4 3 2 1

To my good friends
Fred and Allison Sobotka,
with many thanks

Lo, this only have I found, that God hath made men upright; but they have sought out many inventions.

ECCLESIASTES 7:29

PART ONE

The Death of All Held Dear

ONE

A Funeral Goes Badly Wrong

OFTEN HAVE I thought that undertakers are the happiest of men.

The opportunity to endure one's life over again is a dire prospect; but were it to happen, I might well choose the mortuarial trade, in preference to that which I inherited. My father animated that which had been inert, cogged brass and ribboned spirals of baser metal; that I might lay the once-alive into their coffins and then to mouldy earth, would complete the Ouroboric circle he and I shared.

"Mr Dower…" A voice, dark in timbre, spoke close to my ear. "Everything is to your satisfaction, I trust?"

The man seemed born to follow behind crêpe-decked hearses, skeletal fingers reverently spidered tip-to-tip; the very caricature of his calling – such was the one who, bending forward in the church aisle, peered at me.

My words knotted in my throat. *She is dead, you heartless mummering bastard* – unspoken, but cried out in silence. How *satisfied* was I expected to be?

"All is quite…" My own hands clenched to fists in my lap, where they had been folded atop my frayed gloves. "Pleasing." Life-long cowardice overwhelmed the newly minted rage and grief in my heart. "Your concern, and your services, are appreciated."

He smiled – thus again my conviction as to the cheer of undertakers. Who else smiles at funerals? That which marches toward us, however we avert our eyes and thoughts, its measured tread inevitable and invincible – to that corvine breed it is equally certain, but heart-lifting as the clatter of coins dropped in a merchant's cashbox.

Of course, I hated the man.

And I might even have demonstrated as much – at last – despite the reserve characteristic of our English breed. The scent of him summoned my gorge into my throat; as this person's kind was wont to do, an attempt had been made to mask the acrid scent of those embalming fluids which had over time seeped into his greying flesh, with that musty lavender reminiscent of old ladies' parlours. Better had he not; the combination of chemical and ancient flower was nearly as appalling, or perhaps even more so, than his obsequious manner. If I had brought my whitened knuckles hard upon his invasive nose, the blow might have been launched by not just anger, but the need to draw an unencumbered breath into my lungs.

The appearance of an angel, bobbing just beyond the other's hunched shoulders, forestalled such an attack.

Cherub, technically; I knew that much. The lack of Christian instruction in my long-fled youth was filled instead by acquaintance with the paintings of those old masters viewed in museum galleries. Often have I gazed upon scenes of saints and their Saviour, and noted the depiction about them of fluttering, chubbish creatures much like that which now hovered closer by.

"Wondrous little thing, is it not?" Pride sounded in the undertaker's voice, as he glanced behind and above himself, eyes avidly gleaming at that which I had just spotted. "I do hope you find them to your liking, Mr Dower; they are but recently acquired. This occasion – and a very sorry one it is, I assure you – is their, shall we say, *inaugural* flight."

I was not as entranced by the device as he was; if he had set out to prod me toward either murder or suicide, he could not have more efficiently done so.

"Indeed. It is... distinctive." Of course, I could scarcely have said that such an apparition was unprecedented in my experience. The curse that had seemingly been laid upon me in the cradle was that in manhood I would encounter a dismayingly numerous assortment of machinery, the clacking gears of which propelled their aping of human form and motion – or angelic, as in this particular case. Glass eyes have peered into mine, as if they could see as well as those of fleshly creatures; steel-hinged jaws have parted and clapped together again, the leathery bellows in the chests below forcing air past throats strung with violin-gut, emitting words which I must admit were often wiser than mine. Thus our contrivances surpass our own, weaker kind; I take some sullen comfort in the awareness that my encounters along these lines were but the forewarning of that general misery which all Mankind might suffer beneath someday.

The seraphic construction bumped against the side of the undertaker's head, as though seeking a kiss upon its painted lips. He drew back, the better to regard the softly ticking thing, allowing it to drift closer to me. I brought my hand up, to bat it away–

"Take care," spoke another voice. "My understanding is that the dear little thing is somewhat fragile."

I turned about in the pew and found myself gazing into a narrow, boyish face. The Anglican collar below confirmed that the village priest had sat down next to me.

"My pardon–" I made my reply as stiffly as possible. Why clergymen seek to interrupt one's obvious grieving with their fatuous chatter is a matter beyond my comprehension.

"There wouldn't be some other duty to which you should be attending, would there?"

He ignored my suggestion, his gaze drifting toward some unseen prospect.

"There is, one must admit, some cleverness about them." A larger and altogether plumper specimen of the pinkly glistening cherubim floated into his purview, as a billowing cloud might grace that horizon on which his attention was fastened. "I looked a bit into the enterprise – well, actually, there was an article in the *Times* about it. Perhaps a few imparted details would divert your thoughts from their present melancholy course."

"Those thoughts, I assure you, are exactly where I wish them to be." That my interlocutor was not, I attempted to convey by an awkward shifting about of my body, as though the confines of the hard-slabbed pew were pressing cruelly against its occupant's bones. "If you would be so kind…"

"We live in an astonishing age–" The Reverend Weebsome – for that was his name; proximity summoned it from the recesses of memory – pressed on. "I am sure you would agree about that."

"To be astonished about this age, I would first need to care about it." One of the cherubs, with its simpering smile, floated closer to my face; I swatted it away with the back of my hand. "Such is not the case."

This sour comment prompted a glance from my unwanted companion, away from me and toward the coffin supported on rude wooden trestles between the pews and the church's altar. The unadorned wood planks of that box, containing the silent deceased, was a reflection of not just the meagre state of my pocketbook, but as well my disdain for pointless show – even if I might have been able to withstand the expense of a grander and more ornate casket, I would likely have foregone its purchase. The village undertaker might have been hopeful of such, but in this he was fated to disappointment. Having despaired of profitable conversation with a grieving widower such as myself, he had retreated to a vestibule at the farther side of the rustic chapel, from which point he busied himself setting aloft more of the pre-pubescent mechanical angels. The effect perceived was very much similar to that afforded by one of those itinerant carnivals, which advertise their presence in the rural countryside by releasing colourful paper balloons to the sky, their elevation made possible from the heat of an ignited ball of pitch dangling beneath, and only occasionally setting afire a hayrick or thatched-roof cottage when descending at last to the ground.

"Of course…" The reverend scarcely allowed my grumbling to interfere with his continued reflections. "These devices do seem to appeal to a regrettably common taste, which is a bit less seemly than what the Church of England might wish to encourage among the parishioners. But then, a mawkish sentimentality has always been a characteristic of the lower classes…" He directed a thin, conspiratorial smile toward me. "I'm sure you have observed as much, Mr Dower."

Before I could reply, Weebsome lifted his hand and prodded a fingertip against the pinkly rounded belly of one of the devices drifting just above his head.

"But then," he mused, "why would God have made such ingenious creatures of us, if He did not intend for us to make use of those gifts?"

"This deity of whom you speak…" Against my own will, I rose to the bait of this discourse. "If it indeed exists, also made us remarkably skilled at assassination and general mendacity. You might as well say that we were designed to be lying, thieving bastards, and we have done a fine job of proving ourselves as such."

My blasphemy seemed to disturb the man as little as did

my general gloomy irritability. Perhaps he was starved for conversation – he possessed some obvious refinement and education, ill-suited for his clerical posting upon the bleak Cornish coast. I had overheard a few of the natives remark, with either derision or superstitious dread, upon his habit of wandering about with his sharp-pointed nose stuck in – of all things! – a book.

"I hope you don't mind," Weebsome continued, "if I tell you a little of how they came to be?" By now, the space confined by the church's buckling ceiling was thronged with an airy flotilla of the infantile angels, propelled in wandering course by the flutter of the mainspring-driven wings mounted on their naked backs. "You especially might find it of interest."

"This is the second time you have indicated a desire to impart such information. Short of physical violence, I see no way of dissuading you."

"An Irish cleric once achieved a small measure of scandal with a proposal for alleviating the immemorial poverty in that dankly miserable land." Reverend Weebsome launched into his exposition. "Perhaps you might even have stumbled upon it, in those journals of which you are most fond."

"I read little for pleasure," was my comment, "and even less for enlightenment."

"Not altogether a foolish course to pursue, Mr Dower – the author was by all accounts a scurrilous and mocking fellow. He advanced the proposal – the satirical intent of which was not so obvious, that everyone was able to perceive it – that the surfeit of the Irish population, and their consequent general destitution, could be mitigated by regarding their infants rather more as comestibles than as children."

"Indeed. I have heard something of this sort before. The supposed humour escapes me."

"As for many, I assure you. This fellow accomplished little but to make himself even less esteemed than before – but that was perhaps what he had desired all along. Humanity has among its numbers more than a few who strive for their fellow man's disdain."

"How they must envy me, then." Not for the first time did I make this observation. "I have managed to achieve a great deal along those lines, with hardly any effort expended at all."

"You flatter yourself, Mr Dower, if you fancy this Irish dean was less reviled than yourself. Much of this particular writing I mention was given over to the supposed succulence of Irish infants, and recommendations as to the most appetizing ways to prepare the dishes containing them. I fear this is where the bounds of good taste were exceeded; whatever propensity for cannibalism there is among the educated English public, it would likely be, as with so many of our other vices, one that is enjoyed discreetly."

"No doubt," I said. "Our aristocracy has had centuries to cultivate the loathsomeness of its eccentricities. But I fail to see the subject's relevance to our present situation."

Which had become perceptibly more dire, even as we had conversed. The undertaker had taken his responsibilities to what seemed a maniacal level – from the narrow alcove in which he had stationed himself, increasing aerial phalanxes of those damnable clockwork cherubs had taken flight. The sombrely dressed figure had another brass-bound chest behind him, adorned with bills of lading from a London commercial shipping firm, which I had failed to discern before. With its lid flung back, he rummaged through the fibrous wood wool, extracting ever more of the winged figures; possessed of some innate buoyancy, they seemed to almost leap upward from their confinement, so that all he needed to do was wind the machinery at their backs, then turn about and release them, as a pigeon fancier might with his homing flock.

The result hung ominously close above our heads. It is one thing to see a few, or even a dozen or so, artificial cherubim fluttering around – but altogether quite a more dismaying phenomenon to witness the closely massed ranks roiling above us now. An observer of a more credulous and spiritual disposition might well have supposed that war had commenced in the nursery division of Heaven, its inhabitants butting each other head to naked bum, fixedly smiling and simpering as they squabbled for primacy against the ceiling.

I was not their only observer – in the church's doorway were clustered a number of the local villagers, who had come here not out of any respect for myself or the deceased, but in the expectation of those alcoholic spirits which were by tradition dispensed at christenings and funerals. They scarcely seemed in need of such infusion; the gaping mouths and blinking confusion in their upturned faces, as they goggled at the minuscule angels, signalled that they credited this apparition more to their own drunkenness than to divine intervention in their affairs. At their back stood two sturdier individuals, shovels in hand and clothes daubed with damp clay and muck, having freshly returned from digging the appropriate hole in the graveyard next the church. A bit more sober, having spent their time labouring rather than drinking, they observed all that was happening with some degree of skeptical disdain, complete with whispered comments in each other's ear, and subsequent guffawing laughter.

"There is admittedly a slight connection," riposted the Reverend Weebsome, "but a true one, nevertheless. The Irish cleric might well have been jesting when he wrote of stewing and fricasseeing the children of the wretched poor – but they exist in fact, do they not?"

"Ever so," I allowed. "But it is my own wretched poverty that has been the greatest concern throughout my life. And as such, it has left little time to reflect upon others' hardships."

"As it has been wisely written, Mr Dower, *The poor are always with us*. The corollary being that their deceased infants are as well – so if one wishes to search out dead babies, one needn't travel as far as Ireland; we have enough of them close at hand."

"I little doubt it. Your reminding me of that dismal fact, at a moment when others might well have left me to my private mourning, gives rise to some concern about the propriety of your interest in these matters."

"Be that as it may." The Reverend Weebsome indicated little response to my chiding comment; settling back into the pew, he increased his comfort and lessened my own, as he continued in the mode of a Sunday afternoon lecturer at some posh London gallery. "Often before, it had been noted by persons of a certain – shall we say? – *necrophiliac* curiosity, that unembalmed corpses delayed from burial, either by neglect or intent, would take on grossly distended proportions due to the gaseous vapours produced in their decomposition." The individual sitting beside me took an unseemly relish in expanding upon these details. "Stories of ghastly explosions were commonly bruited about, the abdomens of the deceased splitting asunder and releasing a nauseating stench. If a candle had been left flickering nearby, even worse might be the case, with the fumes igniting in a ball of flame sufficient to throw bystanders upon their backs, denuded of eyebrows and any other facial hair."

"Good God, man." Even more appalled than before, I shrank back from him. "At a time such as this, do you really think–"

I had scarce enough time to voice that much objection, before the reverend pressed on with his obsessions. While he had been speaking, a greater number of the rustic onlookers had entered into the church, the better to gape open-mouthed at the throng of tiny mechanical angels above their heads. So little happens in these remote parts of the British Isles, each day being but a soggy reminder of those gone before, that any novelty at all evokes a stupefying fascination in its observers – and certainly these cherubim with ticking, fluttering wings were more than sufficient in that regard.

"A merciful Providence," continued Weebsome, "had always before ensured that the sour emissions of the dead were not sufficiently buoyant to lift them bodily into the air, while still pent within their frames; any such mounting toward the heavens would still await the end times promised to the faithful. That changed, as so much does, with the unforeseen import upon our island's shores of novel creatures from foreign lands, as the black plague is thought by learned doctors to have been introduced to Europe by rats swarming down the hawsers that tethered merchant vessels in those northern harbours, holds filled with silks and tea from sultry Asian latitudes. The fleas in the vermin's fur held the pestilence in their minute forms, scarcely bigger than black poppy-seeds; how great a consequence from such tiny specks!"

I was distracted by the jostling bodies surrounding us. There seemed so many of them, all possessed of an excitement increased in no small degree by the liquors which they had already consumed, that I was concerned that in their agitation they might topple over the trestle-mounted coffin of which I had lost sight. As I rose from the pew, to ascertain if such were the case, the Reverend Weebsome was bold enough to seize me by the arm and drag me back down next to him.

"Or so it is maintained by the accounts I have read." Weebsome nodded slowly, as though savouring each word. "Imagine the consternation that must have been aroused, when our own English dead began swelling up, then rising bodily into the air. Tongues must have been wagging a great deal."

"This is the first I have heard of any such thing." Shifting about, I had succeeded in peering between the close-pressed bodies and catching a glimpse of the casket, for the moment still secure in its position. "Perhaps this was not a true history that you came across, but a fiction of the sort scribbled out at a penny per word or less, by those wretches whose disordered imaginations are their sole way of wresting a living from their fellow men."

"No one could make up such fantasies, Mr Dower – for they are not fantasies, but have the ring of veracity about them. And here you have the proof before your very eyes!" Without releasing his grip upon my arm, with his free hand he jabbed a finger toward the ceiling – or rather, to the bobbing cherubim who were now several pink layers deep, obscuring the ancient, bowed rafters. "For you behold the point where entrepreneurial minds ally themselves with modern science. The mystery of those levitating corpses was dispelled by research, which indicated that the unstoppable engines of global commerce had brought this upon us."

"Perhaps..." I essayed a weak jest, as I futilely attempted to escape from him. "Perhaps then, it would have been better for us to have stayed at home, and tended our own familiar gardens."

"Too late for that!" His formerly mild demeanour was now completely extinct, replaced by that furious enthusiasm for all things new, which I had observed so many times before in those besotted with what they term the Future. "Those microbes and other tiny organisms, too small to be seen with the naked eye, which feasted on British corpses before – they were but puny things compared to those who have now arrived amongst us. All those legends and travellers' tales brought back from India, of Hindoo mystics levitating at the topmost end of a vertical rope, while all the marketplace stands amazed – easily explained once it is grasped that the airborne form was not that of a *living* man, but a *dead* one tethered to prevent its escape upon the winds."

The clergyman's words made me consider, not for the first time, of how great a mercy it was to live on this beleaguered island, rather than some even more Godforsaken region. For indeed I had heard those scarcely credible stories, predating the Venetian wanderer Marco Polo, of auto-inflated corpses rising from funeral pyres before the torches could be set to the dry tinder beneath, or the discovery in mausoleums set in verdant jungles, of recently deceased royalty bobbing about the stone ceilings like Montgolfier balloons – now those tales seemed to have come true for us as well. That such things were now happening here, whether we wished them to or not, seemed but one more instance of the world imposing its hulking, unlovely self upon us.

"I anticipate what more you wish to tell me." I spoke, rising from my own dark meditations. "Some person – a man of business, possessed of more cleverness than forbearance – perceived what use could be made of these newly elevating corpses – or at least those of the deceased infants."

"Exactly so. From the accounts that have come to my notice, it seems that the general public had a less than enthusiastic response to the spectacle of adults whose souls had passed over to the other side – as some politely describe the transformation that awaits us all – however artfully done up as angels, complete with beating wings. Apparently, many regarded the effect as being somewhat – shall we say? – macabre."

"*Shall we say*, indeed." Over the mounting hubbub of the crowd inside the church, I expressed my assent with this reported opinion – remarkable for being one of the rare instances in which I had ever agreed with anyone about anything. "You evoke a ghastly vision, Reverend – I have seen more than a few of my fellow human beings who had been deprived of animation, and I cannot think of any of them whose appearance would have been greatly improved with a tin halo dangling over their heads, and mechanical wings ratcheting at their backs, careening above like a flock of bloodied albatrosses."

"Just so," allowed Weebsome. "I personally consider myself fortunate not to have witnessed the sight. But these transfigured infants–" With his index finger, he directed my attention once more to the clumsily bobbing forms above us. "They do seem to possess some eerie charm. I imagine that the great mass of humanity has an innate sympathy for the faces of innocent children, especially those of such tender age as these."

"If so, then such is another difference between myself and others. Thus I have remained childless throughout my unfortunate existence, as much from preference as circumstance."

"A pity, Mr Dower; perhaps the bleakness of your lot would have been lightened by the opportunity of paternal solicitude."

I made no reply, other than the contempt manifested by my narrowing gaze settling upon the man's young and preternaturally foolish visage. The chances of his ever achieving fatherhood, I was confident, were negligible – not so much due to his priestly vocation as to his membership in that brotherhood whispered about since Grecian times, whose communion with the fairer sex was limited to spoken discourse.

"But I digress," continued Weebsome. "Pray forgive any impertinence, while you are in the midst of your sorrows – my remarks were not so intended. My only thought was to perhaps distract you for a moment from the contemplation of your loss."

"I think not." So clamorous had become the jabbering of the voices about us, the villagers stoking each other's excitement to an ever greater pitch, that I was forced to raise my own voice to be heard by the person sitting next to me.

"You merely seized an opportunity to carry on about your own obsessive interests, believing that I would be too polite to check you in that pursuit. Very well; perhaps I have failed to do so. But it is not from any tender regard for your feelings, but rather my disdain for humanity in general. You wish to prattle about dead infants transformed to mechanical angels? Oh, by all means, *do*." My study of the man turned virtually murderous. "No doubt this seems wondrous to one with limited experience of the clanking, grinding world into which mankind has been thrust, but I assure you – I have seen, and grappled with, contrivances of such size and lethal ingenuity as to diminish all these trite marvels that so astonish you, to motes and flyspecks barely worth the notice."

"I am aware, Mr Dower, of your – shall we say? – *unseemly* personal history." The reverend's smile was unsuited to but typical of his clerical profession. "You are a character of some distinction in this remote provincial nook to which you have fled, no doubt to escape the notoriety that would otherwise pursue you like Tisiphone and her chthonic sisters. But in fact you have not eluded the Furies of local gossip; your village neighbours are a tight-lipped breed, not given to conversation with those they consider strangers–"

"Which is something I admire about them." All this learned cant, with its laboured references to ancient myth, told me nothing of which I was not already aware. "They keep to themselves and their immemorial tribe; would that all men did. If while doing so, they also choose to whisper about me behind my back – what concern is that of mine?"

"Seemingly little," answered Weebsome, "by your account. But among my sinful propensities, I freely confess, is that of inordinate curiosity. In that regard, I have made you the subject of my research, aided to the degree that village folk are willing to confide their suspicions and gossip to their local priest – perhaps they seek a fellow conspirator in one who is enjoined, as I am, to forgive as well as listen. I frankly doubt if you are capable of either one of those."

"How utterly insightful of you. You read me like a book, Reverend."

"Be that as it may. But for myself, I brought with me, upon assuming the responsibilities of this parish, some general knowledge of that life and career which you understandably would prefer to have kept hidden. The name of George Dower is connected with some momentous events – wreckage and plunder, devastation on a colossal scale! Great swathes of London reduced to rubble; certainly an impressive achievement, I am certain you would agree."

"Scarcely any of my doing–" Only the passion of my defence allowed my words to be discerned above the clamour of the jabbering, gesticulating mob pressing so closely about us as to rock the pew upon its worn wooden feet. "Your knowledge is sadly deficient, if it fails to disclose that whatever part I played in those notorious happenings, my efforts were directed more to preventing rather than inciting them."

"True; I allow you that, Mr Dower." Once more, he prodded away one of the clacketing winged angels that had bobbed close by his head. "To paraphrase the poet, the good that men do is oft interred, but before that it is somehow transmuted to slander. Just as though we were all some sort of misguided alchemists, who had stumbled upon the knack of turning gold to lead, rather than the reverse. Ah, well; human nature is a pit of infamy, is it not?" He spoke blithely, as one might describe a rose bush's spotted leaves. "We are all sinners – if it were otherwise, I would very likely be unemployed."

"Always have I found it to be so." That much I had in agreement with him. "On many–"

I was prevented from completing the sentence. Once more, as so often in my life, incendiary chaos erupted.

The screams of hysterical women had the salutary effect

of interrupting my increasingly irritated conversation with Reverend Weebsome. Equally panicked shouts from male throats, coarsened by pipe and tankard, set the church's close-pent air trembling at my ears. My startled gaze swung around from the clergyman's face; after a mere second or two of eye-widened confusion, I perceived what had happened, and its unravelling consequences.

Weebsome's brushing away of the mechanical cherub nuzzling his brow had been but a simple reflexive action, with no other intent behind it – but by doing so, he had unleashed a good deal more, as one might innocently unlatch a barn door, unaware that maddened stallions, muzzles flecked with foam, pressed behind.

Something had malfunctioned with the clockwork wings attached behind the naked shoulder blades of the particular cherub – I recognized it by the unnaturally prominent blush upon its rounded cheeks. Perhaps the reverend's insignificant blow had triggered an already existing flaw in the aerial machinery; whatever the cause, the result was that of the cherub veering at an unprecedented velocity down toward the church's altar, past the coffin laid upon its wooden trestles.

"'S truth! Bluidy thing be p'ssessed!" That had been the cry of one of the onlookers, falling backward from both inebriation and a more sensible desire to put as much distance between himself and this new apparition. "*Day*-mons 'n' sich!"

No doubt the New Testament account of the Gadarene swine and their careening rush toward the cliff's edge was uppermost in the minds of at least a few of the closely assembled onlookers. The rosy pinkness of the cherubs' ceramic shells, encasing the slowly decaying flesh within and the levitating gasses thereby produced, was indeed similar in hue to that of those familiar barnyard animals. The completely understandable desire to not be trampled by demonic pigs was perhaps triggered by the sight of this singular cherub crashing into one of the brass candlesticks upon the altar, with enough force not only to topple the light, but crack itself open like an egg upon the upturned edge of the candlestick's base. Further disaster might not have ensued, had the candle-flame not come into direct proximity with the cherub's ruptured form; however, that being the case, it quickly became apparent that the gasses generated within not only had sufficient levity to bring this small weight aloft, but were flammable as well.

The result was indeed impressive, and much remarked upon by the assembled crowd, their previous marvelling clamour now changed to utter hysteria. For the damaged cherub had not exploded, as likely would have resulted if the break in its ceramic casing had been a bit wider; instead, the gas leaking from within had been ignited into a jet of flame nearly a foot in length, searing blue in colour where it was not tinged with yellow at its farther edge. The gas's combustion seemed to have a considerable propulsive force to it, sending the broken cherub on a rapid vertical course, at a rate of speed sufficient to tear the tiny mechanical wings from off its back. The violence of its doing so evoked screams of terror from the village women and a few of the smaller children who had not yet been trampled by the press of their elders; the shouts of the menfolk were considerably coarser in nature, laced with apparent profanities in an otherwise impenetrable Cornish dialect.

If the ascent of the artificial angel had been sufficient to provoke such reaction from the throng of onlookers, little wonder that the quickly subsequent events roused an even stronger response. As I have described before, the low and roughly timbered ceiling of the church was crowded now with a pink armada of the cherubim's naked forms, bobbing against each other, their wings interminably clacking and fluttering, the idiot smiles on their rosily painted faces remaining unaltered.

"God save us," spoke the Reverend Weebsome beside me, the blood draining from his already pale features. "This is–"

Whatever his assessment might have been, I was spared it. I too had craned my head back, spine pressed against the pew's boards behind me, so that with all the rest of humanity's rough specimens close about, I witnessed the impact of the fire-spouting, rocket-like infant, possessed of a greater vitality in this manner than likely it had ever possessed in its brief and sickly mortal life. The gentle bumping and jostling about of the other cherubim had not been of enough force to damage their naked carapaces, but all that changed with the sudden arrival of this one in their midst. Vaulting upward from the altar below, it collided with a few of its mechanical brethren, cracking open the thin shells that had been pasted upon the softer decaying flesh inside. Jagged fragments, as though from shattered tea cups, rained down upon the onlookers' upturned faces – but that was the least of the escalating calamities.

"Flee!" My undesired companion well anticipated what was to come. "Save yourself!" Weebsome leapt to his feet, but was unable to exit the pew, prevented from doing so by the close press of villagers in the church aisle.

His foresight proved accurate. With my gaze angled toward the equally crowded ceiling, I could see that the blue flame still jetted from the aperture in the cherub's form, thus thrusting it with undiminished velocity against the others like it. But their innate gasses, released by the cracks in their brittle abdomens and rounded buttocks, proved to be equally volatile. A few of the cherubim exploded like bombs, with deafening burst and pyrotechnic display; the others were transformed into arcing missiles like the first, fiery tongues of varying dimensions and strength propelling them into the ones beyond.

Those in turn suffered the concussive impact that their predecessors had, and were similarly converted to razoring shards with brilliant fire and billowing smoke at their centres, or shooting infantile figures, striking others of their sort farther on, with predictable impact and transfiguration. A horizontal cascade, ever louder and more glaring in its violence, spread across the ceiling, as though the onlookers were witnessing some apocalyptic battle in the heavens, foretold in the Book of Revelations.

As above, so below; while the villagers had previously been caught in place by their own numbers within the church's narrow confines, and rendered gape-mouthed and stupefied by all that they saw happening above their heads, now they sought escape from what they considered, with some justification, to be their own imminent deaths. The heated debris from the overhead conflagration rained down upon their heads; the flames and continuing explosions were close enough to singe hair and skin. From a number of the cherubs which had been completely vaporized, the fluttering mechanical wings remained relatively intact and went clacking through the smoke-filled air like the giant moths of some Amazonian jungle.

What had been dreadsome apprehension on their part, now turned to mindless panic. The church's doors, barely wide enough to admit one broad-shouldered man at a time, were instantly blocked by and made impassable by those fighting for exit. Thus trapped within, the people were further terrorized by the disintegrating rockets of the cherubim, hurtling down upon them with fire but no swords, the idiot simpering faces aglow with apparent delight at the havoc provoked.

Not for the first time, I witnessed the degree to which individual specimens of humanity can be converted to a conglomerate, witless mass. Rebounding from the blocked doors, the villagers were an ocean wave, comparable to those that capsize ships and send them hurtling to the depths. The pew in which I was trapped now toppled backward; I lost sight of the Reverend Weebsome, as he made an ill-advised attempt to remain standing against the surge of shouting, weeping bodies. I gave no mind to the chances of his surviving their trampling boots, preoccupied as I was with my own safety. Desperation alone drove my clinging to the seat and back of the pew, fingernails dug into the smooth-worn wood; for a few seconds at least, the rude structure served as a barricade against the terrified mob. Then it became rather more of a canoe, as the simple boats of the primitive Americans are termed, being wrenched from its moorings upon the church floor and lifted a considerable distance higher, bearing me with it. From this vantage point I glimpsed the church entire; of Weebsome there was no trace, but I caught sight of the undertaker, trapped in the alcove from which he had sent aloft his mechanical cherubim. The expression upon his elongated face was that of a man horror-struck, his funereal solemnity riven less by the spectacle of the embattled people before him, than by contemplating the loss of the devices upon which he had spent so much, and which he had set aloft from his own hands.

I had little if any time to reflect upon the undertaker's plight. As a swimmer rising upon the highest point of a tidal swell might soon anticipate being tumbled down its face, I looked over my shoulder and saw the church's rear wall quickly approaching. The structure was of whitewashed stone, substantial enough to have withstood centuries of neglect. I could imagine the impressive force of the crowd breaking apart the seams of the wall and tossing my impromptu craft out to the relative safety of the night air and the surrounding mossy loam – but that hope was rendered vain by the certainty of the stones remaining intact and my helpless form, surrounded by the pew's splinters, being crushed like an insect slapped against the plastered wall of one's bedchamber.

Squeezing shut my eyes, as I had before when expecting my doom, I braced myself for an annihilating blow—

To all the din confined by the little rural church, was suddenly added another sound. The shattering of glass has a particular timbre, able to cut above the shouts of men and screams of women – that was what I heard, to a startling degree of loudness. Bracing myself against the back of the tottering pew, I could see another destructive event, illumined by the combined flames of the mechanical cherubim still swarming and diving about. The church's sole ornamentation was a stained-glass window, the funds for which had been donated by a charitable society in London, dedicated to bringing enlightenment to the heathen, Cornish peasants qualifying as such by their standards. Multicoloured leaden glass depicted the region's patron Saint Piran, surrounded by the bear, fox and badger that had been his first disciples, the local human inhabitants having been rather less enthusiastic about adopting Christianity. Or at least the window had depicted such; as I watched, it burst into pieces, the bright shards scattering above the heads of those trapped within the church.

So maddened by terror were the villagers, that it had not occurred to any that smashing the window might have afforded another means of egress; my first surmise upon seeing its demolishment was that some unknown party outside had come to this fortunate conclusion, and acted upon it. Thus it came as a considerable surprise, to witness a small number of able-bodied men fighting their way into the church, climbing over the stone lintel of what had been the stained-glass window and laying about themselves with fist and upraised shovels. The latter instruments of violence confirmed my recognition of the grave-diggers who had earlier come to the door of the church. That these men had some singular purpose in mind was indicated by the accuracy and frequency of the punches they threw into the faces of the crowd, as they drove themselves wedge-like to the area in front of the altar.

The close press of bodies had prevented the coffin from having been toppled over from the trestles upon which it rested. With a shoulder-first push, the grave-diggers managed to surround the simple wooden casket, then hoist it above their heads. Exiting with their prize was more easily accomplished; the crowd, still driven to witless panic by the fiery cherubim diving upon them from above, surged *en masse* to the apparent safety afforded by the star-lit open air visible where the window had been moments before. The grave-diggers, bearing the coffin aloft, needed merely to join with that flow, like swimmers being carried out into the ocean by a retreating tide, and then they were outside with the others.

All this I observed in what seemed like less than a minute – then I was able to observe very little more. Where the pew in which I rode had been caught against the church's farther wall, now it dropped precipitously, being no longer held in place by the formidable strength and number of the maddened crowd. The pew crashed to splinters, among which I lay dazed...

Silence is a soothing balm, particularly when it follows such a riot of screaming and cursing, punctuated by various exploding infants.

I could have remained for a while longer in the battered church, listening to no more than the beating of my heart. A storm had seemed to pass over me, leaving a desolate peace in its wake. Enough cold moonlight angled through the empty window aperture, glinting on the shards of stained glass scattered across the church's floor, that I could make a general assessment of the situation, even as I reluctantly gained full consciousness once more.

"Reverend Weebsome?" I struggled to my feet, brushing away various bits of debris as I gazed about the dim interior.

"Are you still here? Alive?"

No answer came – likely, his corpse was hidden in the wreckage, trampled to a gory state, or charred by the now-extinguished fire that had consumed a good deal of these sacrosanct premises.

My bootsoles crunched upon ceramic fragments, the remains of those small, ignited angels that had wrought such terror. Stumbling outside, I drew the chill and ocean-smelling air deep into my lungs, a subsequent coughing exhalation bringing the taste of smoke and those rotting, flammable gasses onto my tongue.

From the starlit distance came a faint sound of human voices. Lacking any other guide, I directed my steps toward them. At the crest of a mossy rise, slick with saline dew, I glanced over my shoulder and saw the church below, its roof timbers redly smouldering; no doubt there would be nothing but ash and blackened stone remaining when the morning light broke over the scene.

The murmuring voices grew louder, then suddenly ceased as I drew near.

"Oy!" One of the men had evidently spotted me. I saw the forms of three or four of them, silhouetted by the lantern set upon the ground. "There be grieving wid'wer now!"

The remark was inflected with both surprise and some small degree of sympathy.

"Begging yer pardon, sar–" The individual addressed me further. "Would've gun back and rescued you and all, 'cept for being fair certain you was daid already."

"Would that I were." I joined them at the edge of a deep, freshly excavated hole. "I have few ambitions remaining, but that one."

"Suit yerself," spoke one of the others. "Ye've come at good time, though. If there be some proper words to speak, it'd have to be yers to speak 'em, no priest being 'vailable at the moment."

The situation which he described was clarified by the simple expedient of one of the men raising the lantern, so that its flickering beam fell into the hole by which we stood. I saw there, at an appropriate depth, the coffin which had so recently stood before the church's altar.

"How decent of you..." I realized now that I was in the company of those grave-diggers, who I had last witnessed bursting through the stained-glass window and fighting their way through the panicking crowd. "You have saved from desecration all that remains of one who was dear to me."

"'F we did, so be it." The first who had spoken to me now began coiling the ropes by which the coffin had been let down into the earth. "But in truth, weren't so nobly mot'vated. Plain and simple, don't get paid until she be planted. And hole bin already dug, so seemed shame to waste it."

I said no more. I watched dully as the men picked up their shovels and began filling in that cold doorway through which we all must pass someday, the damp clods drumming hollowly upon the casket's nailed lid.

Then I was alone once more, the men nodding their respects to me, then shouldering their tools and departing, the lantern leading their steps along the winding way back to the village.

For a moment longer, I stood in wordless contemplation at the grave's mounded edge. I heard the sound of wings fluttering above me; looking up, I saw against the stars a small form, the last of the mechanical cherubim, having escaped the church's wreckage and now making its way to the rolling, accepting sea.

When all was silent again, I turned myself away from the broken ground, and trod in darkness toward that place where no one waited for me.

TWO

Memories & Mysteries

MY WIFE – for so I thought of her, who had come to share my labours by day and our bedchamber by night – kept secrets from me. This in itself was no secret, for what husband is deluded otherwise? The fairer sex is a tribe of mysteries, and we are happier for leaving them undisturbed.

"Miss McThane; what see you there?"

So I addressed her, when we were in our private moments – which amused her, and invariably elicited a slight smile. I believe that all women, whatever their age and station, enjoy being reminded of those times when they were most innately beautiful, and sly and rascal-like because of their beauty's invocation of men's desires...

Such a wandering discourse reflects the state of my mind upon returning from the graveside of the one I describe above. I found myself sitting upon a punitively straight-backed chair in the parlour of an otherwise uninhabited inn, which had been both shelter and livelihood to myself and my late wife – or companion, however you may prefer; our union was not of the sort blessed by the church. My boots were still muddy from the journey home, burial ground and ruined church in the darkness behind me.

My thoughts circled again to the one I had left there. There had not been time enough for age to rob her of the beauty that was still vivid in memory; she would have been considered by most, and certainly myself, to have still been in her prime when the grey hand of infirmity had struck her down upon her deathbed. How much of a life can be encompassed in so short a span! Had we really two or so years together, before the indulgences of her previous existence caught up with her, like a daggered assassin who treads only a step behind? Measured by a calendar's discarded pages, seemingly so; by the depth rather than length of our private comfort, that time had been greater indeed.

The loss of which left me sensing myself as an old man, in spirit if not in bodily frame. Less than a decade had passed from Miss McThane's first entrance into my affairs, to that of our conjoined escape here to Cornwall. Of that intervening time, she had been far from my presence – though admittedly still close in my thoughts, as one might recall a lightning-filled storm that rages for a night, then leaves a dull and prosaic peace in all the subsequent days. That our brief domestic idyll had followed even more calamitous events – such might only indicate that her fiery passions had been tamped by the first awareness of her own mortality…

Now that I was alone – utterly – I wished that I felt my own approaching.

I admit that in the not too distant past, I had embraced a suicidal frame of mine. But to pursue one's own destruction requires at least a residual measure of vigour, and my heart was too battered for that final energy to be summoned. Perhaps in the morning I would feel better, and I could kill myself then.

From these dark thoughts I was diverted, to the degree such was possible, by the singular object that sat upon my lap, its dimensions framed by my clammy hands–

A ticking box.

Others might have had some concern that the device was some sort of bomb; such is the world in which we have come to live, that anything of unknown purpose can be surmised to be of lethal intent.

The item had been constructed of some smooth-grained exotic wood, perhaps mahogany, geometrically inlaid with thin intarsia strips of what I took to be macassar ebony. The box overall possessed a square form, a few inches deep, its length and width perhaps a little less than a foot or so. On that side touched by my fingertips were silvery hinges, somewhat tarnished, chased with an intricate engraved pattern. On the side facing my chest was a hasp and lock of the same metal. Any attempt to disengage the lock, thus enabling me to throw back the ornate lid and reveal the box's contents, was frustrated not so much by my lack of that key which would fit it, but even more so by the apparent absence of any keyhole upon the lock's small face. Its operation then, as with so many singular devices I have encountered, remained a mystery to me.

Grey morning light seeped through the inn's tatty curtains as I pondered the matter, my thoughts seemingly prodded along by the soft, persistent ticking of whatever mechanism, of whatever purpose, was concealed in that which I held.

"It is nothing." I spoke aloud, my words listened to by no one save myself. "Either be rid of the thing – the ocean is near at hand, and has received larger than this in its depths – or break it open by brute force, and satisfy yourself as to what it holds."

My reluctance to do either was occasioned by the thought of how the mysterious box had come into my possession. For it had been given to me by my late wife.

Her last gift, and the last act she had done. I had discovered it resting upon her breast, as she lay motionless on her deathbed but a few nights ago. I had been absent from her side for only a moment, but when I had returned to the chamber, I saw that the closet door was open, though I knew it had been shut for days. As well, a number of its contents had been scattered across the floor nearby, as though someone had been rummaging in haste through the closet's furthest reaches. Some extraordinary passion had driven her, in that weakened state, to crawl out of the bed and across the chamber, pull open the door and fetch out the object – never seen by me before – that I found clutched to her breast.

She was gone now, buried; thus was left the box, to ponder. Had Miss McThane wanted me to have it? As remembrance or incumbrance – which? No doubt there was some trick to opening the box, that she had known – but she had left it closed, for me to find where her chilling hands clutched it against her bosom.

The box stopped ticking. An ominous silence filled the parlour in which I sat.

I felt the hair prickling upright along my arms and neck. My unease increased as I sat trapped by the object on my lap.

Its lid opened.

With a caution that is both innate and bitterly learned, I placed a fingertip beneath the lid and lifted upward, the hinges behind making no protest as I revealed the box's contents.

I beheld sheets of paper, of various dimensions and condition; not printed or legal documents, but hand-scripted correspondence. Some of the pages, folded together, appeared to contain expositions of some length; others were but scraps with torn edges. I recognized my writing on none of them.

What widower would not stay his hand, and consider it a wiser choice to light a fire upon the grate, and toss a box such as this thereon, leaving all that it held still unread? She kept secrets – fine, so be it; all women do. To discover this evidence convinced me of nothing which I did not already know. But why had she made it her final act in this world, to make sure that I would discover them in this way? I could not credit any desire of hers to drive a knife through my heart – she might have been mischievous by nature, but never cruel.

I still held the opened and now silent box upon my lap; in regard to its workings, I expected little more. So when a further discovery was afforded me, it was by way of that which lay beyond the box.

As I had sat, darkly musing, the parlour itself had lightened, the sun mounting high enough for its rays to break over the crest of the surrounding hills. One bright, near-horizontal beam pierced the tattered curtain of the window behind me, falling upon the inside of that lid I had tilted back with my finger.

A brass plate was there, elegantly engraved, no doubt by the clever hand of he who had crafted the box and its mechanisms. A date was given, of the device's manufacturing, and below that, the place where it had been done: *Clerkenwell*, a London district with which I am more than familiar, having once been the proprietor of a watchmaker's shop therein.

Then finally, the incised signature of the box's fashioner–

Which was – how could I ever have expected otherwise! – that of my father.

I set both my hands upon the lid of the box and pressed it close, not caring whether its lock might engage once more, preventing my inquiry into those pages it held. For I knew, with sinking heart, that one more dire chapter in my own fate had been unsealed thereby.

We imagine our sins are such that all the world knows of them. That we are Napoleons and Caesars and Alexanders of black deed and destruction, much talked about – it seems rather a shame otherwise, to have ruined a life as certainly as I have my own, and not gotten at least a thrill of gossip from the endeavour.

I did not start out by seeking for as much disdain, little or small, as I have earned. I would rather have preferred to remain anonymous as the great run of men, or perhaps a little less – when one is in trade, as I had hoped to be when setting out upon my life's course, a bit of notice is desired; one has no customers otherwise. I had inherited a few such from my father, as well as all the stock of mechanical devices in the shop that had first been his. I little realized then how much else was my inheritance from him, and how undesirable the bulk of it, for someone desiring a quiet, modest life.

Be that as it may. My adulthood preceded his demise by only a few years; I assumed my legacy with perhaps a vague notion that among all the ticking, whirling contrivances that had been his creations – the least of which had been the watches and clocks, which admittedly kept excellent time, due to a patented improvement in the escape wheel's configuration – there I might find some trace of him, a key to his personal nature that I might recognize in my own.

I did not. What I discovered was that the elder Dower had been both a genius and a madman – neither of which I am, though the world has taken its best shot at maddening me.

Thankfully, my own fumbling inadequacies with all things mechanical kept me from outright villainy, though they did little to prevent my enmeshment in all manner of frightful schemes. Thus I made the acquaintance of Miss McThane and her then-consort and fellow conspirators. There would have been no possibility of my foreseeing that one day she would become dear to me; when the destruction of this world had been averted by means of an improbable congress between the two of us, I had little expected – or desired – to ever see her again.

But see her I did, and in the midst of even more wickedness occasioned by my father's legacy, and my own connection to those devices. After the culmination of *l'affaire Bendray*, there might have been some hope of retiring into anonymity, free from surrounding humanity's speculation and gossip. But subsequent events into which I was swept, propelled by both my own impecunious state and the machinations – how suitable a word! – of that loathsome woman Mrs Fletcher, who was less woman and more a terrifying engine of ambition – literally so – when I encountered her, put a stop to any such vain chance. Scarcely can one be involved in the destruction of a good deal of London, with the reduction of much of the Houses of Parliament to smoking rubble alongside the Thames, and expect to be spared public notice.

If I am responsible for that, to even the smallest degree, I scourge myself more for it than any of the precedent death and destruction. To the extent that it resulted in my lingering disrepute, such that busybodies as the possibly late Reverend Weebsome could amuse themselves by ferreting out my past – then perhaps I deserve that lash and burden.

"Very well, George; you see your father's name. You have seen it many times before. Why such trepidation now?"

Reader, I have indicated above some of the bitter reflections that were spurred by the sight of that name, my parent and inventive deviser of the box which was seemingly the last gift from my heart's companion – if gift it was, rather than some elabourate curse. For I had seen the name attached to more fearsome devices than this, great clanking machines of intimidating power.

A mystery, though, was dispelled by the recognition of my father as the box's creator. I had learned, in the course of my lifelong trials, that various of my father's machines had their chief functions based upon the subtle principle of sympathetic vibrations. Many have had occasion to see this phenomenon illustrated by the string of a violin trembling of its own accord, in response to another at a slight distance, playing a note of the exact same pitch. Where my father's genius had excelled, among other areas, was in applying this principle to vibrations more ethereal than those of mere sound traveling through the air that surrounds us. Certain of his creations were so finely tuned as to be able to detect and operate upon the vibrations of human thought, moving from out our skulls and through some medium otherwise unknown to us, but real nevertheless. Indeed, I bear witness to such; I had acquaintance, *tête-à-tête* as it were, with the device known as the *Paganinicon*, as human in appearance as myself, and possessed of every ability of speech and motion just as though it were my fleshly brother, rather than a construction of gears and even more intricate machinery. And in some ways, it was more than mere brother to me – for within the metal skull concealed beneath its artfully waxen head had been wires thinner and more sensitive than the hairs upon a housefly's back, all tuned to the vibrations emitted by the soft grey jelly inside my own head. Take it as a sign of my father's regard for me, his only son, that he would use my infant cranium as an adjunct to one of his mechanical devisings – but such was his nature, to place no limit upon the productions of his fecund genius.

I surmised that the enigmatic box left to me by my beloved Miss McThane operated on the same principle, though on a less dramatic scale. Some connection had apparently existed between it and her, communicated through that same insubstantial medium. Thus the box's ticking – though sharper and more mechanically regulated in nature, I was sure that it had been responsive in some way to the beating of the heart in her breast. Somewhere in the box's hidden machinery were the fine wires that had at some time been tuned to a frequency constantly flowing out from her. While she lived, the box listened to her and knew, in its slight way, that she was alive – this no doubt allowed her to operate its lock and turn back its lid at her convenience, though no one else would have been able to, including her husband. Thus, while her breath and heartbeat continued, her privacy was ensured and secrets maintained – but then upon her demise, the box's concealed mainspring slowly wound down and finally stilled, allowing inspection of the box's contents by other hands and eyes. She would have had to have known that this would be the case; her working knowledge of my father's devices exceeded my own.

Thus I felt there was no violation in my tipping back the lid once more, while keeping my eyes averted from the brass plate with my father's name incised upon it.

That the box held papers, I had already ascertained; there were in fact fewer than I had initially supposed, upon my earlier and cursory glimpse inside. A remarkably thin sheaf indeed, given the number of years that Miss McThane might have spent storing up documents important to her – their lack of uniformity indicated her correspondent had apparently employed whatever had come to hand, when he – or perhaps she – had taken an opportunity to communicate with her. There were no envelopes or other appurtenances included with the lot, from which clues to the missives' origin might have been obtained. A small deal table, much scarred and ring-marked from tankards set down by the inn's thirstier guests, sat close to my chair. I drew it over and sorted out the papers upon its surface.

Until this point, I had delayed a close examination of the letters themselves, dreading any confirmation therein of the dire suspicions that had already been raised. But I could put off the task no longer...

Little effort was required on my part to place them in

at least rough chronological order; she had done as much, however frequently she had perused them. Some of them, which seemed to have been more carefully prepared by their author, were dated at the top margin; the others, showing some evidence of haste at the time of their writing, were interleaved between.

My heart sank upon examining the first of the pages to bear a date, for it did indicate a time subsequent to our retiring together to this remote locale, after her life and mine had been so thoroughly and notoriously endangered in London. It is one thing to accept, as all men must, the secretiveness common to all women – but quite another to confront the secrets of one woman in particular. Had she continued not just thinking of, but corresponding with, another man while I had been beguiled into thinking that I alone had claim upon her affections?

In the gloomier mood thus provoked, I continued my inspection of the thin hoard. In doing so, I garnered no more indications of their source. None of the letters was headed with a familiar salutation; evidently, Miss McThane's correspondent had felt no need for any, the two of them being in a condition of familiarity with each other. The concluding lines of certain pages were, to a slight degree, more revelatory; one or two of the scrawled notes, and the majority of the longer missives, were signed with a single initial S.–

How my heart staggered within my chest, as though from a blow by a mailed fist, at the sight of that serpentine capital! In truth, it might have been an actual snake of fatal breed, and it could have come no closer to causing my death. Espying my father's name engraved on the box's lid had been bad enough, as an indicator of what might be its dire contents – to have that premonition so swiftly confirmed set a chill in my bones.

As I sat alone in that dark room, a consuming spectre of great fires was summoned within my memory – but it did nothing to elide the past's icy grip upon my spirits. As though intervening Time itself had evaporated, I seemed to find myself on the bank of a great river, my gaze lifted to a human figure silhouetted by those flames, falling to what I had assumed then would be his certain destruction...

To what degree I could, I thrust that appalling recollection from my thoughts. Perhaps another had written the letters before; certainly there were more scoundrels in Britain whose names began with that initial, than he who I so remembered.

As the matter turned out, I was somewhat relieved of the concerns that had tormented me before that first discovery. The letters were devoid of those terms of endearment, and detailed reminiscences of sweet assignations, that would have indicated a continuing romantic relationship between their author and Miss McThane. If lovers they had ever been, that ardour had cooled to mere friendship by the time this correspondence had commenced. What reprieve was thus provided from my own jealousies, it was obviated by what else I detected in the letters – I could almost hear aloud their nervous, breezy tone, somewhat slangy in the words chosen, though their subject matter was scarcely light-hearted; that manner was more than familiar to me, recalled as the herald of what been the most dreadful moments of my life.

I soon discovered that there was but one subject contained within the letters, and that obsessively so: they described the author's search for another, unnamed person. This quest was both seemingly arduous, and with fruitless results. The place names mentioned, I was able by my own geographical knowledge to locate in the North of England and in the farther reaches of Scotland. I had some small familiarity with those provinces, having been abducted at a time early in my career to the remote Hebridean isle of Groughay – little more than a muddy flyspeck in those frigid waters. The person who had written these letters to Miss

McThane – this enigmatic *S.*; an enigma due most to the reluctance to name him to myself – was apparently at ease in disreputable circumstances; some of the events experienced and individuals encountered in his search, particularly of what he recounted as happening in the darker alleys of Glasgow and Edinburgh and even grimmer towns to their north, were specified to a hair-raising degree.

Dark meditations engulfed my brain, like a nocturnal tide sluicing through and engulfing the stern rocks only a short distance from where I sat. Reading through the grim details of the search for the unnamed person, I came at last to the final missive in the collection.

A single sheet of paper, torn in half and in what seemed to be evident haste. There were but two words upon it, and scrawled hand similarly evinced some considerable agitation on the part of their author:

FOUND HIM –

That was all. No more than that; perplexed, I turned to the box on the small table beside my chair, pried open its lid once more and prodded my fingertips through its slight depths, as though there might have been some other scrap of paper that I had overlooked. But there was nothing of the kind.

Shuffling the papers into a more compact assemblage, I leaned back and regarded them with unavoidable suspicion. Genuine, they appeared to be; that Miss McThane's correspondent was real, and had been engaged in this scouring of the northern countryside for an equally unnamed person, I had little doubt. For her to have fabricated the documents attesting to the man's endeavour – that seemed to be elaborate lengths to have gone to, in order to perpetrate a hoax upon me. Though of course, I reminded myself, there was always the possibility that Miss McThane, here in Cornwall and so far distant from her correspondent, had been misled by him as to the actual events. How much confidence had she reposed in him, as to what he related in these letters? If his identity were in fact that which I bleakly suspected, then it was an out-and-out rascal with whom she had dealt, no matter the degree of conspiracy that had once been maintained between them. Perhaps she had been the victim of deviousness on his part – he might have been sitting at his ease in some public house, penning at his leisure an entirely concocted epic. Which he might have been motivated to draw out at as much length as possible, if she had been sending him money to continue his search. But if that were the case, why would he have imperilled the continued fleecing of the poor woman, by indicating that he had at last located his quarry? My various surmises about the matter failed to coalesce into anything that made sense.

My wearied thoughts stumbled from one blind, fruitless alley into another. Whether Miss McThane had been the victim of he whose correspondence she had preserved so carefully in the box ticking in time with her own heart, or whether I was meant to be cozened by a scheme that she had painstakingly assembled before her death – perhaps in league with this *S.* person, perhaps on her own – I had no way of knowing.

And – a possibility I was forced to acknowledge – perhaps I might never know. At least on this side of the grave; she who would have been most able to elucidate the matter, now lay buried some distance from the church that had been despoiled by those fiery cherubim. Genuine angels, made even more fearsome by the flaming swords they carried, might as well have been stationed about Miss McThane's grave, to keep me from interrogating her…

Thus the day after her interment passed, with myself no wiser than when it had dawned. Bleak speculation had produced meagre results. Stiff from long sitting, I creakily stood upright; surrounded by the night's advancing shades,

I leaned over the small table and deposited the papers back into the repository from which I had taken them, and closed the lid. If some hidden mechanism were set to spring into action and irrevocably seal the box once again, preventing me from further examination of those sordid pages, I would have considered it small loss.

Sentiment seemed to encase my feet in lead, an unseen weight stopping me from mounting the stairs that led above. The memories of those few years, now at an end, in which I had not been alone in this heartless world – they flooded my thoughts. It was yet too painful for me to seek rest either in the bed we had shared, or even one in another chamber, so close to that narrower bed by which I had sat, nursing her through her final days. The inn's public area held among its furnishings a short, sag-bottomed couch, suitable for the use of those who drank here with a companion, usually of the opposite sex. Wrapping a woollen throw about my shoulders, and drawing my shod feet up, I curled myself on the threadbare item, considering myself no more discomforted than I would have been upon a palace's feather mattress.

A storm was rolling in from the Atlantic. Eyes closed in the dark, I listened for a moment to the wind-driven creaking of the surrounding timbers, and the clattering of the shingles and shutters above – and thus at last fell asleep.

THREE

Mr Dower Receives Some   Unwelcome Visitors

TRAVELLERS WHO ARRIVE by night are an innkeeper's curse.

Or thus it has always seemed to me. Perhaps if I had been born to this trade, both hospitable and mercenary, I might have resigned myself more easily to such nocturnal guests – but I was not so. To pry a living from the inn which had also served as home for Miss McThane and myself, I had been forced to open the door at any hour, day or night, to those who had either been adventurous or unfortunate enough to have found themselves on this stretch of jagged coast.

Perhaps I should have posted a notice on the door-front: *A private grief forestalls our furnishing bed and supper to the public; pray forgive the inconvenience.* How else might they have had any inkling that I had but recently buried my wife, and desired no visitors?

The sounds that had woken me continued; I raised my head from the stone-like arm of the couch and listened. On this occasion – with my thoughts jumbled up with dreaming fragments of infant angels leering inanely as they burst into flame, and cryptic letters tumbled from out a thundering box the size of Saint Paul's Cathedral – some moments of

blinking confusion were required before I could make even
partial determination of what had woken me from exhausted
slumber. Not jingling bridlery in the courtyard before,
or footsteps damply approaching the inn's doorstep, but
something altogether wetter and more amorphous, as though
it were some element of the enveloping rain itself, and the
waves surging in the distance.

I had no candle or lantern close at hand, thus my hearing
was the only sense I could employ. For the span of a few
seconds, I detected nothing beyond those noises of wind and
pelting storm that had become so usual in my experience,
that they were as easily disregarded as dead silence itself.

On the verge of reapplying my head to the couch's arm,
I closed my eyes and tugged the wrap closer about myself
– and at that moment, heard more undeniably that sound
which had woken me. No auditory spectre this, and distinct
from the rain and other relentless weather to which I had
become accustomed, but at the same time possessing a
certain aqueous timbre. Words so often fail me; the closest
I am able to describe that which I heard outside is as being
similar to what one would hear if standing upon the shore,
the heaving motion of the constant waves lifting up a
mass of seaweed and slapping it upon the rocks nearby,
then dragging it back into the ocean depths as the waters
retreated.

Again, the wetly flapping sound came from the dark
beyond the walls, ominously nearer this time. It ceased, as
though whatever were its cause had reached the point that
was its intent.

Then – my hair prickles upon the back of my neck even
as I relate this history – another sound, of different nature; a
soft, hooting call, disturbing in its mournfulness, as might have
been emitted by the post-horn of those riders who had once
carried the mail, had the one who forced this brazen cry been

at the edge of death, and about to topple from his horse's back.

My initial impulse was to draw the woollen throw over my head and curl into a ball upon the couch. I have encountered dreadful things – more than my share, frankly, if there were any justice in this world – and facing them with whatever courage I have been able to summon has not, for the most part, worked out any better than attempting to ignore them. Cowardice is a greatly underrated virtue.

The dying call sounded once more, perhaps a little louder and more insistent. Refuge there was none; despite my reluctance, I would have to confront this storm-borne entity.

"Where are you?" Having unlatched and drawn open the door, I received the full brunt of the rain onto my face and chest. Shielding my eyes as well as I could, I peered out into the darkness. "If you seek George Dower, you have found him. But if you desire some other unfortunate, then go your way."

The winds from off the sea are often so violent, that they are able to tear vast rents in the clouds overhead, even as the rain continues to lash the hills and valleys. They did so now, allowing a shaft of moonlight to penetrate, silvering the ground about me. In that radiance, I spotted something clinging to the corner of the inn, its rounded bulk having mounted partway toward one of the upper windows. By the fragmentary lunar spectrum, my unwanted visitor appeared glassy and jelly-like, and blurrily transparent, so that through it I could see the sticks and branches of the untrimmed hedges beyond...

That steam has transformed our England, and the world beyond, is undeniable – or rather I should write *Steam*, as one might style the name of some intimidating deity, so as to emphasize the monstrous power it has become. Mere steam we had before, a humid vapour from the spout of a teakettle on the hob, or the mist rising from the sweating flanks of draught horses resting for a moment in the yokes of heavy-laden carts. A natural phenomenon, such as lightning or the occasional tremors of the earth beneath our feet, but from which we had no more to fear than the accidental scalding of our skin. All that has changed now; Steam has become the engine that draws the hurtling train of the Future toward the Present Day, laden with freight both awesome and appalling, its iron wheels relentless upon tracks from which we cannot unbind ourselves.

I admit what had been my own ignorance in this regard; as I have written in other pages, the rural isolation to which I had fled years ago, after my first acquaintance with my father's more fearsome creations, had sufficed to shield me from knowledge of the changes wrought in my native London. When I foolishly returned, I saw for myself the hideous great tubes and pipes mazing through the streets of the City, as though it were a nest of brass serpents. The constant heat and damp radiated thereby transformed the physical climate, as though the alleys and wider lanes were those of some forgotten empire deep in the Afric jungles.

But another climate had changed as well – the one within men's minds. The fever swamps in which they now found themselves had a correlative effect on their thinking. If *this* was possible, then why not *that* as well? Why stay one's hand, when tempted to grasp what had been previously thought impossible – or forbidden? Our strictures melt away in this new, enveloping heat, and monstrous things are born. And worse, they are not thought monstrous.

Such had happened with the breeding of animals; the cleverness that my father had brought to bear on constructions of brass and iron was now applied, in hidden workshops outside London, to softer and living things. Unnatural conjugations, between species that could never have coupled in the natural world, led to bizarre progeny…

I saw one before me now, as I was pelted by the rain. Through the fingers of the hand I raised in a vain attempt to shield my face, the gelatinous mass was still plainly visible. Its murkily transparent form possessed no colour other than that imparted by the thin angle of moonlight that fell upon it. Possessed of no means of locomotion other than the tendrils that spread out from the edges of the bell-shaped creature, it had still managed to travel some considerable distance, through sea and over sodden ground, and now clung to the inn by means of the suction provided by the cup-like features on the bottom of its appendages.

This much I knew, from some sensation-mongering periodical that had been left behind by one of the inn's guests – that at least those responsible had confined their efforts to denizens of the sea, specifically the octopus and its rather more flaccid neighbour, the jellyfish or Portuguese man-o'-war. That two so dissimilar animals could produce a mingled offspring – indeed, some scientific figures there were who maintained that the jellyfish was not even a single entity, but some sort of conglomerate assembly – was an indicator of not just the mad determination of this new world's relentlessly inventive minds, but the sweltering temperatures in which they lived and pursued their fervid enthusiasms.

Once created, a use must be found – thus the restless wheel of progress to which we are chained like whirling Ixion, whereby needs are fulfilled that we did not even know we had, so that even more urgent needs must be discovered. And thus the advent of the *aqueous couriers*, with one of which I was now confronted. For that part of humanity given to secrecy and plotting, the postal service so wisely instituted by Her Majesty's government, with its penny stamps and red pillar boxes, is not sufficient; another means of communication over great distances, suited to conspiracy and stealth, is preferred. And for that, the loathsome hybrid before me was ideal; the cunning of the octopoid species, often remarked upon by fishermen and sailors, was keen enough that it could be directed to a specific location, and could be relied upon to find its way while minimizing its risk of being observed – thus its propensity for arriving at its destination in the dead of night, and if during an obscuring storm, even better. The wobbling balloon form of the creature afforded the means by which it could navigate not only the coastal reaches, but make its way along rivers and canals as well, with the least expenditure of its store of energy. When progress over dry land was required, the tentacled legacy of its octopus ancestry enabled it to do so. Delivery of messages by these damp and squamous entities might not have been accomplished at the same speed as that of the mail coaches that hurtle across our British nation, but it was seemingly performed with greater secrecy, safe from the eyes and prying fingers of those human intermediaries who might have been prompted by curiosity or hope of gain to unseal any of the missives they carried. Further protection was enabled by the eerie appearance of the couriers themselves; on the rare occasions when one was spotted late at night – silently passing along riverine waters, or through fen and forest, heaving itself forward like an animate blancmange – the effect upon the observer, whether drunk or sober, was such as to provoke feelings of dread and horror, leaving it unmolested as it continued its errand.

Observing the one which had sought me out, I experienced much the same emotions. A shiver passed over my flesh, not evoked by the cold wind and rain that battered me. I was further oppressed by the realization that its primitive organs of perception, hidden somewhere within its gelatinine bulk, had caught sight of me. Once again I heard the low hooting horn-call, more insistent this time, summoning me to take delivery of that which had been so moistly carried to me.

After a moment's revulsed hesitation, I stepped forward into the courtyard. As I approached, the soft courier released its hold upon the building's corner, thereby sloughing itself back into a skirted hemisphere upon the ground. The remaining moonlight glinted from a circled brass tube with flaring aperture, fastened to the leathern harness that girdled the shape. This was the source of the horn note that had thrice sounded, its mouthpiece – or so it would have been to a human player – inserted into a puckered sphincter on the courier's rounded flank, through which air could be expressed in a manner similar to the squeezing of a bagpipes' bladder.

"I take it…" A moment was required for me to find my voice, this being the first occasion on which I addressed a faceless mound of jelly, faintly luminous beneath the rainwater over its surface. "That you have something addressed to me?"

The courier made no response but to raise one of its slithering appendages and lift the flap of the pouch on the other side of its harness. The flexing tip prodded about inside for a moment, then re-emerged with a waxen envelope stuck to it.

I took the stiff flat item reluctantly. The envelope separated from the suckered tentacle with an audible pop, and I came close to falling backward in my haste to put distance between myself and the creature as quickly as possible.

Its interest in me having ceased, the wobbling wet bulk shifted about, the appendages at its lower edge rooting in the mud. Whatever clouded gaze had rested upon my face was now turned toward the darkness from which the creature had journeyed. My mute visitor would be at greater comfort there, returning to the secretive postmasters who had dispatched it to my door.

For my own part, I retreated back inside the inn. A widening puddle of rainwater formed about me, as I stood sodden in the middle of the unlit parlour. My hands were so stiff from damp and cold that some time was required before I could fumble open the tiny box of Swan Vestas on the shelf above the wainscoting, and light the wick of the lantern on the nearest table.

The envelope's waxy sheath had prevented any damage to the contents; so tightly sealed was it that I needed recourse to my penknife to pry open the flap. Once done, I was able to extract a single folded sheet of paper.

Which I recognized, to some degree – in actuality, it was but a partial sheet, having been roughly torn in half; the frayed edge was evident to both sight and touch. I had seen the like before, and quickly confirmed my memory by lifting the lid of the enigmatic box that Miss McThane had bequeathed to me, and removing from it the last of the pages that I had placed in sequence. That paper was of the same coarse texture and yellowed tint as that which had just been given me by the departed aqueous courier. By the glow of the lantern, I held both pieces beside each other; their ripped edges exactly matched.

I laid both pieces down upon the table, brooding as I tapped my finger upon them. One obvious difference I espied between the two messages, as I gazed upon them: as I had noted before, that which I had found in the box, the final one of the lot, had but the two words *FOUND HIM* scrawled upon one side. The one just received was inscribed in the same hand, with the same colour ink, but more densely so – the considerable verbiage flowed from one side to the other. By this evidence, the earlier one had been dispatched in some haste; very likely the subsequent message elaborated on the previous terse communication.

I had more urgent needs at the moment than to see what the missive contained. I was chilled to the bone, and the unlit interior of the inn was scarcely more warming than its exterior. My greater requirement was to start a fire upon the hearth, strip off my clammy garments, and thaw out my flesh. In these regions, the failure to do as much was a frequent cause of death.

But more than that, I knew, delayed the satisfaction of my curiosity. My spirits were oppressed by the discovery that had been forced upon me, as to the nature of how my wife, the late Miss McThane, had conducted her correspondence with this party, whose suspected identity was woefully, bit by advancing bit, growing more certain to me. I had been prompted before to wonder how the pages in the box had been amassed over the last few years, without my having been aware of their arrival, one after another. A functionary of the postal service making his way to this remote location would have been so rare an occurrence as to have etched itself in my mind. Nor had Miss McThane been in the habit of frequenting the village, there being little need for her to do so – thus there would have been no opportunity to have had the letter placed in her hand by some helpful intermediary. But whatever fruitless conjectures I might have previously formed were now set aside by the certainty that the aqueous couriers had been employed, their rounds completed in the deepest hours of nights such as this. While I had lain slumbering, *she* had been awake for at least some of those times, in her night-dress and robe at one of the inn's upstairs windows, watching through the sombre hours for another of those jelly-ish messengers, like the one I had just encountered.

"Spare yourself," I spoke to no other, "at least for a time." Fear masks itself as fatigue, I was well aware – nevertheless, I decided to tend to these matters when I would have no excuse for quailing before whatever revelations were next in store for me. I gathered up both halves of the page that had been sundered in twain, and placed them separately – that one which had been the last I had read, and the other that I had yet to. The first I deposited back in the now-silent box, and closed the lid. The other just received I tucked inside my jacket pocket, to have it ready to hand in the morning. I would then be, if not refreshed in mind and body, at least better resigned in spirit to my fate.

With the coarse woollen throw about my shoulders, I awoke to the smouldering ashes on the grate.

The small fire I had lit, and left unattended as I slept, had imparted a measure of warmth to my bones. So much so that I was deluded for a few blessed minutes, that all the riotous and grim events of the last few days had only been my self-inflicted dreaming, and that I would shortly be able to rouse myself into that ordinary domestic state, with its small quotidian pleasures, that sufficed well enough as happiness for one of my experience.

But that vague illusion was not destined to last. Somebody – damn him! – was pounding upon the door.

"Oy! Dower! Be y'in?"

I winced at the sound of a voice other than my own. The hammering upon the door was suspended for a moment, so whoever was responsible could add to it with the grackling sound of his call. The constant application of strong drink had coarsened the man's throat, a condition not unusual in this region, but the accent marked him as being other than a local; I had heard much the same tone and inflection many years ago, when I had lived in London.

"Bluidy 'ell, Dower–" Whoever the person, he possessed little patience. "If ye be *daid*, then fookin' say so! Otherwaze, open fookin' door!"

These comments were followed by more pounding, even louder than the unseen person had previously managed. Better, I reluctantly decided, that I confront the person while still he stood upon the doorstep, than after he had battered his way in. I picked up the iron poker from beside the fireplace, and went to sort out the trouble as best I could.

"*Fie*-n'ly!" A pair of eyes, pink-rimmed from gin and tobacco, glared at me – or rather, up toward me, as the individual stood so hunched forward that he was rendered a good head shorter than myself. His squinting visage was shaded by a broad-brimmed hat, or the remains of one; it was as much wadded and abused as his crevassed face. "Why keep in'stution for the comfit o' weary trav'llers such as meself, if can't be bothurrd welcome in?"

"I am afraid you have been misdirected." Gripping the poker in both hands, I barred his way. "We are not open for custom at this time. Please seek shelter elsewhere."

"Ooh – *custum*, is it?" A skewing grin spread across the man's face. "Very posh, indeed! Frae looks place, had no idee be so grand. But if can't 'ford bed, a swodge o' floor'll do me, pref'bly nigh kitchen." Hands so begrimed and hairy-backed as to resemble diseased badgers pawed at the greasy vest he wore. "And nae fear, me fine Mr Dower – can pay!" He held up a coin of indeterminate denomination. "See?"

"We have no beds available, nor floor." I spoke in as stern a voice as I could summon. "The day is still early; if you continue by the Penworth road, you will come to another establishment by dark – one that will show you more hospitality than I can at this moment." I was struck by a further thought as I faced the man. "Just a moment – how do you know my name?"

"Why bluidy 'ell should'n' know yer name? Name *be* Dower, innit?"

"Whether it is or not, that is no concern of yours." I regarded him with mounting suspicion. "To my knowledge, you have never come this way before, and if I had made your acquaintance at some earlier time and place, I am sure I have no recall of it."

"Hold yer kettle, mate; no need git all bolshie with honest man as meself." With a sooty-nailed index finger, he pointed over his shoulder. "Folk in village ga'e me yer name. Be a figure of much d'scussion among 'em."

The proffered explanation scarcely relieved my doubts concerning this individual. And indeed, having had greater opportunity to study his appearance, I became even more convinced of his innate rascality. The upraised gesture made toward the distant village had allowed the ragged cuff of his dirt-embedded coat to fall to his equally grimy elbow, thus revealing a forearm emblazoned with tattoos, of the blurry and amateurish sort inscribed to the flesh with lamp-black and push-pin, a decorative craft much practiced by those serving at Her Majesty's pleasure in various houses of detention – I could just discern on this person's skin a dagger and ribbon memorializing his blessed mother, a piratical skull-and-crossbones, and various obscure prisoners' curses. The elabourateness of these markings indicated that he'd had ample leisure to devote to their tedious creation, there being little other diversion while behind bars and stone walls.

My days of London residency were sufficiently behind me that the connection was slowly formed in my mind between this person and others of his breed that I had encountered then. Not a tribe in the sense of the wandering Romany, much excoriated as gypsies, to whom a great many misdeeds were commonly and falsely attributed – but rather that motley and incorrigible assortment of Englanders who were no doubt native here before Caesar's legions came and went. It is difficult to keep a shop in Clerkenwell or any other of the city's parishes, without having to continually chase one or more of their ilk back out onto the street. Ever given to sticky-fingered theft and more elabourate swindles, they were a familiar urban plague – or so I had thought them; to encounter one here in the Cornish wastes afforded some surprise to me.

"So then, me foin Mr Dower – if take no offence at callin' by own damned name – is munny good enow for ye? Moyt come in?"

His voice broke into my dark reminiscences, and I discovered that he was no longer before me, but rather alongside, his small but determined form already insinuated between myself and the door frame, in the manner of those terrier dogs who will brook no obstruction between them and a place by the hearth, or whatever dish of scraps might await them in the kitchen.

"Cease at once." Some hasty action was required on my part to prevent his entry. The poker was caught between his chest and mine as I pushed him back; so close were we that the ripe pong of tramp sweat and undergarments long unwashed rose and filled my nostrils. "Quit these premises, or I will not account for what might happen next."

"Dicky inhosputtable sort, an't ye? Bluidy scandal on yer trade, I'd say." His scowl, peering up at me, softened into a gappy smile that was scarcely more pleasant. "Have it yer way then, *Mister* Dower – bin beaten nigh death in foiner places than yer poxy crib. But if ye please…" A cringing tone informed his words. "Gie jest smalles' peek inside, will ye? I'm shurre yer furnushings be magnufficent indeed." Ducking his head, the smaller man attempted to peer around me to the inn's rooms beyond. "Be a great kindniss, it wud, as be able to tell all me mates as to whut fookin' palace have here."

"You exhaust my patience, sir." Summoning my strength, I forced him backward, off the doorstep and into the muddy courtyard. "There is a constable in the village–" In actuality, there was no such office-holder. "I would just as soon not call his attention to your unwanted persistence here. But if you insist…"

"No need aw that; no need!" His obsequiousness nearly bent the man double, his head little higher than the level of his knees as he backed away. "Nivver bothurr the awthor'ties – it's all guid!" A keener and cleverer spark lit up his yellowy eyes. "'Tis foin place, too foin for likes o' me – ye're correck about that. I'd only disgust yer el'gant patrons – of which ye have a great many, I'm shurre. Ye do, don't ye?" The emptied smile split his face as he gazed studiously up at me. "A great many – all sorts comin's and goin's…"

"Whatever are you talking about?" I still held onto the poker, ready to employ it if need be.

"*Only*, Mr Dower, whut village-folk told me about – nowt more'n that. Watchful like, an't they? Sees all *sorts* o' things, they do. Those as come 'ere for lodgin', and… for othurr purposes." One of his eyebrows inched upward. "Very *strenge* viz'turrs, the village-folk regard 'em; very strenge indeed."

"Your meaning is obscure – if you have any. Leave me, at once."

"Ah, well; so be it." The unpleasant individual made a show of resignation, consisting of a shoulder-heaving sigh and a pigeon-like shuffle from one foot to the other; the leather of his ancient boots was split enough to reveal the blackened rags inside. "But if 'ave it in y'art, p'raps cud jist *tell* me like…"

I should not have responded – already I'd had more conversation with the person than I desired – but I foolishly did so. "What is it you would have me tell you?"

"Yer viz'turrs – as did munshun – I've a pow'ful cur'osity on those. Fair *mad*-dund on subjict, I be. Sich a kindniss be doin', 'f tell me 'bout 'em – ye ken the wuns I mean." He angled his head close to sideways, intently peering into my face. "Th'wuns come round when 'tis dark… bringin' thairr liddle messages…"

A sudden apprehension seized my thoughts. *He knows* – of this I was certain; there could be no other meaning to his words. Whoever the person was – and I had thought him until now to be no more than a wandering tramp, his odd actions and remarks the product of long indulgence in cheap alcohol, and worse – he possessed some awareness of events about myself and my circumstances that indicated a darker agenda on his part. Whether this came through his spying upon me – entirely possible, as the crags surrounding the inn afforded ample scope for stealth and concealment – or by some other avenue of revelation, it little mattered.

I realized more. All of his sly words and feigned curiosity – their purpose was this: he had wanted me to know I had been the subject of his scrutiny. For how long? And by who else? What other incisive gazes fixed upon me, even at this moment?

A violent passion stirred my limbs. Outraged, I lunged forward and swung the iron poker in a slashing downward arc. I would have been a murderer if the man had not sprung aside with surprising agility. The poker struck the ground with sufficient force to bury its hooked tip inches deep into the mud. I was thrown off-balance, the velocity of my errant blow nearly tumbling me forward.

By the time I regained my upright stance, the target of my fury had scurried several yards away. Safely beyond my reach, he turned about and jeered at me, his weathered face radiant with delight, relishing my discomfiture.

"Foin host y'arre, Mr Dower! Ever so *gray*-shus!" He drew himself to his unimpressive full height, as though surveying the battlefield he had strode across as victor. "Seems news come late t'yer ear – well, 'ere's anutherr fer ye chaw on. There be more – yea, there will! There 'asn't bin last letter to come to yer hand – not by long shot. Anuther there be, soon enow!" His coarsened voice cracked into a shout. "And whun comes, then – *then* ye'll be asking questions o' *me!* Ye'll see!"

Turning on his heel, the figure strode off and was quickly vanished, the dirt of his shabby garments concealing him in the landscape even before he would otherwise have been out of view.

I drew the poker out of the mud; brooding, I struck it against my boot, knocking away the clots of earth. As quickly as it had flared, my temper was now abated – somewhat.

An odd sentiment came to me. If my life had been otherwise, less coloured by irruptive chaos, I might have been rattled by this disagreeable person's threats and warnings. But if the world about me were to once more transform itself into an engine of encircling mystery and imminent disaster–

Then I felt strangely at home.

I turned myself about and headed back into the inn, to await whatever sinister event came next.

FOUR

Mr Dower Accepts an Unusual Invitation

T HROUGH ALL THE next day, nothing of note happened. This came as something of a disappointment to me – as might a soldier feel when summoned, musket loaded, to his position of battle, only to discover that the long-awaited enemy had unaccountably decided to turn about and go home.

I awoke the following morning, if not restored, then at least grimly determined.

Any further revelation was held in abeyance by the simple expedient of leaving the letter in the inside pocket of my jacket, the one which I wore most often by the combined force of poverty and habit. That the missive I had received so eerily from the jelly-ish courier contained much more information than its immediate predecessor's two words – *Found him* – had been indicated by my cursory glance across the torn but thickly lined sheet. When securing the letter, my intent had been to read it in full at a later time, with the contents of my skull relatively less exhausted, so I might study it in depth, wringing all possible meaning and possibilities from the words inscribed by that distant, unknown person. And so I had commenced upon that plan, the day after my confrontation with the direly insinuating vagrant – but something had stayed my hand and eye from further action. My wife – for so I still fondly and foolishly thought of her – was so lately in the ground; what further tarnishing of my memories of her could I endure? If there were further secrets to be exposed, let it not be on this one day more – such had been my decision at last. Refolding the letter, I had deposited it inside my jacket, its unexamined narration a constant weight upon my thoughts, like a wound from which we hesitate to remove the bandage, for fear that it would be far from healed.

When night came, once more I fitted myself to the couch near the grate, fireless this time; I remained fully dressed and shod, anticipating that I would be roused by some urgent situation, impossible to foresee, and requiring all haste on my part to confront. The evening light, grey and pallid, faded as I allowed my eyes to close…

I dreamt, knowing that I was dreaming all the while.

Miss McThane – younger, as I had known her – turned to me, smiling as she did so.

What see you there, Mr Dower?

I made no reply, fearing that if I spoke, I would wake.

In her hands was the box, softly ticking. She tilted back the lid, and showed me the interior.

What see you?

There were no letters, no scraps of worn, much-read paper, but only a starless dark, vaster than the world's night.

I bent down, to discern what I could.

And fell…

I was still falling, when I started awake.

Gripping the threadbare back and cushions, I stared wide-eyed at the ceiling above, my heart pounding in my chest. That all I had just seen were but the mind's phantasmata, with no more substance than ghosts and other imagined afflictions, was no comfort to me.

The last traces of the dream – Miss McThane's voice and smile – ebbed away and were gone. In their place came a sound, distant and haunting, though contained in this more solid world–

It was the post-horn, the simple brass instrument affixed to an aqueous courier, such as had announced the arrival of the one which had visited me before. How many times must I have slept oblivious to that small, hooting note, while my wife had lain awake beside me, waiting for its call!

I swung my legs from the couch and stood up. If my slumbers before had kept me deaf to the courier's wavering note, now I was exquisitely attuned to it.

This night was blessedly free of the rain that had pelted me on the previous occasion. A faint luminescence greeted my eye as I stepped out to the darkness. Some distance away, on the rock-strewn path winding to the courtyard's gate, sat another of the gelatinous messengers – or perhaps the same one as before; I thought I recognized the marks inscribed across the glistening surface turned face-like toward me.

I was still yards away from the courier, when the night was cracked with the sharp report of a rifle being fired – I glimpsed, from the corner of my eye, the flash from its muzzle out somewhere in the surrounding hills. At the same moment, a shrieking cry assaulted my ears, its high-pitched noise overwhelming the echo of the shot.

For a moment, I had involuntarily ducked low, as though attempting to evade the unseen marksman. When I raised my head, I saw that I was not his target; instead, the aqueous courier had been struck by the bullet. Before me, but still beyond my reach, the creature flailed upon the ground, its various appendages in a writhing paroxysm; the shrill note I heard was emitted by the ragged tear widening through the jelly-ish substance, as might a child's inflated rubber balloon whistle when punctured by a hat-pin.

The sound from the shredding laceration faded in pitch and volume until all was silent once more. That diminution took but a few seconds; when finished, the creature was but an empty, transparent sack, weighted to the earth by the leather harness it had borne while alive, festooned by the small brass horn.

I took but a single step forward, my hand reaching for the pouch, uppermost on the collapsed and motionless form – but the instinct for self-preservation overrode my desire to secure whatever letter might have been contained therein. Another shot rang out, and sparks flew up from a stone close beside me. Whether the shot had been meant to kill me as well, or merely warn me away from the deflated corpse ahead, the effect was the same in regard to my actions. I dove from the path, taking refuge in the shallow ditch at its edge. The person with the rifle, hidden in darkness, might still have had me in his sights; I could not be certain if I had managed to sufficiently obscure myself from his firing another bullet. Thus it seemed the wisest course to crawl as hurriedly as possible, away from the spot and back toward the inn.

This I accomplished, without injury; either I had somehow managed to elude the other's searching gaze, or he considered that his goal of driving me away from the fallen courier had been accomplished. I risked lifting my head and looking over my shoulder to the spot from which I had fled. The moon's faint radiance seemed to have brightened a bit, enough that I could just discern a shadowed figure, rifle in hand, stooping over what remained of the aqueous courier, and lifting open the flap of its harness's leather pouch.

I took advantage of the person's attention being fixed on obtaining that which I also had desired; I sprang from the ditch and ran, not halting until I had slammed the inn's door behind me, my back pressed to its timbers.

At least I now had the advantage of being on my home turf. True, my only weapon was the iron poker that I at once seized from where I had left it propped beside the door, but I would be able to employ it from any number of hiding places close at hand, striking the miscreant if he were so bold as to enter the premises familiar to me, unknown to him.

My defensive preparations proved unnecessary; I heard no approaching step from outside. I took to the stairs, heading to the storey above so that from one of the upper windows I might better survey the landscape.

I saw nothing of the murderous individual, but I did ascertain the cause of that greater illumination that had previously silhouetted the man. Whereas before, during my previous encounters with the aqueous courier, the creature's faint radiance had made it appear as a softly amorphous moon fallen from the sky and mired upon the ground below, now that same silvery-blue light was multiplied many times over. From my vantage point, I could scan across a considerable expanse of the landscape, to that point on the path winding away, where the courier had been slain by rifle-fire, and some distance beyond to the clashing sea. This territory had been transformed, so that I could see it in as much detail as if it were blanketed with the last crepuscular minutes of the fading day. For where I had once seen one lunar-ish form, now I saw many; all along the path, and over the hills and crags, there were more such apparitions, their innate luminance combining to a glow seductive to the eye. I was captivated, breathless for a moment, by such uncanny beauty. And they were not rooted to those places where first I saw them; they were slowly moving, with that slow, lumpish grace that one might expect from ocean-going entities stranded for the moment on the relatively dry land. Nor were they silent; to my ear came a multi-throated keening, the horns affixed to their wobbling flanks sounding notes deeper and more mournful than the call I had heard when the first of their number I encountered, nights ago, had announced his arrival.

Slowly, the straggling ranks of the aqueous couriers – so many of them! – made their way to where their slain fellow lay, a dark and flaccid form on the path. A number of them assembled about the corpse; their appendages were not made for lifting such a pliant shape, but they managed to pull it up from the mud and drape it across a pair of their rounded, bell-like masses. The dead courier seemed like a ragged banner there, trailing the torn edges of its fatal wound.

I had sadly misconceived the nature of these creatures, based upon the brief contact with the one whose slaughter I had witnessed, and the reports which I had previously read. I had thought them to be mere dumb animals, bizarre miscegenations that would never have occurred in nature unaided, but restless human cunning had brought forth to a world overheated both physically and mentally. That they might mourn and retrieve the body of a fallen comrade, being made aware of its death by some subtle etheric vibration – surely this would argue that they were close to being as intelligent and sensitive as ourselves.

As I watched, the blue effulgence that had been cast over the landscape began to fade, just as the greater orb in the sky might diminish through the night hours. The soft procession bearing the dead courier had reached its destination, carrying its deflated burden into the lapping waves. The number of similar creatures visible to my gaze had lessened as well, either by escorting their mournful fellows into the sea-water, or by returning to the hidden paths by which they travelled across the land. Out upon the ocean, the spots of light dwindled, becoming gradually smaller and then disappearing as the luminous shapes returned to the depths from which they had risen.

When all was darkness again, except for the stars and that larger orb with which we are more familiar, I started to draw back from the window… and then held that motion in abeyance. I thought I had spotted something else out in the hills, another witness to the eerie procession I had just watched. A figure wrapped in shadows, unrecognizable, at the jagged crest of the highest stone outcropping that overlooked the fields below – perhaps it was the marksman who had slain the courier with a single bullet. I could not be certain; a dull gleam could have been the reflection of the moonlight off the barrel of his rifle, held slanting downward beside himself. Had he returned in order to survey the scene of his lethal deed? Having thus stolen that which had been meant for my hand, did he have further villainous intentions? I leaned forward, straining to see if I could detect any clue as to his coming movements, whether he would turn and retreat down the other side of the rise, and thus out of my view, or whether he would make his way toward the inn.

I saw neither indication; the figure had disappeared, if he had in fact been there at all; the possibility existed that what I had glimpsed had been no more than a production of my overwrought nerves, taut as violin strings after so many unsettling occurrences in rapid succession.

Once more, anticipating the worst, I forwent the much desired rest that my bed would have provided. Iron poker in hand, I took up my station, bolt upright on the couch downstairs. If figures wrapped in night were to advance upon me, I would be at least this much prepared for them.

"Do I have the privilege of addressing the Honourable Mr George Dower?" These words were accompanied by an ingratiating smile, of seemingly unimpeachable sincerity. "A Londoner by birth, but a resident of this locale for some time now?"

I found it difficult to decide which question to answer first – they had fallen upon my ear in such quick succession as to seem like an artillery barrage. Added to my befuddlement were other factors: the first, that I had been roused from sleep by the knocking upon the inn's door; the second, that being confronted with a cheerful and seemingly well-intentioned countenance, after the hostility and slyness of so many of my recent meetings, was sufficient to take me aback.

The poker was in my hand, ready to wield upon some assailant; I had snatched it up from the floor, where it had dropped when my vigil, seated upon the couch, had been overtaken by exhaustion. The gentleman outside, while still maintaining his smile, gave the implement a nervous glance, as though he were reconsidering the wisdom of arriving here unannounced.

"I am George Dower." Reluctant to set aside the poker, I held it instead behind my back and out of worrisome view. "Though you err in addressing me with any superfluous honorific – I have few pretensions to gentility anymore."

My attention was sufficiently awakened as to be able to gather what clues I could from his appearance. He was no booted and tweed-garbed hiker, of the sort who flee the city for a strenuous – and costly – holiday, traipsing about the British wilds. To the contrary, he was dressed in a genteel manner considerably at odds with the surrounding countryside; his gloved hands and finely tailored morning jacket were such that he might well have stepped out of an elegant salon and directly upon my muddy doorstep, if there existed some form of transport capable of instantaneously accomplishing that. Younger than me – as is an increasingly greater percentage of the population – and possessed of one of those ruddy-cheeked faces to which a smile comes naturally; I do not possess the same.

"Begging your pardon – but allow me to disagree." The

man's own words seemed to amuse him, the smile becoming even warmer and more ample. "The opprobrium which chafes upon you – understandably so – is not universal; I can assure you of that, my dear Mr Dower. Permit me to present myself – the name is Rollingwood; Herbrace Rollingwood – as one of that party who are, to a small measure, aware of your services to the greater community."

The words of this Rollingwood person aroused a measure of suspicion in my breast. The chances that he was sincere in his admiration were small, based upon my previous experience with those who professed such an emotion; all of Rollingwood's predecessors in that regard had been scoundrels intent on wickedness, usually hoping to employ me as a cat's-paw in advancing their schemes. But still – breathes there a man so jaded in his assessment of others' motives, that he cannot hope, however foolishly, for some bright spot amongst them?

"Forgive my asking..." I was not yet completely convinced as to his relative innocence. "But what exact *services* are they, which you speak of?"

"I am sure, Mr Dower, that you recall the havoc and subsequent damage to London city, with which your name is associated–"

"Forgetting those events would be difficult. Even at a point this far removed from them."

"Exactly so," allowed Rollingwood. "But with the re-establishment of order, there has been a blurring of memory; I am certain that for the majority of people, even those who were directly affected – I mean the survivors, of course – there would be scant recall of your identity. We forget, do we not? Perhaps laudably so. But as I indicated, there are some who still recall that affairs might have gone very much worse, had it not been for some of your efforts."

"Very well, Mr Rollingwood." I set the poker down, angled

just inside the doorway, and stepped back to afford entry to my visitor. "I assume you have some other purpose here, other than informing me that not all the world considers me a total blackguard. If you would care to inform me as to how I might assist you, please do so."

"I will not trouble you long." Gazing about himself where he stood in the centre of the inn's parlour, the gentleman removed his gloves and tucked them into the pocket of his coat. "My errand is simple. I merely wish to remove your wife hence, and take her to London."

"My wife is dead, sir."

"Of that sad circumstance, I am aware." Rollingwood's smile had already disappeared, now replaced by a spaniel-eyed expression of sympathy. "Allow me to express my deepest condolences upon your loss."

The gentleman's sentiment was only exceeded by the apparent sincerity that had engendered it. He was of that breed possessing a surfeit of human warmth, which suffered others' pangs as sharply as though they had been his own. Such persons must be constituted of sterner stuff than is the general run of Mankind; how could they survive in this cruel world otherwise?

"That is all very fine, Mr – Rollingwood, is it? – Mr Rollingwood, then. All very fine." I regarded him askance, as though prepared to witness his kindly mask whipped away, and replaced with a rather more cunning one. "If you had come all this way merely to express that commiseration, then you are certainly welcome; I do appreciate it. But you speak of *removing* that person whose loss I am still grieving, as though she were a chest of drawers that has become inconvenient through disuse. You will have to pardon me if that remark gives me some pause."

"No, no; forgive *me*, Mr Dower." He slightly bowed his head, revealing through his thin, fine hair the scalp which had been pinkened by the morning sun; by the time he was past his thirties, he would likely be balding. "Perhaps I spoke hastily; I meant no rudeness – but I know as well that you are a busy man, with a great many duties to which you must attend. Life must go on, even as we mourn."

"Just so," I said. "I do indeed have a number of... pressing concerns." I was hardly about to inform him of being beleaguered by amorphous, water-borne postmen bearing enigmatic messages, and being shot at in the night by unknown persons; I could scarcely see how any of those things were his business. "So if there were some other matter which you wished to discuss with me, I would appreciate your informing me of it."

"By all means." He placed his hands behind the small of his back and drew himself taller, as though on military parade. "I have the pleasure of representing the Gravitas Maximus Funerary Society, and it is on behalf of that esteemed organization that I appear before you today."

"Forgive my ignorance, Mr Rollingwood; I am sure that your... society, or whatever it is... would rank as high in my opinion as it does in other people's, if I knew what it was. I lead a secluded life here, of my own choosing; many famous things happen, of which I remain happily unaware."

"I am certain that is the case; I harbour no intention of disturbing your solitude here – which is rather to be envied, I assure you." Another tilt of the head, this time with the ingratiating smile having returned to his face. "As you might have surmised from its name, the corporate entity with which I am associated has a great deal to do with the dead – indeed, it exists for no other purpose."

"The dead seem to be taken care of well enough, by those means which Mankind has employed for quite some time now – at least, that is, I am not aware of many complaints coming from those who have passed on."

"But are they, Mr Dower? *Are* they?" My visitor spoke with a sudden passion. "We live in a modern world–"

"Unfortunately."

"Precisely my point! Times have changed, and we must change with them."

"I was rather hoping to be dead myself," I averred, "before that became a necessity."

"But you are not, sir; and thus you bear a duty to those whose terminated circumstances render it impossible for them to defend their own interests. Think of your wife, whom you loved while she was with you. Is it fit that she not be memorialized in a fashion commensurate with your tender, sacred memories of her?"

"Very likely not–" His words evoked some agitation in me. "But there's little I can do about it now."

"Forgive me–"

"Why should I?" The full fury of my temper was set free, like maddened horses unstabled. "You turn up on my doorstep unannounced, which seems to be a privilege that the whole bloody world grants itself, and then you go blathering on about my poor dead wife. You profess yourself to be well disposed toward me, and then you speak as if I were exactly the same heartless bastard that everyone else has determined me to be. Very well then; I *am* that monster! Have you satisfied your curiosity concerning that? I sincerely hope so, as I fail to see what other business there is to transact between us."

"If not business, then pray let there be peace between us, Mr Dower. I meant no insult to you." Rollingwood wrung his hands before himself now, in a perfect agony of abasement. "If you wish me to depart, with my having given you nothing but my deepest apologies, then so be it – what a clumsy, blundering idiot I am! But say the word, and I will burden you no longer with my presence."

"Never mind." I was somewhat mollified, as one would be when confronted by an errant hound, grovelling in shame. "You were brought here for something you obviously felt important; something to do with this Funerary Society in whose service you are – *and* something to do with my late wife. I can scarcely see any connection between the woman and your organization – or any organization, for that matter; her earthly affairs are at an end. But I am capable of giving you enough courtesy, and a few minutes, for you to state your exact purpose."

"I appreciate that, Mr Dower; I will endeavour to be brief. Our world, as you and I seem to agree, is full of modern contrivances, the wizardry of newly unleashed forces. Alas, the mastery of them lags behind their advent; much consternation is brought about by bumbling, well-intentioned souls, who throw switches and engage gears without fully comprehending how these devices operate, and things that might go wrong with them."

"Trust me." I spoke sourly. "I have some experience in that regard."

"Indeed; I know to which you refer. But a few days ago – your wife's funeral service went badly awry, did it not?"

His words prodded one of my eyebrows up into a gaze of suspicion. "How do you know about that?"

"We have resources, Mr Dower. Though not all have yet heard of the Gravitas Maximus Funerary Society, we are in fact a well-funded organization. This allows us to employ operatives in many parts of Britain – even, I might say, in as remote a corner as this. They are ever alert for instances of memorials to the dead, which could have – to say the least – gone better."

"Why so? It strikes me as a peculiar preoccupation for anyone, let alone an organization of some substance, as you claim yours to be."

"Permit me to explain." Rollingwood graced me with his easy smile once more. "I believe my information to be accurate, that the service in the village church – which stands no more; I have gone by its charred remains – was marred by those modern contrivances to which you profess such an aversion."

"If you refer to those damnable mechanical angels, with the corpses of dead babies stuffed inside, then you are correct, sir. Fluttering about like a swarm of pink bats – *that* is what the modern world has brought to us? Better that we had stayed in the caves that our fur-clad ancestors inhabited."

"Ah, but the failure was not that of *Modernity* – the fault was in the hands of those who too weakly grasped its possibilities. It is a common condition." Rollingwood spread his hands wide. "Even here among your rural neighbours, the enthusiasm for all things futuristic is but in its early stages. A few years hence, one might come to this place and find that it resembles more the London metropolis that now is, rather than the backward village that it was."

"I confess that this has always been beyond my understanding." His mild comments elicited from me one of those rote monologues by which I am so able to convince anyone listening as to what a gloomy bore I am. "This mad desire for the Future – what folly! People believe it to be a Paradise within close attainment, in which all that pleases – and more! – will be granted them. And then the Future does arrive, as it has for all Men before, and we find that it is the barren wasteland in which everything we had, and cherished, is taken from us, and buried in the sod."

To his credit, Rollingwood left me alone with my grim meditations for a moment. After a few seconds, he discreetly cleared his throat.

"Sir, your opinions are shared by others – though I confess, not many. But it is greatly for the benefit of those such as yourself, that the Gravitas Maximus Funerary Society was founded. To the degree that we are able, we seek to ameliorate the suffering of those who have witnessed the sad last memorials to their loved ones being transformed into riotous calamity, such as happened to yourself. Perhaps a day will come, when the new technologies applied to funerals will have been fully mastered, with appropriately decorous services the result. But until then, we strive to rectify the unfortunate situation that exists for a growing number of people."

"Indeed?" I gave him a sidelong glance. "And how exactly do you and your *society* go about doing that?"

"We amend whatever damage had been previously done, by performing another service, warranted by us to be of extreme tastefulness and consideration for the feelings of the deceased's survivors."

"That," I said, "sounds like an expensive proposition."

"Yes–" Rollingwood made his admission with a nod of the head. "There are some costs involved."

"Then, sir, you are talking to the wrong man. What resources I have were nigh exhausted by the simple insertion of my late wife into the ground here. To do more than that would likely pauperize me."

"Put your mind at rest, Mr Dower. Our services are offered to you *gratis*, as it were."

"Your organization is of a charitable nature?"

"By no means–" With an upraised hand, Rollingwood disavowed the notion. "The Gravitas Maximus Funerary Society is captained by entrepreneurs who seek to turn a reasonable profit. And yet they are civic-minded as well, and wish to improve the general lot of Mankind."

"That is a vain endeavour."

"I understand your believing so," said Rollingwood. "Nevertheless, I assure you that the Society's directors are practical men."

"And yet–" My skeptical eyebrow arched upward again. "They wish to do me some elabourate favour, and for no recompense. When I was a man of business, with my little watch shop in Clerkenwell, I did not dispense my wares for free."

"To you, sir, the services are given – but they are in fact paid for, by a benefactor who wishes to remain anonymous."

"Does he, indeed?" If my eyebrow could have gone any higher, it would have been near the top of my head. "I hope you will pardon my doubts as to this person's intent – but those extraordinary experiences with which you credit me have also led to a belief that secretive people generally have reasons for wishing to remain so, and they are rarely good ones."

"I wish that I could ease your apprehensions in that regard, but alas! I cannot. The generous person's exact identity is unknown to me – but of his motives I have been modestly informed. Your late wife–"

"You may refer to her as Miss McThane; you will not offend me by doing so."

"Yes… well, then; as you wish." Rollingwood was visibly discomfited, but recovered himself. "The late Miss McThane had… hm; how shall I put it?… a rather *colourful* career before making your acquaintance."

"*Now* you are coming close to offending me."

"My apologies, but I do wish to be frank with you. Her associates in that previous existence were not all of the most impeccable nature–"

"I am aware of that. One of them I had known, her most intimate. He was a greater rascal than ever she had been – but not, I had once hoped, irredeemably so."

"Exactly, Mr Dower. Practitioners of vice rarely become paragons of virtue, but they do sometimes repent at least a small bit, and seek to make amends for their misdeeds. Such seems to be the case here: I am not certain whether your *soi-disant* benefactor is acting upon his conscience alone, and out of his own purse, or whether he is in communication with a number of the late Miss McThane's other admirers–"

"*Admirers*, are they?" My eyebrow descended sufficiently as to allow for the upward roll of my gaze, accompanied by the slow shake of my head. "If any there remain, this person would have needed to take up his charitable collection along the rows of cells in Her Majesty's Pentonville prison, as I would imagine that the majority of them reside there and nowhere else."

"Perhaps so," allowed Rollingwood. "Your knowledge on the point exceeds mine. Regardless, the upshot is that payment has been made in full, and that the relocation of your wife's body – excuse me – to a more suitable final resting place can proceed immediately. Accomplished, of course, with the more decorous memorial service provided by our Society."

"You set a low bar when it comes to decorum; merely refrain from burning the chapel down and you will have succeeded at that much. But I am puzzled: where do you intend to take her? And why?"

"To London; the cemetery at Highgate, to be exact. And our doing so would be at the express wish of the person who approached us about the matter. Miss McThane's residence here on the Cornish coast was a relatively brief episode in her life, be it the last of them; she was more a Londoner to her bones, thus a burial within the city might have seemed more appropriate to her memory. And – I speculate here – perhaps another, more sentimental reason exists. The man's generosity is spurred by a certain fondness he must have had for her while alive; perhaps he wishes to be able to pay his respects at her graveside, in private and at times convenient to himself. Allowing him to do so seems little to ask."

Rollingwood's speech kindled no rancour in my breast. Another, I knew, had been the greater love of this woman's life – but I had been the last. If yet one more had remembrances of her affections, so be it; God knows she had been a generous sort.

"This elegant memorial of which you speak–" I persisted with my questions. "Am I to be witness to it?"

"It is hoped that you would agree to do so. Those arrangements, for your comfortable transport and lodging, have also been provided for."

I mused upon all that had been presented to me. My inclination was to allow this *post mortem* shuffling about to proceed as Rollingwood had indicated. As matters stood, my late beloved was planted weed-like in a rather forsaken patch of graveyard, with more trampled mud than grass about it. The location hardly seemed suited for one who had possessed such vivacity while she had been above the ground, however diminished that energy might have been in her last declining days. And if all of London's charlatans and criminals came there to give their bare-headed tribute... very likely, she would have enjoyed that.

Still I hesitated, perhaps more from fatigue than doubt.

"An interesting proposition you lay before me, Mr Rollingwood. I promise to give it my most earnest consideration, though it might be some days or even weeks before I can give you an answer. It seems an undertaking – so to speak – that would require some effort, and preparation, to bring to a satisfactory conclusion. There are arrangements to be made; I would imagine that the disinterment of the casket would require both some civil as well as clerical permission – and at the moment, I am not certain whether our village priest is available, or even alive."

"How happy I am then, to be able to provide some comfort to you!" My visitor's smile became a veritable display of sunbeams, lacking only the singing of larks upon leafy branches. "All has been arranged, even as we speak. Permit me–" He stepped back from me to the door, drawing it open and gesturing for me to come and stand beside him. "Behold!"

I did as I was bidden, and viewed a surprising apparition. A carriage was present in the centre of the inn's courtyard, bearing an oaken catafalque ornamented with ebony inlays and gilt curlicues about its corners. Strapped to this was that simpler wooden construction which I recognized as the casket holding my wife's mortal remains. A pair of harnessed steeds, of a quality unavailable to be hired in any local stable, stamped the mud from their black-lacquered hooves.

"If I and my associates have erred," said Rollingwood, "you have our apologies. But we anticipated that you, as the grieving widower, would have no objection to our plans – and we proceeded on that assumption. We were able to do so with some alacrity – as I told you, the Society has funds more than sufficient for its purposes; that which is accomplished slowly, and with foot-dragging delays in the ordinary course of business, is done at lightning speed when money greases the wheels."

Of that, I had little doubt; I had witnessed as much in the course of my previous dealings with the grand conspirators of the world. Notions which men of lesser wealth would have taken years to bring to fruition, if at all, were by the wealthy sent headlong into our midst, like brakeless drays hurtling down steep inclines, with cries of *Damn the consequences!*

"If you are in accord with us," continued Rollingwood, "there is nothing left to arrange here; all has been taken care of. We may depart immediately, with yourself and your late wife."

I stood silent, musing upon this unexpected development. It presented a certain opportunity to me – namely, escape. If I had only been besieged by the mysteries presented by Miss

McThane's correspondence with that other – an enterprise that had previously been unknown to me – then I would have had little concern for my own safety. All that might have been at risk would be that tranquillity of mind of which I had precious little before. And the possibility had remained of leaving this puzzle unexamined, as with so many others that had confronted me, thereby preserving what sanity I had. In this world, wilful ignorance is often the wisest course.

But all that consideration had been set topsy-turvy by the introduction of violence to the scene. Shots had been fired from a shadowy assailant's rifle; one had come near enough to send me scurrying away in fear for my life. Perhaps that had been the intent behind the bullet, to frighten me only – but perhaps the marksman had misjudged his aim in the night's darkness, and failed in his more lethal ambition. If so, how likely was it that one who had set out to be a murderer would be satisfied to leave that ambition unfulfilled? The person might be skulking about nearby, rifle in hand, awaiting his opportunity – which he might have acted upon this very morning, if it had not been for the arrival of Rollingwood and his casket-laden entourage.

Perhaps an unusually kindly Providence had sent this representative of the Gravitas Maximus Funerary Society to my door, and thus given me the chance to flee from my present circumstances. While alone, I had been at the mercy of the stealthy marksman, only being able to hide myself here at the inn and await my assailant discovering some means of entry; when that occurred, my trusty iron poker would likely be of little avail. Were I to abandon the building and attempt to make my way to the village, either by day or under cover of night, I would be a relatively easy target.

But Rollingwood had presented me a means of exit, without his even being aware of my predicament. Unless the marksman was willing to engage in wholesale slaughter, of myself and Rollingwood and whatever associates had accompanied him here, their presence would secure my safety all the distance to London, by whatever route had been already arranged. And once in the distant capital? Whatever dangers might await me there – and I could easily imagine a great many – I would at least have whatever safety could be found in the mass of people, of whom there were even greater numbers. If my stalker followed, he would not be able to pursue me at his convenience, my being a quarry surrounded by an empty landscape; in addition, there were still officers of the law going about their duties in London, who would very likely impede his pursuit.

Another consideration came to mind: whatever mysteries in which I was engrossed, regarding the woman whose transfer from one grave to another would be the engine of my escape, I might well have more ability to unravel them there than here; having been more a *habituée* of that great metropolis, Miss McThane had left her former associates in its twisting alleys, not in any Cornish village. Would I be able to locate any of them, and interrogate them as to any knowledge they might possess, relevant to the mysterious correspondence I had been bequeathed? I had no idea, other than a reliance on the cynical old maxim, *Bad pennies always turn up*.

"Mr Rollingwood–" I drew myself from my circling calculations. "The case you make is persuasive. How soon would we be able to depart?"

His smile broadened. "Immediately, sir."

"Very well." I turned toward the stairs. "I need to pack a bag."

Some few moments later – my habitual wardrobe is not so extensive, that its assembly for travel requires more than a small valise – I stood beside that bed, which I would never share again. Wide as a world, it had seemed, when another's tender regard had encompassed me. It was not diminished in my memory by these recent revelations of domestic subterfuge.

Which did, however belatedly, prompt me to a duty I had already forestalled too long. So many injurious circumstances can overwhelm as we journey from point to point, or upon our arrival at what turns out to be an unfortunate destination, that it would have been remiss of me not to have put at least my mental affairs in order, as best I could, before departing these premises.

Thinking thus, I reached inside my jacket and drew out the letter which had been so eerily delivered to me. Unfolding the single torn sheet contained within the waxen envelope, I cast my gaze upon it–

No need to peruse all the words contained therein, for its most dreaded confirmation to be lain upon my heart and thoughts. Seeing clearly no more than the bold-scrawled signature at the bottom – and that affording not surprise, but rather confirmed suspicion – I folded the letter back up and deposited it from where it had just been extracted.

"So, Mr Scape..." I murmured a greeting to my late wife's correspondent, as though he were standing now before me, with the same wicked, knowing smile that I recalled from before. "You are a durable fellow. How it has come about, I do not know – but you yet live."

The import of that, I did not know. Perhaps whatever interest he took in my affairs had come to an end, at the moment of Miss McThane breathing her last...

I could only hope.

Latching my bag, I lifted it from the bed and headed downstairs with it, to the coach and whatever else awaited me.

PART TWO
Again, the Urbane Mr Dower

FIVE

Another Funeral, with Worse Prospects

I CONFESS – IF YOU will allow me – that I expected something rather different."

"Your pardon, Mr Dower–" Rollingwood turned his inevitably sympathetic gaze toward me. "But I am not quite sure I follow your meaning."

At the time of this exchange, he and I were standing in the midst of the cemetery at Highgate, or rather what it had become since last I had seen it – a considerable span of years intervened since that time, predating the unfortunate introduction of the Moloch-like force of *Steam* upon the city of London. The idle curiosity of a young man – I strain to recall how I had felt in those innocent days – was all that ever brought me to these sombre environs; I shared that popular fancy for strolling about this notable graveyard's Egyptian Avenue and Circle of Lebanon, admiring the ornate tombs and mausoleums, the permanent residents of which were sadly unable to appreciate. A pleasure it was then, on a summer day, to espy the occasional fox slinking through the rampant park-like foliage, the bright coat of the animal seeming to stake the claim of Life upon the precincts of the dead, and irrepressible Nature at the limits of the sterile city. But the changes that had occurred since then – the Future once more become Today – oppressed my heart again, as they had before. Time's passage had not inured my sensibilities to malignant Change.

Granted, I had not been in the best of temper before I had accompanied Rollingwood and the other associates of the Gravitas Maximus Funerary Society to Highgate. On the previous occasion on which I had travelled from the wastes of Cornwall to London – not that many years ago, and prompted by other concerns and conspiracies – the vast interconnecting web of rail transport had not yet reached my point of departure, an indication of how remote and insignificant it was; thus, I completed the greatest extent of the journey by means of hired carriage, as would have been done by those we like to think of as our primitive and benighted ancestors. Now that system was complete, yet still expanding like some veinous growth; soon the day would come, if not already arrived, in which the privilege of being in any way disconnected from the rest of Humanity would be reserved only for the wealthy, who can purchase with their riches the isolation and quiet denied to us mere rabble.

(Though I fear worse awaits our descendants; that conniver Scape had professed an ability to see far to the Future, aided by another of my father's devices. He had described to me an age to come, in which all members of society walk about with little flat boxes in their hands, to which they bend their unceasing attention so as to never be without the image of another's face in their own, and another's constant yammering voice in their ears, scouring away whatever private thoughts they might otherwise have been forced to attend to. Scape himself had not been keen on this distant prospect; he had once cynically commented to me that the devices seemed to possess the almost magical power of transforming grown men into chattering adolescent girls.)

What greater comfort I experienced, and the degree to which the journey was more quickly accomplished upon the iron tracks laid across the nation, was obviated by the view from the train compartment's window, as Rollingwood and I sat facing each other in the narrow space. That which I had glimpsed years before, and even had been able to inspect at closer range when the carriage had stopped upon the road to London, had been transformed from its first encroachment – which had been appalling enough – to its complete fulfilment, utterly oppressing my soul. England's once-verdant fields, divided only by hedge and brook as far as the eye could see, were now overlain with a vast net of pipes and tubes, interconnecting with and branching off from each other; some were no greater in diameter than the span of one's hand, others were of terrifying girth, fully capable of swallowing anaconda-like the train in which I sat.

"You seem a bit ill at ease, Mr Dower." Ever the soul of sympathy, Rollingwood had leaned forward, peering with concern at my face. "Shall I open the window a bit–" He pointed beside us. "To allow some fresh air to enter?"

"God, no." That had been my response; I even reached forward to stay his hand. "As stifling as it might be in here, I fail to see how conditions would be improved by exposing ourselves to those outside. We seem to be passing through the humid climate of those jungles that afflicted Livingstone as he searched for the sources of the Nile."

My comment was prompted by the vapours that condensed upon the exterior of the glass, only slightly dissipated by the rapid passage of the train, and the billowing clouds blurrily visible beyond. The pressures contained within the snaking pipes were such that rents and tears in their bolted construction were constantly being exposed, allowing jets of steam to issue forth. What human figures could be discerned in the overheated landscape, where once yeoman farmers had tilled the earth, were engaged in the sweltering labour of maintaining the pipes and tubes as best they could; stripped to the waist, their sweating backs and shoulders reddened as though boiled, they seemed but dwarves to the monstrous forms they served.

I should have expected similar transformations, upon our arrival in London. Once Miss McThane's coffin, nailed up in its shipping crate, had been unfreighted by the labourers in the employ of the Gravitas Maximus Funerary Society, our party immediately had set out for Highgate. The journey from the centre of the city to what had been its outskirts had afforded me a similarly depressing view of the changes wrought by Steam, our new master. The London I had last seen but a pair of years ago had suffered enough by the advent of this technological regime, even before calamitous ruination had been visited upon it – or so I had believed then. But those stifling alterations had been but the vanguard of the greater ones that had now come. *Steam* still had been an invader then, however imminent its triumph; the outlines of what had been, the city built by Wren and Barry and the historic others, were still visible through the roiling mists and past the fiery pipes laid through the streets. But now it was a conqueror, secure in its dominion; little of the world I had known, when I stood inside my Clerkenwell watch shop and scanned through its bowed window, hoping desperately for custom, now could be seen unobscured. All damage from fire and destruction, that might have served as a useful admonishment against foolish enthusiasms, had been repaired more quickly than I would have imagined possible. The Future had now arrived complete, in all its crushing might.

"I mean, Mr Rollingwood, that I expected some respite from modernity – here, of all places." Such were my thoughts, now that I stood within the beloved cemetery's precincts. "Is there no reverence left anywhere, any regard for the Past and our departed?"

"Ah." My companion gave a slow nod. "I confess some familiarity with the sights that you now behold – our Society has been busy of late, conducting memorials here. I have become such a frequent visitor to Highgate, that its present appearance is one to which I am now thoroughly accustomed."

"More pity for you, then." With my garments already sodden with my own perspiration, I gazed about the grave-studded scenery, once an image of tranquil solemnity, now a riot of overgrown foliage. "I often think that we do not *accustom* ourselves to anything; we merely devolve to a state in which we no longer notice how thoroughly rotten things have become."

"Perhaps so." Rollingwood indulged me with his patient smile. "I won't dispute you. Suffice it to say I'm somewhat relieved that your response to these surroundings is more – shall we say? – *choleric* rather than *morbid*."

"What meaning is that remark intended to convey?"

"Very little, in the event. Only that I had been advised, by those with some prior knowledge regarding yourself, that there have been occasions in the past when your vital spirits had drawn to such a low ebb, that putting an end to your sorrows – by your own hand – had been contemplated. If being in a place such as this had prompted your taking such final action, I should be prepared to intervene, to the degree I would be able."

"Your gossiping sources should mind their own damned business." As so often before, I was nettled by others' presumptuous interest in my affairs. "Rest assured, that however much I entertain passing fancies – just as other men do – that particular one is in abeyance for the moment."

"I am gladdened to hear."

"And more importantly – why is it so infernally *hot*?" I again mopped my brow with a handkerchief that I could have wrung out like a dish-rag. "I would swear that the temperature is greater here than down in the city proper."

"The reason for that phenomenon is simple," explained Rollingwood. "Some time ago, a great entrepreneurial project had been undertaken, by which a system of boilers – immense apparatuses, larger than any ever before constructed – were sunk below the earth on which we stand." With a stamp of his foot, Rollingwood indicated the location of which he spoke. "The intent was to provide London with even more copious amounts of that steam power which it demands."

"As if it were needed," I observed sourly. "I would have thought it had plenty enough."

"The appetite is seemingly insatiable. Alas, the enterprise foundered; its authors were too ambitious, attempting too much – and too hasty, precautioning too little. A fiery subterranean explosion was the result, not breaching the earth's surface like a new Vesuvius, but confined to the vaulted chambers beneath us. Nearly all of the labourers tending the furnaces were instantly consumed, and the company had some difficulty in securing replacements for them."

"How unsporting of our lower classes, to be so reluctant to have themselves turned to ash."

"Indeed." Rollingwood seemed oblivious to my sarcasm. "Such selfish attitudes only impede progress. The upshot in this case being that the buried furnaces roar on, burning the fuel that had been stockpiled for their operation. Unattended, the vertical apertures providing the air necessary for combustion have shattered from neglect, permitting the heat and vapours to escape directly here – thus, the elevated temperatures that you have noted."

Indeed, other changes than that had come to my attention. The sultry climate contained within the cemetery's walls, the constant radiation welling up from the earth itself and the humid clouds roiling just above my head, had resulted in a consequent transformation to the foliage. No longer did Highgate represent an English park, verdant but well-tempered; Nature had run wild here, spurred by the tropical climate that had been created. The ground and every stone, every tree trunk, was carpeted with spongy lichens, so thick and grotesquely coloured as to resemble an Arab rug merchant's wares, overlapping in such profusion as to dazzle an adventurer's eye. Riots of vines tangled in the branches overhead, looping about each other in serpentine congress. The modest and well-trimmed underbrush between the tombs had been usurped by botanical monstrosities, with pendulous shield-like leaves as broad as the ears of elephants, shiny as though their dark-green tint had been lacquered upon them, water dripping from the lowest points.

The resemblance to some malodorous rain forest, of the sort more commonly found about the globe's equator rather than in our otherwise chilly latitudes, did as much as the encompassing heat to muddle my thoughts; the scalding mist caught in my lungs prevented drawing a full enough breath to clear my head. I kept myself close to Rollingwood, so I might grasp his arm for support, in the event of a swooning loss of balance–

"Good God, man; what is *that?*"

A moment was required for me to realize the voice that had spoken was my own; it had sounded distant and dream-like – or more properly, nightmarish – from the tepid fog settling upon my brain.

Another moment passed before that which had prompted the outburst came fully into view – dismayingly so, as though one were to discover the apparition that had tormented a night's sleep was in fact real, and sitting at the foot of the bed in the morning sunlight.

"Think nothing of it," said Rollingwood. "The creature is harmless."

"It might very well be, while it is over *there*–" I pointed toward a spot several yards away, and a particularly overgrown section of foliage. "My concern is about what happens when it and its fellows come over *here*."

For what I had spotted was some sort of canine, of a not inconsiderable size, with a slinking gait and hunched shoulders, and a spotted hide. The muzzle of its lowered head displayed a distinctly unpleasant and slavering grin, as though it were relishing the discomfiture that its appearance had produced in me. So unexpected and outlandish was its presence upon nominally British soil that the name by which such an animal was called – for I had seen engravings in naturalist tomes depicting it – had been driven from my mind.

"It is merely a *hyena*." My companion helpfully supplied the vanished word. "They can be a bit nasty, as adventurers' reports have related – but can I assure you that we have nothing to fear."

"Bloody hell." Alarm evoked a coarser vocabulary to my speech. Two more of the beasts had appeared – perhaps there was a whole pack of them close by. Their eyes glittered with a malign intelligence, their exposed teeth giving the appearance of fierce delight, as though they were already anticipating being able to sink their yellowed fangs into the throat of their prey – presumably me, given how they had fastened their gaze in my direction. "What are those devilish bastards doing here?"

"What do wild animals do anywhere, that is home to them?" Rollingwood's shoulders lifted in a shrug. "I am not conversant with their exact habits, but I rather imagine they spend their time either lolling about to no great purpose, or killing and eating whatever is smaller and more hapless than themselves. Nature is a grim business, over all."

"For God's sake, man, I wasn't inquiring as to how they occupy themselves – I meant, how did they come to *be* here? Hardly a native species, are they?"

"By no means, Mr Dower; the hyenas were imported to this spot. Some years ago, one of London's new breed of entrepreneurs, made wealthy beyond our ability to imagine, indulged the fancy of having a private zoölogical garden set up on the grounds of his estate nearby. The man had an entirely laudable aversion to iron cages, though, feeling it cruel and unnatural to pen up beasts that had been freely roaming about the African plains before their capture and transport here to England. Thus he allowed them to run free in the gardens surrounding the Georgian-period mansion he had erected – with not always salubrious results, from the reports I have heard. His dinner parties became increasingly ill-attended, ladies of genteel taste being particularly put off by the screams of various herbivores being torn apart, and the scenes of general slaughter that were visible out the dining room windows."

"I can well imagine." Not for the first time, I speculated on the peculiar fascination that the moneyed classes had for exotic animals, not being content to go peer at them in whatever foreign clime was more suitable to them, but absurdly keen on bringing them back as well, thinking them to be no more inconvenient than slightly larger lapdogs. I had experienced for myself the fruits of such folly, having once been pursued with carnal intent by a mechanical Orang-Utan, the deranged replacement for a sad creature that had sickened and died upon being shifted from temperate Borneo to the chillier wastes of Yorkshire. "But your explanation," I persisted, "does not suffice. What are these hyenas – and God knows whatever else – doing here in the cemetery of Highgate? Surely the beasts procured by this foolish individual are kept safely penned within the limits of his estate."

"Well… they *were*." Rollingwood seemed abashed himself, as though another man's foolishness had been his own. "But… events happened of their own accord, as they so often do in our affairs. The gentleman in question was somewhat distracted by the apparent failure of his zoo-keeping enterprise – very well, a great deal distracted by it. So much so, that in the turmoil of his subsequent thinking, he paid little attention to those matters of business that had afforded him the funds for such pursuits. He came to ruin, as one might expect; his rivals picked clean the bones of his financial carcass. Despair led to suicide, in the particularly grisly manner of a pistol shot to the head, in the presence of some of the larger carnivores prowling about on his mortgaged estate – which beasts availed themselves of the opportunity to consume those mortal remains that his bankers and creditors had overlooked." A slow shake of the head indicated Rollingwood's innate sympathy. "Very sad, indeed. The circumstances of the gentleman's death made it difficult to find a purchaser for the mansion and its grounds, which thereby fell into neglect. Impelled by hunger, the uncaged beasts knocked down the fences which only had sufficed to hold them as long as they were well-fed. The warmth of the environs here at Highgate attracted the animals – no doubt it seemed reminiscent of those more equatorial regions from which they had been brought. And the cemetery offered the additional advantage of – how shall I put it? *Prey*; yes, that would be the word."

"Do you mean to say that the native English foxes and hedgehogs – and mice and the lesser vermin – are sufficient for the appetites of African lions?"

"No… not exactly. The larger predators – including the hyenas, which I would advise you to steer clear of – remain a bit hungrier, shall we say, than they would if they were back in their native land. A few of the larger herbivores, having escaped the quarters in which they were previously pent up, still survive; if you look there–" He directed my attention with an outstretched forefinger. "Just there – you can spot one."

I looked where Rollingwood pointed; after a moment of peering scrutiny, I made out in the distance an elongated muzzle, the attached gaze possessed of a bovine tranquillity as the head bobbed above some low treetops.

"That," Rollingwood helpfully commented, "is a *giraffe.*"

"I bloody well know what it is. They might not be all that common a sight in Cornwall or even London, but people have still heard of these daft beasts. Are there many of them wandering about here?"

"Not enough to satisfy the appetites of the other creatures who prey upon them, and so their numbers are continually diminishing – a circumstance which has led to certain unfortunate... incidents."

That last word seemed evasive to me. "Such as, precisely?"

"Allow me to inform you that Highgate is no longer as popular a destination for the casual stroller, out for the day from the city, as it once was. And let us leave it at that."

"You are insane–" I stared at Rollingwood with a sudden and alarmed comprehension. "The whole lot of you – Gravitas Maximus Funerary Society and all the rest. *This* is your notion of a more decorous funeral service?" Looking away from him, I quickly surveyed the overgrown foliage encircling the spot where we stood; I fully expected some snarling beast to spring from its concealment at any moment, intent on my throat. "How do you expect to get my late wife safely into the ground, if we are all going to be gnawed upon at the side of the grave?"

"Calm yourself, Mr Dower – provisions have been made for your security." Rollingwood turned partway about, in order to gesture toward the party that had accompanied us to the cemetery. "These individuals are more than adequate to ensure that no harm comes to you, from man or beast."

"But they are nothing more than your hired mourners!" I had previously given but scant attention to the dozen or so black-clad figures who stood about the coffin some yards behind us on the path. They seemed an unimpressive lot, as might be expected from their willingness to be engaged for the purpose of expressing sham grief over the interment of one whom they had never met in life. "I see no great advantage in having them here, unless you somehow are capable of directing the lions' attention first to them, then once the beasts' appetites are satiated, we would be able to make our escape."

"These men possess virtues other than merely being edible." Rollingwood smiled with smug assurance. "If they appear somewhat disreputable to you, it is because they are drawn from those ranks of society in which harsher conditions prevail, than those to which you and I are accustomed."

"To be frank–" I gave them closer scrutiny. "They look like criminals."

"Oh, to be certain; have no doubt about that. But when recruiting associates who will not flinch from necessary action, however violent, one will not find many saints among the candidates. But they are reformed at least a little bit, by the application of ready pay."

The doubts I entertained were not lessened by Rollingwood's easy assurances. I could not refrain from further studying these employees of the Gravitas Maximus Funerary Society. Even from this distance, habitual villainy was apparent in their faces. The unfortunate circumstances of my career have given me ample – alas! – opportunity to note such: the ill-shaven cheeks and lantern jaws; the narrowed squint shifting about in all directions, searching for the least chance of illicit gain, whether it be an apple palmed from a monger's cart or the dynamited vaults of the Bank of England; the shoulders hunched into armour against the cudgels of prison guards, the great knobby hands dangling before, emptied for the moment of some victim's throat. The Society might have garbed them as best it could, into grieving black suits and top hats adorned with ribbons of mourning crêpe, the latter already shrinking and coiling snake-like in the cemetery's heavy mists, but the result was no more convincing than if wolves were draped with a fancy dress of lambs; the pointy teeth remained still apparent.

"Hold on–" Another apprehension seized me. "Are these men armed?"

"But of course," said Rollingwood. "Would you expect them otherwise?"

"My expectations are not at issue. Do you think it wise?" My continuing scrutiny had revealed to my eye the tell-tale shape of those instruments weighting the men's coat pockets, suitable for assaults on other persons. "I would not be startled to learn that some of them are murderers, who have somehow evaded the final punishment for their misdeeds."

"Very likely they all are, or at least the majority of them." My companion spoke of the matter with unnerving calmness. "Why would we have hired them, if they lacked appropriate experience for the job? If the need arises for defence against a voracious wild animal, then this crew will not flinch at the sight of blood."

I remained unconvinced of all about which Rollingwood had attempted to reassure me – it was a subject of conjecture as to whether I was more ill at ease contemplating the sudden appearance of those wild beasts which were presumably skulking about unobserved behind the cemetery's lush fronds, awaiting the best opportunity to assuage their hunger, or the possibility of a felonious insurrection among those who were supposed to be guarding us. That of which I entertained little doubt was that this entire memorial expedition was an episode of folly, ill conceived and unlikely to end well, with the risk of disaster increasing exponentially, the longer we remained here.

"And of course," continued Rollingwood, "such creatures as these, and the larger and more vicious ones, are not the only dangers that threaten, and against which you should be protected."

"What the devil are you talking about?" I eyed the man with a newly incipient suspicion. "What dangers do you mean?"

"My dear Mr Dower – let us just say that I was not greatly surprised when you accepted our invitation to come here to London. I'm certain that your residence in Cornwall is at most times imbued with tranquillity. But when that quiet is broken – say, by a rifle shot – then it's understandable that you were alarmed."

"You know of that?"

"Well…" He gave a noncommittal shrug. "One hears of things."

I debated with myself, as to demand from him the identity of the marksman who had taken aim at me that night. After a consideration only requiring a few seconds, I decided to refrain – either he knew no more of the assassin, and thus could tell me nothing; or he did, but would dissemble in the evasive manner he had already displayed.

"Very well." I saw no point in wasting any more time than necessary. "Perhaps we should commence with the service. Given the circumstances, I don't believe that a little haste would be all that unseemly. I am the one who is best acquainted with the deceased, and I can assure you that my late wife was never one for lingering farewells."

"But of course; I agree with you entirely." Rollingwood gave a small nod toward the others. "Our mourners – and in their additional capacity of our bodyguards – are engaged by the hour. And while your benefactor placed no limits on his expenditure, I see no reason to abuse his generosity. We are only waiting for Jamford to arrive; when he is here, we will commence with all due alacrity."

"*Jamford*?" The name rang no bells with me. "Of whom do you speak?"

"The clergyman who will deliver the eulogy. Our Society enlists his aid whenever possible, for just such memorial purposes. We find him to be eloquent and unusually tasteful in his choice of words. Which is an important consideration, as not all of our clients are of – shall we say? – the *common* faith. Some of them are in fact rather eccentric as to their beliefs, if they profess to have any at all. The Reverend Jamford is accommodating in these matters – but then, he is free to be, as strictly speaking he is no longer associated with the Church of England."

"Did he leave of his own accord, or did they throw him out?"

"I believe the relationship was sundered by mutual agreement. He had apparently been outspoken – to an embarrassing degree – on certain obscure points of theology."

"I take it then, that he was able to find some other, perhaps nonconformist denomination that was more to his liking?"

"There are several such from which to choose, Mr Dower; we live in unsettled times, with many finding no comfort in the old ways. As to the specific peculiarities of Jamford's faith – I've heard him say that the group is called the More Loving Embrace, or something like that – I'm not quite sure what they would be."

"*More Loving Embrace*? Sounds dire, to be frank. But never mind; it makes no difference to me." The fellow could have been a naked devil-worshipper, painted and prancing about to the drums of some Caribbean isle, and I would have found him no more objectionable than the last cleric with whom I had conversed, the lately incinerated Weebsome. "I imagine this person will perform as decent a job as any other – if he ever arrives."

"Punctuality is not his long suit, I fear. His thoughts reside for the most part in the world to come."

"Is there no way we can dispense with his services? I would not mind, and at this point, the likelihood of Miss McThane being disappointed is minimal."

"No–" Rollingwood gave a shake of his head. "Not without contravening the wishes of the benefactor who is paying for all. I was informed that he gave quite explicit instructions as to how we were to proceed."

"Damned cheeky of him – it is *my* dead wife that we are re-burying. I would have thought that I had a greater say in how it is to be accomplished."

"Perhaps, Mr Dower, it is precisely your feelings that he took into account."

"If he had, then his doing so is a rarity in my experience. There have been few if any times that–"

"Hold." Laying a hand upon my arm, Rollingwood interrupted my oft-repeated tirade. "Your prayers – if I believed you had any – have been answered. We need wait no longer to proceed with the service; the man has arrived."

Looking back down along the path, encroached on either side by the unnaturally steam-lushened foliage, I saw the group of those who had been hired to protect as well as mourn, however unconvincingly they might, divide like a respectful Red Sea before a promenading Moses. The figure who passed through their midst was not robed in chasuble or other liturgical vestments, as one might have expected at a more ornate London funeral; in his black serge coat and trousers, the only sign of his clerical vocation was the simple white-linen dog collar about his neck. Simplicity ended there, however; his visage was of a grimly commanding sort, a fierce chin raised like the prow of a ship cresting Life's stormy seas, a forehead crevassed by the constant severity of his thoughts, a squinting glare like chips of ice embedded in flesh hardly more pliant. The unbridled state of his snowy hair gave further testament to his eccentric convictions; it sprang uncombed and untrimmed from his brown-spotted scalp, in the manner of those who no longer feel bound by society's conventions, thus appearing rather like the prophets of old. Tucked in the crook of one arm was a ponderous morocco-bound Bible, its pages festooned with tattered slips of paper, scrawled with enough memoranda and emendations as to have completely rewritten the labours of King James' committee of Hebrew and Greek scholars.

"You are this Dower?" Speaking with blunt aggression, he thrust his leonine physiognomy an inch away from mine. "Speak up!"

"Yes…" Already cowed, I drew back a step. "The Reverend Jamford, I take it?"

"*Right* Reverend to you!" His scowl curdled even further. "You'll be obliged to observe the conventions."

"Have you become a bishop then?" Beside us, Rollingwood lost none of his amused air. "The promotion was long overdue, I imagine. You should have granted it to yourself before now."

"Wipe away that smirk, you young fool–" Jamford's gnarled hands clenched white-knuckled on the tome he carried, as though preparing to assault Rollingwood with it. "My Godly work continues apace. The world does not yet recognize me as it should – but it will! If I say I'm *Bishop*, then bloody well I am."

"Consecrate yourself as *Pope* then, and be done with your upward progress."

"Soon enough," muttered Jamford darkly. A paucity of fellow conspirators seemed no impediment to the vaulting ambitions of his soul. "We live in tumultuous times, Mr Dower–" He fixed upon me once more his intimidating glare; I felt skewered as a specimen beetle by an entomologist's pin. "You find yourself in the company of scapegraces – such as this sweet-faced idiot, and his lot."

"Which would be the lot who *pays* you," Rollingwood mildly protested. "When there are not many else who would."

"The untransfigured flesh must eat – thus we are caught on the prong of this wicked world." The hard set of the cleric's expression was scarcely less murderous than that of the disreputable mourners nearby. "Prepare yourself for the next world, Dower; it comes soon."

If the apocalyptic event had happened in the subsequent minute, I would have been happier; anything to escape the attention of another lunatic, of the sort which seemed to constantly gravitate toward me.

"Perhaps," I spoke, "if we are all assembled now – that is, if there is no one else whose arrival we are waiting upon – then is there the possibility that we could proceed with that for which we are here? If the hour is late in general, Reverend Jamford, then surely it is in the specific as well."

One concern motivated me to prod the others in this way; about us, the shadows of the vine-strangled trees and memorial statuary had already lengthened with the sun's declining from the noon hour. The ability to perceive shapes and motion through the humid mists had correspondingly decreased, evoking some apprehension on my part. The flesh-rending beasts who had taken up the cemetery as their habitat could very well be keeping their appetites in check until such time as a stealthier approach upon their quarry – including my own person – would be more likely to produce a satisfying result. The irony was not lost upon me that I had fled my hiding-hole on the remote Cornish coast, seeking greater safety in London, and now found myself threatened by animals rather than men, and which – to their credit – made no dissembling bones about their intentions. Ever thus; to paraphrase the metaphysical Anglican cleric, *We run to Death and Death meets us as fast.*

Poetry, however, provides greater consolation when one is secure behind the locked door of one's study; at the moment, I was adrift in what had become the wilds of Highgate, nerves tautened by listening for the pad of clawed feet in the surrounding undergrowth, and the glint of slitted yellow eyes through the wet fronds.

"Very well." Jamford gave a single nod of his shaggy head. "I have no desire to tarry here; I find this idle chatter disagreeable. Let us begin, and be done."

In short order – facilitated by Rollingwood's directions to those others loitering nearby, no doubt discussing various criminal enterprises and jailhouse reminiscences – our company was assembled at the gravesite some yards farther on. The coffin had already been lowered into the deep earth, its muddy sides trickling with more tears than from any of the stone-faced onlookers; a pair of grave-diggers, the apparent cousins of those I had last encountered in Cornwall, leaned upon their shovels a respectful distance away, until the completion of the ceremony and the resumption of their labours.

At the head of the grave, Jamford began his oration, voice growling and stentorian; the immense leaves at our backs trembled as though frightened at the portent of his words. I overheard some snickering among the hired mourners; this was a performance with which they were evidently familiar, its repetition being a subject for coarse humour. The cleric – or bishop, as he styled himself – clasped the leather-bound book in his roughened grasp, but did not open it, the contents having been engraved in memory some time back.

My attention being diverted elsewhere, the exact content of Jamford's eulogy was lost on me; I assumed that it was no more than the usual collection of pieties delivered on such occasions, in which the sentimental manage to find some comfort. I listened distractedly, as one might to the rumblings of thunder beyond a distant hill. Under the lid of the coffin, already specked with damp clods from the crumbling earth, was as much comfort as I had ever found in this life; that she might also have dispelled, with but a few words and a smile, these exasperating puzzles entangled about me – that was of little consequence.

Jamford's voice grew louder, amazingly so; he had started at such a pitch that I wouldn't have thought it possible before. I had lost track of time's passing, as persons of my age are wont to do, either from the depths of our musing or the threadbare fabric of our brains. I brought my gaze up from the grave and its contents; blinking, I listened for a moment before those sounds assumed meaning.

"Await ye the great machinery of resurrection!" He seemed a man possessed; he saw no one about him, sight lifted above our heads, his eyes fastened onto private visions in the roiling mists. "The teeth of those awesome gears – think ye your flesh is not meat to them? Shall the mainspring of the universe, unwinding but never unwound, be not slaked with your blood? Your bones are not iron – shall they not snap like twigs upon the rack of the escapement that never ceases to count the slow hours of eternity?"

The man is mad – the thought leapt completely formed to my mind. So often have I voiced to myself that suspicion, only to have subsequent events confirm it in every detail; to hear those inner, unbidden words once more was like the tolling of that long-familiar steeple bell heralding one's return to native soil. For better or worse, the land of the insane was home to me.

"Consider, ye wretched, ye heirs of blundering Adam!" To my dismay – a flicker of hope, that I might be wrong, was extinguished like a gnat between thumb and forefinger – the man continued in like manner. "Cog and flame are the instruments of the Lord's wrath – the first grinds, the second consumes the grist produced thereby. Your feeble repentance will not suffice to save you. Would the Author of this world have designed it with such precision, with such evident annihilating purpose, yet allowed some means of escape? The prisons built by men's hands are dark, doleful places, but a stray thread of sunlight still penetrates their stones from time to time, a lark's cheering song floats through the iron bars and succours a weary heart – but God builds more mightily than these! *He* is the Great Watchmaker! The screws *He* drives into place do not rust or fail! The mainspring *He* has wound ticks to Eternity!"

The frame of the erstwhile bishop's dementia came further into view, like some dread sarcophagus advancing through the mists, containing within the scraggy remnants of what had once been his sanity. To my ear, his funeral oration sounded as if his mind had been rendered captive of that which the German philosophizers term the *Zeitgeist*, or – if they had the decency to speak proper English – the *Spirit of the Age*. As surely as the great machines of Steam had encumbered the nation, so the landscape inside his skull had been transformed thereby. If any Saviour remained to him, it would be one with no bloody wounds upon His crucified hands and feet, but rather one who would open His chest as the Paganinicon had done so many years ago, to reveal whirling gears and wheels rather than a thorn-bound heart.

I glanced over at Rollingwood standing beside me. The hired mourners displayed no untoward reaction to Jamford's pealing words, but the customary smile had disappeared from the face of the Gravitas Maximus Funerary Society's representative. As had much of the colour that his eager young blood had brought before to his cheek – the man looked grievously appalled, as though this turn of events had not only been unanticipated by him, but was scarcely endurable.

With the point of my elbow, I managed a surreptitious nudge to his ribs. "Tell me–" I whispered from the corner of my mouth; my words were masked from others' detection by the bishop's continued roaring, "do these events usually go quite like this?"

"No–" An expression settled on Rollingwood's face, the like of which I had not previously seen there. "An interval of some weeks has passed since the reverend has conducted one of these – indeed, it might have been months; I would have to consult my business diary. But it seems as if some alteration has come over him in the meantime–"

"Oy! 'Ave a care, mate." One of the mourners, perhaps the most villainous in appearance of the lot, issued a barely *sotto voce* rebuke in our direction. "S'posed to be respeck'ful and all, and two of yez blath'rin' away like a pair o' magpies, y'are."

"Too right, Cecil." The next over, equally unshaven and disreputable, leaned forward in order to peer disdainfully at us. "And thet'un there be the fookin' widower! Plantin' 'is ball and chain in the sod, we are, and the bastid can't even stay shet up for couple minutes. Dis-*grace*-ful's whut it is."

Rollingwood ignored them. His continuing distress revealed a sterner element, which his previous cheerfulness had kept masked.

"Jamford was always a bit on the eccentric side–"

This concession seemed hardly necessary to me.

"Actually," continued Rollingwood, "more than a bit. But there were still at least a few bounds of propriety within which he managed to stay. But now he seems to have gone completely off the rails – I had not heard him speak in quite this manner before." He observed and listened to the bishop for a few seconds more, then turned back to me. "Once more, my sincerest apologies; I imagine this must be rather distressing to you."

"Whatever feelings I have in that regard are of little consequence." My statement was the truth; after so many occurrences of a similar nature, my sensibilities were numbed to a considerable degree. Men do not resolve to become stone-hearted; our lives calcify our tenderest elements, whether we will it or not. "And given that my wife is dead, I scarcely imagine that she is taking much offence, either." My exchange with Rollingwood went on unabated, despite the glares from the hired mourners. "But my endurance is an issue, however; how much longer do you think this will last?"

"It could be some time." Rollingwood shifted about uncomfortably. "He is of a long-winded tendency, which always before represented good value for money; few previous clients ever complained about him delivering a perfunctory account. For many people, the worth of such services is measured by their length."

In this, as with so many other things, I was not of the same opinion. That old maxim, *Brevity is the soul of wit*, could profitably be amended to include funerals as well. The enjoyment which others derive from their own public weeping was nothing in which I cared to indulge; the sooner we all could escape Highgate's damp, predator-infested environs, the more satisfied I would be.

This was, in point of fact, more than mere inclination on my part; as Jamford rolled onward with his increasingly demented speech – more blathering about machinery and God, and some apparent similarity between them – my anxiety increased. Already I had been concerned about the wild animals which had taken up residence in the cemetery, of which creatures I had already obtained a glimpse; I very much doubted that the mourners who had been engaged for the memorial service would do much more than save their own hides, if the occasion arose. New worries, however, advanced upon my thoughts and seized a position there. As we stood by the gravesite, the daylight had rapidly diminished, casting the scene into a twilight aspect even more sepulchral than before. Though our sector of the world had entered into its afternoon hours, there was yet considerable time before sunset – but while I could still distinguish Rollingwood next to me, and the forms of the others gathered about, the shadows of the surrounding foliage had been completely engulfed by the enveloping gloom.

I tilted my head back, seeking some reason for this phenomenon; I pay little attention to calendars of astronomical events – indeed, who does? – so I would have been unlikely to have been aware of an impending solar eclipse. Such did not seem to be the case; while the sky directly overhead was completely shrouded by the mists rising and condensing from the heated earth below, some blurry yellow light from the paled sun was still visible about the surrounding horizon. The occlusion across the cemetery grounds was more in the nature of a partial shadow, cast by some enormous object far above, of such scale as to darken the landscape for miles in any direction.

A fear of large, hovering things is not unreasonable, by my reckoning; surely I am not alone in estimating that little good can come from them – worse yet, if their visible aspect is shrouded from one's view. If my general apprehension had been unloosed by the sight of wild animals in the vicinity – and the indication of larger and hungrier ones, which I had not yet seen – it now bounded forward with no restraint.

"Look – you see that, don't you?" I made no attempt to keep my voice to a decorous whisper as I grasped hold of Rollingwood's arm with one hand and pointed upward with the other. "There! Above us!"

"See what?" He had glanced to the deeply overcast sky, but displayed no reaction to what he might have seen; indeed, he returned a puzzled expression at me. "What do you mean?"

"Are you blind?" Both amazed and appalled, I stared back at him. "You are unable to perceive... *that?* Bloody huge! Blocks out the sun! *There*, you imbecile!"

"Well, tears it, that does–" The hired mourner who had previously admonished me now began to roll up his jacket sleeve, the muscles of his forearm drawing tight his upraised fist. "If a sinse o' propri'ty won't shutter yer gob, then I'll demned well 'ave to."

"Do 'im over, Cecil–" His companion nudged the man in the small of the back. "Bluidy rude, 'e is."

"Oh!" At the same moment, comprehension dawned upon Rollingwood. "Yes, of course – impressive, isn't it?"

"This is insane–" To me, it now seemed as if the self-styled bishop's lunacy had become contagious, infecting everyone in the vicinity. I dropped my hand from his arm and stepped backward. "We should flee, at once–"

"By no means." His smile appeared once more, a luminous instance in the deepening gloom. "I see where I have erred, Mr Dower – I should have informed you at greater detail about the particular nature of this service, and all that it entails."

All this while, Jamford's funeral oration had continued unabated – if anything, his thunderous voice had increased in volume, in an attempt to drown out the hubbub which had broken out before him. I discerned further reference to *machines* and *gears* and *God*, but had no superabundance of attention with which to join all together and make sense of them. Whatever was taking place in the heavens, or at least that part immediate to us, it had no inhibiting effect on either his vigour or dementia.

"Oy, Cecil – this bluidy great galloon's all aj'tated o'er nowt." The threat of violence was forestalled by the one mourner deciding to restrain his more pugilistically-minded comrade. "Ign'rant bastid, 'e is, but more t'be pitied, seems."

"Informed me of what?" Thus goaded, I demanded explanation. "I came here at your invitation, expecting no more than a proper funeral – which is what you assured me would happen." To my concern about the security of my person was added a mounting anger, over once more having been cozened into others' bizarre schemes. "And now–" I gestured toward the increasingly ominous sky, "what monstrous event do you mean to inflict on me?"

"Pray calm yourself, Mr Dower – your fears are understandable, but ungrounded. What a fool I've been!" Rollingwood's smile persisted as he heaped obloquy upon himself. "I did not sufficiently take into account the length of your exile from this our modern world. That which you have seen of it, at such a telescopic distance, is but a fraction of the advances that have been reached by Mankind in your absence."

"True enow," agreed the loquacious mourner. "Be whut 'appens, when yokels like this'n brought to the city. *Most* disor'enting, must be!"

"I swear…" Now it was my hands that were clenched into straining fists. "If no explanation is forthcoming, I will not be responsible for what happens next."

"Then how fortunate it is, that you will be able to witness for yourself – at this moment! – that our intentions constitute no harm to you." Raising his arm, Rollingwood directed my attention toward the figure at the head of the grave. "I do believe that our chosen cleric is approaching the climax of his speech. All will be revealed in short order, once he concludes."

A sense of disgust overwhelmed me, evoked more by my own failings than the moral deficits of those in whose company I found myself. Surely I had experience enough, that would have enabled me to foresee the entangling snares that others set before my feet. What was the point of embracing a hermit's life, as much as I had been able to, and then forsake it at the first enticement? I should have been of sterner resolve, and confronted whatever dangers lurked there, rather than fleeing to London and finding myself in circumstances of greater hazard.

I turned on my heel and stalked away, to put as much distance between myself and the person who had inveigled me here, as well as to lessen the impact upon my eardrums of Jamford's increasingly apocalyptic rantings. Several yards from the gravesite, I stationed myself on a slight rise, overgrown with vines and damp fronds; scowling, I folded my arms across my chest, as much as daring any lion or other predator to approach me in my present sullen mood.

"Lord, do carry on, don't he?" An amused voice spoke from close beside me. "Some types in this world, love the sound of their own voices. Be one of that breed, surely."

"My desire for companionship at the moment is greatly diminished." I did not bother to glance over and determine who had accosted me. The humid mists were so thick, and the shadow so thorough from whatever enormous object loitered overhead, that the individual might easily have approached without me noticing, or perhaps had already been standing at the spot – and I, preoccupied, had not even discerned him. "If you desire conversation, you had best seek elsewhere."

"Palaver's fair enough, suppose – most the species rattle away, whether have something to speak of or not." The individual, whoever he might be, sounded highly amused by his own observation. "Myself, speak as much or more than the general run of humanity – but then, I've cause, being industrious sort and all."

Strangely, this man's voice seemed familiar to me, though I could not immediately summon from memory the occasion on which I might have heard it. Curiosity as to his identity got

the better of me, overbalancing my previous nettled disdain.
I turned and studied his face, seeking some clue there. A
younger person, presentably attired – more than presentable,
to be truthful; his swallow-tailed suit was of ostentatious cut
and expense, trimly fitted to his slender form. A silken, bottle-
green cravat knotted at his throat, trousers of an extravagant
hound's-tooth check, more suitable to salon than funeral –
the effect produced was that of someone not only given over
to fashion, but who could afford the most *au courant* tastes.

"Nick Spivvem, at your service–" He gave a slight incline of
his head, with a lopsided smile rather more insinuating than
the constant and honest one I had become used to seeing
on Rollingwood's face. "Did promise, Mr Dower, that we'd
a meeting again – soon enough, seems, that haven't forgot
already!"

The contrast was jarring, between the costly attire of this
Spivvem character – if such was his actual name; my suspicions
were already aroused as to everything about him – and his
slangy patois. A criminal sort, perhaps, his habiliments both
an indicator of the success of his felonious enterprises and an
aping of the moneyed classes upon which he was most likely
to prey, either as a thief or a swindler.

"You!" This perception was enough to trigger my
recognizing the man, and recalling the time when I had last
seen him. "That was you who came to the inn – and who I
had to chase off, with threat of violence–"

The man's sly, narrow face was the only similarity between
his previous incarnation and the one which stood beside me
now, and even that had been greatly transformed; before, his
visage had been scruffy and ill-shaven, seemingly weathered
by the exposure to the elements that vagabonds suffer as a
consequence of their wandering lives. Had that been some
artful disguise, along with the ragged, dirt-blackened garb and
worn-thin boots in which he had appeared at my doorstep,

put on with some intent to deceive? And to what purpose?

"Indeed, was I." The pleasure Spivvem took in his masquerade was evident. "Didn't get along very well then, did we? But all's forgiven – imagine had great deal on your mind, and not given to usual ways of hospitality."

Back in Cornwall, during our regrettable encounter at the inn, his manner of speech had been considerably coarser, evidently assumed as another facet of his disguise; it remained odd and elliptic, a cant typical of his thieving breed.

"There is nothing," I said, "which requires absolution. My manners are not the issue, you blackguard–"

"Eh! Uncalled for, that!"

"What is your purpose in coming here?" I could feel the temper of my blood mounting up my neck and into my own face. "Nothing well-intentioned, I'm certain." Under other circumstances, I might not have been as quick to anger – but the man's unexpected appearance on the site, along with the continued battering of Jamford's oration, and the sky's ominous and still unexplained darkening, had frayed my nerves to a snapping point. "Explain yourself – do you mean to aim another bullet in my direction, with a pistol rather than a rifle this time?"

"Bullet? Bluidy hell, Dower – never fired gun in life, and not likely start with target such as yourself. Kindly disposed toward you, am I."

"Pardon my skepticism in that regard – but if you were not the marksman skulking about in the night, then who was?"

"Very good inquiry, much worth discussing. Would enlighten you, given chance. Time on hands? Say, once done hereabouts? The Flask down High Street's private enow."

"I have no intention of accompanying you to any establishment." I drew back, fixing a colder glare upon this Spivvem. "What reason have I to trust you? Privacy is what you speak of – but you have intruded upon mine twice now.

You come here uninvited, and you came there in Cornwell with your form disguised in a peculiar and loathsome manner. And now you assure me of your friendliness? I think it rather more likely that you intend to separate me from my present companions, so that you can *privately* do me some harm."

"If all's wanted, do it easily enough, without all that bother." Spivvem's expression hardened into something less cordial. "Gents about grave – know 'em?"

"Other than as hired mourners, I do not. I have been informed, though, that they are also functioning as the guardians of my person, in case of various beasts intruding upon us. That being the case, they might as well be usefully employed in ejecting yourself from the premises."

"Yes," said Spivvem, "would for certain. Be acquaintances of mine, so know proclivities – can be counted on not just for fists and boots, but for enjoyment of using them. Fun-loving types, they are. But if wanted do *you* over, easily have slipped few quid in their pockets, and goner you'd be."

"But they are not currently in your employ?"

"As said–" Spivvem gave a shake of his head. "At moment, no. Didn't think necessary, mission being more to help than hinder."

"I am glad to hear you have not purchased their allegiance." I turned from him, preparing to stride back toward Rollingwood and the others, my interest in whatever else this intruder might say having come to an end. "Perhaps you should count yourself fortunate that your presence here has not yet been noted by others than myself. Before, you forced yourself upon me when I had few if any allies to forfend your unwanted meddling, and my own efforts were insufficient to put a stop to it. The situation is otherwise now; these rowdy mercenaries, engaged on my behalf, are undoubtedly prepared to alter your mind in this regard. Whatever advantage you sought by contacting me, either here or elsewhere, I advise you to abandon its pursuit before lasting harm comes to you."

"Speak very well, Dower, you do–" Spivvem called after me when I was but a few steps away. "Concern for my welfare *very* noble. But be better off, thinking of yourself. In worse mishaps than can imagine, and walking blind into 'em. Great deal could help you with – spurn me at your peril."

"That is a risk I am prepared to assume." I halted and glanced back over my shoulder at him. "It seems no greater than the others from which I must choose."

He shouted no rejoinder as I continued walking away – which was just as well, for I would have paid no attention, had he done so.

SIX

Mr Dower Disdainfully Regards the Future

I CONTINUED ON MY short way back to the grave. Reaching it and the assembly gathered around, I looked again to the spot from which I had returned; the mysterious Spivvem had disappeared, having either completely departed from the area or been swallowed up by the intervening mists and deepening gloom.

The latter of which had increased to such a profundity that lanterns had been lit and placed at the head of the grave, their upward glow illuminating the Right Reverend Jamford in a spectral manner, and allowing the rest of the company to be discerned.

"Where did you go?" Rollingwood's anxiety visibly diminished when he perceived my reappearance beside him. "I told you – we approach the final moments of the service."

"Calm yourself," I said. "I but went for a brief stroll, being overcome with my emotions; I am certain you sympathize. And rest assured – I would not have missed this for all the world."

What I had missed, and for which I was grateful, was a considerable amount of Jamford's eulogy – a mild term for his performance, now even more agitated and discomforting than when I had strayed from the full force of its delivery. If my suspicions had been aroused before as to his mental state, further attention confirmed that his grip upon sanity was a precarious thing.

"Light springs from the earth's depths!" Wild-eyed, hair in greater disarray as though electrified, he thundered on in a mounting passion. "The machinery of Grace abounding! The dead shall not be mired in cold clay – they rise to the heavens! And not on some day which our old outmoded faith promised but never delivered – *the promised day is upon us now!*"

That final and rather startling announcement seemed to act as an initiating signal to all those congregated about the gravesite – save myself, of course. An excited hubbub coursed through the hired mourners, as though they anticipated some desirable event with which they were familiar from previous funerals. Rollingwood shared in this emotion; craning his neck, he joined with the others in raptly gazing up at the darkness over their heads.

As did I, scarcely being able to do otherwise, given the apparition above.

The awesome shadow was rendered more intimidating by the advent of a swelling wind, as though the proximity of the object had summoned the forces of Nature. One moment a freshening breeze, lessening a margin of the steaming humidity about us, then the next a veritable gale scouring in from the hills, strong enough that I needed to brace myself shoulder-first, to keep from being knocked off my feet.

"What is happening?" I shouted to make myself heard. About the grave, the hired mourners had assumed similar stances, heads lowered and hands clutching the brims of hats tight against their brows. Jamford remained eerily upright, rock-like in a transport of ecstasy, his widened eyes gleaming and the leather tome clutched against his chest. "Is this some part–"

There was no time for me to pursue the query, or for Rollingwood to reply. The wind had the effect of dispelling the mists, sending ragged clouds scudding over the ground, and revealing much of what had been hidden before. I saw no beasts waiting to pounce; very likely they had been frightened away, not so much by the increasing wind, but by the grinding mechanical noise I now heard coming from somewhere above. The gears and pinions capable of producing such clashing, deafening noise would need to have been on a scale commensurate with that which cast the immediate world into shade.

My vision had adjusted sufficiently that I was able to discern some details of that immensity. The impact upon me was vertiginous in the extreme – for a dizzying moment I felt as if the landscape had somehow been inverted, with the boggy soil beneath transformed into a sky solid enough to prevent my plummeting through it, and the vista overhead now comprising the earth from which I had been removed. For above me – or was it below? Disoriented, I could not tell – I saw a vast expanse of tombstones and marble statuary, all of the cemetery's aspects reproduced to perfection. If the graves my gaze swept across had opened up, their grisly contents might have tumbled upon my head, or I might have fallen into their embrace.

"There!" Pointing ahead of where we stood, Rollingwood crowed in triumph, his expression even more radiantly happy than before. "Did I not tell you this would be wonderful?"

That to which he had directed my attention was a set of thick hempen ropes, that had come tumbling and looping down from the aerial cemetery overhead. Two of the mourners, it appeared, had been engaged for additional duties; they sprang into the open grave, and with practiced speed secured these lines to the iron hardware on either side of the casket. But a few seconds later, I was set aback, witnessing that which I had never expected–

Its weight tautening the ropes, higher and higher the casket rose from out of the earth, the wooden form swaying in the unabated wind. For a moment, I could gaze directly at it, suspended with the mortal remains of my late wife contained within. Then the coffin's upward progress resumed, drawn inexorably toward the vast graveyard occluding the sky above.

"Unbeliever!" A cry incisive and brutal as a trumpet call struck my ears. "Doubt you now?"

I looked across the emptied hole in front of me and saw the Right Reverend Jamford, greatly magnified in triumph. His maddened eyes locked upon mine.

"I told you!" He jabbed a blunt fingertip toward the dangling coffin. "*The Resurrection comes!*"

"I had hoped you would like it–" Sitting upon a boulder rendered bright green by overlapping badges of damp lichen, Rollingwood was the image of utter dejection. "So many others before you have expressed their appreciation for the services we provide."

"*So many others* are bloody idiots." I stood some distance away, having turned my back to him and folded my arms across my chest. "How else did the world get this way?"

"Rail against the modern as you wish, Mr Dower." A defensive note sounded in Rollingwood's voice. "But I do believe you regard the Gravitas Maximus Funerary Society in an unjust manner. We have endeavoured to raise the standard of human practices that have been the same since our naked ancestors hunted with sharpened sticks and stone axes. We would all regard customary burial practices as filthy and disgusting – shoving our beloveds' remains in the wormy ground, then tamping the dirt upon their faces! – if we were not jaded by the long centuries' usage. Have we been doing any more than merely removing them from view, so that they might moulder and rot unobserved? Were you to ask my opinion, crypts and mausoleums are scarcely more reverent, the only difference being that they rest upon the surface of the earth, rather than being assembled in its depths."

"So *this* is your great innovation?" I glanced over my shoulder at him, then angled my gaze up to the sky. The mists and clouds had partially gathered once more, but the immense burial ground I had witnessed floating above, its inverted landscape thickly studded with simple tombstones and more elabourate memorials, remained in sight. "That our dead should not repose peaceably in the ground, but instead be deposited in the air?"

"And why not, if we have the means to do so?" Rollingwood's words became a bit more heated. "We wish those departed from us to ascend to Heaven – skeptics such as yourself might sneer at the notion, but such is still the common creed – and if so, what is the purpose of miring their bones and cold flesh somewhere beneath our feet?"

"I rather believe that blessed abode, if it exists at all, is some distance away." I spoke my objection as drily as possible. "Given the miles and miles that the deceased would have to ascend in order to gain their wings and harps, the interval from *here*–" I pointed to the damp ground "–to *there*–" my forefinger indicated the aerial cemetery "–it hardly seems noticeable."

"Perhaps so; I will not debate these finer theological points with you. People's souls are immaterial things – they are unlikely to tire, no matter how far they have to go. But consider a matter of practicality for us, the living, who remain behind. This world is a material object as well, and there is only so much of it. To the degree we fill it up with coffins and corpses, there is correspondingly less room left for those still animate. Whereas the sky is, to all intents and purposes, infinite; the dead we place there do not crowd and encumber us."

"I had not heard that we are now cheek-to-jowl with our ancestors." I shook my head at the man's sophistry. "You continue to astound with your revelations. To me, it had seemed that we still had some empty space left, in which we could deposit a few stiffened parcels."

"Mock me as you will, Mr Dower – you are able to do so only because you despise the days to come. My employers and I take a longer view, and a kinder one."

Our conversation had reached an impasse, beyond which I did not feel it worth pursuing, at least for the moment. Falling silent, I gazed across the expanse of Highgate, its features obscured as much by my deep brooding as by the overgrown foliage and slowly tumbling waves of steam. My late wife's funeral, such as it was, had been concluded for some time; the coffin containing the unbreathing body of Miss McThane had been lifted to that vast cemetery above – literally an unearthly thing, separated from the world most familiar to us – and was secured in some inverted grave there. Or so Rollingwood had assured me; on this point alone I did not doubt him, as it was unlikely that he could have devised an account that would have been more distasteful to me.

His job done, the Right Reverend Jamford had departed, to tend to other functions of his new faith, and to its acolytes; the lunatical imagery of his booming words no longer assaulted my ears, for which I was grateful. The hired mourners had departed as well, after having received some discreet payment from Rollingwood, pound notes in plain, unlettered envelopes; they were probably drinking away the proceeds from their minimal labours, down at one of the nearest pubs in the district of Highgate proper. I had chosen not to leave at the same time; whatever protective services those ruffians had provided, I felt I had no further need of them. Let the beasts prowling about Highgate's grounds rend me limb from limb, and feed upon my flesh; this would not be the first occasion upon which disgust prompted the judgment that my own life was a mere trifle, discarded without regret.

Somewhat to my surprise, Rollingwood elected to remain with me, at least for a time; I would have thought that concern for his own safety would have prompted a hastier exit. But as I had noted before, he was of that breed of men who esteem sociability as much as I disdain it.

"Tell me, then…" A degree of pity, as well as my own idle curiosity, prompted my turning toward him again. "The events which I witnessed a little while ago – the appearance of that great airborne burial ground – how did such come to be? You wished to talk to me about *practical* matters – surely an enterprise of such immensity was not readily achieved."

"Much was required, indeed." He visibly brightened to a degree, evidently relieved that I had abstained from haranguing him further. "But from small endeavours, great profits might flow, leading to exponentially larger endeavours, and even larger profits. Such was the case with the notion of setting the dead to rest in the sky, rather than in the ground. The first attempt was but with a single corpse, the tragically young daughter of a gentleman with inventive talents – much like your own father, I would imagine."

"It would be difficult," I said, "for me to vouch for that, as I did not know the man – my father, that is. But if there are indeed others similar to him, then God help us all."

"Perhaps I misspoke; I meant no offence." Rollingwood continued his exposition. "As is often the case, the inventor to whom I refer was also an entrepreneur, industrious to attract both enthusiasm and capital to his endeavours. He and his backers seized their moment – as the Bard might have described it, one of those tides in the affairs of men that leads to fortune. The great changes in our world which you have observed, and which you continually bemoan – they have had their effects on the sympathies of the general population, as you might also expect. The Right Reverend Jamford might have placed himself sufficiently beyond the pale with his outright statements of his beliefs, so that he can no longer be endured by the old and staid Church of England, but a good deal of what he espouses is shared by a great many – likely the majority, in fact. The Second Coming, the End of Days, the Apocalypse; whatever you wish to term it–" Rollingwood waved a dismissive hand. "Since those cataclysms to which you yourself were a witness, that prophesied event is much on people's minds. Many believe that our world is changing only as a precedent to its coming to a conclusion. That being the case, a certain evangelicalism has taken flight amongst them, which welcomed this new mode for burial of the dead. The feeling seems to be that Resurrection is near at hand, just as you have heard Jamford so strenuously proclaim, then surely it's better to have deceased loved ones up in the sky, where they are likely to experience a happier and more elevated return to living form, than down in the cold, clammy earth."

"What nonsense," I grumbled. "If the end of the world managed to put a stop to such delusions, then it would indeed be a blessed occurrence."

"You are welcome to your opinion, Mr Dower. But that which you decry has been a commercial opportunity for others, and one of considerable scope."

"By others, I take it you refer to the Gravitas Maximus Funerary Society, by which your own bread is buttered."

"A modest share of its profits is paid to me – you are correct about that. But I would think well of its operations, regardless. As do many of our fellow citizens." Raising a hand, Rollingwood pointed to the immense shape of the aerial cemetery, unavoidably visible through the clouds, its grave-studded bulk obscuring a large measure of the sky.

"And by many, I wish to indicate not just the good folk of London, but all the regions about it – and beyond! All the way to Yorkshire, and Scotland to its northernmost Hebridean fringes. The enthusiasm for upward interment has swept the nation; it speaks a great deal for the isolation of your Cornish redoubt, that you had not been made aware of it before now. But these advances will sweep across your neighbours there as well."

"I have little doubt of it; they are not clever enough to resist, and will embrace them as fervently as the rest." A disapproving scowl formed on my face as I regarded the hovering monstrosity. "But do you actually mean to tell me there are more of these hideous constructions? That every district in the British Isles has one installed above it? What a gloom-inspiring prospect."

"No, just the one; it is sufficient for the purpose. You view it at a distance, and are impressed by its size; were you to make a closer inspection, to actually go and walk about its upper surface, I am sure that you would be completely astounded. And in fact, it is continually expanding about its periphery – a great many corpses are produced on a daily basis, in this world below, and accommodation must be made for them in their elevated and permanent residence." Smiling once more, Rollingwood gave a small nod. "I anticipate your question to follow, Mr Dower. Why *one* greatly centralized cemetery, rather than many lesser ones scattered about our skies? It is because the technical means providing such levitation requires this concentrating of the dead. You are familiar with those means, even though you had not seen before this awesome application of them. At your late wife's previous funeral service – surely you recall those floating cherubim, with their mechanically beating wings?"

"How could I forget them? Though I have indeed tried."

"There you have it," said Rollingwood. "The gases generated within the ceramic casing of those dead infants were barely sufficient to set them aloft. With this–" He pointed once more to the airborne cemetery visible in the distance. "The process is brought to a state of perfection. We err when we believe that the Age of Steam, this Future that has hurtled upon us and become our Present, is epitomized by gigantic, clanking machines and engines, their iron gears towering above us. I assure you, Mr Dower, that such is not the case; a wiser perception will understand that Steam is the great solvent of the world's mysteries; all that was rigidly glued, one solid mass to another, comes apart with the application of sufficient heat, releasing all manner of wonders. Organisms from other lands, invisible to the naked eye, are bred and nurtured in covered glass dishes, until they are of a dazzling potency. You know of those, I take it?"

"I do." Even to my own ear, my words were frostily uttered. "A different clergyman told me of them."

"Then you understand how it is done – and more; how it is accepted. Once we would have been appalled at seeming conjuror's tricks being applied to the otherwise lifeless forms of our loved ones. But Steam has loosened Mankind's hoary old convictions as well; now we think it marvellous." Rollingwood's smile was now a signal of relished triumph. "The Future is upon us, Mr Dower; if you choose not to embrace, that is but your choice."

"Spare me your mercenary enthusiasm – but elucidate this. The dead who are entombed and buried and otherwise encysted in this hovering cemetery you find so marvellous – they are at the same time the source of its ability to stay aloft?"

"Exactly so. Their decomposition is managed in a discreet way, the gases emitted being harvested and compressed so as to produce the results you observe. Which are sufficient, as I previously indicated, for one great aerial cemetery, which is both tethered and moved about by a system of iron cables extending from the edges of the construction, and anchored at appropriate points all across Britain." Rollingwood lifted his hand and indicated a distant point. "You can see one of them right there."

He was correct about that; I had previously discerned the tautened line perhaps a mile or so away, visible through the mists only due to its immense cross-section. I had not realized its significance, though, as the more elevated banks of clouds had concealed the doleful construct floating above.

"By a simple expedient," continued Rollingwood, "the cemetery is relocated from one place to another above this nation. Powerful engines drive the winches aboard the cemetery; by paying out the lines at one side, and drawing up those opposite, it travels about as needed, so that all might have their turn at enjoying the spiritual comforts it provides. Ingenious, I'm sure you'll admit."

"I will admit nothing of the kind–" I seethed now, words crawling through clenched teeth. "For what you have told me, when translated into honest words, is that your filthy invisible bugs feast upon the corpses that you have inveigled into your possession, and their rotting stench sends this whole ghoulish construction up into the air, as one great putrefying mass, that you can then shift about for the sake of attracting more customers from the recently bereaved."

"I must protest, Mr Dower. You describe these matters with the ugliest possible locutions–"

"And this," I persisted relentless, "is what you mean to do with my late wife's body?"

"Most people have no qualms about the arrangement. Indeed, they generally find some poetic satisfaction in the thought that their deceased elevate themselves, so to speak."

"Sir, you disgust me." I might well have murdered the man, if I could have endured the touch of his throat between my tightening hands – but the stink of corruption I detected about him made it impossible. "I can no longer stand your company; I will make my own way hence."

I strode away, not glancing back at the man.

"You are placing yourself at considerable danger–" Rollingwood called after me. "These are not safe premises in which to wander alone."

"That risk is preferable to me." I continued on, forcing my way through the banks of mist mounting to my waist. "See to your own person, as you wish."

Of course, I was completely lost within a matter of minutes.

I expected as much; whatever memories I might have retained of strolling about Highgate, from younger and happier days – or at least less annoyed – they were eclipsed by the transformations that had been laid over the cemetery. What had been winding, tastefully manicured paths – lined by marble angels and other memorial figures like weeping sentries – were now a jungled maze, suitable for more intrepid explorers than myself. I realized now that the route which I had taken to the gravesite prepared for Miss McThane's casket, accompanied by Rollingwood and the protective mourners hired by the Gravitas Maximus Funerary Society, had been widened and cleared by frequent traffic and the regular application of those broad-bladed implements known as *machetes*, by which passage through snaking vines and choking foliage can be achieved. I had thought at the time that the environs were oppressively close and bewildering – but straying farther, I perceived that those spaces had been of cathedral-like emptiness compared to those in which I was now entangled.

To make the situation worse – as if that were necessary! – twilight was at last falling upon the surrounding hills. What illumination could penetrate the clouds and mist was tinging red, and would soon be extinguished completely. I had entertained the thought of climbing to some higher point from which the lanterns of Highgate village's shops and homes might have been sighted, allowing me to navigate an exit from the cemetery – but those hopes were dashed by the towering height of the greenery about me. I might as well have been plunged to the bottom of some Alpine crevasse, its narrowing walls unclimbable even with rope and axe.

When total darkness ensued, an event only one or two hours distant, I would be utterly lost. At one time, before the advent of monstrous Steam, it might have been a chilly prospect – but now, I was more likely to be suffocated by the interminable heat seeping from the ground, produced by the raging of the abandoned engines that Rollingwood had described to me. Already my stifled breath caught in my throat; freed from any necessity of maintaining decorum, I tore open my shirt collar, though to little avail. My laboured panting for breath was so loud in my own ears, that a moment or two passed before I perceived a more ominous sound close at hand.

A deep growl, emitted by some beast hidden in damp foliage ahead – there was no longer any need to anticipate the long hours before dawn would break again over Highgate; my gnawed bones might be exposed to that dim light, but my living flesh would not.

The noise altered to a rasping snarl, signalling that the unseen animal was about to spring upon its prey. I stood frozen to the spot, aware that any attempt to turn and flee would only result in that crushing weight falling upon my back, pinning me face-down upon the sodden earth as those fanged jaws snapped my neck like a bundle of twigs.

With appalling suddenness, the crepuscular gloom was blotted out by the dreaded shape leaping upon me. I toppled backward, my hands futilely straining against its weight, a sharp-toothed snout only inches from my face…

Then matters became very odd, indeed.

Tiny bits of metal, glittering in a narrow shaft of moonlight that had managed to penetrate the clouds above, lay scattered all about me. Teeth I saw, but not the white crescents of a carnivore's jaws, but rather those of brass gears, interlinked with each other – I might well have been attacked, not by a lion or some other fearsome animal, but by a pocket watch grown to enormous proportions, its gilt case sprung open, or a similar ratcheting and ticking mechanical construction.

That I was deranged, either temporarily or now permanently – this was a very real possibility. It would not have been the first time that the stress of events had resulted in the disordering of my thoughts and perceptions. That I maintained any degree of sanity at all, for any length of time, was a small tribute to my generally stolid and unimaginative nature.

Whatever my mental state, I was not bodily injured, however, or not in any manner immediately apparent. Sitting up on the ground where I had landed, I looked about me; in what rapidly decaying light was still available, there were in fact gears and springs and less identifiable metal pieces arrayed all about. Some were still connected to each other, and displayed a jittering animation, clicking and whirring before finally expending the last of their motive force.

A larger construction had toppled onto its side, a foot or so away from me. I could discern that it was roughly shaped like a lion, with forelimbs and hindquarters assembled of jointed iron, and a massive head in which one fiercely gleaming glass eye was still embedded, the other having been dislodged and rolled under some low fronds, from where it regarded me with an unblinking stare.

I rose unsteadily to my feet; bending down, I prodded the artificial carcass with a cautious fingertip. Much of the device's innards were exposed; deep within the space where a heart would have beaten, if the thing had been a creature of flesh and blood, a mainspring as large as my doubled fists trembled and spun, its faint churr the only noise impinging on the encompassing silence. The growling snarl I had heard, when the *faux* beast was hidden from sight, had been emitted by the accordion-pleated structure I could see at its throat; that intimidating note would sound no more, the armature compressing the pleated leather having been dislocated from the workings behind.

The rest of the mechanism's intricacies were concealed beneath what had first seemed to my touch as a frayed carpet, stitched about the form so as to give the impression of the tawny hide of a marauding predator. A looser, more tangled fabric portrayed its mane, coursing from the head and onto its back. All was damp and rotted; the long exposure to the cemetery's humid mists had rendered the substance into one great patch of mildew and corruption, through which my finger could penetrate with no more resistance than that given by matted cobwebs.

My proximity to the construction disclosed further details of its operation. Its hindquarters were connected to a larger iron armature, at the point where its tail might otherwise have been; this mechanism extended back into the foliage which had previously concealed the device, and from which it had sprung upon me. The much-rusted beam had thrust the simulated beast forward, upon the release of the coiled springs mounted upon an equally corroded plate anchored to the ground. This convulsive action had been triggered by a snaring cord against which I had inadvertently stumbled in the dark.

"So *this*–" A wild exhilaration burst within me; I spoke aloud as I straightened up, still gazing upon the closely wrought machinery lying stilled at my feet. "This is what we fear! We tremble before junk! Nothing but scraps of metal and tattered rags!"

There were no wild animals prowling about the cemetery, hunting whatever prey their jaws could seize upon – of this surmise I was immediately convinced. Their purported existence was but a giant hoax, of which Rollingwood was a fellow conspirator or a victim of others deluding him – it hardly mattered as to his exact role in the scheme. If ever living creatures had escaped from a private zoölogical garden and taken residence in the overgrown cemetery, they had likely starved to death, once the weaker had been consumed by the stronger, or sickened from the constant damp, coughing out their lungs in fatal bouts of pleurisy or some other infection – these had been, after all, beasts more accustomed to the somewhat drier veldts of Africa than to actual jungles. That general demise having occurred, no doubt some criminal-minded entrepreneur had seized upon the opportunity; in league with the sort of clever tinkerer with which England seemed to abound these days, this person – I could well imagine his sly, smirking visage – had studded Highgate with contraptions such as the one that was now greatly disintegrated before me. Incapable of actual harm, other than what would be suffered from being knocked off one's feet, in the cemetery's perpetual mists they would be intimidating enough that a profitable swindle could be enacted, in which confederates would feign to protect those attending funerals here – just as had those miscreants which been hired to attend the graveside service for my late wife. But in reality, no one was ever truly threatened by anything other than poorly maintained clockwork and hissing steam valves.

Shaking my head, I studied further the corroding wreckage, swaddled in its ripped and frayed pelt. I took offence at the sight – this was not a device which my father had any hand in constructing, but obviously of recent devising. As much as I regretted my filial association with the author of so many hideous machines, which had wrought so much damage upon the world that no longer existed, and been so inspiring of the wretched one we now inhabited, still I had always felt some odd pride in the products of my father's industry. The man had been a genius, as I was not; the precision and grace of the handiwork shown in his technical legacy, incomprehensible to me, often seemed more like art than mere craftsmanship. But this mock lion was a wretched piece of work, cobbled together by rude mechanics; it was a wonder that such a clanking shambles had ever frightened anyone other the few wandering children who might have encountered it.

Once past my spasm of disgust, that other emotion returned and welled greater inside my breast. I felt liberated of more than fear; much that had oppressed me before now seemed to dissolve into phantasms as insubstantial as the tumbling vapours surrounding the spot. At that instant, Life no longer seemed an oppressive burden, from which one might be freed at the first conflux of opportunity and wearied sulk. Coat unbuttoned, I stood with legs spread and arms akimbo, as though conqueror of a craven realm.

"The Future, then–" No shame attended my booming voice; I only regretted that there was no one else to hear me. "What a fraud! What a clanking, hissing parade – one crippled, patched-together contrivance after another." I scornfully kicked the iron head of the manufactured lion. "The great machines, the ones which rightfully deserved our awe – those are gone, as are the hands that built them." My memory still retained the vision of those ambulatory lighthouses, one of which had towered over the destruction of the Houses of Parliament, and so much else in the city of London; with my eyes opened, however, they were no more than a figment of recall. "What we have left, my dear sirs–" Flinging my hands wide, I addressed my imagined audience. "Are the dwarves scuttling about in the deep footprints of vanished giants – we shall not see my father's like again! And for that, I confess..."

A darker musing tinged my thoughts, as though a raven had winged by, obscuring for a moment what dimming light was left.

"I confess I am both thankful and saddened." My voice dropped lower, as did my nodding head. "The World to Come might once have been some furious monstrosity bearing down upon us, with its thundering wheels set upon unswerving rails, and its gleaming arms poised to strike the World That Was to bloody flinders – but at least it had been a thing of vaulting ambition and enterprise. What have we now?" More pityingly, with the toe of my boot I nudged the broken gears and disconnected springs. "Toys and gimcracks, cheaply made, and for low ends; soon falling apart from their own inadequacy. Nothing more than that. And thus we have the World we created, and the Future we deserve."

Reader, that is as much threadbare philosophy as I can provide; you have struck a poor bargain if you came to these pages hoping for any greater insight than that. All very noble, I am certain, to moan and whine about Mankind's dreary, distracted fate, but one achieves as much thereby as does the frog in the ditch, cursing and shaking his little webbed fist at the tines of the harrow that are about to skewer him. The virtue of old Zeno's stoicism in this regard is that at least one keeps futile rantings to oneself.

At the moment I had spoken as much, I perceived that another appeared to be listening. I looked up and into the placid gaze of a giraffe, either the same or another, as I had previously viewed at a greater remove. Being closer now, I realized that the creature was as much a mechanical construct as the motionless, partially disassembled lion at my feet; what tranquillity was in its eyes was no more than that radiated by idiot, unseeing glass. The boldly dappled skin of its elongated neck had been greatly eroded by moth and rot, revealing the bolted iron gantry within, specked with rust.

"You, sir–" I sourly amused myself by addressing the artificial beast. "You are more the natural heir to this world than I am. My kind once had souls; take comfort that yours never did."

No doubt I would still have been standing there in the humid mists of Highgate Cemetery, making other foolish orations, when the sun rose again; I might well have provided some instructive example to an early-rising passerby, as to the perils of too much thinking about weighty matters – but events spared me from that salutary fate. The first was that my more exalted mood returned, as a glittering shore might be revealed by the withdrawal of a sullen tide. Again, the Future and the World both seemed but puny things, easily disregarded. To the degree my aging bones could manage, I capered a bit, as would have some proud African warrior who had just speared and dispatched an actual lion, strong of tooth and claw. Such are the advantages of solitude, that even an Englishman might indulge in a little triumphant dance, unhindered by others' observation.

As might have been anticipated, glad exertion in such a tropic climate – artificial as it was – evoked a corresponding flush of overheated blood throughout my body; in the dark of a British night, I was quickly drenched in sweat. Having already loosed my jacket's buttons, I grasped its lapels in both hands and opened it wide, as though giving myself rudimentary wings to assist in my eccentric dance–

So giddy was my renewed spirit, I was but slightly amazed when I glanced down at myself and saw that a perfectly round hole, about the span of my thumbnail, had mysteriously appeared in the fabric of my coat, a few inches from where it was extended from my damp shirtfront. A puzzling occurrence; the hole had not been there a moment ago, I was sure, and now I could quite plainly see through it to the moonlit clouds beyond me. Had the cemetery's transformed environs spawned a new breed of moth, capable of taking such a bite, then darting away rather than fluttering nearby?

The mystery was quickly resolved, though not to my liking, when my bounding mania ebbed enough that I could perceive a bit more of my surroundings. An echo faded against the flanks of the nearby hills, and I realized that my ears had been struck by the sound of a rifle shot – if I had not been gyrating about like a fool, I would have heard and known what it was.

Within short order – no more than a split-second – I was face-down upon the earth, my chest pressed against whatever moss and mud upon which I previously had been standing. This instinctive response proved to be the wisest course, for no sooner had I flattened myself than the air was split by the sharp report of another bullet being fired. It passed above me, and through the space which I had occupied; judging by the impact striking shards from a nearby headstone, the bullet would have penetrated my chest if I had still been upon my feet.

Raising my head, and with mind racing, I attempted to calculate some avenue of escape from the spot. Only a few seconds might pass before my unseen assailant – surely the same as had stalked me before on the Cornish coast – would correct his aim to where I now lay prostrate. My only hope, it quickly seemed, was to flee the relatively open space in which I was exposed, and plunge headlong into the thick foliage massed about me. Concealed by those elephantine leaves and overlapping fronds, I might evade the marksman long enough for him to abandon this latest attempt at assassination before the village constables, alerted by the rifle-fire, would arrive to investigate – or I might be able to struggle through the cemetery's overgrown terrain to a point where I would be able to scale its surrounding walls and sprint to greater safety in the darkened fields beyond.

Having a rough notion of the direction from which the shot had come, I raised myself onto my hands and knees, preparing to dart with as much rapidity as I could summon, toward the greenery opposite. My action was stymied, however, when another shot sounded – I even saw a spark of light from this weapon's muzzle, somewhere in the distance to which I had oriented myself. Perhaps it was only my overwrought imagination, but I perceived the bullet passing directly above me, close enough to part my hair; a draping vine was snapped in two by its impact, just behind where I crouched.

Had my assailant a confederate, similarly stalking me? Or more than one? A distinct possibility, for yet one more shot struck the ground by my hand; this more accurate aim, so much closer to its target, was afforded by an angle to my left, and a closer proximity than that from which the other rifle-fire had emanated.

I could afford no more time to plot my own trajectory hence. All directions seemed equally dangerous, there being perhaps any number of lethal-minded marksmen surrounding me. Such being the case, I rolled onto my side, away from the splattered mud into which the last shot had struck. Scrambling into a hunched-over posture, I dove into the leaves dangling only a few inches from me.

The rubbery branches were so thickly entwined as to support my weight; that, and their wet surfaces, gave a bewildering sensation of having actually plunged into ocean depths, my limbs entangled in seaweed. I sank enough that the green elements closed above, shuttering away what little illumination had come from the cloud-masked moon and stars. In utter darkness I swam, or attempted to, feet kicking and arms desperately flailing. I could only conjecture that it would be a matter of a few seconds before my stalkers assembled at the spot from which I had fled, and perceived where I had made my escape.

My floundering limbs achieved little progress until I stumbled upon a more efficacious mode of propelling myself forward; I realized that I could seize upon the vines and branches before me and then employ them to bodily drag myself farther into the concealing foliage, just as if I were clambering along a ladder laid horizontal. As I did so, ominous sounds came from behind – I was certain I heard quickly muttering voices, likely those of my stalkers arriving upon the scene I had abandoned, and conferring as to where I had disappeared.

Thus motivated, I redoubled my efforts, giving little thought if any as to what noise I made thereby; those intent on my life might direct their rifle-fire into the bushes and fronds, but I was already so well concealed within them that it could only be a fortunate shot that might strike me. My sole consideration now was to put as much distance between myself and these pursuers–

To that end, I achieved some considerable velocity; panic is an inspiring emotion. So much so that when the foliage through which I thrashed, one hastily grasped vine after another, became less abundant and incapable of bearing me further, I flew for a good yard or more before crashing upon the ground of another open space. I lay sprawled and somewhat dazed, but only for a moment; bounding to my feet, I attempted to discern whatever course of escape I could attempt from this point.

To my dismay, those possibilities seemed scant; the opening into which my efforts had flung me was at the base of a masonry wall, its crenellated top too high for my fingertips to reach, however I strained or leapt. Passage alongside it, to my left, was impossible, blocked by a solid green mass more impenetrable than that through which I had just passed.

During my hurried contemplation of options, no more than a second or two ticked away, but in that time I also heard what could only be the sound of another person fighting violently through the dense foliage behind me, accompanied by liberal cursing – evidently, at least one of my pursuers was even now following the most direct route to where I stood, and would soon be upon me.

Pressed by necessity, I took the path that remained; placing my flattened hands and chest against the wall, I managed a scraping, inching progress through the narrow gap between it and the tangled growth at my back.

Within a few uncomfortable yards, the mortared stones came to an end, succeeded by wrought-iron gates, the bars of which were too closely set to squeeze past, secured by a rusting chain and padlock. Tarnished gilt letters at the top proclaimed the name – SMEDLEY – of the family whose fortress-like mausoleum stood within, its marble flanks festooned with crawling ivy. Between the imposing structure and the gates stood a massive memorial statue, typical of the grieving wealthy; upon an alabaster pillar, a winged angel gazed down, its noble face full of compassion and pity for the bulk of Humanity, who had been so untimely deprived of all the deceased Smedleys deposited in their marble niches.

My survey of the robed figure was quickly curtailed, however–

"There he is!"

The shout came from somewhere to the right. My situation was immediately evident; the other pursuers had not chosen to follow me directly, but had instead circled about, thus cutting off any continued flight on my part.

Though I could see no more than fragmented shadows in the dark, the men's lethal designs were made obvious once more, as a hail of bullets rained upon me. A searing pain burst upon my shoulder; its impact both stunned and slammed me against the iron gates.

Dimly aware of events as I was, the bright sparks of bullets striking the gates' iron bars surrounded me. Whether one such resulted in the disintegration of the padlock or one of the chain's links, or whether my sudden weight thrown against the corroded metal was sufficient to snap it apart, I could not tell. It little mattered; whatever the cause, the result was that the gates parted from each other, creakily swinging open and sending me sprawling within.

Rolling onto my back, I awaited my terminal fate. To seek refuge inside the mausoleum, I knew, would be a waste of what little time remained to me. Whatever might be the reason for these persons' stalking of me, they had accomplished what they had set out upon. Haste and darkness had spoiled the accuracy of their earlier rifle-fire; now they could slay me at their leisure. If they did so here in the open air or in the mustier quarters of those already dead, I little cared.

And that they would be enabled to do as they wished, now seemed obvious. For a great radiance had sprung up around me, bright enough that when I raised my head, I could see the distinct shadows of my outspread fingers cast upon the base of the statue against which my shoulders had lodged. Perhaps this sight was some delusion engendered within a disordered brain, for surely only a fraction of the night's hours had passed in the chase, now concluded. To further disprove that the growing illumination was the breaking of the dawn, I perceived that the light appeared not in the sky above, but – weirdly so – from the ground beneath me.

Braced upon my elbows, I saw the faces gathering near me: those of my stalkers, approaching at the periphery of my vision, rifles in hand; they were threatening in appearance, even beyond the weapons they held. Their eyes narrowed upon their prey, and thin, cruel smiles played upon their lips.

But there was another face as well; tilting my head back, I saw the visage of the marble angel, rather more serene in aspect, one delicately wrought hand raised in blessing, great feathered wings spread behind.

Then the figure toppled toward me, as if intent on swooping down and rescuing me from my peril. I heard a startled cry from one of the men around me, as the earth buckled and heaved beneath myself and them. In an instant, the light grew blinding, a brilliant eruption in all directions. From memory, I heard the Right Reverend Jamford's clarion voice again, both promising and threatening that some new radiance, never seen before, would spring from the bowels of the earth, annihilating all that had come before–

The marble angel, with its gentle seraphic gaze, plunged toward me. Upon the dancing earth, I prepared for that impact.

SEVEN

In a Gondola, with Americans

I AM A MAN not of Byronic passions – to put it mildly. To others, I leave the great excitements, and both the calamities and triumphs that wilder, more ambitious temperaments seek. Or rather, I would have left them, if events and conspiracies had not intervened to thwart my simple desires. I had hoped, when much younger, for mere survival and a certain degree of comfort; instead, I have had detestable adventures, one after another. Someone else received my quiet life, and longs for excitement instead – the fool.

Thus the reader might excuse my *post mortem* bemusement at finding myself in an apparent afterlife more reminiscent of Italy than England.

Venice, to be exact; my body – that much at least was familiar to me – lounged against a bank of pillows, at an angle halfway between vertical and horizontal, in one of those distinctive narrow boats known to travellers as a *gondola*. I was aware of the term, as well as the distinguishing features such as the toothed prow-head I could see some distance before me, having perused in my idle hours various peregrinatory accounts written by those countrymen of mine who fancied warmer climes to the chilly ones of their native land. Such of course is the typical longing of a certain type of literary aristocrat, hobbling about on his clubfoot while perusing his own near relations for suitable sexual conquests, all the while dreaming that both his dire poetry and dissolute habits would be facilitated by the beams of an alien sun.

Which was oddly lacking here; I was in no great rush to assume full consciousness – and who could blame me for that reticence, after the circumstances of my death? – but I was able to perceive that no daylight of any temperature fell upon me at the moment. Nor was I under a night sky – the moon and stars were absent when I gazed upward, but also those roiling banks of mist and cloud that had concealed them most recently in my memory. In addition, the air felt close and fetid about me; I was under no illusion that the lagoons into which every Venetian chamber pot was emptied would smell as fresh as an open countryside stream, but I might have expected at least a saline breeze from the nearby ocean.

I had neither strength nor inclination to pursue this mystery; if translation to an incorporeal state of being was mine now, it did not seem to be accompanied by relief of the bruises and scrapes suffered while fleeing through the cemetery of Highgate. And worse: my arm felt like bloody hell, the ache from the bullet wound I had received – a superficial injury, to some degree, there being no apparent shattering of the bone within – was perceptible all the way to my wrist. My assumption was that some sort of dressing had been applied, as there was only a little dried blood staining the rent in my jacket sleeve, dangling empty at my side.

"Mr Dower – you're awake! How wonderful!" An unfamiliar voice summoned my attention. "Crackerjack!"

My companion in the minute craft had much of the personal effusiveness that I recalled from Rollingwood – wherever that gentleman was now – but possessed of an even heartier forcefulness, such that I felt literally pushed

against the pillows at my back. What was more disconcerting
was that the person, identity still unknown to me, was an
American; this was evidenced not just by his odd vocabulary,
but also the way in which the flat twang of his accent
murdered the language we shared. I had heard such before,
years ago, when I still had been attempting to make a living
from my watchmaker's shop in Clerkenwell; I had received
the occasional customer from across the Atlantic, more
often than not drawn into the premises by that unapologetic
curiosity the breed possesses, allowing them to delightedly
prowl about any spot they regarded as sufficiently antiquated
and therefore charming.

"Please… a moment." I weakly held up my hand, to fend
off a further effusion from the man. "I am a bit… out of sorts."

"Take your time, pal." The sparkling white of his teeth was
revealed by his widened smile. "We got plenty of that!"

A suspicion crept into my thoughts, that I was not actually
dead – or perhaps a hope; if the events concluding my stay
in Highgate had also terminated my life, then the prospect of
sailing about in a gondola's cramped space, in the company
of an American, would indicate that my sins while alive
had been judged grievous enough to sentence me to Hell or
somewhere similar. I was not so convinced an atheist as to
dismiss that possibility out of hand – and, I am chagrined to
admit, this would not have been the first occasion on which
I had been mistaken about my demise. A morbid turn of
mind is indicated by the fact that I had once before come to
my senses while drifting in a boat, only then it had been the
Thames near London, and I had made a similar conclusion
about no longer being numbered among the living.

I took advantage of the other's relaxed manner, and the
slow clearing of my head, to make what examination I could
of my circumstances. That I was not in some Italianate version
of the afterlife, so attractive to poets and other wastrels, was

quickly confirmed; true, this was a gondola about me, but upon closer scrutiny its shabby fraud was apparent. By the light of the lantern above me, I could see that the waters through which the boat glided were so shallow as to enable their bottom reach to be perceived. The gondola itself did not continue its motion of its own accord, but rather by means of the iron-wheeled carriage on which it was mounted, rolling along on submerged metal rails. The long paddle at its side, by which the boat might have been assumed to be sculled forward, was a similar artifice: a rudimentary system of cogs accounted for the implement's back-and-forth motion. It would have continued to do so regardless of the *gondolier* – that term I recalled as well – who stood on a tiny platform just above and a little behind me.

And who was – to my surprise, I admit – another human being, rather than an automated mechanism in the guise of a man. He wore the traditional costume – horizontally striped shirt, red neckerchief, and flat straw hat with dangling ribbon – that was required of his water-going trade. More disconcertingly, as I twisted about in my seat to gaze up at him, the gondolier gave me a conspiratorial wink and smile.

The lopsided manner of that expression, with just one corner of his mouth twisting upward, triggered my recognition of the person. I had seen him twice before, once at my door in Cornwall, then but some short time ago at the side of my wife's grave in Highgate, before her casket had been hauled up to that other cemetery floating in the sky. On that later occasion, he had introduced himself as *Nick Spivvem* – if that were his true name; I had my suspicions on that account, given his generally roguish demeanour.

Before I could make any expostulation as to his presence with the boat, he raised a finger to his lips, admonishing me to silence. Thus I remained without speaking; given the mystifying circumstances into which I had somehow been placed, it seemed the wisest course to accept him as, if not a friend and ally, then someone who might be able to enlighten me to a degree – if I played along with whatever charade in which he was engaged.

"Hope you're feeling better–" The American's dismayingly hearty voice broke into my considerations. "Heckuva blow you took up there; would've sworn it was enough to knock the brains right out of a guy's skull."

I swivelled my gaze back toward him, giving closer scrutiny now that some of the fog had dissipated from my head. The figure I saw was dressed in a garish plaid suit, of an orange colour never seen in Nature or the Scottish Highlands; across its vest and the ample stomach beneath was draped a gold watch-chain, festooned with the medallions of various civic-minded organizations. White spats with intricate closures revealed the heels and squared toes of glistening patent-leather boots. His ample face was adorned on either side by the sort of mutton-chop whiskers that gave the impression of someone attempting to push himself headfirst past the hindquarters of unsheared sheep; at its centre was a tuberous nose reddened by gin, or whatever other potion was more imbibed in the former colonies.

"Here, lemme fix that for ya." He transferred an immense cigar to the corner of his mouth, so as to be able to lean forward and adjust the jacket back upon my shoulder, from which it had slipped off. "Hope that doesn't sting too much–" Leaning back again, he used the cigar to gesture toward my wounded arm. "It'll be fine, though. Trust me, just a scratch."

"I appreciate your concern." With some awkwardness, I managed to wrestle my arm into the empty sleeve, without dislodging the reddened linen bandage. "Am I correct in assuming that you ministered to the wound, however slight it might be? Then I owe you for your kindness, and shall endeavour to repay you whenever I have the chance, Mr…"

"Blightley," he responded to my hinted inquiry. "Edward Blightley, and definitely happy to be at your service, Mr Dower. Been hoping to make your acquaintance for quite a while now; *quite* a while."

"I see." As best I could, I kept hidden my reaction to that announcement; anymore, it was exactly the sort of thing I dreaded most. "And might I enquire as to *why* you have sought me out?"

"Well, of course you can!" Grey ash spilled upon a cravat of startling bottle-green iridescence as he gestured with the outflung cigar. "I'm a man of business, Mr Dower – just as you are. So pretty damn likely, ain't it, that it's a business matter I want to discuss with you."

"Hm; yes, well. I am sorry to disappoint you, Mr Blightley–"

"Call me Ed; all my friends do."

"Mr Blightley," I repeated more firmly. "Given that you might very well have saved my life, though I am not certain as to how you managed that–"

"I had help."

"Please let me continue. You have my gratitude, but it is not sufficient to alter the fact that I am *not* a man of business. Any attempts along those lines, I abandoned years ago. My sole business, such as it is, has been reduced to merely attempting to live out my days in as insignificant a manner as possible. I assure you that any other activity in which you might have observed my participation, including that from which you apparently made some rescue, was all thrust upon me against my liking."

"Oh, sure; believe me, I understand. A quiet life – don't we all want that?" Blightley smiled and nodded. "I got a little piece of land in New Jersey, up near Piscataway. Day'll come, when you'll find me there, just sitting on the front porch, rockin' and smokin'." He regarded the glowing ember at the tip of his cigar for a moment, then looked again at me. "But right now, in my line of business, I gotta seize the opportunities when I can. They don't come around too often – not like this!"

"And what line of business would that be?"

He gave no answer, but instead rooted inside his own brilliant jacket, withdrawing a folded sheet of paper. Smoothing out the creases, he then extended it to me with a flourish.

The item appeared to be some sort of advertisement; I could see as much, from its bold lettering, as I took it from his hand. By the yellow glow of the lantern above me, I made a closer examination of its particulars:

BY TUMULTUOUS PUBLIC DEMAND

THE THEATRICAL PARTNERSHIP OF

BLIGHTLEY & HAZE, LTD.

AFTER TRIUMPHANT TOURS OF

BOSTON, NEW YORK, MOOSE JAW,

& OTHER INTERNATIONAL CAPITALS OF CULTURE

IS PLEASED TO ANNOUNCE

THE BRITISH APPEARANCES

OF THEIR CELEBRATED

DRAMATIC & COMEDIC AUTOMATA TROUPE

CURRENTLY ENGAGED FOR EXTENDED

PERFORMANCES IN BRIGHTON, BLACKPOOL,

AND FRINTON-ON-SEA;

ENQUIRE BELOW FOR FURTHER BOOKINGS

An illustration accompanied the handbill: a steel engraving of two soldiers fiercely glaring at each other, bayoneted rifles poised in their hands. The uniform of one of the figures was light-coloured, the other dark; I did not immediately recognize them, though I had a vague memory of having seen something like them before.

"No, no – keep it." Blightley waved me off as I attempted to return the sheet to him. "We've got piles of 'em. Pretty much blanketing the countryside – won't be long before we're the talk o' the town, in every little English burg." He took a deep draught from his cigar, savouring the inhaled smoke for a moment while contemplating some rosy vista he could discern in the darkness beyond me. "They've never seen anything like it – a spectacular entertainment! Suitable for all ages as well, and morally uplifting; I can promise you."

"Of that, I have no doubt." I surreptitiously laid the advertisement on the gondola's floor beside my feet, having no actual desire to keep hold of it. "A partner is mentioned – does he accompany, or did you leave him behind to attend to your affairs in the States?"

"Mr Haze! Bestir yourself!" These words were not addressed to me, but to someone behind my interlocutor, as he turned himself about. "Not being very sociable, are you? Man here wants to make your acquaintance."

That I had not been aware of one more passenger in the gondola was quickly explained by the disproportion between Blightley's expansive bulk and the meagreness of the figure who now peered at me. At my first glance, I had the uncanny impression that the other was not a human being at all, but some sort of spectacled owl, so magnified were his eyes behind thickly distorting lenses. The effect was heightened by the sombreness of his unsmiling expression, as he raised his head past Blightley's shoulder and peered at me. His face might have been a child's, were it not for its wrinkled, crêpe-like skin; his diminutive form seemed to have never advanced into adolescence, either.

"Good evening." Wetly blinking, this Haze creature pronounced an emotionless greeting, but said no more.

"Are you sure?" From his vest, Blightley extracted a pocket watch – not gold-cased, but cheap gilt, rubbed bare in spots to expose the pot metal beneath; with my experience, I could detect this difference in quality. "Thought we'd be getting on toward morning by now." He squinted at the dial, then laid the watch by one ear, to determine if it was still ticking. "Doesn't really matter a heckuva lot, though, does it? Not in a place like this."

I knew full well what he meant, awareness of my surroundings having achieved a greater extent. The gondola was not the only sham contrivance here, rolling about on its submerged iron wheels rather than gliding free on the surface of the waters. Further away, there were the outlined silhouettes of a *faux* city, its structures modelled – not very convincingly – after those of the Italian locale I had first assumed it to be, complete with low-arched bridges over the canals branching from this one, and an ostentatiously positioned replica of the famous dome of Saint Mark's Basilica. The faint, artificial light behind what were likely no more than plaster flats, of the sort used for stage scenery in any grimy music hall, indicated no verifiable time of day; dawn or dusk, it would be all the same in this sadly timeless locale.

"You're right about that." Blightley had perceived my disdain. "Pretty shabby, ain't it?" He returned his watch to its niche on his rounded gut. "My stage carpenters back home would've done a better job. But sometimes we just have to make do with what's available, and throw in our hand with the best folks we can scare up. Just as you'll be able to do now, Mr Dower."

"Perhaps." In my life, so many ruinous propositions have been advanced to me, that I have developed a preternatural awareness of when another is in the offing. "But I doubt if that will be the present case. You appear to follow the theatrical trade, Mr Blightley; I have nothing to do with that, nor any wish to be so associated. Therefore, the possibility of any mutually advantageous collaboration between us would appear to be slight."

"Don't underestimate yourself; it's amazing what folks can get up to, given half a chance. And show business is a glamorous life – I can tell you, for sure. Travel the world, adoring audiences, money by the bucket–" He glanced behind himself at his partner. "Am I right about that, Mr Haze?"

That undersized figure made no reply, displaying no more reaction than might have been shown by a stuffed mannequin. After a moment of silently regarding Blightley through the weighty lenses of his glasses, he turned back to studying the gondola's course through the waters ahead.

"Your associate is a man of few words."

"Well, kinda…" Blightley acknowledged my comment with a nod. "Can talk your arm off, though, if you get 'im on the right subject. Technical matters, mainly – somebody's got to keep all these gadgets working, right? That's what he does, and a bang-up job at it, too. That's what makes us such a good team – I handle all the talking to people as is necessary, which leaves his brain free to concentrate on gears and springs, and all those other bits and pieces as makes our modern mechanical world the wonder that it is. But of course, you'd know more about that sort of thing than I would."

"I fear I must disappoint you in that regard." This was not the first time I had heard comments of this nature. So many times, others had sought to inveigle me into their schemes, either daft or felonious, based on the assumption that my father's genius was an inheritable trait, and that I could either devise or operate his creations with an equal facility. "You overestimate my abilities, just as you have my interest in whatever you care to propose."

"I'm willing to take my chances." Blightley grinned as he spoke. "I've cracked some pretty tough nuts in my time. Maybe I'll be able to change your mind as well, if you'll hear me out."

"Very well." If there were an alternative to listening further to the man, I would have seized upon it, but I saw none. The surrounding waters were so shallow that I might well have clambered out of the gondola and paddled at little risk, if some wet discomfort, to the artificial shore by which we passed – but then what? I had no idea of what subterranean chamber this was, or exactly how I had come to it, or whether the pursuers who had fallen upon me in the cemetery of Highgate were still waiting there or somewhere else close at hand, readying themselves for their next opportunity of doing me harm. With those circumstances in mind, I considered it best to endure these persons' company for a while longer, until some aidsome clarification presented itself. "You have something of which you wish to speak to me–" I gestured with an expansive wave of my hand. "By all means, proceed."

"We're halfway there already!" Blightley launched into an exposition that had every mark of having been rehearsed before. "Sir, we are entrepreneurs–"

"As so many of your countrymen are."

"In America, it's considered a virtue. We can hardly sit still, what with all the grand endeavours we launch on a daily basis."

To one of my inclination, this seemed a dreadful prospect, but I restrained my tongue.

"Sure," continued Blightley, "the ambitions of myself and Mr Haze are pinned to the sphere of popular entertainment – and why not? It's what people like – wouldn't be *popular* otherwise, would it? And folks do pony up for something that amuses them. Maybe in the future – who knows?" The man's broad shoulders lifted in a shrug. "When we have more of a name, and a bit o' capital, then the world would be our oyster! But for now, we seem to be on a good thing."

"Which is?"

"As you might've deduced from our publicity–" He pointed to where I had dropped the handbill onto the gondola's floor.

"Our particular niche, so to say, is in performances using mechanical reproductions of human beings. I expect you're familiar with such."

"Lamentably so." The extent of my own father's skills, and the depraved ambitions in which they were employed, had been revealed to me by that devilish Paganinicon, which had been able to play upon the violin with virtuosity rivalling that of the performer from whom its name had been derived. The blasted thing possessed other abilities by which it had been able to pass itself off as a man of actual flesh and blood, resulting in a good deal of immoral behaviour, before it had come to well-deserved ruin. "You advertise your spectacles so forthrightly? I would not have expected there to be much of an audience for such open imposture."

"You'd be pretty surprised on that score, then. People love the stuff, and hoot and holler when they're watching machines got up to look as real as themselves. It's a fascination, is what it is, and we can sell tickets fast as we can print 'em up. Of course, the shows have got to be well done – that's where my partner Haze is so valuable, though he won't boast of it himself. Bit shy, he is, as you might've observed already. But he's a clever fella – can make a hunk of brass and tin prance 'n' dance about, just as if it'd been birthed natural-like, rather than cobbled together on his workbench. Don't take my word for it, though – you can see for yourself." His blunt finger pointed above me. "That's one of ours right there, acting just as if it were poling this barge along. Fooled you, didn't it? Bet you thought it was a real person, just like yourself."

The American's words took me aback; had I been somehow mistaken in my previous apprehension of the gondolier as being human, and my recognition of the particular individual as one with whom I had some brief exchange, both in Cornwall and here in London? The possibility existed, of course – it would not be the first time that I had been unable to distinguish the essential difference between the merely mechanical and the truly animate. And those earlier occasions had often been when I was in greater command of both my senses and my thoughts, and not befuddled by whatever explosives and upheavals had brought me to this still undetermined location.

With my mind in such a state of wonderment, I involuntarily twisted about where I sat, once again glancing behind myself and upward to the gondolier in question. My doing so, however, did not confirm that of which Blightley had just boasted, as to the artificiality of the figure; even in the faint glow from the dangling lantern, he appeared exactly as I had identified him before, the knavish Spivvem. His fleshly human nature was again indicated by the sly smirk at the corner of his mouth, to which was added the upward rolling of his eyes, signalling his mockery of what the other man had just said.

When I turned back around, I could tell that Blightley himself had not seen these small betraying clues; Spivvem, in his disguise of Venetian boatman, had kept them subtle enough as to form a private communication between himself and me. Thus I was made his fellow conspirator, for the moment at least, in league against the others in the craft. I briefly pondered revealing the deception to the two entrepreneurs, weighing whether I would derive some advantage by thereby ingratiating myself further with the odd pair. But, I quickly reasoned, they were already attempting to flatter me into some commercial enterprise with them – perhaps this was a sincere overture on their part, or they were scoundrels with some ulterior agenda in mind – I could not yet discern which was the case. Where it was obvious that Spivvem's honesty was a doubtful matter, but he still might be of some aid to me – he had, after all, somehow managed to substitute himself for whatever mechanism that Blightley and his partner Haze had installed on the gondola, and which they believed to be still in operation there. Had he done so in order to spy upon them, or upon me? Whichever it was, his having done so revealed some considerable ingenuity on his part – an alliance with him might serve me better, if my threatened skin were still to be saved.

"Impressive, indeed." Returning my gaze to Blightley, I made a show of feigned appreciation. "Little wonder that you and Mr Haze have been able to achieve success in the theatre. If I had not been informed otherwise, I might well have mistaken this creation of yours for a living man."

"Coming from such as yourself, that's a grand compliment." Blightley hooked a thumb into the armhole of his vest, while brandishing the cigar with his other hand. "Given your expertise, what with mechanical figures and all."

"It would seem rather, that your knowledge of the subject greatly exceeds mine. I could never have assembled such a convincing simulation."

"That's all Haze's doing, as I said. Was the making of my fortune, the day I hooked up with him. But then, I like to think that there's some mutual benefit. Clever as he is – and you hardly know the half of it, Mr Dower! – he doesn't have quite the same head for business that I do." Blightley gave a sage nod. "Pardon my boasting, but a partnership such as ours isn't seen everyday."

All the while Haze's loquacious associate discussed their individual peculiarities, the other man gave no sign of giving attention, or even having heard. Haze remained as he was, perched in the gondola's prow, owlishly contemplating the water through which the craft rolled, while he very likely dreamt of even more intricate contraptions.

"I'll cut right to the crux of the matter, George – mind if I call you George?" Eyes glittering, Blightley leaned toward me. "I figure we should be friends, seeing how we've got so much in common. Same business and all, if you know what I mean."

"Address me as you wish." Whatever the other man's full name might be, I had no interest in learning it. "Standing on formality is not a trait of mine."

"George – you strike me as a stand-up sort of fella. The fact that with your keen eye for fancy machinery, you approve of ours – that's icing on the cake. Just makes it all the easier to tell you, that there's room for one more in our enterprise. Man of your talents – why, you'd fit right in."

"You certainly make it sound enticing." In actuality he didn't, but right now I wished him to believe otherwise. "Do tell me more."

"Gotcha! Hook, line 'n' bob!" His delight was infectious, or would have been for someone less sourly disposed than myself. "I knew you were a savvy type – always on the lookout for a snapping good opportunity. That's how we get on in the world, ain't it? Well, you'll remember this as being a red-letter day, no doubt about that!"

"Already, it is engraved in my memory. But I still lack details as to its exact wonderfulness."

"Let me fix you up on that score, George." We faced each other so close, that Blightley was able to lay a comradely hand upon my knee. "Here's what Haze and I have been up to, that's led to our present success. I take it you're aware of the great – bloody great, your lot would say – bloody great conflict going on in America, even as we speak?"

"The affairs of other countries matter little to me, Mr Blightley–"

"Call me Ed."

"I can scarcely be concerned with what happens in my own. But yes, even for one as solipsistic as myself, word of your nation's turmoil has reached my ear. The daily journals are replete with accounts of your North and your South being divided by some enmity, the causes of which are obscure to me."

"Yes, George, and quite a sad thing it is, too. Civil wars are the bloodiest, and there's been some awful battles in this one, and worse to come before it's all over." Sombre for a moment, Blightley soon resumed his cheerful aspect. "But it's an ill wind that doesn't blow somebody some good, as the old saw goes. Other folks' misery creates some bang-up opportunities – and it's a businessman's prerogative to take advantage of them, am I right?"

"I suppose – but how exactly do you accomplish that?"

"Easy as pie – at least it is for people who've got as much on the ball as me 'n' Haze. All those accounts of deaths and slaughter, that your English folks lap up when they read about 'em in the papers here? Well, that's at a considerable distance from the events – so you can just imagine how much more compelling they seem, when they're happening in your own backyard, and the soldier boys getting killed and maimed are your own kin, and your neighbours', as well."

"This immediacy, I take it, is something you employ to your advantage."

"Right in one go, George. People read of these tragic events – or exciting, depending on how you look at 'em – or they hear of 'em; much talked about, they are, you can bet your bottom dollar on that – but they can't actually *see* all the great battles and bloody goings-on, can they? Imagination's a fine thing and all, but it has its limits."

"So it would appear," I said. "And this deficiency is a matter that you seek to correct, with the performances of your–" Glancing down to the discarded handbill at my feet, I again read its bold words. "Your troupe of automata?"

"Bang-up job they do – I can tell you that!" The cigar in Blightley's hand drew a flaming arc as he flung out his encompassing gesture. "You should just see 'em – and I expect you will, soon enough. Haze 'n' I have spared no expense, to achieve a degree of verisimilitude never before witnessed on the stage. Why, the costumes alone that we stuff Haze's machines into – grey uniforms for the Southerners, and blue for the Yankees, just like you see there on the paper – they didn't come cheap; nosirree! And the rifles and the sabres – even cannons! – those required a damn considerable investment; you should've heard my backers squealing when I handed 'em the bill!" He laughed, slapping his own knee this time. "Had one fella tell me that it woulda been cheaper to've hired the actual Union and Confederate armies to whup it about on stage, with all the shooting and banging and what-not."

"Did you consider that possibility?"

"Truth of the matter, George – I did." Leaning closer so as to achieve more confidentiality, Blightley dropped his voice, and glanced quickly over his shoulder to ascertain whether the figure sitting in the prow could hear or not. "But I was sure it woulda broken poor Haze's heart, not to use all those clever machines he'd put together – he might not strike you as being exactly an effusive sort of fella, and most times he's not, but I've been hooked up with him long enough to know he's got a sensitive side. Probably why he finds it hard to speak to ordinary folk, least till he gets to know 'em; he'll warm up to you, I promise."

"My own words can scarcely describe how I look forward to that day."

"Glad you feel so." Blightley gave no sign of perceiving my sarcasm. "So there's the personal issue, all right – but from a business point of view, we'd already sunk a packet into the machines. And they do have some advantages to 'em – they can be replaced, right? We put a lot of effort into the staging of our shows, with a great deal of realism to the depiction of the battles. If it was real, live, flesh-and-blood soldiers up there on the boards, we'd probably lose a few at every performance. That'd make it difficult, I reckon, to recruit new ones. Kind of young men who sign up to go marching off with real armies, and get their heads blown off, are strangely reluctant to do the same in a theatre. Not sure why, given that the effect on 'em is pretty much the same."

"And your audiences?" I raised an enquiring eyebrow. "I presume they appreciate all the attention and effort you expend, to make these portrayals so convincing."

"You bet they do! War's a wonderful thing, George – if there weren't any, impresario types such as myself would've had to invent them, to come up with anything so all-fired interesting. Sometimes I even wonder if all our nation's leaders, with their strutting and posing and big talk, all their high-flown ideals and rhetoric – maybe that's all they do! And for no other purpose but to keep folks entertained – but that's a cynical notion, and one I don't pursue further."

By this point in the American's exposition, the gondola had proceeded on its submerged iron tracks to what seemed to be the position where I had first regained consciousness in it. I recognized the particular sham constructions, flat rigged plaster that they were, of the artificial Venice past which we made our way. The long-handled paddle at the craft's side continued its regular cogged motions; the human being I knew to be the capped gondolier above, and which Blightley assumed was one of his own theatrical machines, went on with his sly eavesdropping of our conversation.

"May I ask you a question, Mr Blightley?"

"Sure – but the moniker's Ed. Really."

"Very well. What I would like to know is – why are you here?"

"Huh?" The other man blinked in perplexity. "Where else should I be? I mean – I wanted to have a talk with you, and this is where you're at. Kinda obvious, isn't it?"

"Not quite what I meant, Mr Blightley. What I wish to determine is why you and your associate have come here to England. The civil war of which you speak – I am certain it is all very fascinating, but you admit that is greatly due to the audience's connection with the forces that are involved. In this country, those connections are largely absent, and our interest is consequently diminished. I very much expect that whatever seeds you and Mr Haze wish to sow here, they will fall on stony ground. Rather than seek to enlist me in your theatrical enterprises – to what purpose, I fail to see – surely you would be better off by returning home and reaping the profitable harvest you have planted in those larger and more enthusiastic fields."

"Would if we could." Blightley's expression darkened to a scowl. "Kind of a problem with that, I'm afraid."

"*Problem?* When is success ever a problem?"

"When it's the kind me 'n' Haze have had. No wonder the poor bastard's so tetchy – must feel like he's been kicked in the teeth, and after all his hard work. To be honest, that's how *I* feel."

"Your meaning escapes me."

"Maybe if Haze *wasn't* so all-fired clever." The man before me visibly sank into the morass of some bitter recollection. "Maybe if the mechanical actors he puts together *weren't* so lifelike – is it our fault that people are so fooled by 'em?"

"I take it that something untoward happened, because of your machines' uncanny resemblance to humanity."

"Right you are, George – you see clear to the heart of the matter, you do. Damn! And we were so close–" Blightley wrung his large-knuckled hands together, as if he were strangling the author of his miseries. "If things had gone just the least bit different, our fortunes – our *real* fortunes – woulda been made, and I wouldn't be sitting here jabbering with you, in this phony lagoon. Haze 'n' I'd be back where we belong, swanning it up at the Fifth Avenue Hotel, eating pressed duck and swilling champagne by the bucketful."

I said nothing, feeling no need to. The American's confession having begun, I was certain that I would not be able to escape the complete unburdening of his woes.

EIGHT

The Hazard of Theatrical Enterprises

"ERE'S WHAT HAPPENED." Blightley did not disappoint; he hunched forward, unblinking gaze fastened onto mine. "Haze 'n' I made a dreadful mistake – we shoulda waited till the war was over, before we started up our theatrical recreations of its famous battles. But we were impatient fools about that – and can you blame us? It's only human nature, isn't it, George – you see a gleaming pile in front of you, just waiting to be grabbed – why, you're gonna jump for it, aren't you? And we did!" His previous gloom was supplanted by a fevered agitation. "I wish you coulda seen it, George – it was magnificent. Two full regiments of mechanical soldiers, the blue and the grey, with cannons and even cavalry – cavalry, George! Those horses must've been Haze's masterpieces – very convincing, they were."

"I worked on them," came a low, muttering voice from the gondola's prow, "for a long time." Haze himself did not turn to face us, but continued gazing sullenly at the dark waters. "All ruined now."

"A certain impression is being formed in my mind," I regarded both men more closely, "that in the event, things did not proceed quite as you anticipated."

"You can say that again." Blightley's words were emphasized by a ponderous nod of his head. "We shoulda started out small, with a show we could've fit onto a regular theatre stage. But – my own stupid notion, I confess – why not something huge, that the whole country would notice? Hell, maybe the whole world! So we launched with a performance out in the open, with a whole valley for our contraptions to bang around in, and the mechanical horses charging back and forth – quite a sight, you can be sure. We put the audience up in the hills, with the top-dollar viewpoints right up close to the action, and the nickel seats out in the boonies – but higher up, so's they could still see just fine. Packed 'em in, we did. 'Course, we advertised like blazes, so we weren't surprised we got such a mob – people took the train all the way from Chicago, just to see. So as much as ticket sales went, we had a rip-roarer on our hands."

"I have no doubt of that." Indeed, I didn't; the American not only had the sunny optimism of his national breed, only briefly eclipsed by passing darker moods, but an apparent egoism beyond that tendency, which bespoke an innate talent for self-promotion. "Then what could have gone amiss?"

"Well, hindsight's a lovely thing, ain't it? You see so much more when you're looking backward." Blightley emitted a quick, barking laugh. "Chiefly, I'd reckon it was our choice of venue – you know, where our grand performance all took place. That damn valley – cute little place it was, too; very attractive – but just too far southernly inclined. Of course, that'd seemed something of an advantage at the time – my thinking had been we'd not only get the audience we mainly expected, of folks pretty much welded to the Union cause – but I'd calculated we'd also do well with those more sympathetic to the Confederacy, of whom there seemed to be quite a number in the surrounding region. And then, of course, there was a reliable contingent of those who just enjoy the spectacle of people shooting at each other – in the States, there's always been quite a few of those. The problem, however, when appealing to a mixed lot like that, especially at a time when passions are running high – they do become a bit, you might say, excitable."

"That comes as no surprise," I noted. "My understanding is that the Americans are, as a rule, of a volatile temperament."

"Certainly proved themselves so on that day! Truth to tell, George, once things got going, it would've been hard to determine, save for the uniforms on Haze's machines, whether the battle was taking place there on the field, or out where the audience had been gathered. Awful it was, what with all the hollering and cursing, and even gunshots – and that was just the women! Oh, the men in the assembled lot, on either side, gave a good account of themselves as well, but one mighta expected as much from them – or I should've, but didn't, fool that I was. It pretty much seemed that our performance, once underway so that folks could actually see the blue-clad soldiers exchanging hostilities with those wearing the grey – that was but a safety match set to the dry tinder of the popular imagination. Maybe if my partner Haze's creations hadn't been so convincing – but frankly, it seems to me now that they could've lacked a great deal in that regard, and any deficiencies woulda been more that overcome by the audience's feelings being strung to such a high pitch."

"But surely, this turn of events would not account for the disastrous blow to your fortunes, of which you have previously complained." I sensed that the American had not yet made a full account of the circumstances that had impelled his escape here to England. "Theatrical riots have occurred before – indeed, there was a time in this country, that such were so frequent as to chase the Bard from the stage, and imperil his life. Englishmen might be a good deal more placid now, but reports of similar havoc, at least in the lower sort of music hall, are not completely unknown."

"Right you are, George. If that'd been all that happened, our enterprises might well have recovered – or even prospered; as businessmen like us say, there's no such thing as bad publicity. But as it turned out, there were more disadvantages to the venue's location than just the audience being hot-collared and all. And for that, how was I to know? I'm no military expert, 'cept to the degree I can put on a good show, and I'd been so preoccupied with all it took to get ready for our inaugural performance, that I'd paid no mind to the reports in the papers as to the various manoeuvrings of the Union and Confederate armies. Just our luck, then, that we'd managed to plunk ourselves down right betwixt the two of 'em! And of course, they'd been too busy with their strategies for slaughtering each other, that they weren't paying any attention to what a couple of impresarios were getting up to with their mechanical soldiers and horses."

"The dimensions of the *contretemps* are becoming apparent to me."

"See it coming, can't you, George? Our whole venue was already in a complete uproar, and the next thing you know, real cannonballs were whizzing through the air, and blowing up a good number of the performing machines, and the spectators as well. Dreadful sight, I can tell you, especially from a business aspect – your chances of getting repeat customers are greatly diminished when so many of 'em are lying on the ground, all bloody and in pieces. And then things only got worse, when the real Union and Confederate armies, with bayonets fixed on the muzzles of their rifles, came pouring over the hills and mixed it up there in the middle. Considerable confusion ensued, to describe it in the mildest terms, compounded by there being genuine bullets fired, instead of just the blank rounds that Haze's machines employed. That resulted in a good deal of our performing stock being damaged beyond repair–"

"The bastards," came a darkly muttered comment from the prow. "It wasn't *fair*."

"No, it wasn't, Haze; very unsportsmanlike, if you were to ask me. But if fairness is the issue, then I have to admit that those flesh-and-blood soldiers took a beating as well. Seems there was a plethora of bewilderment on their part, when they figured out that some of their fellows, wearing the exact same uniforms, weren't human at all, but things moved along by gears and cogs. So a regrettable conclusion was reached in the minds of the rank-and-file, that they were trapped in some devilish intrigue, in which no one could be trusted, no matter what the colour of their fighting garb. Well, you can just picture what came of *that*! The surrounding audience was already in a panic, most attempting to flee for their lives, but a good number in a more bloodthirsty state of mind, and throwing themselves into the carnage they saw before them. Which had by that time devolved into utter chaos, every man for himself, and likewise every machine. By the time it was all over, and the little valley was quiet again, there were no victors on the battlefield, and precious few survivors."

"Not counting yourselves, of course."

"As I said, George, we're businessmen, same as you. And it's extremely hard to stay in business if you're dead. So yes, prudence dictated a hasty retreat from the scene. Once it was pretty clear that things were out of hand, and there'd be no bringing down the curtain to end what'd become of the performance, we'd scooped up what we could of the financial proceeds, and removed ourselves to a place of safety. And one from which we could take further flight if necessary, which we quickly concluded was the situation, given what we were told by various informants as to the *denouement* of our grand performance."

"I would imagine that those accounts were dire."

"Worse than that," said Blightley. "They were *incomplete*. A calamity like that, and already it was being hushed up? I had to assume the worst – which was that our theatrical performance had come to the attention of the government, and its interest in the matter was not likely to go pleasantly for me 'n' Haze. A considerable embarrassment for both sides of the conflict in which the nation was embroiled, right at a time when both the Union and the Confederates were desperately bent on keeping up the popular morale – hard to see how that could be accomplished while you're telling folks that their heroic brothers and husbands just annihilated themselves in a phony battle with a bunch of clanking machines. Say what you will about the gullibility of the common folk, they do have some standards as to what they'll swallow."

"Quite a predicament," I commented. "Obviously, you could not remain in the North, from where you had initiated your theatrical enterprise, nor could you flee to the South, having become equally despised there."

"Being despised I could handle, George – a businessman spends most of his life having that much on his plate. But Haze 'n' I were facing criminal charges – this is wartime in the States, and you can't be responsible for blowing up that many men in uniform and not have people thinking you're guilty of sabotage. They *hang* people for that! And a Northern rope fits as snug about your neck as a Southern one – no thank you, sir! I'll take my chances adrift in the great wide world, rather than find myself dangling with my toes above the ground."

"I would do more than that, if I were in your position. Might I suggest that you and Mr Haze take what funds are available to you, and invest them in an enterprise more respectable than that of presenting public entertainments? Perhaps a small shop – a tobacconist, say – in a remote English village would provide you both with a means of living, as well as a degree of anonymity that the dramatic stage could never afford you."

"Those are words of wisdom, George–" Blightley gave an emphatic nod. "I've said as much to myself, and to my partner Haze. But damn me, the theatre's in my blood! I'm a natural showman, and I can no more put down the trade than I could stopper my own breathing."

"How unfortunate for you. Given all that you have told me, it seems more like you are the captain of a ship that you would rather run upon a rocky reef, than set a course for some more modest but sunnier isle."

"Be that as it might, George, and I won't gainsay it. But our course *has* been set, and our sails are full, even as we speak. Never say die!"

I held my tongue. It struck me that if those Union and Confederate soldiers he had spoken of, who had been killed in pointless battle – as though History showed there to be another kind – if they had been less dogged in character, they would now be alive, rather than buried in their nameless graves.

"And the tide has turned," continued Blightley, "in our favour. The mere fact that we're sitting here together, having this little talk, shows as much. Why, you're alive, George – think of that! Took some doing, I can tell you, to get your hide pulled out of that little predicament you'd gotten yourself stuck into, up above. Those scoundrels were fixing to plug you – granted, there's some fine irony in being murdered in a cemetery, but I'm sure you'd rather have avoided it. So I'm glad we'd been keeping an eye on you, and determined where those Funerary Society folks were planning to drag you to, so we could get our trapdoor arrangements in place – you can thank Haze for it all working out so well."

"You were lying in wait for me?"

"Don't make it sound so scoundrel-like, George; we meant

you no harm, but only good – you can see that, can't you? We mighta been a bit secretive about it, and most times people go skulking about in the dark, that's an indicator of something nefarious in their intention – but our circumstances forced our hand that way. Those scallywags that were shooting at you – they're a bad lot. If Haze 'n' I had been out in the open with getting ahold of you, very likely they'd've put a couple of bullets through our heads as well, and not just yours."

"Those persons – the men with the rifles, hunting me – you know who they are?"

"Well …" This time, the American's shrug was of a more noncommittal nature. "A bit."

"And why they pursue me, with such lethal design? Does your knowledge include that?"

"Mr Dower, I have to tell you – these are trivialities you're stewing your mind up with. We've got more important matters to think about."

"*Trivialities?*" I regarded him in amazement. "They tried to kill me! More than once!"

"Right there's the problem with someone not having plied the theatrical trade – if you had, a smidgen more perspective would be yours. Why, if I spent my time mulling over all the reasons folk might have for doing me in – from stiffing 'em on a contract, to being a bit free 'n' easy with the cashbox – I'd be thinking of nothing else. What a waste of time!" Blightley wagged an admonitory finger at me. "Here's my word of advice, George – I just assume that *everybody* wants to take a shot at me, and it's only a matter of convenience as to whether they act on the notion or not. They can keep their reasons, whatever they might be, and I'll just go about my business. You should do the same."

I considered the possibilities presented by the man's advice. The first such was that he was an idiot, or otherwise deranged – I have had so much experience with the like, for it to have become tiresomely familiar. That madmen walk freely about is a reflection upon the nature of the world; these persons are more comfortable here than those of sounder mind.

The other alternative striking me was that his blithe dismissal of murderers in general had a more specific intent; that being one of concealment. My suspicions were aroused; in all probability, Blightley knew a good deal more about those stalking me, but for some reason did not wish to divulge what he knew. For now, his reasons were unguessable; if he were in league with those others, why hadn't he simply left me to their dubious mercies, rather than going to such lengths to rescue me? And if opposed to them, why not expand upon their villainy, and thereby induce me to repose greater trust in him?

His words having set this mystery before me, I decided to leave them where they lay, and make no further inquiry on the point. Having already refused the divulgence of what he knew, he was unlikely to acquiesce if pressed; better to wait for a later opportunity to present itself.

"Very well," I said. "On to, as you say, more important matters."

"That's the spirit!" From pure enthusiasm, Blightley swung a fist across his chest. "I *knew* you and us'd get along. We can get a lawyer to draw up the papers somewhere down the road, when things have settled down a bit more. Important thing is for all of us to get to work – we're friends now, but when the money's rolling in, we won't just be business partners – more like brothers, if you know what I mean!"

"A moment, please. Mr Blightley, I have no memory of stating an intention to join you and Mr Haze in any commercial venture."

"Huh – well, I'll be damned." The other man frowned in perplexity. "I just kinda assumed... why wouldn't you?"

"You must understand – I have had similar offers before. Some I have accepted, and others I have been bludgeoned into; the ones I refused, or managed to escape, are the only ones of which I have a comfortable memory. Those who desire my assistance with their various mad schemes – and I confess that your previous endeavours seem to be cut from the same cloth – they do not seek me; they seek my father. Who is dead. A great many of his creations live on, however, in their clanking, grinding way – he must have been busy indeed while alive, ceaselessly bolting together one device after another; so perhaps the neglect of his familial duties toward his son are understandable. But if I did not inherit any affection from him, then neither was his genius bestowed on me. You and the partner you already have – together you have conceived the notion that your fortune lies with placing mechanical performers on the world's stages. Perhaps you are right about that, though the dire history you have related would seem to indicate otherwise. Be that as it may; my meagre talents are not such that I can assist you to tumultuous success or calamitous ruin."

"Selling yourself short, George – that's what you're doing!" Blightley shook his head. "But you can't buffalo me; I know as much about your history as you do – maybe more. And I'll be honest as I can with you, since there's a coupla things you're a little confused about. One, it's not your *talents* or your *genius* that's so attractive to me – those are pretty overrated things, in my opinion. Haze's cleverness will have to suffice for both of us, since I don't have much along those lines, 'cept an eye for the main chance. But you have something of better value'n either of those, and that's your *name* – or to put it another way, your *reputation*. Maybe there was a time – I believe it so – when that Dower moniker you carry 'round was something of a secret, known only to the *cognoscenti* of clockwork marvels and steam-driven wonders, and of course to those in the employ of Her Majesty's various bureaus, whose job it is to keep all sorts of disasters and fearsome occurrences hushed up. And of course, you did a fair bit of keeping yourself anonymous, by burying yourself in that damp little hole out on the coast of nowhere. But things as enormous as these can't be covered up for long; giants have a habit of stomping out into the open with their incredible large boots laced up to the knees. Which is pretty much what happened, figuratively speaking, when your associates set loose that enormous walking lighthouse up above in London town."

"Please…" Pained by his words and the memories they evoked, I held up a hand as though to shield my face from their further onslaught. "If I have not managed to evade that infamy, it is not for lack of trying."

"*Infamy?* Damnation, George – little wonder you're not rich! That's not infamy we're talking about – it's *fame*. A golden crown, just waiting for you to pick it up and set it on your fool head. There's no greater advertisement than death and destruction, leastways after a little time has passed, and people have gotten over their petty personal tragedies, loved ones being kilt and stuff like that. And you've achieved a great deal in that line, whether you like it or not. A coupla years've gone by, and now all that people remember is the splendid excitement they had, seeing the Houses of Parliament get smashed to flinders. Let's face it – the theatre wouldn't exist at all, if it weren't for people desperately requiring some escape from their plodding daily lives. Me 'n' Haze, even with that fiasco we set off back in the States, we'd have to go some to match the kind of performance with which your name is linked."

The other's peroration, I knew, had been intended to sway me to his cause, as trumpet calls are employed to inspire soldiers – the flesh-and-blood ones, that is – to deeds of martial glory. But it had the contrary effect, oppressing me even deeper; he might just as well have thrust me under the black waters surrounding the gondola, and held me there until no more breath bubbled from my lips. In times past, I confess, I had contemplated the sin of suicide; once again, I regretted that circumstance and the infirmity of my self-destructive resolve had swayed me from that extinguishing course.

"I beg of you..." My gaze lifted imploringly to his. "Desist from your entreaties. You wish to flatter me, I know, and bind my fate to yours. It is a vain hope on your part; you mistake me for someone of both greater mettle and wider ambition."

"Stuff and nonsense!" Blightley would not be turned aside so easily. "Whatever greatness you personally lack – and we're all cowards to some degree – your *name* has it in spades. And that is all that we require from you, to press forward with our joint enterprise. You're not the genius of machinery that your father was – so what? Haze can supply whatever clockwork jiggery-pokery that we'll need along the way. Why, you'd be virtually a silent partner in our company; we do all the work, and you can mope about all you want, but with a decent share of the proceeds in your pockets to console you."

"If my name is all you require – then take it!" I spread out my empty hands. "I freely give it to you. Trumpet about the land whatever association you wish people to believe I have with you, and you will not hear me saying otherwise. Just leave me be, to seek out some dark concealing corner, and you and Mr Haze can split your profits between you, without a single penny coming to me."

"Doesn't work that way, George." Blightley shook his head. "The name has to have a body attached to it, and that'd be you. The grand entertainments we have in mind for the public, they'll be unlike anything ever seen before – but other entrepreneurs have already attempted the same, and they've dismally failed, for the lack of exactly what you can provide. Not everyone hooks up the name Dower with clanking huge machinery, but they haven't yet forgotten the thrilling chaos bestowed upon 'em by those gears and cogs that your father first concocted. We have both History and Truth on our side, which is not always the case when it comes to promotion, I can tell you that much! But to make the sale – to get the punters, as I've heard 'em called in this country, to demand that we take their money – for that, we need a living and verifiable Dower to front for us. Without you, George, we'd be sneered at as frauds and charlatans, and all our dreams 'n' hopes would be smashed to bits on the rocks of public indifference." His voice had risen considerably as he had spoken, but now he let it fall to a more sombre pitch. "You have to help us out, George – why, we're nothing without you."

"I'm sorry –" In truth, I wasn't; the man's maudlin self-pity steeled my determination to find a way free of the pair. "But you fail to understand the forces you are attempting to unleash. Did your own experiences, on your American battlefield, teach you nothing about the dangers involved with these machines? It is one thing to be an observer of bloody chaos, as someone buying a ticket to one of your shows might delight in, but to be the instigator of it – this is *hubris*, Mr Blightley, as the ancients warned of; you bring about your own destruction by indulging in that folly."

"George, my pal, you do us wrong. I'm sure you think that we're just colonial bumpkins, pawing at machines we don't understand, the way a monkey would with a wind-up clock, 'cause he's enchanted by the ticking sound it makes. But we're a bit smarter'n all that, I'll have you know; we're more'n able to learn from our mistakes. Sure, tinkering with devices such as your famous father created, and the like that my clever partner can come up with, it has its dangers; nobody knows that better than us! But worse than danger, it has something

far more terrible – it has *expenses.* Damn clanking things cost
a packet to build – 'specially if you do it at the level our Mr
Haze does."

"Excuse me." The person mentioned gave another
unsmiling glance over his shoulder. "I did no more than give
you what you asked for."

"And a damn fine job you did," Blightley hastily replied.
"I meant no disrespect. But I have to tell you–" His further
comments were directed to me. "It wasn't just the law that
my partner and I fled from; it was our creditors. Even with
all the sums that our backers ponied up, we were in the hole
so far as you wouldn't believe. We coulda turned over all the
receipts from our inaugural performance, just handed the
cashbox to 'em, and there'd still been enough red ink to be
drownded in. Facing ruin, we were."

"And you wish to re-enact that situation here in England?
I thought you said that you had learned from your errors."

"So we have!" Enthusiasm returning, Blightley once more
bounced upon the gondola's plank seat. "And you can see the
result, right here about you."

I turned my head, following the direction of the American's
extended index finger, out over the side of the narrow
gondola. His gesture indicated the shabby cut-out silhouettes
of the simulated Venice by which we passed.

"Grand, isn't it?" He beamed with pride. "Our enterprise is
already underway, and our cash resources aren't exhausted
yet. We should be able to finish up and be open for business,
with hardly any trouble."

"This is it?" I regarded our surroundings with considerable
dubiety. "You have abandoned your notion of presenting
battle scenes?"

"Perhaps for the moment, George – that was something
much more suitable to tastes of the folk in my own country.
They're rather more excitable – violent, even – than you

lot over here. Even with all the changes that've happened, there's still something... well, *calmer* in the English blood."

"You might be mistaken about that. I have had more experience with my own countrymen, and much of it has been neither calm or pleasant."

"Nevertheless, I reckon we're on to a winner here. Brits're always dreaming about Italy, aren't they? Perfectly understandable, given the general state of your weather. Maybe things've gotten more steam-heated here in London, but go beyond and it's still pretty dreadful. So why wouldn't your kin jump at the chance for a sunny holiday, without the bother of actually having to travel abroad and deal with the rude foreigners elsewhere?"

"Surely you jest." I scanned the Stygian environs once more, before returning my gaze to him. "Sunlight is notably absent here."

"It's a work in progress – should be fine on opening day. Haze 'n' I had a lucky break when we stumbled upon this spot. Seems like there's some huge underground boilers close by – and they're still hissing away! Got all the power and heat to do whatever we want with, and for free. Can't beat that!"

I knew more about the origin of the engines he spoke of, having been informed by Rollingwood concerning them and their humidifying effect upon the local climate of the cemetery in Highgate, but I held my tongue; I had no wish to distract Blightley from the revelation of his plans.

"So you see–" He proceeded to expound upon exactly that subject. "We've been busy, and we've spent quite a bit of the capital that we... *withdrew*, so to speak... from our concluded enterprises in America. There are still a few finishing touches we need to work on, but in short order we'll have a very accommodating subterranean resort here – our guests'll never have to worry about a rainy day, that's for sure! All the pleasures of an Italian sojourn, with minimal inconvenience."

"For those who wish – and I am sure there would be many – they are welcome to it." That of which Blightley had spoken seemed a ghastly notion to me, but then, I have never had an understanding of popular taste. "But you told me only a moment ago that you had at last discerned the folly of reliance upon animated machinery – do you therefore intend to leave this *faux* Venetian capital, with its canals and *palazzos*, completely uninhabited by anything that moves? How enjoyable would that be? Surely the attraction of journeying to Italy is not just to experience the relief from English weather that its sunshine affords, but to converse with its effusive natives, and listen to their incessant song. I had always been instructed that Italy was a land graced with music, just as we are not – but would you have your guests pay for the scant pleasure of wandering about this silent wasteland?"

"Is that all that sticks in your craw, George, about our schemes?" Blightley tilted his head back and laughed, slapping his palms upon both knees this time. "Then you're as good as ours! For there *shall* be machines – or at least folks will believe it so. Because of course, that's the linchpin of our business – people are vastly entertained by machines walking around and talking – and singing! – just as if they were real human beings. And the more convincing is the imitation, then the greater the entertainment, and the bigger the audience – and the box office receipts. So it struck me – and a powerful revelation it was – why bother with the machines at all? If verisimilitude is the goal, then why not give it to 'em? And who'd be better at playing the part of a human being, than another human?" He bestowed a conspiratorial wink on me. "Brilliant, you gotta admit."

"Let me see if I understand you correctly. Your intention is to hire actual flesh-and-blood persons, to play the part of the machines which are constructed to act and in every way seem like human beings?"

"Sure, why not – at least, once you get your head settled on the notion. People want to be fooled, and enjoy the fooling, so why not fool 'em the best way possible? And who's to know otherwise? You could *tell* folks this was what you're doing, and they wouldn't believe you – 'cause it'd spoil the fun! The only ones who'd be convinced at all would be those you hired to perform this little masquerade – and there's no shortage of them, eager for a day's wages. All this steam power that's been unleashed, it's thrown a lot of men outta work. Why pay for someone to use his muscles on your behalf, when you can crank open a valve and – *Whoosh!* Just like that! – you got ten times the force at your command. We can get all the performers we need – at least at the beginning – right up above in London. Need any more, we'll just go out to your home counties and do some recruiting."

"So this is what we have come to." I have never pretended to have any great fondness for Humanity; what little I possessed when young has been eroded by bitter experience. Still, Blightley's exposition of his plan for business, made ghastlier by that perennial American cheerfulness he exuded, filled me with sadness. Had it been such a little while ago that I had been exhilarated by my encounter with the shabby artificial lion up in Highgate, and had pranced about like a fool, so certain of Mankind's dominance over our own creations? An idle fancy, that seemed now. "The machines have the better of us, and now we seek to slough off our fragile carnal form, and become as them, just as they ape us. Men pretending to be machines, pretending to be men; surely we have vaulted headfirst into madness."

"Oh, it gets better than that." My gloom did not infect Blightley. "Seems as there's already a good many of your countrymen, who've already gone 'round the bend regarding things mechanical, what with all these changes and upheavals everybody's going through. So they believe that they're machines already – kinda tetched in the head, but harmlessly so. But I figure I'll make a personal effort to hire as many of those loonies as I can find, since it would seem likely they'd have a natural affinity for the work. And then we'd have men who think they're machines, paid to act like humans who're pretending to be machines that can act just like flesh-and-blood persons. By that point, I imagine the whole lot won't know *what* they are, or even care."

An involuntary shudder trembled my frame. It seemed to me now that the unmoored gondola had drifted free of all reality, the iron rails on which it rode relentlessly steering its captive passengers alongside crumbling pasteboard.

"Buck up, George–" The American leaned forward and slapped me on the shoulder, with sufficient force to almost topple me out of the boat. "You'll get used to the way things are – it's a new world! And it's up to us to find our places in it."

"To be honest," I spoke weakly, "I would just as soon not."

"Not as if you have a say about it all. Haze 'n' I need you on this endeavour. Like I told you, it's the name that's the important thing, and the face 'n' all to back it up. Our audience will want to be sure that they're getting the absolute best in mechanical entertainment, whether it's brass 'n' steel singing those Italian arias, or folk like them – won't matter which it really is. But you'll just have to accept that *Dower* is the brand name *par excellence* in that line, and that's what'll put us over the top."

"I think you underestimate the degree of my reluctance–"

"And you, George – you think you've got a choice in the matter. Well, you don't!" Blightley's amiable manner dissipated, his voice becoming sternly harsher. "You're not the only requirement for our success – there's more, you might say, technical details we've got to get down pat – but you are necessary all the same, however much we both might regret that being the case. You've got some lily-livered squeamishness about machines – well, fine, I can understand that; not everybody in this world is going to be lucky enough to be endowed with some Yankee grit. But whatever you lack in spirit – which seems to be quite a lot, frankly – Haze 'n' I'll be more'n happy to make up for it. So you have nothing to lose, do you? And a lot to gain – I'm sure you'll find that being a damn moody sourpuss is a lot more enjoyable when you're rich, rather than poor." Beaming once more, he thrust his hand toward me. "So let's shake on it – we be partners now, launched upon a great enterprise!"

"Actually, Mr Blightley, we are not." I drew back from him, both my hands firmly tucked at my sides. "I owe you my gratitude, for having rescued me from my pursuers; your reluctance to tell me what you know about those persons does not diminish that debt. But if you think me churlish now, for refusing your kindly meant offer, that is something I cannot help. I have tried to demur as graciously as possible, but your persistence forces me to speak more rudely than I would otherwise have wished. So then, my answer is *No*; I will not associate myself with you and Mr Haze. You have my best wishes, for whatever those might be worth – but your success or failure must be determined without any intervention from me."

"Hmm." Blightley stroked his chin. "Is that your final word, George?"

"How can I make it more certain for you? It is indeed."

"No way for me to change your mind?"

"None."

"Well, then…" He reached inside his jacket and drew something out. "Maybe this will."

I found myself gazing at the pistol in his hand, one of the intimidatingly large variety that American gunsmiths are so skilled at crafting; within the narrow confines of the gondola, it appeared immense as an artillery cannon.

"What do you mean by this?" The pistol's long-barrelled snout was directed straight at my chest. At such close distance, a bullet from it would likely obliterate my heart, drilling a hole straight out through the spine. "You can't be–"

"But I am, George; I'm very serious." Blightley's voice was level and calm, as though the weight of the gun he held were sufficient ballast to bring his temperament down to earth. "We made you an offer – and a good one – and you chose to refuse it. But as I tried to make clear, you really don't have that option. You're going to be part of our business, whether you like it or not."

"What rubbish." After my initial startlement when the gun had been produced, my own reaction was one of exasperated disgust. "Do you intend to point that thing at me twenty-four hours a day, seven days a week, from now until whenever – and still somehow manage the affairs of your theatrical enterprise? I rather suspect you are bluffing; if I were to jump over the side of this boat right now, and swim or wade to that flimsy harbour you've constructed – what would you do? Shoot me before I reach it? So much for your being able to advertise to the public that this particular Dower is somehow associated with your performances."

"I'd be doing you a favour, if I put a bullet in your back." A sneer showed on Blightley's face as he shook his head. "Think you could find your way out of here? It'd be snowing in Hell before you managed that trick. And even if you did manage to get back up to the surface – then what? Did you forget that there're still some folks out there who're looking to shoot you, even more than I might like to? I know a little about 'em, and I can promise you that they haven't gone away – if anything, they're scouring the bushes for you, even harder than they were before. Only this time, when they find you, there won't be me 'n' Haze conveniently rescuing your ungrateful hide. So sure, jump out and splash for it if you want, but I might as well save the bullet – you'd be a dead man, no matter what. Frankly, that'd suit me just fine, as then there'd be no worries about you joining up with one of our competitors – and there's a few of those – if you decided somebody else'd made you a prettier offer."

Blightley's exposition of these realities was sufficient to render me silent. His rising choler had extinguished whatever amiability he had possessed before. Clearly, he had anticipated that I would with alacrity embrace his business proposal, and that the three of us would already be celebrating our joint venture. My rejection of it had triggered a childish wrath on his part, and the desire to seek the vengeance of those spurned by others.

"I'm sick of all this yakking." He confirmed my surmise as to his fiery thoughts, by elevating the pistol higher; now its muzzle was pointed directly at my brow. "Nice talking to ya, George–"

Anticipating the worst, I squeezed my eyes shut – I make no pretensions to bravery in the face of death. Thus I did not see, but heard what happened next.

"Keep head below, Dower–" A shout, but not Blightley's voice was raised; in a fraction of a second, I recognized it as that of Spivvem, coming from above and behind me, where he stood in his gondolier costuming. "Oy, yank – how's *this?*"

Something whooshed above me; if I had not instinctively crouched, it would likely have cracked the side of my skull. The sound was terminated by another, that of a resounding thwack as one object struck another; a moment later, a plume of water was great enough to drench my trousers as I sat in the boat.

My eyes flew open, and I witnessed a greatly transformed scene.

Blightley had vanished – there was no one sitting before me. The noises of water being thrashed about continued, though; turning my head, I saw that they were caused by the figure that had been toppled over the gondola's side, and whose limbs were now flailing a yard or so away. It was the American in the dark water, gasping as he struggled to keep his face above the agitated surface; a stream of blood trickled across his wet face, from a wound he had suffered at one corner of his brow.

What had inflicted the injury was soon apparent to me, as my gaze darted above. The gondola's long-handled oar had been withdrawn from the water, and then swung about as a club, with sufficient impact to have propelled Blightley out of the boat; the flattened paddle-end of the oar was still for a moment, having reached the furthest point of the horizontal arc through which it had been wielded.

I had been so imbedded in my morose reaction to the American's attempt to draw me into his business plans, and then my entire attention being compelled by the weapon being thrust into my face, that the surreptitious presence of the person Nick Spivvem aboard the gondola had been driven from my mind. Now it took a central place in my perceptions: however much I had failed to mount a defence against Blightley's lethal intent, Spivvem filled that void. His quick actions had displaced the ribboned gondolier's cap and sent it flying; bare-headed, he continued his assault upon my would-be captors, drawing back the pole in both his hands and then thrusting its farther end straight into the chest of the startled Haze, with similar results to that which his partner had suffered. Both were now flailing about, churning the water to froth as they sought to save themselves from drowning.

Blightley's efforts along this line met with rather more success than did Haze's; the smaller man's startled, wide-eyed visage had already disappeared beneath the surface, marked only by the last few bubbles of his gasping breath. His partner displayed an admirable loyalty to him; having recovered some from being capsized from the boat, Blightley had the presence of mind to apprehend the other's desperate situation; splashing over to where he had last been seen, Blightley dove beneath and secured a hold under Haze's shoulders, by which he was dragged back up into the air.

Unfortunately for myself and Spivvem, that rescue needed only one of Blightley's arms; in his other hand was the pistol, of which he had instinctively managed to keep hold, even while struggling in the water. His sodden appearance, mutton-chop whiskers plastered to the sides of his face and neck, did nothing to conceal his anger; as he bobbed with Haze pressed against his side, he raised the weapon and fired off a shot.

Given the man's lack of footing, there was no wonder that the bullet went wide of its intended target; that it came close enough to strike and bury itself into the gondola's prow indicated that Blightley might well be able to better aim his next shot.

"Get head down!" The rocky ceiling above was still echoing with the gun's first sharp report when Spivvem shouted at me. He had little need to; I had already flattened myself as best I could into the space between the gondola's plank-like seats. "And *stay* down!"

Even from that lowered angle, I could see that Spivvem's only weapon, the long-handled oar with which he had knocked both men from the boat, was useless now; the spot at which Blightley kicked himself and his partner afloat was too distant for the pole to reach. My expectation was that Spivvem would cast it away, then dive alongside me in order to shield himself from another bullet from the American's gun–

That did not happen. Instead, I witnessed Spivvem hoisting the pole to a vertical position, then jabbing it straight down toward the gondola's submerged wheels and the iron tracks on which they rolled. The boat's progress before had been so steady and slow, as to scarcely raise a ripple in the surrounding water – no more; with a jolt that slid me back toward the perch on which Spivvem stood, the gondola leapt forward, and continued to accelerate.

Whatever disarrangement had been caused to the mechanism beneath, it was more than sufficient to extract the gondola's remaining occupants from our previous danger; from somewhere behind us, Blightley managed to fire another shot, but it went farther wide than the one before. Foolishly, I raised my head and caught a last glimpse of the two Americans bobbing in the gondola's wake, the smaller still panting for breath and his red-faced partner shouting a curse at us, the exact obscenity swallowed in the echoing distance.

As is so often the case, one hazard was evaded, only to be replaced with another. The damage that Spivvem had caused to the gondola's propulsive mechanism did not lessen in its effects, but in fact increased, perhaps to a greater degree than even he had anticipated. As the boat sped faster, its motion became more erratic and violent, shaken by both the malfunctioning apparatus to which it was fastened and the impact of its prow against the water ahead. Flinging out my arms, I seized hold of the gondola's sides to keep from being pitched out of it.

Spivvem had no such recourse available; having engineered our escape, he fell victim to the means by which he had done so. I saw him toppling backward, dislodged from the perch on which he had been standing. With no time for thought, I reached to grasp one of his pinwheeling hands; I nearly succeed in securing him – my outstretched fingertips brushed against his, before he disappeared into the dark behind. If there was a splash as he struck the water, I could not hear it through the battering noises of the boat's now rocket-like progress.

The dangling lamp swung free of its hook, sailing in a comet arc before it too was extinguished. I could see nothing from where I had pinioned myself, but only sensed the gondola beginning to disintegrate about me. A black wave swamped over me, and I fought to fill my lungs through it, as I hurtled toward some unknowable destination, which I knew I would never reach.

PART THREE
A Seaside Idyll

NINE

An Acquaintance from the Past is Met Again

S O OFTEN HAVE I suffered under the misapprehension of my own death, and of having been translated to whatever world awaits us beyond the grave, that I am no longer amazed to open my eyes and find myself in circumstances unknown to me.

At least there was daylight upon this scene; an immediate comfort, given that the most recent memory I could summon was of being engulfed in unlit waters, wracked by the velocity of my passage through them. Evidence of that terminated journey lay strewn about me; as I raised my head, blinking, I spotted fragments of gaily painted wood, one of which was of sufficient size to indicate the curved prow of the gondola in which I had ridden as captive of an uncertain fate. Other remnants were scattered about the sandy foreshore upon which I lay; as I raised myself upon my elbows, my sodden garb clinging coldly to my frame, I could see that my arrival here – wherever *here* was – had been accomplished with some violence. The iron tracks on which the gondola had ridden, with such velocity as to render me unconscious, came to an end closer to the lapping water's edge; an upright wooden barrier had been driven in two by the impact that had thrown me several yards farther.

Craggy rocks, festooned with tangled seaweed, mounted stepwise to demarcate the shore's limit. If my senseless form had struck them, no doubt the result would have been fatal, or at least crippling; to have somehow avoided that fate was as much good fortune as I could have hoped for – that, and to have awoken before any tide had risen over this little cove, at a depth sufficient to have drowned me.

"Better you *had* died, Dower–" In this lonely circumstance, my predilection for addressing myself returned, there being no one else to burden with my thoughts. "You have not escaped a sorry fate, but merely exchanged a bad one for a worse."

This musing was prompted by the grimness of the scenery surrounding me. The coastline of Cornwall is harsh enough, but my memories of it were almost tropical by nature, compared to the bleak strand on which I had now been abandoned. The sun might have been shining, and even uncloudedly so, but not with force enough to keep my skin from shivering. Yet – oddly – at the same time, a sense of something like *comfort* came over me. I was not as apprehensive about my lot as I had been on similar occasions, most recently when I had found myself in the gondola, still intact then, in that shoddy subterranean Venice that the Americans Blightley and Haze had constructed. The more that my disordered thoughts reassembled themselves inside my skull, the less concern I seemed to have over the situation; my inward tranquillity very much resembled this place, still and silent after the turbulent ocean had retreated to its ponderous depths. My spirits actually rose to a fractional degree, as I gazed about myself; that elevation was accompanied by my own marvelling at the lack of anxiety I possessed. Perhaps – or so I placidly thought – I had suffered some otherwise undetected injury during my rapid transition here, specifically a blow to the head, such that some cerebral organ had been dislodged, as persons suffering similar traumas are reported to lose any sense of fear.

But as immediately as I entertained that notion, I dismissed it; some other cause was in play here. As luck would have it, the mere effort of speculation evoked the answer. Which was *memory*; I knew this locale; I had been here before. An impressive span of years separated the previous time from this moment, but I was now certain that the world's mysterious workings, with its seemingly endless panoply of schemers and machines, had somehow contrived to deposit me on the island of Groughay, far from the nearest human habitation, in the Outer Hebrides north and west of the Scottish mainland.

To be sure, this happenstance would present some problems for me; my recall of Groughay was that it was the very definition of the word *desolate*, possessing little in the way of shelter from the elements, and even less in the way of bodily sustenance, other than the scraggly gorse upon the rock-strewn hills, and a few ill-tempered sheep – unless, of course, the passage of years and the harsh climate had rendered those extinct. I cared not for their fate; I resolved to face these difficulties relating to my further survival as they pressed themselves upon me. For now, I was simply glad to be alive, however battered by the mode of transport that had brought me here, and in a place – if not exactly home – the contours of which were familiar enough that I did not have to speculate as to what fresh Hell I had been thrust into.

"Then–" I spoke aloud once more. "If I am *not* dead – for if I were, I don't imagine I would be so bruised and battered – then this, while not necessarily an improvement in my conditions, is at least not the worst I could imagine."

"You are not dead, Dower–"

A deep, guttural voice intruded upon my meandering thoughts.

"This, I can assure you."

Startled, I gazed wildly about myself, attempting to perceive the person who had spoken to me. I had thought myself blessedly alone; to discover otherwise was a shock.

"Here," said the unseen other. "You are close enough to touch me, if you wished."

The possibility was raised once more, that I had suffered some derangement, either in the tumultuous flight from the subterranean chambers beneath the cemetery in Highgate to this far-flung point, or in my sudden casting upon the shore on which I had found myself. I saw no one; I seemed to be addressed by a person invisible.

My bewilderment was both lessened and increased by what happened next. The voice's source was revealed: what I had taken to be one of the cove's dark rocks, slick with the ocean water that has washed over it, bestirred itself. I saw that it was a figure human as myself, who had been sitting this whole time upon the sand, arms crossed upon his knees as he had silently observed the castaway before him.

"A long time." He reached out and laid his hand upon the side of my face. "Do you not know me?"

That I had mistakenly assumed the person to be stone rather than flesh-and-blood was explained by the garb that enveloped his body. Tightly fitting to his torso and limbs, of a thin monochrome substance that extended glove-like over his hands, but encased his head as well, masking his face; the only indication of his features was the narrow slits through which his unblinking gaze encompassed me in.

"I never knew your name–" For now I did recognize the human-like figure before me. "But I always thought of you as *the Brown Leather Man*."

"As you wish." His voice was slightly gentled – or such was my fancy; perhaps the passage of time had rendered his memories of me less harsh, enough that he could greet me in a fashion friendlier than that by which he had last departed of me, so long ago. "It matters little."

Reader, indulge me this; if meeting again this singular creature cast me into a reflective mood, I issue no apology for that. For I had lost so much, of things both great and small, that for this one to be unexpectedly restored... as a bankruptee finds a lost penny in his pocket, and considers himself absurdly wealthy thereby, so my emotions ran. In the scales of the larger world, the loss of one's wife is a minute thing, scarcely noticed by any save the widower – but I had lost a world as well, and the ticking, clanking one which had been substituted for it seemed a poor exchange. The Brown Leather Man was a dark shade from out my past – but still from mine and not another's, and for that I found myself grateful.

Of course, this occasion was not the first on which I thought he had re-appeared before me. In Cornwall – before Miss McThane became my wife, and I was but a defeated and suicidal bachelor – a person strode out of the ocean and confronted me, and I had mistaken him for this one. In the event, that intruder in my life had turned out to be a scoundrel named Stonebrake, clad at that time in a diving costume that enabled him to pursue his devious errands unobserved in the ocean depths; he had come dripping out upon the land to draw me into various schemes, all of which I came to regret. But no matter now; the man was dead – but this one, the actual Brown Leather Man, was seemingly alive, though I had believed I would never lay eyes upon him again.

"You are surprised, Dower." He accurately read my thoughts, as though they were visibly swirling behind my eyes. "Need you be?"

"Apparently so," I said. "You have ever surprised me."

No truer statement could have been uttered by me. The erratic course of my life, from one disaster to another, had been launched by this creature, other than human as he was; had he not turned up on the doorstep of my watch shop in Clerkenwell, so many years ago, I might have led a decently placid existence, as free of excitement as any proper Englishman might have wished. The world's vast conspiracies would have passed over my head, like clouds that appear darkly massive from a distance, but dissolve to mere occluding mist when they lower themselves to earth. I could not hold him accountable as author of all the schemes and follies in which I became enmeshed; many had been required, including my own deceased father, to engineer all those interlinked machinations. But just as ships are racked by tumultuous seas, the events had been first augured by the appearance of this stormy petrel.

"And you surprise me now." I studied the glistening blank mask that served as the Brown Leather Man's face, searching for some clue there. "I might not be dead – your word I take for that – but I confess that I believed you were; or as good as."

"Your kind thinks in such a way." His gaze turned from me for a moment, gazing upon the grey, sullen waters. "Humanity, as you call yourselves – if other beings are not in communion with you, wisely keeping to themselves, then you believe they have no existence at all. So then, most that lives is a secret to you."

I was not prepared to debate the point; I knew from our previous acquaintance, that his was a soul given to deeply brooding concerns. Perhaps it was a characteristic of his species, if any survived other than himself; the Atlantic depths in which the *selkies*, as known to the Scots who on rare occasions encountered them, had made their sunless home would seem well-suited for producing such a race of gloomy philosophers.

"Such might well be the case." I looked out upon the ocean, the slowness of its lapping waves evoking a peaceful effect. "I suspect that I resemble my brethren in that regard – the less I know, the happier I am for it."

"The sentiment expressed does not surprise me." The dark slits of the Brown Leather Man's eyes regarded me again. "Your nature, when first we met, was one left untroubled by mere events. The world treats roughly such placid souls – much has happened recently, that would have thrown those of common temper into sheer panic."

"Age and fatigue have confirmed that petty wisdom I possessed when younger. No one seems to be firing a rifle toward me at this moment, so I might as well savour it. And..." I nodded slowly. "I have just now reached a more profound conclusion, which casts a great many things in a different light."

"And what is that?"

"I find myself here on the island of Groughay." My outflung gesture took in the surrounding lichen-embossed rocks, and whatever bleak terrain lay beyond them. "Circumstances brought me here once before; outlandish ones, to be certain. Why then should I believe that I ever left this place? My memories are of even wilder events that extracted me hence, and deposited me back in a veritable maelstrom of unfolded conspiracies and their seemingly insane agents; I remember a certain Lord Bendray, who had the absurd notion of exploding this world to flinders, so that he might communicate with those entities he believed to be in existence on other planets – but though he might have been the first of such I encountered, he was hardly the worst of them. Rather than considering Groughay as a place of exile, perhaps I should more properly regard it as one of refuge. Having escaped, however unwilling I might have been at the time, from a maddened world to this peaceful rock, perhaps all those subsequent lunacies were but constructed by my imagination, and never took place in reality at all."

"Indeed?" If the Brown Leather Man's masked face had been able to display an expression, it would have been a quizzical one. "So you believe that you have somehow dreamt everything that happened to you, from your first arrival here onward?"

"Actually, it would have had to have been my *only* arrival here, if I never left. But yes, everything – the contents of my memory are so jumbled up, and so chaotic in nature, that they do seem dream-like. Or nightmarish, rather, to use a more precise term." I plunged my fingers into the damp sand beside me, and drew up a handful, sifting the grains as though to determine whether they were more real than all those now-vanished events. "Perhaps they were the labour of but a single night, my overwrought brain churning up one phantasmal vision after another as I slept, and this is my first waking morning upon the island."

"And what of those?" A dark finger pointed toward the splintered fragments of wood strewn nearby, the remnants of a brightly painted Venetian gondola. "Do dreams usually leave bits and pieces behind, that you can see and pick up?"

"Hm." I felt my own brow crease. "I will have to think about that. But in all honesty, that seems like a detail of little significance compared to the logic I have pursued." My mood had been so upraised by the revelations that had struck me, I was not about to let another deflate them. "And indeed, why not chase the notion further? Perhaps the issue at hand is not whether, having once come to Groughay, I have ever left this place – but having dreamt of a chaos of wild events, I have ever woken up, or whether I continue to dream still." I waved a dismissive hand toward the wooden shards. "Such things would require precious little imagination, compared to all the rest that has seemingly been produced by my night-fevered brain. You yourself seem impressively real, and so my conversation with you – but then, so did all those other, vaster articles and events."

"All of which," observed the Brown Leather Man, "you
have now convinced yourself to have been phantasms, mere
wisps cavorting inside your skull as you slept, and continue
to sleep. If so, then I might be such as well – would that not
be the case?"

"There is no call to be offended by it." I lifted my shoulders
in a shrug. "If offence you do take, it is no more than my
dreaming that you do so."

"Allow me to inject a counter-argument to the discussion."
My sable companion rose to his feet, a few rivulets coursing
off the tightly fitting garb that kept his body safely encased in
the vivifying fluids of his native sea. He stepped closer to me,
then leaned forward while swinging one arm in a swooping
arc. His fist struck a blow to the side of my head, with
sufficient velocity to knock me sprawling upon one shoulder.
"There–" His narrowed gaze fell upon me. "Does that cause
any reconsideration on your part, as to what is real and what
is dream?"

"Damn your hide–" Raising my own hand, I rubbed the
injured spot, which continued to throb painfully. "I hope
you realize that it is possible to voice a disagreement with
someone, without necessarily resorting to violence."

"Do you concede my point?"

"I fail to see where you have made any. A man can as easily
dream of being struck, as any other event."

"If I have not yet convinced you of my reality–" The Brown
Leather Man displayed his fist, still tightly clenched. "Then
perhaps I need to repeat my assertion, with greater force."

"No, no – that's quite all right." Digging the butt of my
palms into the sand, I pushed myself as far away from him as
I was able. "For the sake of argument – or rather, for the sake
of concluding this one – I admit the validity of your position."

And in truth, this was no mere cowardly evasion on my

part. To myself, and unspoken, I had to acknowledge that this eerie, man-like figure was utterly correct as to the solidity of the circumstances in which I had discovered myself. All that I wished had never happened – it had indeed. To think of it as fantasy, concocted by those ceaseless mental engines that take the upper hand while one's rational part is buried in slumber – *that* was the dreaming, fondly embraced, and sadly abandoned now that I felt myself fully awake. To dream of dreaming, chasing one imaginary rabbit after another down its unending burrow – what silly creatures we are, as a species. I could hardly fault others for so often attempting to deceive me, when I was so obviously willing to do as much to myself. In that sense, the Brown Leather Man's blow had achieved a salutary effect, that of knocking over the painted screen that I had erected before my perceptions, obscuring the true state of affairs about me.

"Very well," I spoke aloud. "On this epistemological battlefield, you are the victor. You are as real as I am, as surely as this island of Groughay is real beneath us. Now what?"

"I despair of you." He shook his glistening, featureless head. "That I am real and no dream – that all that has ever happened to you, those things took place in the world in which all creatures live, and not inside your head – this much is undeniable. But you advance a baseless assumption, when you conclude that *everything* about you is true. Observe, Dower."

Involuntarily, I gave a flinch as I saw him squeeze his gloved hand into a fist once more. But it came nowhere near me – instead, as though indulging in one of those fits of temper in which a person damages himself more than any other object, he struck an outcropping of rock close beside me.

To my surprise, he did not curse himself for a fool, and rub his bruised knuckles with his other hand, attempting to alleviate the pain of the futile blow. Startled, I turned to look, and saw it was the rock instead that had suffered. A cracking, splintering sound had come to my ear; to my perplexity, I could discern that the Brown Leather Man's fist had penetrated the damp, lichened surface, nearly to the extent of his wrist. The white edges of the hole that had been produced by the impact contrasted sharply with his forearm.

"Why... it is nothing but plaster!" I bent forward, peering more closely at the damage. "And *papier-mâché*–" When my companion withdrew his fist, I could see within the hole, and note the glued sticks and angled board pieces that formed the hollow structure, and upon which the imitation rock surface had been artfully laid. "Why would anybody have deposited such an artifice here?"

"Hardly the only one." The Brown Leather Man strode to the vertical cliff-wall bounding the cove; with a quick thrust of his upraised boot, he punched a similar hole in it. A resultant crack ran jaggedly up higher than his chest, causing a small avalanche of pebbles and papery dust. "If I had a mind to, I could crush everything you see here–" He gestured toward the visible extent of the island beyond. "The whole place is as phony as a three-dollar bill."

The last of the words he had spoken startled me. There was some other pretence going on here, other than the shabby falsehood of the terrain that had just been revealed to me – and I was now certain what it was, as though the delayed effect of the blow from the other's fist had arranged my thoughts into a new and more accurate order. I had noted before that while the Brown Leather Man appeared just as I remembered him from long ago, he did not speak now as he had then. When I had had conversation with him before – always oblique and abbreviated, but filled with dreadful portent – his manner of speaking had been stilted and odd, with inverted phrases and accents, as of a foreigner to the British realm. Now his enunciation and phraseology was much like my own, as though he had spent the intervening years in close proximity to native English speakers, absorbing their speech and making it his own – yet the last time I had encountered him, he had with irrevocable bitterness renounced the prospect of any further contact with the human species, determining to return to his own doomed kind in the frigid waters of the North Atlantic, and die with them there. Of what might have induced him to break that vow, I had no idea, but this change in him remained apparent. Even more significant, though, were his lapses into mystifyingly obscure cant, such as *three-dollar bill* – an Americanism, it seemed, such as I might have expected from the entrepreneurial Blightley, now departed from my life, or so I hoped. In what circles would have the Brown Leather Man been a communicant, that a usage of such type came easily to his tongue? It might have been a puzzle indeed, had not the answer already formed within my thoughts, that the source of this wordage was not one displaced from here by location, but by Time.

"What is the purpose of these sham constructions?" Rather than voicing anything more accusatory, I feigned the pondering of another question, yet unanswered. "The island of Groughay already possesses genuine rocks – I stumbled across many of them when I was here once before. What purpose is fulfilled by crafting and depositing fakes, when the real ones abound alongside?"

"There is no Groughay," said the Brown Leather Man, an unseen sneer turning his voice even more guttural. "Or at least not here. You have been deceived, Dower – yet again. It is not a matter of *this* rock–" He pointed to the smaller one near me, through which he had punched his fist. "Or *this*–" His gesture swept across the vertical face beside himself. "You are not on Groughay; everything you see is a replica, designed to make you believe that you had been transported from those chambers beneath London, with its sham Venetian canals, to a remote island in the Hebrides. If you were to shovel just a few feet through the sand beneath, you'd come to sheets of bolted iron; the waters you see there – no more an ocean than what you'd find in a bathtub, only on a somewhat grander scale. And the sky?"

The Brown Leather Man – for so I continued to term him, leaving his true name unspoken even in my thoughts – bent down and picked up a substantial stone, enough to fill his hand; he weighed it for a moment in his palm, then flung it upward. Though presumably as artificial as the one in which he had previously crushed a hole, it had enough weight and mass to strike what I could now perceive as the painted ceiling above us; a rectangular tile was dislodged by the impact and fell with the stone to a spot close beside me.

"There–" With the toe of his boot, he kicked the flat object. "Do you need further proof?"

I looked from the tile – one of its four corners had been chipped away – and then up to the expanse above. The only wonder now was that I had ever been deceived by it at all, and had believed myself to be out in the open air. That I had, and so easily, occasioned another of those brief, self-flagellating meditations of which I am such a *soi-disant* expert, dispensing them like penny candy to all who are so unfortunate as to be reading these pages: *Thus it ever is with Humanity, that we are not deceived by what others wish us to believe, but by that which we wish to believe*. I had desired to consider myself cast upon some remote and chilly Hebridean isle – such has been my life, that this is what passes for ambition with me – and the desire had placed itself between my perceptions and reality, blinding me to its obvious ramshackle artificiality. Even what I had taken to be the low murmur of the ceaselessly rolling ocean upon this concocted shore, I perceived now to be the thrum of *Steam* once more, those relentless boilers and pistons that powered these self-inflicted deceptions.

"This is, I take it, some further contrivance authored by those godforsaken Americans Blightley and Haze?" My thoughts, having penetrated the mock island's thin veneer of verisimilitude, pressed on to note more inadequate details – what I had believed to be the thin grey sunlight of the Northern latitudes was actually the flickering illumination of gas jets tucked into various niches above; the clammy mists that I recalled from my long-ago sojourn on the actual Groughay were in fact somewhat more tepid than those, indicating that they were but leaks from the various pipes and valves that no doubt underlaid the scene. "Judging from my previous acquaintance with what they had so proudly proclaimed to be their handiwork, what I see here has every indication of being more of the same."

"Got it in one, Dower." Another oddly breezy expression was uttered by the Brown Leather Man. "That pasteboard Venice from which you were extracted, with its mildewy atmosphere and boggy canals, is hardly the limit of their ambitions. They and their backers – of which Blightley has an indisputable genius for finding, and milking funds from the same – have a grand scheme for creating an empire of amusement parks–"

"What would those be? I have never heard such a term."

"Don't perplex yourself over it," he replied. "The words will soon enough be in vogue. The world – the real one – does not provide enough entertainment for those who desire nothing but; so there shall be special places to cater to that taste. Blightley and his partner are but the forerunners of an entire breed of like-minded entrepreneurs. Having come to ruin in America – mostly because their various contraptions are pretty much junk; I'm sure Blightley told you something else, though – they have an ever greater ambition here in England, to build giant underground locales such as this, in which various famous adventures would be portrayed, so

that throngs of visitors would pay to experience all those
thrilling events for themselves. Thus Blightley and Haze,
and their financial associates, would reap vast fortunes based
upon diverting the public's fancies."

"I'm certain they shall; few men have *lost* money by
indulging others' folly." Frowning, I gestured toward the
shoddy landscape surrounding us. "But if such is their design,
why did they go to the bother of recreating the island of
Groughay? The real island is a miserable, insignificant place,
markedly more so than is the norm even for Scotland. That I
was gladdened for a moment, to have thought myself there,
only illustrates how dire the general run of my circumstances
have become. But as to the history of the place, no famous
adventures have ever occurred on Groughay."

"You err, Dower; there is one such."

"And that would be…?"

"None other but your own." The Brown Leather Man's dark
gaze remained fixed upon me. "You believe your life to be one
of little note, that the world regards with no more interest than
you might invest in the fluttering of a mayfly, deceased after a
single day. Well, you're wrong about that – no surprise. While
you've been crouching in your hidey-hole down in Cornwall,
the engines of publicity have been churning night and day,
with your life and times being the grist for that particular mill.
I imagine you thought that Blightley fellow was handing you
some kind of line, about how important it would be to have
your name associated with his various half-cocked schemes.
Actually, he wasn't – I can assure you that there is some
considerable value to the name of Dower, but not for the
purposes of assuring the theatre-going public as to the quality
of the mechanical performers they'll be viewing."

"You've heard him talk about that?"

"I hear *of* a great many things," the other ominously
hinted. "But Blightley's schemes are hardly a private matter

– he yaps about them to anyone who'll listen, and who might have coin in his pocket to contribute to their advancement. But what he tells the backers who fall for his pitch, and what he told you – those are two different things. The actual reason he sought to enlist you in his cockamamie enterprise is because of the public interest in your adventures, and the money they'd pay to vicariously enjoy them in just such artificial locales as the one you see here."

"My *adventures*?" His words stunned me more than the blow of his fist had. "Hardly how I would describe those unfortunate experiences."

"Everything's a misfortunate for you, Dower – but yes, other people regard them differently. And to his credit – or blame; however you wish – Blightley is largely responsible for that. While you slept in your remote bed, dreaming of anonymity, he has been busily thwarting your every desire. A vast army of hacks, those ink-stained wretches who'll scribble anything for money, has been employed to promote the wonderfulness of the life you've lived – you might not believe it to have been so, and very likely it was just as much a smoking pit of disaster as you perceive it, but once those hunched-over, paid-by-the-word plodders had laid down their worn-out pens, your biography had been transformed into as much the stuff of heroes and derring-do as anything old Homer and Virgil ever spoke of."

"Good God." To say that I was appalled would have been the grossest of understatements. With these few sentences, the Brown Leather Man – if he indeed had been the creature he was but pretending to be, rather than another – had turned my previous nightmares into airy, skipping fantasies, full of sunlight and innocent children's songs, but now all swept away by this evil prospect. "Tell me," I implored, "that this is but a malicious fabrication on your part, designed to torment me beyond endurance.

The malice I forgive – easily – if only you confess that the unwanted notoriety of which you speak – this monstrous possibility – is a lie."

"I speak nothing but the truth, however little you wish to hear it–"

"It cannot be." My own hands squeezed themselves into white-knuckling fists. "I do not believe you."

"You'll bloody well believe, when I have proven it to you – which I can. Wait but a moment." He turned and strode a few paces away from where I sat, toward another of the plaster-and-pasteboard outcroppings of rock which formed this artificial cove's underpinnings. Reaching behind it, he pulled forth a satchel made of the same dark, glistening substance as his own aquatic garb; carrying this pouch by its broad strap, he returned to me. A moment was required for him to unseal the flap by which the penetration of any moisture was prevented, but when he had accomplished this, he extracted an object of flat rectangular dimensions. "Here–" He thrust the item toward me. "Take it, and see for yourself."

With the greatest reluctance, I allowed him to place it in my hands. A book, of obviously cheap manufacture, shoddily bound and with the visible edges of its pages already yellowing. Its garish exterior depicted a hodge-podge of various imagined machines, drawn skilfully enough by some nameless artist so as to present their most threatening aspect. Gilt letters, already peeling, luridly shouted the volume's title –

INFERNAL DEVICES

"What a ghastly thing." Shaking my head at what I saw, I opened the book – I took no notice of the author's name, if there were indeed any person shameless enough to claim it as his own. When I had read only the opening lines of the first chapter, I was unable to conceal my revulsion. "The bloody cheek – this is written in the first person! As if *I* had written it!"

"That is the conceit of Blightley's commission." The Brown Leather Man radiated an air of smug triumph, even through the blank mask which concealed his face. "If your life is to be presented to the public as a series of heroic adventures, all the better to entice people to a reconstruction of those events, then he who lived through them must also be seen as a hero. That would be *you*, Dower – and what you hold there is your dashing, but tastefully modest as well, account of famous deeds."

The impulse that rose within me, to fling the volume – wretched in appearance, even more wretched in content – into the concocted sea nearby was almost overwhelming. Such a violent lash of my arm was stayed, however, by the horrid fascination that seized hold of me; I continued turning the crudely printed pages, as though I suffered the same compulsion that forces one to stare unblinking into a writhing pit of snakes.

It was with some gratitude that I felt the urge ebb away, after a cursory perusal of the outlandish narrative. Any resemblance to my own life – the one I had actually lived – was slight; certain facts and details remained, but all buried beneath the writer's meretricious prose, which I took to be his imitation of my own more measured way of speaking. And all the while, on every page, the bastard sought to portray every stumbling accident that had befallen me in reality, every prankish scheme that had been cast as traps before my feet, as some sort of thrilling exploit. If the account had been represented as mere fiction, it would have been bad enough – but for it to be employed to gull its readers into believing me a person worthy of renown? Within my breast, both shame and fury burnt.

"I wish I could give you my thanks–" Closing the book

without glancing at whatever might be its tedious and inevitable denouement, I held it up toward the one who had so hatefully bestowed it upon me. "As a general rule, I am grateful to anyone who is so kind as to tell me the truth, however little I might wish to know it. But in this instance, that response is beyond my capacity."

"Keep it." He dismissively waved off the volume. "Or throw it away. There's plenty more where it came from."

"*More*?" I had not thought it possible, but I was newly aghast. "How much more?"

"You'd be surprised, Dower – or perhaps not. At any rate, a vast body of literature has been created – if you'd care to call it that – recounting not just your supposed adventures, but a great deal of others as well. There appears to be a voracious audience for tales of steam-driven devices and other machines of dubious purpose, and the halfwits who become entangled with them. Very likely, the day approaches when there will be nothing *but* such books as the one in your hand, and nobody will bother reading Shakespeare and Milton and all the rest of that creaky lot. Some might consider that a blow to civilization, but–" His dark shoulders rose in a shrug. "For me, that's just how it goes."

Once more, a sense of unease was evoked by the manner in which he spoke, so different from that which I recalled from my first experiences in his company – and increasingly so, as if some concealing veil had inadvertently slipped from his featureless visage, beyond the one through which I had already glimpsed his true identity. But at this moment, I did not have the leisure to mull over the matter, searching for whatever significance it might possess.

"Before, I thought I might have dreamt a great deal, which you have convinced me were things that actually happened, alas." My face was set into a mournful expression as I gazed at the loathsome book in my hands. "But this raises another wonderment to my thoughts, as to whether I have ever existed at all, or am merely the creation of some marginally talented scribbler, grinding away in some garret redolent of gin and stale tobacco."

"You'd be a lot better off, Dower, if you gave up this endless questioning as to what is real, and what is not–"

"If your observation is a preface to another blow... then really, you needn't bother." I pushed myself back away from him, as far as possible, just to be on the safe side. "My resigned attitude toward reality, or whatever it appears to be at the moment, is quite secure; I can assure you of that."

"Fine; keep it that way." While the diction of the person behind the mask might have altered from when I had first encountered him, a general air of glowering menace seemed newly born. "You have more pressing matters to be concerned about. For one, there are people who want to kill you – I might've guessed that would be at the top of your thoughts."

"It does preoccupy me," I said, "to a certain degree. But you will have to excuse some confusion on my part. For it seems that no sooner than various parties of a mysterious nature threaten my life, then equally strange persons come to my rescue. I confess that I am beginning to find this recurring process a bit tedious."

"Grateful sort, aren't you?"

"I would be more so, if I were not so certain that you and your associate – that disreputable Nick Spivvem fellow – did not have your own agenda that prompted your saving my hide, just as Blightley and Haze had theirs in mind when they had previously done the same."

"*Spivvem*?" The Brown Leather Man's outburst was accompanied by a derisive snort, only slightly muffled by the glistening sheath that hid his face. "I have nothing to do with that sonuvabitch – he's exactly the sort that gives criminals a bad name."

"The meaning of the word you employ is obscure to me – but I have a sense of what you wish to imply. There are many rapscallions in the world; why do you view this one in particular so harshly?"

"You have no need to hear my reasons." A sullen tone tinged the other's voice. "Suffice it to say that you're well quit of him. The only favour he might ever have done you is that he triggered the process that extracted you from those phony canals that Blightley and Haze had created, and brought you here so that I could pound some sense into your head. But don't concern yourself about ever having to thank him for that – the man's dead."

"How can you be sure of that?"

"Trust me," the Brown Leather Man spoke grimly. "It's enough of a miracle that *you* survived the journey – and you wouldn't have if I hadn't been here to drag you ashore."

"I take it that your presence was no mere coincidence."

"You're getting smarter all the time, Dower; there's hope for you yet. Let's just say that the people who've been trying to kill you aren't the only ones interested in your comings and goings. I've been keeping my eye on you."

"So it seems. But my worries are hardly dispelled by that being the case. Those others you mention, who have indicated such a concern for my whereabouts, showing themselves as they did in Cornwall, and then in London – why should I not assume those assassins will turn up here, wherever this place might be, just as they have surprised me before?" I glanced about the artificial cove, as if there might actually be some sign of such an intrusion. "Those persons have displayed a remarkable persistence in attempting to do me ill."

"For the moment, you're safe enough – you might not have been transported all the way to the Outer Hebrides, but you're still quite a ways from London; if they managed to track you from Highgate Cemetery to that fake Venice underneath it, there'd be some time before they could follow you out here."

"And this location is…?" I peered more closely at him. As I did so, I congratulated myself upon the ruse I had succeeded in perpetrating. My pretence of still being gulled by his masquerade, and concealing what I knew in certainty of him, had stirred his natural volubility and yielded a good deal of information he might not otherwise have related. "Exactly how far have I been removed from that previous spot?"

"You are in the Lake District, or that which was termed as such before having been transformed by those technological advances I know you abhor. I doubt if Wordsworth and Ruskin would recognize the place now, if they were to return from their urban exiles; precious few lakes remain, or at least there are none visible on the surface. Ullswater and Windermere, and all the rest that were considered so scenic and charming – they've all been drained into those underground steam mines, that furnish so much power to London and the other sprawling cities. Blightley and Haze sought some advantage for their enterprises by seeking to construct portions of the amusement park empire here – a good number of vast subterranean chambers are available for their purposes, having been hollowed out and then abandoned as the mines continue to be excavated downward. In addition, the tunnels containing the pipes and tubes that pump the steam to its destinations are easily expanded to accommodate the human passengers that the Americans seek to lure to their new entertainments – it was through the prototype of one of those, that you were rocketed out from underneath London and deposited here."

"Pardon me, but that raises in my mind some doubts as to my security. Wouldn't it be likely then, that Blightley and Haze, or some agents in their employ, might show up at any moment? If they had been murderously inclined before, surely they would now be twice as disposed toward that end."

"Calm yourself, Dower. Their resources are limited – the capital they brought with them when they fled their native land, and the funds they have managed to raise here in Britain, have largely been exhausted, and with little profit to show to their increasingly impatient investors. Blightley's attempt to recruit you into his schemes is an indication of just how desperate he is. Having failed at that, and with scant ability to send anyone else in pursuit of you, he and his odd partner will be more likely preoccupied with keeping their heads down and out of sight, while they calculate their next moves."

"That," I said, "is welcome news. Events have come upon me at a fearsome pace, and I no longer possess what little youthful strength I once had, by which I might have been able to endure their frantic rush. You have proven that this island is a lamentable fraud–" I glanced sadly at the broken rock close beside me, with its hollow plaster innards revealed, then back to my present companion. "But it is close enough to the actual thing, as to provide a calm respite for me. I could quite happily remain here at peace, for a considerable length of time."

"Don't be an idiot," growled the Brown Leather Man. "Any hiatus in your dire circumstances will soon be concluded. Those who were previously in pursuit might not be upon your back at this very moment, but they will be soon enough. For accomplishing their lethal goals, the means they have at their disposal are greatly magnified compared to anything that Blightley and his associates can get up to. The worst of your assailants, and the forces that command them, have but toyed with you up until now – they underestimated the degree to which others are interested in saving your ass, plus the amount of sheer dumb luck that has kept you alive up until now."

Again, that strange disjunction of the words spoken in his deep-pitched voice, as though one manner of speaking was as much a sham as this locale to which I had been transported – but I already knew which was the falsehood, and which the authentic.

"You won't always be that lucky, Dower." He continued his stark assessment of my situation. "And whatever time you've got left, it's quickly running out. You need to get your act together, and quick."

"Very well–" My own voice became heated; his prodding had succeeded in raising my ire. "You speak of these greater and more ominous forces arrayed against me – who are they? I might not be able to prevail against them, but I would wish to know the name, and the nature, of those who want me dead."

"A reasonable request." The Brown Leather Man gave a small nod. "Perhaps you have already heard the name before, but had no idea of its significance – but in that, you would scarcely be alone; they keep their true purpose a closely guarded secret, and lull the great mass of people into believing them harmless. *The More Loving Embrace* – is that term familiar to you?"

"No–" My spine suddenly snapped straight and erect. "Wait a moment – I have heard that–" A fragment of memory leapt from the recesses of my mind. "At my wife's funeral, back there in the cemetery at Highgate, the cleric who gave the eulogy–"

"You mean the Right Reverend Jamford?" Another nod was given by the Brown Leather Man. "You're on the right track – go on."

"Odious man – ranting and raving about all sorts of apocalyptic nonsense. The fellow from the Gravitas Maximus Funerary Society – Rollingwood was that name – he said that it was entirely typical of him, which was why Jamford had been ejected from the Church of England as being entirely indecorous; a position with which I find myself in agreement. Even that brief encounter with the person was more than I could ever have wished to endure. But Rollingwood told me of the man's new denomination, and that was the name of it – the More Loving Embrace..."

"And had you seen or heard of them before?"

"Never."

"For once," noted the other, "you needn't blame yourself for any ignorance. That the More Loving Embrace hadn't come to your notice until you were standing at the side of your wife's grave, and that you were not aware of its significance – it is less because of your reclusive mode of life, and more to do with those persons' secretive ways."

"Who are they? What do they want? Specifically, what do they want of *me*?" I slowly shook my head in despair. "Such a wretched species Humanity is! Scarcely a day goes by, without some number of idle, restless individuals forming a new conspiracy, to wage war against all the other conspiracies that came together the day before. Why can't they leave their fellow men undisturbed, so we can creep into our graves at our natural pace?"

"Believe me–" His tone was even more drily composed than before. "If it were to be my decision, I'd happily let you rot as you wish, and just as most men do. And I suspect that a great many others, those who've fastened their attentions upon you, would be more than content if they were not compelled to pursue such an interest in order to further their designs. But there you have it: you possess no virtues that command the focus of the world's covert forces, nor do you even desire to, but nevertheless this notoriety is thrust upon you. Either deal with it as best you can, or let it destroy you as the toad in the ditch is speared by the tines of the harrow."

"Let me inform you of something else I do not possess." My long-simmering anger now boiled over. "I have no need of lectures in regard to Fate, and how it has seized upon me. Perhaps I have not made my peace with the matter, but at least I am not in ignorance of it. If you wish to be of service to me – and perhaps you do; I cannot tell – then do so by ignoring what were merely my rhetorical lamentations, and proceed with answering what you yourself evidently regard as the more important question. Who are these More Loving Embrace people you mention, and what is their aim regarding me?"

"We're on the same page, Dower." Up to this point, the Brown Leather Man had maintained his standing posture, looming over me like those black clouds that amass on the horizon, signalling the approach of doleful weather; now he assumed a more companionable position by sitting down upon one of the rocks close-by, of a large enough construction to bear his weight rather than collapsing into shards of plaster and pasteboard. Leaning forward, he brought his face, featureless except for its slitted eyes, near to mine. "I'll tell you what I know."

"Please do."

"They're a secretive bunch – and don't interrupt me with any complaints about how that makes them just like so many others; there's secretive, and then there's *really* secretive, and the More Loving Embrace falls into the latter category. They started out that way, apparently some time ago – I have no idea of the exact date. And as sinister as they seem to be now, they were otherwise at their beginning – some kind of charitable, philanthropic organization, kinda religious in their thinking; hence the name. But one that strictly adhered to the Christian edict that you're supposed to keep your devotions unknown, and out of the public eye – so even when they were do-gooders, they kept themselves hidden, and remarkably well. But things change, don't they? Human nature's pretty inevitable stuff; the years went by, and the More Loving Embrace became more and more powerful, and even more given to secrecy – but now they had another reason for that. Because, bit by bit, they abandoned all that malarkey about doing good… so let's just say they got interested in *other* things."

"As you say – inevitable. Exactly what sort of things are we talking about?"

"Various," he replied. "A great deal of them criminal in nature, except for those at such a high level that they are no longer crimes, but rather affairs of state – pretty much the same thing, of course. But of late the More Loving Embrace has settled on a particular agenda, which its members pursue to the exclusion of those previous interests."

"And the nature of that agenda is known to you?"

"Well… perhaps." The Brown Leather Man's response indicated an evasive discomfort on his part. "But it's nothing you need to know about."

"I think otherwise. These people have an unnatural interest in me, therefore I have a justifiable interest in return."

"Trust me, Dower – it's better if you *don't* know. The only thing that you need to be concerned about is that the More Loving Embrace is dead-set against Blightley and Haze, and all the plans that those two Americans have managed to rope their backers into. That might not be the ultimate point of their agenda, but it's connected."

"Intriguing…" I nodded slowly. "That makes me think rather more highly of these More Loving Embrace people, whoever they are, and whatever they want. I am no particular friend of Blightley and his partner – the man stuck a pistol in my face, after all. And that came after he had done everything he could to cozen me into his ridiculous schemes. If this More Loving Embrace is so opposed to Blightley, why shouldn't I be on their side as well?"

"They don't like you any better, Dower – the More Loving Embrace is who sent those guys with their guns to track you down in Cornwall, and try to put a bullet through your head. The same ones who followed you to London, and were hunting you in Highgate cemetery. The More Loving Embrace is a real equal-opportunity outfit; just because they don't like Blightley and Haze, that doesn't mean they're not also capable of wanting to do you in."

"I must confess that I find your efforts at explanation to be more perplexing than enlightening." Leaning back, I studied the darkly garbed figure with a measure of skepticism. "We seem to have made some progress; now at least I know who else it is who has been trying to kill me – or at least the name of their conspiratorial organization. But if they have some overriding *animus* toward Blightley and Haze, what in God's name does that have to do with me? If the More Loving Embrace has made as close an observation of my comings and goings as you indicate they must have, being so powerful and omniscient as you describe them, then surely they are aware that I have never had any association with the Americans they so despise. I had never even encountered the men in question until this conspiracy's armed agents drove me away from my home and into the arms of Rollingwood and the Gravitas Maximus Funerary Society – which of course I only did, hoping to find some safety in London; a vain hope, as it turned out. But nevertheless, if the More Loving Embrace had merely let me be rather than seeking my death, I would have continued in my previous condition, with there being no contact between myself and those others. Unless, of course–" Another thought had suddenly struck me. "Unless the More Loving Embrace was acting on some preëmptive logic, and wished to make it impossible that I might ever have doings with Blightley and Haze in the future, through the simple expedient of murdering me. That seems a bit cold-blooded on their part, but nothing you have said about them indicates that they would shrink from such an action. Is that indeed their reasoning?"

"You're on the right track," said the Brown Leather Man, "but you're knocking on the wrong door. There's something that the More Loving Embrace wants to keep from happening, all right, and they're happy to kill you to prevent it – but it doesn't have anything to do with the possibility of your hooking up with Blightley and Haze. It has to do with *you*, and your father–"

"I knew it." Disgust overwhelmed my soul. "That again? Is there never to be any surcease, any end to this constant prying into my unfortunate patrimony? This is an avenue down which I have been prodded before, and only to disastrous conclusions – and that being the case, I find myself very much doubting both the intelligence and the originality of this grand, ancient conspiracy you have talked about. One might have expected, given the notoriety and the extent of the damage caused by other villains obsessed with my father's creations, that this More Loving Embrace association would devise some other, and more likely profitable, pursuit to chase themselves down."

"You misunderstand–"

"No, I don't." My flaring temper prompted this interruption; I wished to hear no more from him. "I understand perfectly. These people, sunk into their own iniquity, have convinced themselves, as others have before them, that there exists some vastly clever machine devised by my late father, the discovery and subsequent operation of which will enable them to amass fortunes beyond imagination, chiefly by threatening other people with some terrifying violence. And of course, the key to that scheme is myself; by virtue of my lineage, I can either locate the damnable thing, or, if they already have it in their possession, I can push the appropriate levers that will set its gears and cogs into whirring motion. Well, sir, I will not have it – this is beyond my endurance. Those who have not lived my life might have some insane desire to repeat the worst portions of it, but I do not. Let them do their utmost, but I will not be part of it."

"Don't be an idiot, Dower – or at least not as much of one as you've been before. Think a moment; why would the More Loving Embrace send its agents to shoot you, if they wished to coerce your assistance in whatever it is they're planning?"

"That is a puzzlement to me, but I have learned from bitter experience not to attribute a great deal of rationality to those who seek me out with such designs in mind. Your history of this organization indicates that they have fallen from the path of righteousness, however noble their intentions might have been when they started out on it; it would not surprise me to discover that they have departed from the precincts of sanity as well. Such seems to be the invariable effect on people, when they spend too much of their time thinking about my father's creations. Their ability to destroy seems to be only exceeded by their capacity to derange."

"They're not crazy, nor do they seek any assistance from you. Face the obvious, man – if the More Loving Embrace seeks to end your life, then obviously they have some other intent. And of that, I am able to inform you: they are in possession of an item of considerable importance – or at least they know where it is, as do I. The reason why the More Loving Embrace's agents are in pursuit with such lethal intent is that they wish to prevent *you* from finding it as well."

"But I am not looking for anything, other than a modicum of peace and quiet." I voiced my protest as strenuously as I could. "Least of all am I seeking another one of my father's creations – my past experiences have more than convinced me that it's best not to have anything to do with them at all. I have no ambition other than to be left alone, free of any entanglement with all the malign conspiracies which inevitably revolve around everything that my father set his hand to while alive."

"You have made an understandable mistake, Dower – for which I am at fault." The Brown Leather Man lowered his voice to a confiding tone, while at the same time bringing his masked face closer to my own. "It is not one of your father's creations that occasions such concern; it is your own."

"Then the mistake is not mine, but those others' – I have never created anything, other than excuses as to why I am not the equal of my father in that regard."

"And this is where you're wrong." He almost sounded sad in his assessment of me, as though he viewed with regret some injury I had done to myself. "You're responsible for more coming into being than you give yourself credit for. Those mechanical creations of your father – sure, they're great. But your mind has been poisoned by this constant thinking about them, just as the minds of others have been – so that you believe that no other kind of creation is possible. For them, that might be true; they have willingly, and happily, bolted themselves to the iron rails they hope will carry them to the Future. But it's different for you; there's another possibility."

"I very much doubt that–" My words were spoken with numb habit, less rueful than resigned. "Possibilities are for fools, or at least those more foolish than I am; if you care to weary yourself with them, as others do, then by all means – proceed. But I have neither interest in or desire for such."

"Perhaps I can spark a little enthusiasm." Once more, he reached out and dragged his glossy leathern pouch toward himself; unsealing its flap, his dark-gloved hand reached inside again. Withdrawing an object, he extended it toward me. "Here – try this on for size."

It was nothing more than a doubled sheet of paper, but one

that possessed an odd sense of familiarity for me. Unfolding it, I was struck by memory; not far-distant ones, but recent – I might well have been in the parlour of my inn, surrounded by the Cornish night, as I gazed upon a similar missive. That previous letter, so reminiscent of the one I now held, had been delivered by one of those aqueous couriers that had so eerily crept about that rugged coastal landscape, the gelatinous messenger then having been rudely dispatched by the same assassins who had turned their attentions toward me. There had been other letters as well, all held in the ticking box that had been my late wife's mysterious bequest to me. All had been addressed to Miss McThane, as was the one that my gaze now fell upon; further, all had been inscribed with the same ink, and in the same distinctive, scrawling hand. A distinction existed with the one that the Brown Leather Man had just given me: it was unfinished, the final sentence trailing off incomplete, and there being no signature initial of its author below.

"What is the meaning of this?" I continued my ruse, looking up with artfully widened eyes at the figure sitting close to me. "How did you come by it?"

Not by murder and theft," he replied, "as others have intercepted similar communications to you. Let's just say… by *other* means." He reached out his hand and tapped a finger on the words written on the paper. "Read it."

I did as he directed, and examined the lines over which I had merely glanced before. No surprise came to me, as I quickly discerned that the contents of the letter dealt with the same subject as had those I had perused upon taking them from the box in which Miss McThane had carefully preserved them. The author expanded upon his having concluded his search for some unnamed individual, detailing his efforts in that regard and the often dubious locales through which he had prowled.

"Am I to assume that this has some significance for me?" I lowered the missive and studied the figure opposite. "If so, I fail to discern it – and whatever meaning it would have had for my late wife is equally as obscure."

"Your incomprehension astonishes me," said the Brown Leather Man. "Do you not know who wrote these letters to her?"

"How could I? The letters which were completed and sent to her, and which she kept, were only signed with a single initial. What was I to make of that?"

"*All* of them?"

I pretended that his question took me aback; frowning, I might have in truth been trolling through my memory, seeking any exception to the statement I had made...

Did any actor ever give such a performance, unseen by all but one? I jerked myself straight, as though an invisible bolt of lightning had coursed upward in my spine, stronger than the shock evoked by any previous inward revelation. My eyes shot open wide; I stared straight before myself, as the flat of one hand struck the side of my breast. Within but a few seconds, the same hand darted inside my jacket–

And withdrew from its pocket another letter, within the envelope which had been given to me by that eerie courier, the night outside the inn.

"What an idiot I have been..." I held the letter in both my elabourately trembling hands. "I forgot all about this..."

"There was a time, when I might've found that hard to believe." The Brown Leather Man's voice was tinged with arch smugness. "But given what I know about you... yeah, I can imagine that happening. It must have – since there's so much that you don't seem to know, and that you should."

I bit my lip, to stifle a shout of triumph. To gull the one who sought to make me the victim of his pretence – I savoured a considerable satisfaction from this moment.

"Perhaps..." I expanded on the absence of mind I had falsely confessed. "If it had been in *her* hand – I would've read it immediately, so that I might have heard her voice again in my thoughts. But it was written by another's..." Lifting my gaze from the letter, I met the other's gaze with my own. "What might be revealed here – I could not contemplate! And so it was expunged from my thoughts."

"Sure–" A trace of sympathy was heard in his voice. "Completely understandable."

I shook my head, conveying an apparent dismay at my own stupidity. With no further prompting, I proceeded with the task at hand. This supposed Brown Leather Man's slit-eyed scrutiny weighed upon me as my fingers opened the envelope; he did not notice that its seal had already been breached. Its contents were damp, but not sodden; whatever exposure to the waters the letter within might have suffered had been lessened, it seemed, by both my coat and my shivering body; perhaps time and what corporeal heat I could summon from within had dried it out a bit. I extracted and unfolded the single sheet of paper; the lines inscribed upon the page were blurred, as was inevitable given the duress of its exposure to the elements, but still readable–

But I did not bother to read them.

Instead, I placed the tip of my finger underneath the final word, the name inscribed at the bottom of the sheet of paper, and held it unmoving there.

"I take it," spoke the Brown Leather Man, "that you're surprised?"

"Yes." Lowering the paper in my hands, I looked over at the figure beside me. My voice was low and quiet, and of an uncharacteristic firmness. "I *am* surprised. That you had a low estimate of my wits, I was well aware. But that you think me so dull-witted as to be unaware of the identity of he who wrote this and all the other letters to my wife – and that you are that same man–" I slowly shook my head. "Often have I been a fool, Scape – but never that much of one."

Behind the slits of the leathern mask, his eyes widened with his own sudden realization.

A surge of anger overwhelmed any further desire for concealment on my part. That furious rage impelled my actions as I threw myself upon the other, my hands grappling for his throat, the force of my lunge toppling us both upon the sands of this artificial cove.

That I wished to murder him, I confess – there is only so much knavery that a man can endure, before some hindering restraint snaps inside him. And perhaps I might have, had my fingers not found the seam of the mask, as I knelt upon his chest. It was the work of a moment to grasp that edge and pull it upward from his throat, then toss aside the flaccid empty form, revealing the face that had been hidden within–

I pushed myself back and away from him, a startled cry escaping from my mouth. For only a second I had thought there was another mask revealed, of a coarser and nearly as darkened substance – then I realized that it was an actual human visage, but one that had suffered hideous scarring from fire.

He got onto his knees, resting his weight upon his gloved hands, then swung his gaze toward me. His eyes were the only aspect of him that was still recognizable in the ruin of his face.

"You're right," said Scape. "I should've known better. When did you figure it all out?"

"From the beginning." I spoke with bitter satisfaction. "From the very beginning."

TEN

What is Found Must First Be Lost

G UESS I'M NOT surprised." Scape flung another stone
across the water. "Pretty dumb to have underestimated
you."

The stone – a small pebble, really – possessed enough
substance to skip a few times, with attendant small ripples
produced, before disappearing beneath the surface. Perhaps
Blightley and Haze, in the efforts to reproduce the island of
Groughay, had not bothered to manufacture the tiny rocks as
they had the larger outcroppings, from plaster and pasteboard,
but had resorted to the simpler expedient of strewing about
a few cartloads of such genuine bits. The ocean, however,
that had been slowly lapping at the artificial shore no longer
seemed as convincing as before; whatever machinery driving
the shallow waves from below had ceased its operation,
rendering the water flat and lifeless.

"I should have never believed you dead." I stood next to
him, gazing toward the constructed horizon. "Even when I
saw you fall to your apparent destruction, long ago on the
banks of the Thames. Your tenacity seems to have no more
limits than your rascality. I might well have stood upon your
corpse, with it devoid of breath and heartbeat, and leaned
down and sawn off your very head; I might have buried your

remains not six feet but six leagues deep, and made my camp upon your grave for years, to prevent your rising – and still I should not have been astonished to answer a knock upon my door, and find you standing there with that perpetual, insufferable smile of yours."

"Well…" His shoulders, still garbed in the darkly glistening outfit that had driven my first identification of him as the Brown Leather Man, lifted in a shrug. "It actually did come as kind of a surprise to *me*. When it happened – I mean, when I discovered that I wasn't dead – what a shock, eh?"

I kept my gaze averted from him and the massively scarred features that masked him as thoroughly as had the garment's slit-eyed hood, now abandoned and lying flat and empty on the sands, like a jellyfish that had been cast up, if any such creatures were so darkly hued. It was not a physical revulsion on my part that prompted my looking elsewhere – after seeing what had happened to him, the result of those fiery explosions in which I had believed him to have been consumed, I felt no further horror at the sight. Rather, it was a feeble attempt at kindness on my part; he had not been a notably handsome individual in that former existence, but had been decent enough in appearance as to have given Miss McThane no pause in being his partner in more than their various criminal enterprises. But now I could not imagine her or any other woman looking upon him with anything other than pity or disgust, so thoroughly disfigured was he. He could not have been unaware of the effect his appearance evoked in others; thus I figured it best not to let any scrutiny of mine weigh upon him, however inured I might already have become.

"When I fell from that stupid walking lighthouse – the Colossus of Blackpool, or whatever it was called – I was sure it was the end. And I was OK with that." Scape continued talking as he bent down and picked up another pebble. "And maybe that's what I wanted – you know? I've really screwed up a lot of stuff in my time – not like I have to tell you about that – and so if finally doing something good for other people got me snuffed, too…" He straightened up and tossed the stone in the same trajectory as the previous one. "Maybe that wasn't so much a bug, as it was a feature."

His discourse raised some uncomfortable memories; for a moment, the artificial vista before me was obscured, replaced by visions of those eruptive conflagrations that had left so much of London in smouldering wreckage, and from which I had barely managed to escape alive. The indisputable fact that Scape had also done, and now stood beside me, might well have reinforced a more religiously minded person's belief in miracles.

"You're right about that," replied Scape, after I had told him as much. "Believe me, there was a long time after I got fished out of the Thames – half drowned, half burnt to a crisp – that I wished I had died. When you're lying in a charity ward, they don't give you much to ease the pain."

"Did you make any effort to act upon that wish? To bring an end to your suffering, by way of your own hand?"

"Thought about it." He shrugged, as though to dismiss the notion now as easily as he might have before. "For maybe a day or two."

"Amateur," was my wry observation. "I've made nearly a lifelong study of the matter – killing oneself, I mean. Not with any great consistency, perhaps, but returning to it often enough as to make its contemplation seem familiar."

"Yeah…" Scape warily regarded me. "You're kinda creeping me out, talking like that."

"Any concern I have for your feelings would be minimal." My round for a shrug; my momentary, idle curiosity on the point had been more than satisfied. "So… having determined to continue with your miserable existence, why did you make no effort to communicate with those who knew you? I myself might have made some effort to assist, even if I could have done no more than direct some of your former associates to your side."

"Right – like any of that bunch would've helped. Most of 'em would more likely have come around to the hospital and stood on my throat, just to off me while I couldn't defend myself."

"There was one," I spoke quietly, "who would have been glad to know, at that time, of your still being alive. But she is dead herself now."

"And what would she have said if I'd turned up, the way I am now?"

"I do not know. But I think you underestimated the depth of her feeling for you, by not giving her that opportunity."

"Maybe so." Scape silently regarded the dull expanse into which the stones had disappeared, without even a ripple apparent now. "But I kinda figured she deserved better – and you seem to have taken care of that all right."

It was a subject I did not care to pursue, and I said no more about it – being painfully aware, as I had been while the woman had been alive and had resided with me as my wife, that there had been another with a prior claim to her affections. *Had been*, and now *was*, as he stood next to me – and this had been part of the last secret that she had kept hidden from me, that he still lived and was in correspondence with her, while I slept on unawares.

"But why such masquerade on your part?" This was my attempt to turn our conversation to other matters, of which there were so many that I desired explanation. "What was the intent behind disguising yourself as that other, the one I knew as the Brown Leather Man?"

"Are you kidding? Jesus Christ, Dower – you were about ready to kill me just now." Scape rubbed his throat, chafed by my recent grasp upon it. "And that's pretty much the reaction I was expecting. Not like we've ever really been friends, is it? Plus – I admit it – I've been sneaking around behind your back, writing to your wife and her writing to me. That's usually the kind of thing that gets even a mild-mannered type like you all riled up. Which I can understand. But there's still stuff I needed to talk to you about – so I figured, hell, why not pass myself off as somebody you *wouldn't* be so set against? Leastways in the beginning. If things had been going well between us, we'd been hitting it off all buddy-buddy – then I could've shown you who I really was. That was just about as much of a plan as I had."

"And a poor scheme it was," I said. "Even if I had not already deduced that you were still alive, I would have immediately known there was something amiss in the portrayal; your manner of speech was a sad imitation of how *he* spoke."

"Doing the best I could." Scape had picked up another pebble and weighed it in his palm. "Figured if I talked the way I normally did – the way I'm talking now – you'd have flashed on it right away, and you'd have known right off who I was. Except, of course, you already did."

"It is a distinctive patois, certainly." The reason for it – or at least that which Scape had told me, when I had first unfortunately made his acquaintance – was that it was not his original mode of speech, but one that he had acquired through his perusal of one of my father's creations, a device of flashing lights at a precisely regulated speed and rhythm, which had the effect of casting his mind into the distant Future, to a time when everyone spoke in such a clipped and slangy fashion, and with so many words of odd derivation and meaning. Miss McThane had spoken in the same way, but I had come to fondly regard it as part of her eccentric charm; from Scape's mouth, however, such speech had struck me as a dreadful portent of a harsher, faster world to come.

"But it seems," I continued, "that you adopted not so much of *his* way of speaking, but rather that of a proper Englishman; I mean one of this time, of course."

"Pretty much had to." Scape held up the pebble between his thumb and forefinger, as though studying its composition. "I was in a bad way when I got out of that charity hospital – well, I didn't get out so much as I escaped. No resources, no friends, nobody I could turn to – or at least no one I wanted to. Plus, the way I'd made my living before, kinda depended on getting into people's confidences, and then ripping them off for as much as I could. But when you look like this–" He didn't bother to gesture toward his ruined face; his meaning was clear. "Kinda hard to get people to trust you, when they can't even bear to look at you. So I had to survive best I could – lotta burglaries, some muggings; anything I was capable of. Like that old saying: *Hard times will make a rat eat a raw onion*. But I managed."

"So it seems," I observed. "But whatever might have changed for you, one thing seems to have remained a constant."

"And what's that?"

"Your mendacity. Even when making these confessions, you are unable to keep from lying. At virtually the same moment in which you piously state how you kept yourself from burdening Miss McThane with the knowledge that you were still alive, you are displaying to me the proof of your continued correspondence with the woman." I had tucked the fully signed letter back into my jacket; I now withdrew it and brandished the item before Scape, as though he were a prisoner in the dock, confronted with damning evidence. "She could not have initiated this contact, believing you were dead; thus you were the one who sought out her attention. So much for your fine resolutions to keep your tragic circumstances to yourself!"

"Give me a break, Dower. I would've, believe me – but something came up." He pointed to the letter in my hand. "And you're the one responsible for that."

"I am? And how do you come to that conclusion?"

"What we were talking about, before you jumped for my throat and tried to throttle me–"

"You have my apologies for that." Folding the letter, I deposited it in my jacket once more. "I was overcome with a fit of passion."

"Guess so – but you didn't give me a chance to tell you what you're demanding to know."

"Then proceed," I said with feigned courtesy. "You have my keenest interest."

"OK – here's the deal." He turned the mass of scars that was his face toward me. "Like I was telling you, both me and the More Loving Embrace know where a certain... *something* is; the difference between me and them is that they're ready to kill you, in order to keep you from finding it as well. That's how important it is to them."

"But I am not looking for anything–"

"Doesn't matter. There's a connection between it and you, whether you like it or not. You're responsible for its existence, as much as your father was for all his creations."

"I fail to understand. How could this be?"

"Simple," said Scape. "We're not really talking about an *it*; we're talking about a *he*. A person, a real one, not any kind of machine."

"That distinction does not come as a complete surprise to me; you wrote about as much in your correspondence with Miss McThane, informing her in so many words that your quest had been completed – that you had, as I quote, *Found him*."

"Just as she had wanted me to."

"And who is this mysterious person, and what does he have to do with me?"

"That's simple as well, Dower. He's your son. And hers."

"Indeed." I turned my gaze full upon the figure beside me. "What appears simple is that the unfortunate events that resulted in your physical condition produced a similar impairment of your mind. Yes, Miss McThane and I lived as man and wife, and yes, we had that relationship between us which might have resulted in a child – but she was the only woman whom I knew in that way. I am confident that if our union had resulted in progeny of any number, I would have been aware of that fact; it's not really the sort of thing that even the craftiest of women can conceal for very long."

"The child wasn't born while the two of you were living together, down there in Cornwall." He slowly shook his head. "Good thing that she can't hear you now – doubt if she'd find it very flattering that you've forgotten the first time that you got it on with her."

"Oh." I was stunned a bit by his words. "I have not forgotten... certainly not. It was a... *memorable* event."

"Yeah, I bet it was. You seemed pretty flipped about it at the time."

I was thus prodded into more vivid recollection. A scene formed within my thoughts, of the richly adorned interior of the lunatical Lord Bendray's manorial estate – which at the precise time that I remembered, was being shaken to bits by the unleashed operation of one of my father's most fearsome creations. Of that machine, it had been convincingly demonstrated to me that it was equally capable of destroying the entire planet on which we stood, and would proceed to do so in short order, unless it was somehow stopped. The utter depravity of my father's creations was finally borne out to me, when it was revealed – however unlikely it might have seemed to me before then – that the only way to silence the machine, and thus save the world, was for me to have sexual congress with Miss McThane. If that act had depended upon my experience in such matters – in fact, I had none – then I would not be penning these words now; and none would be reading them, for we would all be but dust floating in the cold emptiness that lies beyond our present skies. Fortunately for the bulk of Humanity, Miss McThane's feminine skills and determination were more than enough to overcome any deficiency on my part, allowing me to perform this duty, though with a good measure of bewilderment mixed with the act's associated pleasures.

What was not contained within my memory, for I had no way of knowing, was that there had been any result from that strangely ordained conjunction between us, other than shutting down the dreadful machine created by my father, even as rubble from the shuddering mansion rained upon the bed in which she and I were entwined.

"That's right–" Scape had been able to discern the course of the thoughts that tumbled through my head. "You knocked her up."

"Why was I not informed?" I was unfamiliar with the coarse phrase he employed, but its meaning was nevertheless clear to me. "Why am I only hearing of this now?"

"Come on, Dower – she and I were on the lam. We had to make ourselves scarce, and fast, after all that stuff went down. So we got ourselves as far away as possible–"

"I had heard some rumours in that regard; that the two of you were in the far north of Scotland, pursuing whatever dishonest opportunities came to your hand."

"Well, of *course* we were; people gotta eat, don't they? We didn't get a big payout for all those machines of your father's, the way you did. So that's just the way it goes, right? And that's why you didn't hear anything about your having gotten her pregnant; hell, we didn't know until we were up around John o' Groats, freezing our butts off. Hey, and don't give me any crap about how maybe it wasn't you that did it–"

"The question had come to mind," I admitted. "As much as I loved and admired the woman, I am not such a *naïf* as to believe I am the only one who ever had carnal relations with her. The two of you were lovers, were you not?"

"At one time, yeah." The confession was voiced in a grudging tone from him. "But that had kinda come to an end by the time we ran into you. By that point, she and I were just business partners. So when she told me that you were the only one who could be the father of the kid she was carrying, I knew she was telling the truth."

Sadly, I sensed that the truth was being told now as well – ascribing the paternity of this unfortunate child to Scape had been my only hope of avoiding my own condemnation of my misdeeds. True, I had managed to save the world from destruction, by my sexual congress with Miss McThane terminating the sympathetic vibrations generated by my father's creation – but at what cost? Had there been times when I might have wondered if there had been any other consequences of that brief moment between us, and had I pushed those thoughts away into the forgetful darkness, rather than investigating them? In truth, I had to confess there were such – and that our sins of omission, the obligations we fail to perform, are as black or blacker than the crimes we commit.

"The boy you describe as my son…" I emerged from my brooding thoughts, as one might surface from the depths of a lightless ocean, into a night as dark. "In the correspondence you had with Miss McThane, which I discovered only after her death – does your having written *Found him* refer to this child, and to no other person?"

"That's about the size of it."

"But for him to have been *found*, he must first have been *lost* – to both you and his mother. How did that come about?"

"Face it, Dower – the life the two of us were living, it wasn't exactly conducive to domestic bliss. There were times when we were having a hard time keeping ourselves fed, let alone having a kid on our hands. So we figured we were doing the responsible thing by unloading him onto someone else. We went down to Glasgow – that's where she gave birth – and that's where the orphanage was, where we left him. Wasn't easy for her – hey, you know how she really was, under that tough-girl exterior – but that's how it went down."

"She never said anything of this to me. If she had... I might have done something."

"Well, she didn't – but she was going to."

"Really?" I raised an eyebrow as I regarded him. "How are you aware of that?"

"Told me so. When she got hold of me – there were some, we could say... *associates* from before, who knew where I could be found – that's what she said. She'd heard from them that I was still alive, and she wrote and told me that she wanted to find this kid – no surprise there, that it'd been preying on her mind all these years – and claim him as her own son. And... you know... have him with her, and give him a home and all; a real home. She said that she knew you wouldn't have a problem with that. Not just because the kid's your son, too – but because she had kind of a high opinion about you."

"Did she?"

"Look, you might consider yourself pretty worthless – and there'd been a time when I wouldn't have argued with you about that – but this woman you were living with apparently didn't think you were a total jerk. Most guys should be so lucky."

"Then if so, why did she not tell me as much? I take it that she asked you to find the boy–"

"Yes." Scape nodded. "She begged me to. Because she had already managed to contact the orphanage in Glasgow, and they'd told her that not only didn't they still have the kid, but they had no record of him ever having been there. So she knew something fishy was going on."

"And you consented to her request? With no hesitation on your part?"

"Yeah... I mean, eventually. I had to think about it."

"And what," I inquired, "was it that you thought?"

"I don't know, George." His voice softened to a musing tone. "Except... maybe this was why I hadn't killed myself. Back in the hospital, when I'd thought about it. Maybe I knew that there was something I'd have to do. For her."

Though I understood, I said nothing. A similar notion had come to my own thoughts, more than once. The iron links of obligation, which we so often believe cruelly bind us, are the same by which we are restrained from the Abyss – once broken, we are lost.

"Why did she not inform me of her desire?" My interrogating the other man twisted into my own laceration. "She must have been in agonies of suspense about your search for the child, all the while concealing her distress from me. Granted, I would likely have been of no use in determining what had happened to him – I have no skill or experience in such endeavours – but at least I might have helped bear the burden of waiting to hear of his fate."

"Sure – but what if I *hadn't* been able to locate the kid? Then what?" Scape's voice sank to a low pitch. "Or what if I found out that what happened to him wasn't anything good? And *that's* what I had to tell her? What would your life together have been after that? Haunted, that's what, the two of you remorseful for the rest of your lives about what'd become of this son, that she'd abandoned and that you'd never even known. It's why she didn't say anything about it – she wanted to spare you that."

Once more, I was reduced to silence; within myself, I had to admit that he was correct about that. Whatever Miss McThane's flaws of character might have been – certainly no worse than mine – none of them were driven by a deficit of loving kindness; if I had ever done anything for the poor woman, it had been no more than to allow that to become evident. How cruel of Fate to have presented her with the deathbed choice between sparing the feelings of one who had loved her as best he could, and burdening him with the mission of seeking out the child he had never known.

"Very well–" I forced myself to speak again. "If Miss McThane wished me to be kept in darkness before, as she awaited word from you about the search for our son, and then chose enlightenment for me – so be it. I accept her decision, and the consequences it has for me; how can I do otherwise? So proceed; you must have further information for me. You wrote to her – I have seen the letter – that you had found him. But I see no child with you now – where is he? Some secure place, I hope."

"Well, that's kind of the problem, isn't it?" Scape once more mused upon the pebble between his thumb and forefinger. "It's one thing to *find* somebody – I mean, find where they are – and another to actually lay your hands on them."

"So I take it you do not actually *have* the boy. However successful your search for him might have been, he is in some situation from which you have been unable to extract him. Even if his mother were still alive, you could not have returned the child to her; the most you could have done would be to torture her mind further with the knowledge that he lives, but is never to be seen by her again."

"Jeez, Dower; give me a break. It's a work in progress, all right? Yeah, I don't have the kid – but that doesn't mean I can't *get* him. I mean, that *we* can't."

"*We?* I believe I can now discern your purpose at inveigling yourself into my confidences, first by disguising yourself as the Brown Leather Man I remembered more charitably than I did you, and now by making this labourious confession to me. You wish to somehow rescue this child from some dire predicament, the nature of which you have not yet described to me – that he is in such comes as no surprise; orphans, or those presumed to be, have a hard row to hoe in this world, and are often cruelly exploited. The fact that this is your aim speaks well of you – but I would appreciate some explanation of what you expect from me in this regard."

"Fine; if you'd give me half a moment, I'd be able to do that, wouldn't I?" The deeply scarred face of Scape was still able to assume an irritable expression. "Here's the deal. Don't blame me that I don't have the kid, this son of yours; his whereabouts were a lot harder to track down than I thought they'd be when I promised Miss McThane that I'd find him. It took a lot of doing, which was why there were so many letters going back and forth between the two of us; I didn't want her to think I'd given up on the search. Problem, though, when I did find where this kid of yours is, I almost wished I *hadn't* found out."

"Why so?"

"Because, Dower – where he is, and the people who've got him, don't exactly add up to a piece of cake. You know all the bad types you've run into before, including these More Loving Embrace guys who want to kill you? They're *nothing*. Seriously, compared to what we're going to have to deal with to get hold of your son, your life up till now has been nothing but fun."

"I will be the judge of that." His words provoked a deal of skepticism on my part. "Who exactly are these people, of whom you stand in such dread?"

"A secretive organization–"

"Oh, dear God. *Another?*" I shook my head in dismay. "Surely you jest – or worse, you are in deadly earnest. Why should I disbelieve you? There seem to be so many forming these shadowy cabals and conspiracies, it would seem likely that they would have difficulty in finding any unaffiliated persons to recruit to their ranks."

"Laugh all you want, pal, but it's the truth. These Elohim people are nothing to take lightly–"

"*Elohim?* Is that how they style themselves? Seems very Biblical of them. My religious education was spotty, so I cannot say with certainty, but I seem to recall that the word means something in Hebrew – gods, or angels, or such like."

"How would I know?" Scape's irritation audibly increased. "Look, they can call themselves whatever they want – doesn't matter to me. Maybe all the good conspiracy names were already taken. But what I'm trying to tell you is that they're nothing to mess with."

"If you say so; your knowledge exceeds mine on this point. And with that being the case, I would appreciate some further information about them. Who are they? Other than their assumed name, I mean. What do they want? Specifically, what do they want with my son, that they have secured him in their no-doubt nefarious clutches?"

"It's not just *your* son, Dower – they've got a thing for orphans in general. That's why it was so hard to track down the kid. This Elohim bunch has been raiding orphanages up in Northern England and Scotland for years now – all on the hush-hush, of course – and rounding up children and sending 'em down to someplace near London."

"This seems highly unlikely – I would have thought there would be some public outcry, if such were actually happening."

"Well, that's sweet of you, but you're dead wrong. When it comes to orphans, nobody's ever really cared very much about what happens to them – and that was *before* all these big changes in the world we live in. Do you think that machines care about each other? So the more like machines that people become, the less they give a rat's ass about anyone else. That's just the way it goes."

"But what purpose does this Elohim group have in acquiring these wretched children? I shudder to contemplate what sordid interest they might have – as a general rule, an untoward avidity of this nature never results in anything but the most scandalous fates for the children involved."

"Wish I could tell you," said Scape, "but I can't – though I'm pretty sure it's nothing like what you're talking about. They're up to something else. That's why the Elohim are so dead set against the More Loving Embrace group – they've both got their agendas, and somehow these orphans that the Elohim have scooped up are involved. And you, too – somehow the More Loving Embrace have got it in their heads that if you're able to track down your son, and make contact with him wherever the Elohim have got him and the other orphans stashed away, then they're screwed. So they sent their agents out to kill you, to make absolutely sure that doesn't happen."

"I see – or rather, I do not." Wearied by what passed as his explanation, I gave another shake of my head. "Why is it that whenever I press anyone, yourself included, to make clear the mysteries that continually enfold me, they respond with yet more mysteries? I would have been better off by never having sought enlightenment at all."

"Suit yourself – but you asked. And frankly..." Scape tossed the pebble into the unnaturally still waters; it struck the surface with a minimal plunk. "We've wasted enough time talking. We need to get going."

"And to where would that be?"

"Just about anywhere would be better – especially for you, pal. You got out of Blightley and Haze's hands all right, but that doesn't mean your ass is safe. I told you already: the More Loving Embrace wants you dead, and their guys are probably tracking you down here already. You got away from them twice – that doesn't mean you'll be lucky a third time.

And–" Scape directed his disfigured visage straight toward me. "We've got other stuff to take care of."

"Indeed? To what exactly do you refer?"

"What the hell have we been talking about all this time?" Scape's gaze widened in astonishment. "Your son, moron! We don't have him – right?" He spoke with elabourate slowness, as though to a child. "But we know where he is – right? Or at least I do. So we go... *get*... him. Right?"

"No... *we*... do not." I answered him in the same plodding fashion. "You entirely mistake my interest in the matter, to the degree that I have any at all. My primary concern – and my only one – is with preserving my own skin intact. As for rescuing this child from whatever dire situation in which he has been placed–" I held up a forestalling hand, palm outward. "He certainly has my sympathies; I am not entirely hard-hearted about his welfare. But finding him, and rescuing him – that was a promise you made to Miss McThane; I gave no such avowal to her. How could I have? She was dead long before I even learned of the child's existence."

"Wait a minute." Comprehension dawned behind the other's eyes. "You sonuvabitch... she was your *wife*. She told me... that was how you thought of her. And now..."

"Do you think I care about your opinion?" I could hear my own voice turning colder and harder. "If I do, it is certainly to a lesser degree than I care about my own safety. I had little need of your telling me how greatly the More Loving Embrace desires – I had evidence enough of that already; I still do not know why they wish it, but then, apparently neither do you. With these Elohim people, I have had no experience, but if they are as deadly enemies of the More Loving Embrace as you indicate, then I can only assume that they are of an equally grim nature. I doubt if they would welcome me with open arms, if I were to turn up on their doorstep, enquiring about my son; more likely, their reaction would be of a similarly lethal type. If you wish to attempt the rescue of my son, then by all means, proceed. But as my ability to assist you would be negligibly slight, and the cost to me would almost certainly be my life, then I must beg off any participation in such an endeavour."

"Too late for that, Dower." His fierce glare focused more tightly upon me. "You've already been part of it. How do you think you wound up there at Highgate Cemetery? How did that come about?"

"That fellow Rollingwood – him and the Gravitas Maximus Funerary Society. I accepted their invitation to travel to London, along with my wife's casket, so that she be interred there."

"And who arranged with them for all of that?"

"I have no idea; they told me that had all been done at the behest of some anonymous benefactor, who paid for everything."

"Well, he's not anonymous anymore, is he?" Scape slapped one of his dark-gloved hands against his chest. "You're looking at him."

"You? Very well; in some ways, I am not surprised at all. My dealings with you have always revolved around your scheming and plotting, all designed to snare me into your various enterprises; it now appears that you have returned from the other side of the grave, to which I had believed you to have been dispatched, to continue on that course. The problem for you is that I have the sharpest memory of your machinations against me, and thus I refuse to become tangled up in them again, no matter how nobly you state your motivations."

"Dower... it's different this time."

"As always," I said. "You must pardon my skepticism."

"No, seriously – you gotta listen to me." A note of pleading sounded in his voice, that I had never heard before. "You can't walk out on this one. I *need* you – I can't rescue the kid without you."

"I confess I grow weary with this constant indispensability, which I am inevitably assured I possess. How I became so valuable to so many rogues and schemers – it is a mystery to me. But always I am told by low, disreputable persons such as yourself, that their plans cannot advance without me. I would be less exhausted with the world, if this were not so frequently the case."

"OK, fine; I'll tell you – I was planning to, anyway. But here's the deal–"

Whatever revelations Scape intended to make, they remained unvoiced. For at that exact moment, a great deal of chaos ensued, that had no doubt been long impending.

Scape's words were drowned out by a startling eruptive noise, that might have been volcanic in nature except for the fact that it sounded, not from beneath our feet, but out of the sky above our heads. The essential falsity of that expanse was further confirmed by the jagged chasms branching through it like black lightning strokes. Startled by the noise, I had immediately craned my neck back and looked up toward it – a fortunate thing, for it enabled me to raise my arm across my face, shielding me from the rain of broken tiles and other debris that came tumbling down.

"Crap!" The shout from Scape was loud enough to be heard through the tumult, as bits of the crumbling sky struck the sands and the equally artificial rocks about us. "They're here!"

One section of the sky, like a piece of an enormous eggshell, fell end over end, at last striking the surface of the water. Its impact was sufficient to send a low wave sloshing across the shore and washing up against our boots. Neither Scape nor I paid this slight inundation any mind; our attention was fastened upon the sharp-edged opening that had been produced at the limit of our upturned gaze.

Of what lay beyond, little could be seen but the bright pinpoints of the stars in the open night sky – but that was the least of our concerns. While smaller bits and pieces were still plunking into the agitated false ocean, a number of coarse, knotted ropes were flung out, their weighted ends drawing their serpentine lengths close by us. No sooner had the process been completed, than I saw the agents of the More Loving Embrace – recognizable even at this distance, from my previous encounters with them – as they swarmed down the ropes, their rifles slung across their backs. Obviously, they were taking no chances with their lethal intent toward me, preferring to strike at close quarters rather than take aim from above.

"Don't worry!" Scape seized my arm, preventing me from executing any attempt to flee. In his voice sparked a trace of the excited glee that I recalled from long ago. "I've got this!"

I thought him mad, though not for the first time. My instinct to run was tempered by the knowledge that there would be no hiding places in the limited confines of this manufactured cove; I would shortly be tracked down and slaughtered wherever lay its bounding walls. If there had been hope of escape, I might have shaken him off, and taken to my heels–

But his seemingly demented assurance to me proved true, or at least sufficiently so as to throw my assailants' plans into disarray. The noise of the artificial sky cracking open had ebbed, the last of the shattered pieces landing near, even as the More Loving Embrace's dread agents swiftly came within a few feet of releasing their grip upon the ropes, and springing onto the ground. That partial diminishment of the enveloping tumult was ended by a more deafening noise, that drew my vision away from my rapidly approaching pursuers, and back up to the sky.

Or rather, what remained of it. Around its circumference, even larger segments toppled from their moorings at the horizon, and plunged into the water. The illumination from the flaring gas jets was extinguished with a steaming hiss, leaving only revealed stars and a sickle moon to provide any light. All was turmoil; Scape drove his shoulder into my chest, driving me backward and saving us both from being crushed by an immense concave section that imbedded itself into the ground where we had been standing.

The complete destruction of the constructed sky had the salutary effect of forestalling the More Loving Embrace's agents from completing their attempt upon my life – the ropes by which they descended had been secured to some point on the outer surface of the now disintegrating dome; as it crumbled to pieces, the result was to send these assassins falling, and then tumbling upon the sands, the ropes coiling and snaring about their torsos and heads.

My observation of their predicament was suddenly obscured, the landscape about us lapsing into more thorough shadows. Glancing upward, I saw that the stars and moon had been eclipsed by some awesome shape, extending farther than my eye could see. I was struck by the sudden recall of a similar event, when I had stood beside my wife's freshly excavated grave in the cemetery at Highgate, and that great hovering graveyard had loomed into view above our heads. But this time, rather than the casket being drawn up from below and toward that immensity, something else could be perceived falling from it.

The darkness hindered Scape from calculating the object's vertical trajectory as he had done before, so he was unable to make a similar motion to evade it. We were both struck by the object, sending us sprawling backward.

"I was borned in the district of Sauchiehall Street, to loving and hard-wairking parents…"

That I was hallucinating the voice that spoke, in a creaky and sepulchral tone, seemed the most likely explanation, as I lay flat on my back, somewhat stunned. Pushing myself up on my elbows, I received further confirmation that I had been knocked from my proper senses: a cadaverous form, skin grey in *pallor mortis* over protruding bones, stood propped against a nearby stone outcropping. The wind admitted from the opened sky set the ragged shroud fluttering about the cage-like ribs, ribbons of the tattered cloth winding about the bare ankles of the feet that had embedded themselves into the sand.

"Me muther were a wee sma' wummin, but me faither were a gi'nt of a man, nigh six feet tall." The corpse's jaws clacked open and shut, roughly in time to the words scratchily emitted from a mechanism very like a spring-driven music-box, partially visible through the parchment skin covering the throat. "A wheelwright he were, and a secessionist in the Free Church, so he thrashed a great deal o' Biblical larning into me hide when I were young…"

The grisly figure continued mechanically relating its biography, as I gaped at it in astonishment. To my further surprise and horror, I heard a rising murmur of similar voices all about me; gaining my feet, I scanned across the ill-lit landscape. My eyes had adjusted well enough to the darkness occasioned by the vast shape looming above, that I could make out a seeming regiment of other shrouded corpses littering the cove, most sprawled flat on the sand, a few tilted at whatever angle their plummeting descent had left them at; one had landed headfirst, burying its tight-fleshed skull so that only its torso and limbs were visible, skeletal legs waggling in a slow semaphore, its voice muted by the encasing sand. The others, not so encumbered, were free to continue their own narrations, the clockwork devices sutured above their breastbones clattering away the details of birth and baptism, marriage and labour, and whatever

mundanities had been deemed fit to record. A faint aroma of
formaldehyde and other funereal preservatives hung in the
air, to render the scene even more ghastly.

"Come on, Dower–" A gloved hand caught hold of my
arm. "We need to move."

Scape appeared to have had some foreknowledge of this
grisly barrage from above; he at least did not seem surprised
by it, and he had managed to draw the two of us far enough
away that we had not suffered the brunt of its impact. The
assassins of the More Loving Embrace had not been so
fortunate; a number of them had been knocked unconscious
from having been struck by one of these dully yammering
corpses, with their rifles still strapped upon their backs or
cast from their outflung hands. One of these weapons had
been snatched up by Scape; one-handed, he aimed and fired.
The bullet struck into the chest of one of my pursuers, who
had managed to stagger to his feet and swing his rifle in our
direction; he flew backward and landed lifeless in the shallow
waters behind him.

Urged on by my companion, I ran toward the centre of the
cove, dodging as best I could the forms arrayed on all sides,
of the silent living and the loquacious dead. Our passage was
imperilled by yet more corpses falling from the sky, as though
a veritable avalanche of the deceased had been unleashed
upon our heads, but Scape managed to steer us both through
the onslaught with no more than a glancing blow from one of
the enshrouded figures striking the ground beside us.

"Here–" Coming to a halt, Scape cast away the rifle, so that
both his hands were free. In the darkness, I saw that a pair
of ropes dangled before us; these were not the ones by which
the More Loving Embrace's agents had descended, which
had been precipitously loosened from whatever mooring had
secured them to the outside of the cove's artificial sky. These
were fastened somehow to that great bulk floating above,

which blotted the moon and stars from view; swiftly, Scape knotted one under my arms and across my chest, then did the same for himself with the other. "Hold on–"

"This is madness–" My protest could barely be heard above the hubbub of the corpses still recounting the incidents of their lives, mixed with the shouts of those of my pursuers who had managed to regain their capabilities and assess the situation surrounding them. "This can't–"

"You got a better plan?"

I had neither that nor time for a reply, as the ropes jerked tight at our chests. With the monumental grace possessed by immense objects, the shape hovering above had shifted its position, sufficiently that both Scape and I were snatched off the ground and elevated to the open air.

Rifle shots barked from below, as the recovered assailants directed the fire of their upraised rifles at us. That the rain of corpses still continued, their shrouds fluttering as they arced to earth, proved fortuitous; their shrivelled forms were enough to shield Scape and myself from the bullets that might otherwise have struck us as our dangling ascent accelerated.

I knew it was unwise to look down, but I could not do otherwise; we were now so far in our course that I could see the little constructed cove entire, its sands and manufactured stones, and its bottled-up ocean, encircled by the remnants of the dome that had formed its masquerading sky. A few bright sparks of rifle-fire from my persistent assassins, then all was faded into the dark and distance below our trailing feet.

My companion dangled close enough by, both of us at a trailing angle as our speed increased, that I could reach out and touch his arm. Scape faced away from me, toward whatever might be presumed as our destination; I wished to inquire of him – of course I would have to shout over the rush of the wind streaming about us – as to where exactly that was.

In the event, I was spared any need to raise my voice; the prod of my fingers was enough to turn Scape around that he might converse with me – but he could not. Even in the shadow of the great bulk above us, enough light remained that I could see no animation in his dulled eyes, rolled back in the gravely scarred flesh about them. The cause of this transformation was quickly evident to me; the front of his dark leather garb was slick and shining wet from the blood draining from the bullet hole in the centre of his chest. Not merely had the falling corpses shielded me from harm; as cruel luck would have it, Scape himself had been interposed between myself and the assassins' fire, the final one having struck home in this way. I pulled my hand away; whatever questions I might have, there would be no more answers forthcoming from him.

So we flew on into the night, the living and the dead, and toward whatever troublesome fate continued to be mine.

PART FOUR
The Fires of London

ELEVEN
An Uncomfortable Journey

O Y, DOWER – get leg up. Bluidy useless, you are."
A hand grappled under my arm; already I had
suffered the considerable discomfort of being dragged
upward by the rope knotted about my chest, the rough
edge of some elevated platform scraping hard through my
garments. I did my best to comply with the instructions this
unseen figure snarled at me, calculating that my safety would
be increased by gaining some more substantial purchase than
was allowed by dangling in the empty night air.

I managed to lever the upper portion of my torso onto the
flat surface toward which I had been raised; doing so enabled
my rescuer – if so he was – to pull the rest of my body toward
himself. For a moment, only my shins and boots still extended
out into the open; with a kick and a lurch, I deposited myself
at the other's feet.

"Should left you there," he grumbled. "God might help
hapless, but expect more coöperation myself."

From my face-downward position, I rolled over onto my
back, to allow more breath into my gasping lungs, as well as
to glimpse whoever it was so rudely addressing me.

"Be here, though – all that matters."

I was not thoroughly surprised to see that singular

253

individual, who had previously identified himself as Nick Spivvem, standing above me. He bent down with a bare knife blade in his hand – I was unable to shrink back – but he employed it only to slice through the rope bound about me; with it parted, I was able to gain enough air to at least somewhat clear my dazed thoughts.

"Your pardon ..." I forced myself into a sitting position. "But I believed... you were dead..."

"If be dead, every time *thought* dead, be springing from grave every few minutes, like some fookin' jack-poppet." Spivvem loosely coiled the rope in his hands, then tossed it behind himself. "Would hugely interfere with business doings."

No longer in the shadow cast by this immense bulk, but rather on its uppermost surface, I was able to acquire a better perspective of my surroundings. Night had largely passed, with the cold pearl light of dawn breaking from somewhere to the east, the horizon below the clouded expanse in which we travelled. About me was what appeared to be an elabourate graveyard, similar to that of the cemetery in Highgate, from which I had been so recently abstracted, first from above and then beneath it. Impressive funereal statuary, of the weeping marble angel variety, extended toward the centre of this elevated space, and beyond.

"'Course, not everyone so fortunate." Spivvem continued talking. "Poor bastard here, for example – friend of yours, take it."

I glanced back toward him, and saw that the toe of his boot was prodding a lifeless form stretched out on the ground. The glistening dark garb, with a slack rope still knotted about the bloodied chest, and the fire-scarred face turned upward, were all that was needed to confirm the dead man's identity.

"Not *friend*, quite..." I gave a slow nod. "But someone of my acquaintance, indeed."

"Would think you'd better opinion of him," said Spivvem. "As having saved your life, and all."

"Perhaps so – but he did not do that out of warm-hearted charity. He pursued his own agenda, as always."

"Too right, did." Spivvem gazed down at Scape's stilled face. "Know bit of him, myself. Clever sort; would've accomplished great deal in criminal line, if hadn't turned lofty-minded in latter days."

"He didn't speak so highly of you."

"Imagine he didn't; few do." Spivvem turned his lopsided smile in my direction. "Generally, 'cause step ahead of 'em. Does lead to resentments."

"You flatter yourself." Oddly, I felt the urge to defend the deceased. "He was aware that you had stealthily managed to insert yourself into that artificial Venice concocted by Blightley and Haze."

"Might well have. But 'spect didn't know that I'd secured position on this bluidy floating burial-ground. What he'd arranged to secure your rescue from killers on trail, only sufficed to deliver to my hands."

"Into your hands alone? Or are there others here, employed in combination with you?"

"One time, great many hereabouts, labouring away – operation size of this requires deal of work, keep it going." Spivvem's smile continued as he raised a mischievous eyebrow. "Know where are, do you?"

"I have a general surmise." In the grey light, I pointed to the various memorial statues and monuments that were increasingly made visible. "When I was attending my late wife's funeral in London's Highgate, the graveside service was interrupted by – among a great many other unfortunate things – the appearance of just such a vast shape in the sky as I witnessed a little while ago, when I was stranded upon an artificial Hebridean island. Only at that previous time, the aerial prodigy resulted in the drawing up of my wife's casket to it. That dire marvel would have been completely incomprehensible, had not an agent of the Gravitas Maximus Funerary Society elucidated how there had come to be a cemetery floating above Britain, its position in the sky secured by the levitating gasses generated by the decomposition of the corpses so unfortunate to have been deposited there."

"Rattle on, don't you? Know all that, I do."

"The chances of two such airborne cemeteries being slight–" I persisted with my exposition. "I am forced to conclude that circumstances have brought me to that loathsome place as well."

"Right you are, Mr Dower. But if 'specting more company than me, sadly disappointed. Profitability this enterprise greatly overestimated by gentleman you spoke to, though sure he knew also by then. Daft idea, ask me – people might pay have loved ones planted in sky, but that old saw – *Out of sight, out of mind* – applies, and most didn't care to be inconvenienced by all took to come visiting 'em, and lay posies on the headstones. Being why that 'merican Blightley fellow and partner – queer little bugger Haze – took up notion of having deceased natter away, with clockwork boxes stuck inside."

"That was *Blightley*'s idea?"

"Man's head stuffed with useless fancies. Can believe it? – thought folks would be entranced by dead relations reciting tedious biographies, and pay to hear such. Or at least, managed convince your Whack-a-mus Fyoon-ree lot that was great idea. Hired actors and all, to read words. Bluidy idiots – who doesn't know that whole reason dead are so fondly remembered, is that they finally have shut up?"

"I am not certain it is the case for all people. There is at least one who has passed on, that I would give a great deal to have another moment between us."

"Suit yourself." Spivvem gave a shrug of his narrow shoulders. "Any rate, Blightley bankrupted his backers, as has habit of doing. Ones who pulled your wife up like she were a conker on string – they were about last of workers, and easily chased off by myself, so have free hand to do as see fit–"

His concluding exposition almost went unheard by me, for at the same moment a ponderous groaning noise battered the air, deeper and louder than anything that could have been produced by human throats, however massed in chorus they might have been. As it sounded, the ground beneath me shuddered, severely enough to dislodge a few broken bits of marble from the nearest ranks of headstones.

"What, pray, was that?"

Spivvem made no reply to me; that he had been taken by surprise as well was evidenced by the disappearance of his knowing smile, and the creases in his brow as he swung his gaze across the eerie landscape.

"Don't be worried," he said after his scrutiny had ended, with no apparent result of having determined the cause of what we both had heard. "Machinery always making suchlike bother. 'Spect no more than gears needs greasing."

"Seemed rather more ominous than what you suggest–"

"Said, don't fret." His manner turned snappish. "Everything be fine, sure enough. You're one with all the questions; ask away, as want to."

"Very well–"

Another unnerving phenomenon commenced, which delayed the formulation of my query. The air, thinned by our being at such an altitude, had previously been stirred by a constant breeze, strong enough to ruffle the air atop my head; I had assumed this to be a consequence of our passage through the sky, the velocity of which had been sufficient to extract both myself and the late Scape from that false isle where we had been surrounded by the More Loving Embrace's agents.

Now that same wind noticeably increased its force, to the degree of fluttering the lapels of my jacket; the sensation evoked was very like what one might have experienced, if standing at the edge of a Cornish cliffside, gazing across the ocean at the black clouds of an approaching storm.

"Tell me this, then–" I shouted across the stiffening gale. "Where exactly are we now? I mean, other than upon the aerial cemetery. When I had seen before the underside of this construction, it had been where I had stood in Highgate, outside London. But I was informed that a system of cables, their anchors buried deep in the soil, was capable of adjusting its position to virtually anywhere above the British landscape; if that is truly the case, to what latitude has it been drawn?"

"East what remains of Lake District," said Spivvem, raising his voice to be heard. "That having been where you'd been stranded, after gondola had shot you away. And well south of Glasgow, heading 'cross Scottish border."

Hearing that bleak city's name unnerved me a bit, having so recently heard it spoken of by Scape, when he had recounted to me the sad early days of that previously unknown child born to me by Miss McThane.

"Why there?"

"Why anywhere?" Spivvem shrugged. "Truth be, though, Blightley and partner did better with Scots than else, with this bluidy graveyard in sky. 'Spect something to do with national character, so to speak – overly pious, prone to daft religious enthusiasms. Morbid lot, too; wonder weren't already conversing with dead, before this marvel appeared above 'em. Whatever reason, consequence be great deal more these yammering corpses doing so with Scottish accents – why had such an arsenal ready when came time to rescue you."

My gaze followed the direction in which he pointed, and discerned a number of shroud-wrapped corpses, stacked up in the manner of cordwood; the mound was close enough to the aerial graveyard's edge that they could easily be launched overboard, producing the macabre bombardment through which Scape and I had fled.

"Your clever mind appalls me." Though in truth, I supposed the man was no more reprehensible in his employment of the dead for his own purposes, than those who had given them voice, and placed them here at his disposal. "But I am well satisfied to leave these northern climes behind us – not much good has ever happened to me there, and my recent experiences have done little to alter my opinion in that regard. I am concerned, however, as to where we are headed, and whether it is some destination that will be even worse."

"Calm self, Dower; going no place haven't been before–"

The satisfaction of my curiosity was delayed yet again, by the same audible phenomenon as before, only louder and with more upheaving impact. The groaning and grinding noises, seemingly permeating every atom of the aerial cemetery, were deafeningly magnified from before. At the same moment, its constructed ground buckled beneath us, with enough whiplash force as to have nearly toppled Spivvem from his feet, had he not been able to grasp hold of the outstretched marble arm of one of the funereal angels planted nearby. A good minute or so passed before the shuddering effect, coupled with those dismaying sounds, diminished enough that my companion was able to continue his speaking.

"As was saying..." Spivvem attempted to resume his previous cavalier nonchalance, but it was obvious that these untoward interruptions had left him rattled to a degree, though not as much as myself. "I've canny hand with machines, ones that draw up or spool out the cables tethered to earth–" He gestured toward some distant point beyond the towering stone monuments and closely ranked tombs. "Required no great effort on my part, set 'em to bring us to our destination – and at good speed, too."

"I would caution you as to overconfidence regarding such devices." I managed to get to my own feet, though the ground was still trembling beneath us. "They can be fearsomely mismanaged – trust me, I have much more experience with them than you do. The slightest error in their adjustment can result in terrible consequences."

"Fret yourself needlessly, you do." Spivvem scoffed at this anxiety. "Dimensions this beast beyond your imagining – take fair bit shaking to wreck, it would. Soon enough, see London – be sailing over Saint Paul's, before any great damage happens."

"Are you insane?" The other's words aroused more alarm than had the deep-pitched noise – which still continued, albeit at a slightly lower volume – and the trembling of the aerial cemetery's bulk beneath us. "You have us heading to *London*?"

"What said. Have problem with that?"

"Of course I do!" I shouted over the noises, as well as the wind which coursed at accelerating velocity past us; I braced myself to keep from being toppled by its force. "I *escaped* from London – I have no desire to return there. Surely all the conspiracies that seek to do me ill, if not outright devise my murder, are headquartered there. I would not have to await their dispatching more assassins; you would place me virtually in their hands, so they could slaughter at their leisure!"

"Matter of degree, Dower; that's all – folk who've your hide in mind, track down wherever bunkered. If you'd foil 'em, best strike at their heart; only chance you've got."

"I assure you, I am not the *striking* kind." The voicing of my anxiety was counterpointed by further sounds, distressingly close, that seemed like the wrenching apart of iron girders. "There is a capacity for violence which you seem to possess, that I do not – confront these assailants with whatever efforts you wish; I would only be in your way. Whatever survival I have managed in this world, it has been through hiding, and staying hid as best I am able."

"Too late for that," said Spivvem, any smile erased by a grimmer enthusiasm. "You and I, we've business in that city."

"*Business?* What can you possibly mean by–"

Any further description of the fate awaiting me was obviated by what next ensued. The previous shaking of the cemetery's mass was as nothing compared to the shock that bolted through it now; rather than being knocked from my standing position, I was rendered airborne myself, tossed a distance of at least several yards, and landing so close to the edge that I had to hurriedly scramble away from it, fingers clawing into the ground, to keep from falling. Glancing over my shoulder, I beheld a vertiginous sight – the surrounding clouds had parted enough to reveal the earth far below; we were at such an elevation that whole districts of the British landscape were visible, with silvery rivers winding past the hills and fields. If I had been sent over this virtual precipice, I would have had a considerable expanse of time to review my ill-spent life, before I was buried deep by the final impact.

Flattening myself chest-first, with hope of preventing any subsequent loss of balance, I could not keep myself from raising my head and twisting it about, to further regard that dreadful vista. The cemetery, or at least that section of it in which I was trapped, had tilted edge-downward, providing an ability to perceive the cables which had before been obscured underneath. As had been described to me, they stretched taut between their earthbound anchors and the enormous spooling reels of the cemetery's clattering machinery, which I had not been able to see until now.

But something had gone amiss with those – as I watched aghast, an explosion tore open the riveted boilers, their iron walls splitting open as readily as one might crack a hen's egg. A billowing gout of steam erupted, large enough to eclipse every aspect of the machinery behind. But only for a moment – the velocity of the cemetery's passage through the air quickly dispersed the churning vapour, revealing the tangled wreckage of gears the size of houses, now split in half, their teeth snarling into the other mechanical components. Even more dismaying, though, was that a number of the cables, each thick in diameter as a bullock, snapped free of the reels upon which they had been wound; the iron lines slackened, furiously whipping about as they fell toward the landscape below.

The cemetery's horizontal speed had already been dangerously accelerated, even though its bulk had still been tethered to the anchoring points over which it had travelled. Now freed of that restraint, the erratic but still functioning machinery that drew up the cables ahead, motivating the cemetery on its course, whirred and clattered at an even faster rate; with a jolting lurch that ran through the entire construction, it leapt dizzyingly forward.

As the surface beneath me tilted at an even more precipitous angle, I gained my feet, attempting to hurl myself toward whatever marble statue might provide sufficient hold to prevent my being dislodged and thrown over to my death. This I managed, grasping an angel's stiffly spread wing, then hooking an arm about its neck. If I had not, I would have been knocked askew by a shrouded avalanche, the remainder of the corpses that Spivvem had stocked in place for use as missiles upon the heads of the More Loving Embrace's agents, now toppling across the edge and out into the open air.

They were not alone in that chaotic resurrection; the shocks convulsing the cemetery, as its propulsive machinery continued to disintegrate, were strong enough to break open the great districts of tombs and graves at its centre, jagged portions of stone and iron lifting upward as ice floes are seen to do, when the underwater currents thrust the frozen masses against each other. Those who had thought themselves safely buried, if they had advanced to that heavenly abode which their faith promised, would have no doubt been horrified to see their mortal remains so rudely wrenched from casket and tomb, and flung like broken tinder into space. Those still unfortunately living, in the dismal Scottish borders and bleak north of England, would soon be similarly aghast, finding themselves pelted by a rain of corpses, some of them reciting their potted biographies.

But at least the eruptive dead had the comfort of being beyond sensation; I, on the other hand, would experience a more uncomfortable disembarkation from the cemetery. That seemed even more of a certainty, as a sheer chasm broke through its bulk, dividing it in twain. The latter half underwent further transformation, crumbling into fragments that were first the size of hillocks, then into smaller and smaller bits churning against one another. A shock from another mechanical explosion dislodged these pieces, sending them hurtling down and away.

As my continual luck would have it, the terminal edge of what remained of the cemetery's airborne mass – still attached to its forward cables and pulled ever faster by them to a catastrophic destination ahead – ran directly underneath the statue to which I so desperately clung. It swayed precariously, as though the angel were in contemplation of taking wing and flying to more placid skies above; if I had any confidence in its ability to do so, I would have retained my grasp upon the form, but prudence dictated other efforts on my part. Given how convulsively topsy-turvy everything about me had become, I could scarcely calculate what my next action should be–

Something struck the engraved base on which the angel's bare feet stood; I looked down and saw a more familiar face. It was that of Scape, the clouded eyes in the scarred visage confirming that he remained just as lifeless as when last I had seen him. However, the rope was still knotted about his chest; Spivvem had not sliced it away as he had done to that which had bound me. The preciously small bit of ground on which we both had landed, its clods and pebbles shaking with further tremors, now tilted closer to a vertical angle – I saw the rope draw tight, its distant end apparently snagged on some point I could not determine.

It would have to suffice, though there was no telling how secure that anchor might be. I let go of the marble angel and threw myself toward the much darker form lying before me; no sooner was I clear of the statue than its purchase upon the ground was shattered, and it toppled end-over-end to the void.

Thus I found myself with my face against the other's unbreathing one, my arms wrapped about his shoulders and chest as tightly as I could manage. However many times Scape had rescued me before, it had always been with some ulterior agenda in his ceaselessly devious mind; this instance was perhaps as selfless as he could ever have managed. I reached above him with first one hand, then the other, securing my grasp upon the rope and using it to pull myself across Scape's body, and then toward what I hoped would be some position of lesser danger.

Unsurprisingly, I found Spivvem there. I had lost sight of the rogue when our conversation had been interrupted by the battering commencement of the cemetery's destruction, not yet concluded. He had saved himself, with seemingly scant concern about me, by wedging himself shoulder-first into a stony crevice that had broken open behind where he had stood.

"You!" I ventured to loosen one hand from the rope, so I that I might stab an accusing forefinger toward him. "This is all your doing!" The rush of wind – shivered even more by the continuing explosions and grinding of iron against iron, rock upon rock – threw my voice back into my throat, yet I was sure he understood me. "Your clever tampering... the machines... why couldn't you have let them be?"

To my astonishment, he smiled. Thus I realized that he was of that nature of men, who relish chaos even as it crushes them in its jaws.

"Worry too much, Dower." He spoke with no exertion, but it seemed as though he might have been whispering right into my ear. "Should try–"

I heard no more. For he was suddenly vanished, his image replaced by clear, open sky; the rocks about him had crumbled away, their underpinnings ripped apart as a final, shuddering wrench shook through what little remained of the aerial cemetery. Peering over the edge that had suddenly appeared before me, I could see rocks and boulders tumbling downward; Spivvem was no doubt in their midst.

The rope loosened, its anchor having been eliminated as well. I dug my fingers into the shivering ground, face pressed into the dirt. The fragment on which I rode was still attached to one of the cables drawing it to its destination, sparing me from an immediate fatal descent to earth, but preserving me for the bone-crushing impact ahead–

What else could I do but laugh?

And I did, my mouth filled with as much soil and bits of twig as any hastily buried pauper. My circumstances had either driven me from sanity, or restored me to it – for I was struck that I seemed no worse off than ever before. Broken and battered, awaiting certain death, clinging to a rock hurtling through emptiness – in what way was I different from all other men?

TWELVE

The Americans Bid Farewell to Mr Dower

I F GOD'S BRIGHTER and nobler creatures are weary of
me, I am no less of them.

I have been plagued with angels; much of the ongoing
tribulation engulfing me has been heralded by these pesky
representations of the Divine Will. What little tranquillity
I had in this life, after my wife's demise, had been rudely
interrupted by the onslaught of a squadron of clattering,
simpering mechanical cherubim, unleashed at the funeral
service in my Cornish village's little church. That would
have been bad enough, but further appearances of celestial
messengers had continued, principally in the form of that
elabourate winged statuary by which the English moneyed
classes signify their belief that all of Creation is as upset by
one of their removals as they are – I expect their wearied
household staff at least would disagree with them on this
point. Nevertheless, I had been afflicted with those silent and
decorously mournful angelic beings, first in the cemetery at
Highgate, then in that monstrous graveyard elevated to the
skies above – though one of those latter had at least provided
the welcome service of a handhold to preserve my life for a
little while longer.

So to regain consciousness – again! – and find myself face-to-face with another winged form, this was no great surprise; I have managed to become accustomed to such appearances. I have nearly arrived at the point that if there were not such a one, it would be more of a novelty to me.

That I was lying on my back, I was able to perceive as my scattered thoughts partially coalesced. Which indicated that this latest angel was not so much before me, as suspended above me; how precariously so, I was not yet able to determine. But it seemed a bloody large example of its breed, similarly carved of weighty marble, so prudence dictated an attempt to extract myself from beneath, before it fell and crushed me.

Doing so, by rolling onto one shoulder and crawling with my hands dug into the ground, quickly revealed that I was not in the best of physical condition; merely drawing in my breath produced a wave of sharp pains along my upper torso, indicating some broken ribs, if not worse damage. That I was alive, and not dead – a result which I seem never able to achieve, however much circumstances assist me in that direction – was further indicated by the aching of my battered and bruised flesh; my muscles rebelled at the effort to which I put them, and spots of thickened blood dropped from a wound across one corner of my brow. At last, though, I achieved a position of relative safety, or as much of one as my general exhaustion would allow me to calculate. Forcing myself up and sitting, my flattened palms balancing me from behind, I attempted to survey where exactly I was.

A landscape of disorder greeted my eyes; the immense angel, larger than a man, from beneath which I had just escaped, was not the only monument that had been thrown into upheaval. All about me lay instances of engraved stone and marble, some more-or-less intact, but the majority broken to impressive ruins or completely shattered to rubble and white dust. A few nearby tombs and mausoleums had been rooted up and toppled onto their sides, iron doors flung from their ornate hinges, revealing the unlidded caskets within; the surrounding fences and gates lay tangled about them. I had been saved from sleeping extinction by the fortuitous dislodging of two large headstones, complete with the deceased's names and dates, that had been juxtaposed in such a way as to have provided a space beneath the angel falling across them; if not for the bare shelter they had provided, I would have been buried beneath the statue's weight, thus becoming the most recent person to be interred in this sombre locale.

Taking another painful breath, I gathered enough of my senses to realize what place this was, however much it had been altered from when I had last seen it. That I was once again in Highgate was confirmed by those sultry mists that blurred so much of what I discerned; as well, the disconcerting heat that my hands felt as they pressed against the ground assured me that those vast subterranean engines still operated some distance below. The course that had been set for the aerial cemetery before its utter disintegration, rocketing through the skies above the British landscape, had been exact enough to not only return me to London, but close to the very spot from which I had exited the city.

Such an accomplishment further explained the disordered state of the grounds surrounding me. Looking about, I perceived another oddity, of such dimensions that I had previously mistaken it as some geological feature of the nearby hills; I saw now that it was one of the enormous cables by which the aerial cemetery had been tethered to the earth, the adjustments to which had enabled the construction to be shifted from over one part of Britain to another. The cable looped across these ruins as though it were one of those legendary serpents from the Brazilian jungles, of a size capable of swallowing whole not just oxen but entire unfortunate native villages. Snapped free of whatever had remained of the aerial cemetery's mechanical underpinnings, it must have scythed across Highgate with tremendous velocity and impact, scattering the funereal monuments like tenpins.

And not just in this earthbound cemetery; the fact that I was seemingly alone here was explained by the cable's awesome length disappearing from view in the direction of the nearby Highgate district of shops and homes. Whatever wreckage had ensued among the dead was likely exceeded by what had been wrought among the living; tilting my head, I thought I could hear their distant shouts and cries. The apparatuses of succour were no doubt busily engaged with those most able to be assisted by them, leaving me to my fallen solitude.

With an effort that caused my bones and sinews to all but scream, I got to my feet. So many of the uprooted statues were close to the spot to which I had crawled, and leaning at such precarious angles, that I thought it best to find a place of somewhat greater safety, where I could gather my strength as best I could, and calculate my next actions.

My stumbling tread brought me within a short distance, as I cautiously sidled past the largest of the marble fragments, to what appeared to be a gravesite recently excavated; the rectangular hole had been dug, but no casket lay in its depths. A rush of memory came close to overwhelming me, as I realized I had stood upon this very spot; the empty grave was that which had been intended for my late wife, before she in her coffin had been snared from above and lifted to the aerial cemetery which had so startlingly hove into view.

As I stood there, stranger things took place. My mind's engagement in those recollections was swiftly terminated, as I saw a light come springing upward from the grave; I stood close enough that I was momentarily blinded by the glare.

"Well, I'll be..." A voice with a familiar accent sounded from before and below me. "Look who's here, Mr Haze!"

My vision cleared sufficiently that I could discern the

top of a ladder, extending from below, its topmost rungs propped against the interior edge of the grave. Formerly, the hole had been no deeper than the customary six feet; it had been transformed as well, now seeming to extend a great deal further down into the earth. Clambering upon the ladder was a figure I recognized, that of the American entrepreneur Blightley. A smile appeared on his face as he gazed up at mine.

"Things that happen – who would've guessed?" His dismounting from the ladder and onto the ground near me was made more difficult by both one of his arms being encumbered in a sling, and that he was burdened with a large satchel, of the type colloquially known as a carpet bag, its broad leather strap over his shoulder. "Pretty much thought we'd seen the last of you."

He was shortly joined by his partner, who said nothing, but directed toward me a sullen glare through his owlish glasses.

"Come no closer–" I stepped backward, reaching down to scoop up a large rock. "I will defend myself, if I must."

"Hold your horses, Dower; no need for all that." Blightley was visibly weary, chest heaving from the exertion of climbing whatever distance the ladder represented. He took the opportunity of divesting himself of the satchel, and dropping it at his feet. "We've no harm in mind for you."

"That remains to be seen." I kept hold of the rock. "The last time we spoke, you were aiming a pistol in my direction."

"So I was," admitted the other man. "But let bygones be bygones, all right? There was a lot going on then, that's pretty different now."

"Such as?"

"Well…" He glanced over at the sulking Haze, then back to me. "The two of us still had some ambitions we were pursuing in this part of the world – and now we don't. So the urgency of recruiting you into our plans is kinda diminished."

"You are both leaving England?" I had been able to study him with greater thoroughness; his garish suit, as well as that which Haze wore, was stained and even torn in places, giving them both a somewhat dilapidated appearance, magnified by a subtly perceivable air of defeat and discouragement, that undercut his habitually cheerful manner of speech. "Courtesy would dictate an expression of regret on my part – but somehow I am unable to summon as much."

"Yeah, well… same to ya, pal. Me 'n' Haze will be glad to get back home, no matter how much trouble's waiting for us there. Least we'll be among folk who don't have a poker up their backsides, when it comes to embracing new ideas."

"I fear that your new ideas very much resemble the old criminality."

"Have it your way," said Blightley. A bit of his American resolve seemed to have returned to him; having caught his breath, he slung the strap of his satchel back onto his shoulder. "Pretty much on your own now – been a lot better off if you'd thrown in with us. All we wanted to do was make a pile of money; these other folks have got a different agenda, to say the least."

"Those," I replied, "are the chances I am forced to take."

"Come along, Haze–" Our conversation at an end, the American gestured to his partner with his unbound hand. "It's a long way to Liverpool, but a steamer's waiting there, with a captain owes me a favour. Then home's just the other side of the pond."

I watched them go, making their way through the mists and rubble, considerably entwined with the cemetery's jungle-like foliage; having only slightly recovered a portion of my own strength, I had no means of halting them. Whether Blightley might have had some further knowledge to impart to me, which would have been useful in determining my present circumstances – those, I judged, continuing to be dire at best – that would have to remain a matter of conjecture. For the moment, at least, my solitude had once again been restored.

With every fibre of my body protesting, I stumbled to the edge of the grave, from which the departed pair had so surprisingly emerged. Peering over its edge, I perceived that the ladder which enabled their exit, though of a considerable length, did not reach all the way to the bottom of this four-cornered shaft, but only to a rocky ledge farther down, which itself connected to a slanting trail along the walls, narrow enough that Alpine goats would have had difficulty traversing its course; it spoke to Blightley's determination to return home with his partner that he, with his injured arm, had so managed.

Beyond that, I could see little; I might as well have been standing at some Vesuvian aperture, gazing down to the fiery bowels of the earth. The light continued, wavering and ominously tinged, that had first drawn me toward the side of the grave; what it might have signified was obscured by roiling clouds, seemingly of such weighty composition that they were unable to escape and rise into the sky above.

Having once before plummeted into such caliginous depths, propelled by the impact of one more damnable angel, I had no desire to do so again – thus I stayed at a cautious remove from the grave's edge, leaning forward to make my survey of its contents. I therefore reacted with both fury and surprise when I was impelled forward by a sharp blow across the back of my shoulders. Catching my balance a few inches away from a surely fatal plunge, I whirled about–

And spied another, whom I had expected never to see again, yet was not totally astonished to find standing before me.

"Greetings, Dower." The irrepressibility of Nick Spivvem's angled smile was once again apparent. "Keeping busy, are you?"

"Maintain your distance–" I still had in my grasp the rock with which I had earlier meant to defend myself against the Americans, if the need had arisen; brandishing it now at shoulder height, I gave Spivvem fair warning. "Whatever it is you want from me, I do not care to know. Go about your ill-conceived business, and leave me alone."

"Bluidy hell – this how go off?" He gave a shake of his head. "As if had friends other than me! Not so far out the woods, can spare any'd help you."

"I doubt any amicable intentions on your part." Having a little more time to study the other, I saw that he had been similarly roughed up by the impact of the aerial cemetery into the earth; the miracle that I had survived was compounded by his having done so as well. That he had taken some hard blows was apparent; one side of his neck and face was so bruised as to appear almost black; a sleeve of his jacket was tattered to shreds all the way up to his elbow, revealing crusted blood beneath; and he visibly favoured one leg even as he stood, suggesting that some sinew or bone in the other was sprained or broken. "Even if," I continued, "you had been able to satisfyingly answer all the questions I posed to you while we were still airborne, you would not have earned my trust, or convinced me to throw my lot in with yours."

"Shame, that – you've no hope, save me." Spivvem stepped closer, pressing a broken-nailed fingertip against my chest. "Hear me out, Dower; can still achieve not just survival, but deal of profit besides. And more – there's child involved, isn't there?"

"What do you know about that?" I still held the rock aloft as a weapon, but his unexpected words stayed my hand. "And what business of yours would it be?"

"Lot palaver you wish – never tire of talking, d'ye?" He advanced his familiarity, actually wrapping an arm about my shoulders and pressing me closer to him, as though we were long-lost friends, newly reunited. "But time presses – should be on way, 'fore those mean us no good can stop. Can talk later – are you ready?"

"*Ready?*" I stared at him in puzzlement. "Of what are you speaking?"

"No more'n this–"

With sudden force, Spivvem pushed himself against me; balance lost, I stumbled backward to the edge of the grave. Attempting to save myself from any further jostling on his part, I struck at him with the rock, swinging it down toward his brow – but he easily parried my forearm aside, knocking the stone out of his grasp. Thus disarmed, I could not prevent another shove from him–

And I fell, toppling into the hole, my arms flailing wildly. Desperate, I reached for the rungs of the ladder propped nearby, but my fingertips only futilely grazed them. Above me, I saw the clouded sky, framed by the grave's rough edges, and Spivvem receding as he looked down at me. To my astonishment, he bent his legs, then sprang forward, his own arms outstretched. For a moment, he seemed to hang spreadeagled in open space, then plummeted as I was already engaged in doing. Likely he was smiling in that crazed manner of his, though I could not be certain of this, as we both tumbled toward some point far below.

How long I fell, and how far, I am not certain; these are difficult things to calculate when one is in the midst of them. With previous descents, I had the comfort of being battered unconscious before undergoing the final stages of them, and thus been spared the dizzy anxiety that I suffered upon this occasion.

The passage of time distorts when one descends so headlong into the earth, with no support but the rush of air past one's cartwheeling limbs – particularly so in darkness, when there is no reference as to how quickly it is happening, or how much distance has been vaulted through. One part of my mind judged – certainly incorrectly – that I had been falling for hours; to another part it seemed but a few seconds.

Mercifully, the vertical process terminated; water splashed about me. If not for that, I would have been broken lifeless by the impact of some sterner substance. Fortunately, it was not of great depth; sufficient to break my fall, but not enough in which to drown, as long as I quickly regained some footing. I did so, the water coming to my waist, and looked about myself. The place was familiar to me; I had been here before, with the Americans Blightley and Haze. This was the subterranean chamber that contained their mock Venice, in which I had glided along in a gondola with them. At that time, the waters had been deeper; something must have occurred, so that the entire area had been drained to a great degree; the artificial shore against which the waters lapped now stood yards higher above its dark surface. That was not the only transformation; the pasteboard *palazzos* and other structures were in ruins, their flimsy silhouettes toppled over and broken, giving the false city the appearance of children's toys that had been trodden upon.

"There be–" My survey was interrupted by a voice from some distance where I had fallen. Turning about, I saw Nick Spivvem similarly enmired as I was, his clothes soaked and dark hair plastered to his brow. "Well found you."

He made his way toward me, the water parting around him as he approached. I made no attempt at evasion or escape, considering it pointless under the circumstances.

"Come along then." Once at my side, Spivvem tilted his head to indicate the direction in which he apparently meant us to go. "Much to see."

"What happened here?" I remained where I was; my inquiry was prompted by having been able to perceive more of our surroundings. A lurid glow dimly illuminated the prospect, as though from smouldering fires just out of sight. "When last I saw this, it appeared to be at least functional, if not all that impressive; now everything seems to be in shambles."

"Could say." He took a quick look about us. "Confess myself bit guilty, though not my intent. 'Fraid that when tinkered with rigging of that little boat, in which you and Blightley were having chat, disarranged more than was needed to shoot you away from premises. Indicates, it does, how jury-rigged whole construction was – cheapskate Americans slapped together with no regard for durableness. Good sneeze, whole bluidy place falls apart."

"Is that what you wanted to show me? I already had little regard for the pair you mention – you needn't have so precipitously forced me here, just to provide confirming evidence for my low opinion."

"Give rat's hindquarters, what think of them. Scurried off home, they have – and good riddance. Got more important things take care of, than dealing with those fools. Keep up–" He started off, toward the distant point to which he had previously drawn my attention. "We've business to attend."

With my own jacket damply clinging to my frame, I followed after the other man – if for no other reason than that he seemed to know his way about, and I was otherwise without guide in the subterranean chamber to which I had been compelled.

As we advanced through the waist-deep water, the light increased, the flickering tints of red and orange growing brighter and more threatening; it hardly seemed to be the wisest course to be heading toward them, but Spivvem ahead of me displayed no trepidation. At the same time, the mournful quiet of the artificial Venetian city, broken and tattered, was replaced in our ears by a growing din, the hissing and clanking sounds of machinery in operation.

That such would be the case at whatever destination my companion led toward was confirmed by the fiery glow rising to an eye-searing intensity, and the tumulting din mounting to an almost deafening volume. Some dismaying prospect lay before me, though yet unglimpsed; the distant fires, if such they were, cast their heat with sufficient force to draw sweat from my skin, even as I was still mired in the waters through which we advanced; above us, the rocky ceiling of this vast subterranean chamber reflected downward the intimidating radiance and noise.

"Hey up," spoke Spivvem, glancing over his shoulder at me. "Best stop moment, chat a bit here – difficult make clear, much farther on."

Though unable, given the circumstances, to summon up any emotion bright enough to be termed gladdened, I was at least relieved by this momentary lull in our sodden march. A stony ledge close by afforded a perch out of the water, and large enough for two men; I joined Spivvem there, scrambling up beside him.

"Much to tell – hear me well enow?"

"If you raise your voice," I replied, cupping one hand to my ear. "I will do my best to listen."

"Brilliant." Spivvem's shoulder rubbed against mine, as he pointed in the direction toward which we had been proceeding. "Wager like to know, all that is?"

"I have learned to forestall such inquiries, for fear of finding out the answers."

"No avoiding this'n."He prodded me forward with a hand at my back. "Go look, see yourself – I'll wait."

With some reluctance – the distant heat had been lessening the wet state of my clothing, increasing my comfort to a small degree – I allowed myself to slip from the perch, and back into the shallows. As I waded on, the force of the water rushing past me also increased; through the roaring mechanical din, I could make out another sound, that of a rushing cataract ahead.

The subterranean chamber's dimensions were augmented, I now saw, by those of the chasm into which the water fell; this close to its edge, I braced myself to keep from being swept over. Some rusting iron, perhaps of a ladder, had been fastened to the rock wall nearby; I grasped one of the heavy bars, but it came away in my hand, nearly toppling me. But I was able to regain my balance; at the slight distance I maintained from the opening, I was able to view that which Spivvem had wished me to see–

Below lay the source of the churning fiery glare, and the unrelenting noise. I had expected – or perhaps merely hoped – to find a volcanic phenomenon there before me, of greater dimensions than some Ætna or even Krakatau, but of the same lava-spewing nature. Instead, the grinding iron clatter had been more truly predictive – for what stretched out as far as my eye could perceive through the rising smoke and steam was nothing of geological process, but rather entirely industrial. If one had been given *djinn*-like powers to fly above such appalling factories as disfigure our English cities, and peel back a bolted ceiling, something similar might be revealed, though not at the scale which I now witnessed. It was as though all the earth's depths beneath those surfaces upon which the sun shone and the rain fell, and here excluded, had been transformed into one great interlinked factory, every inch a locus of incessantly pounding activity, with no horizon limiting its extent. The fires were those of the furnaces and crucibles that vomited forth streams of molten iron, crusted with black patches of slag; the gouts of steam and smoke were emitted by the boilers quaking from the pressures bottled within. The waters tumbling over the edge of the cataract above were instantly boiled away, or ran beneath the grated substructure in bubbling rivers. Pistons the size of cottages thrust back and forth with frightening velocity, shivering the girdered frames that caged them.

How much time, whether minutes or hours, crawled by as I stood transfixed, staring at the infernal scene rolled out before me – I have no idea. The terrifying images of industry, unremitting in its mechanical fury, were virtually seared upon my eyes, as my face withered in the heat from the ovens of production. And yet there was something even grimmer and more appalling that I perceived at last, when I was all but blinded…

"Rather stunned, you seem." In a relaxed attitude, Spivvem retained his seat upon the ledge above the flowing waters. "Sight afflict so bad?"

I slowly crawled up beside him. My eyes had been soothed by the darkness through which I had plodded, wading back toward this spot; I could discern the other in silhouette at first, then his features became dimly visible.

"Yes…" I nodded slowly. "It was… horrible."

"If used to green fields and pastures, imagine so." He shrugged. "More an urban upbringing, myself – so didn't find quite so shocking, first I saw it."

"What is it, for God's sake?"

"Rather, what isn't?" Spivvem's voice remained calm and unruffled. "Soon everything, everywhere, be like. No more than seen Future, you have."

"*That?* That is the World to Come?"

"Plenty as would wish it so." He nodded with exaggerated sagacity. "Might get their way."

"Nothing more," I muttered, appalled, "than a giant grinding factory – and for what purpose? What is all that supposed to manufacture?"

"Why… misery, 'course! What other purpose needed? Oh,

to be sure, high-minded industrial types and apologists will 'scuse themselves, pointing to mountains of shoddy goods that come out the loading docks – but really b'lieve that's what thrills their innards? Or would be sight of common folk crushed beneath one great bluidy machine, and the boss's manicured finger on lever drives it? There's true reason for what's called Progress, very like."

"No more," I said. "Please – whatever your purpose in bringing me here, and showing me this, I cannot fathom. But if by doing so, you have trapped me in this place – if there is no escape from what lies so close at hand – than I would rather drown myself now, than be faced with the prospect of enduring it any further."

"Suit yourself, Dower. No business mine, what you do – but not yet. As said before, business to take care of. Both have – that's why here."

"What possible business could I have in such a place, but attempting to flee from it, as best I can?"

"Told above, before made our great jump. The child – your son, that is."

"How would you have any knowledge regarding him?"

"Scape told me. Told me quite lot, indeed."

"I find that difficult to credit, unless you are implying that you once had him under some type of duress, and forced him to tell you."

"Hardly necessary," said Spivvem. "He and I were partners – at least for while."

"As I said to you before – he expressed to me an opinion of considerable hostility toward you."

"Not surprised – had fallings out, we did. Recently, too – volatile character, his. Pity he's dead, otherwise might've made amends. But both engaged in finding this sprat of yours. Fact, Scape and I in league when you first laid eyes on me, down in fookin' Cornwall – oy, dismal place that is. If you hadn't so rudely chased me away, might've saved us all a fair bit trouble. *And* mystification on your part – would've known about your boy, and why all this chasing about, earlier rather than later."

"If the two of you had been concerned over the whereabouts of my son – and you had managed to locate him, as Scape had informed me – then why are we here in this dismal hole? Why not take me to where he is, so that I might assist you in whatever efforts are required to extricate the child from whatever situation in which he resides? Scape had made his promise to Miss McThane to effect that rescue; if for whatever reason you wish to fulfil that pledge, why not commence immediately upon it, rather than wasting more time?"

"Daft, you are–" Spivvem rolled his eyes as he shook his head, then looked full upon me again. "I *have* brought you to where boy is. He's here, or rather–" A hand rose, to point toward the appalling scene from which I had just returned. "*There*."

I could make no reply; the other's words oppressed my soul to a point near extinction.

"Bad off, eh?" Spivvem tilted his head, attempting to peer into my averted face. "Weren't expecting such?"

"No…" My voice dwindled to a whisper. "I knew it."

For that was what had so afflicted me, as I had stood at that precipitous edge, the water streaming past me, transformed to hissing steam below. It had not been the ghastly engines that I had espied through the mists and smoke, churning ceaselessly, their enormous cogged gears grinding away, the pistons slamming back and forth with such relentless fury. If that had been all that I had witnessed from above, it would have been a vision terrifying enough. But there had been more, which had required a sharper peering to glimpse, and which sent me scurrying away, horrified–

Human figures among the demonic machines; that was what I had seen at last. So distant had been the elevated point from which I had viewed this sunken landscape, they seemed ant-like, dwarfed to insignificance by the iron constructions maintained by their labours. Whenever some boiler hatch was opened, the glaring light from the flames within glistened on the sweating torsos of the men, stripped to their waists, or on the faces of the women tending the only slightly less demanding wheels and spindles. Elsewhere, in whatever shadows could be found, a few took shelter for a hastily seized respite, or lay prostrate and motionless, their lives' last energies having been finally pressed from them.

And still worse, if such could be imagined! The smaller forms of children, their faces blackened with soot, their fragile limbs withered and bent, spines hunched nearly circular as they scooped cinders and ash from beneath the constructions pounding only inches above their heads, or squeezed themselves through those constrictive spaces that only they were able to, intent on all those interminable errands that the factory demanded of them.

That had been the vision – the sight of those tiny workers – which had so weighed upon me, I could not speak of it until prodded by Spivvem's words.

"He is there?" What I said was no more than what I had already realized. "My son is among the machines?"

"One time, would've been." Spivvem nodded. "But things've changed somewhat; as much valued he'd been by late mother – and perhaps yourself – he's also for certain others. Scape and I found out that much. And why boy's so – very interesting matter, that is. But also reason for *your* importance in all these dealings and scrabbling about."

"Which is?"

"Others can explain better'n I – and they'll have chance, if I have anything to do with. For I've proposition to make you."

"Proceed." My surroundings, and what I had witnessed a little distance away, so darkened my thoughts, that I was ready to consider any prospect. "I am listening."

"Here's deal." In an expectedly conspiratorial manner, Spivvem brought his face close to mine. "Brought you here, can get you out – but have do something for me."

"Very well," I said. "What would that be?"

"Come with, to where this boy is – I'll take there. Don't fool me, Dower; can see well that black rock of your heart. Very perceptive I am, concerning people's natures – why I'm so good at my line of work. If cared enow your son's plight, much as late wife did, there'd be no need to force you go to him; do it of own free will. But – *We are as are*, as folk my particular tribe like to say, and we do as can. Accompany willingly, and no mucking about on your part, and I'll make sure see daylight again."

"Begging your pardon – but why should I trust you in this?"

"You've alternative?"

"I do not know whether I do or not," I said. "That is yet to be determined. Suffice it to say, though, I am concerned as to how lightly you state your proposition. I cannot believe that it would be accomplished as easily as you make it sound, as though it were some stroll through a leafy park to reach our destination – and if it is more hazardous, that you would be capable of successfully guiding me there. This seems a fearsome territory–" I gestured toward the distance, from which the fiery light and grinding, clanking noise continued to wash toward us. "Your familiarity with it is a debatable matter, given what I have previously seen of your deficiencies regarding things mechanical and technical."

"Got us here, didn't I?"

"And barely alive. Which raises another concern, namely the preservation of my life. I have been continuously pursued by the agents of that conspiratorial organization known as the More Loving Embrace, regarding which I was informed by your former partner Scape, now deceased, were intent upon my never making contact with my son, and thus their lethal intent toward me. That being the case – and I have no reason to doubt the late Scape's assurances about it – I could prudently expect more of those assassins here, being so much closer to the boy himself. The More Loving Embrace's agents might already be aware of my presence at this point, and are lying in wait along whatever route you would take me. To be frank, your ability to protect me from them seems limited."

"All this useless fretting…" Spivvem shook his head again. "Something else said by my kind – *Safety's found where's most danger.*"

"A lovely aphorism, and just about as useful as others of its kind. But fine words will not save me from being shot at."

"Ugly sort of cynicism you have, Dower; ill behooves. And had enow this jabbering; offer's on table, and isn't any other. D'you accept?"

"And if I refuse – what then? I rather suspect that this is no *offer* at all, at least not one in any usual sense. I imagine that if I balk, that will merely trigger some act of violence on your part, and I will be dragged to whatever destination you wish; the only question being whether I am conscious or not during the journey."

"Thought had occurred," admitted Spivvem. "Can't deny. 'Twere possible, would've done so already, rather than wasting all this time convincing you. But as luck'd have, bit out of question at moment."

"How so?"

"'Fraid took more blow coming down from above, than was 'specting." He placed a hand on the side of his abdomen, then winced as he gave the spot a slight push. "Shouldn't have been in such hurry, get us both here, but is need for haste. Amusing that *you* bounced up onto your feet so fine, and I'd be one suffered injury – but upshot's that could no more carry you where should be, than could fly to moon. Thus offer, and's true one; do me service of coming along, and I'll recompense as indicated."

"Very well–" I had given as much consideration as I felt was needed, to all that he had spoken of – and his description of his infirm physical state had confirmed the decision I had already been contemplating. "Are we ready to travel, then?"

"Glad you've seen fit; won't regret it, promise you. So yes, let's proceed." He lowered himself off the ledge – somewhat gingerly, in evident discomfort – and down into the shallow water. "Won't have much trouble keeping up, 'spect."

"I suppose not." Letting him take a few paces onward, I then similarly descended from the narrow perch. "But my best will have to do."

His shadow fell across me, cast by the fiery light ahead, as I stepped close behind him. With his back turned, and any sound of mine masked by the mechanical din reverberating through the space, I was able to extract from inside my jacket the iron bar which I had previously obtained. When it had come loose in my hand before, I had retained it, thinking that it might prove useful in some capacity – and when he had just described his relatively enfeebled condition to me, I was sure that I was not in error about that.

With as much force as I could summon, I raised the implement and brought it down toward his skull. Some preternatural sense alerted him at the last second; he turned about, saw the metal in its arc, and dove to his side. Nevertheless, I managed to land a significant blow, the bar striking between his neck and the point of his shoulder. That was sufficient to knock him from his feet, sending him splashing chest-first into the water.

I quickly stepped forward and launched another slashing swing at him. With his form half-submerged, it was difficult to take accurate aim; I was certain I struck him with considerable force, as I heard a gasping cry of pain and surprise – but at the same moment, his unseen hand caught hold of the bar, and wrenched it from my grip.

My purpose had been achieved by that point, giving me time enough to turn and run before he would be able to pursue me–

Or so I hoped. Against the current streaming against me, I summoned all the energy that remained in my body, making what speed I could.

My plan – to the degree that I had one – had been to return to the site of that false Venice, into which I had first dropped when Spivvem had impelled me over the edge of the grave above. Blightley and his partner Haze had somehow managed to ascend to the surface from there; I had seen them do so. Therefore, some route must exist by which they had made that journey, the last stage of which had been the ladder propped against one side of the hole from which they had emerged. Perhaps there was a sloping path carved into the rock framing that area, traversable by one even as handicapped as Blightley had been – I merely had to discover its starting point, and then I could make my own escape.

In the event, I soon realized that however sound my reasoning, its subsequent execution left much to be desired. The dimness of light, when at a remove from that loathsome factory I had glimpsed, served to conceal the complexity of possible routes leading away from it; intent upon following Spivvem as he had led me downward, I had failed to notice that there were other conduits of water linking to the one which we had waded through. Thus, upon fleeing our terminus, I found myself confronted with a branching maze, with every choice between proceeding left or right equally unsigned, and equally capable of leading toward my goal or, more likely, to stumbling frustration.

I confess that panic soon arose in my breast, my heart accelerating uncontrollably, and my gulping lungs labouring as well. My anxiety multiplied as I encountered one dead end after another, where the spaces dwindling to an impassable dimension, or the waters rising to a depth near my face, signalled my error. Retracing my steps, or attempting to, I was keenly aware that both my time and opportunities were limited; the blow from the iron bar in my hands had disabled Spivvem sufficiently to make my escape from him, but only momentarily so. He was not dead, I was sure, and would be intent on pursuing me once he had regained his facilities. He knew these subterranean chambers better than I did, and he would be motivated by a fury more vengeful than his previous seeking of advantage through me – he might very well not renew the offer he had made, but simply terminate my life. I might round any rocky corner in this labyrinth, and come face-to-face with my final doom.

This mad flight, blindly splashing through one course of streaming water after another, continued for some seemingly interminable period; how long exactly, I could not reckon, other than by the measure of my decreasing strength. Which came to an end at last, or close enough that I could not keep myself from stumbling and pitching forward, landing upon my hands and knees – though not into water; my thoughts and perceptions had become so dazed that I had not been aware that I had entered upon a passage sloping upward, so much so that I had left those shallows behind me.

After a few moments of panting rest, my head hanging low, I clumsily got to my feet once more, and surveyed the scene about me as best I could. I immediately abandoned any

notion of turning about and descending as I had just made
my way; my efforts at finding the passage by which I had
originally entered this bleak world, and the point from which
I might have been able to directly mount again to the surface,
had produced no such circumstances, and pursuing them
further would likely yield no better results. But this place,
to which my sodden steps had led me – it at least continued
upward, to the degree that I could determine; enough of the
fierce glow from that demonic factory penetrated here, that
I could see my own shadow wavering on the cavern wall
beside me. Might this narrow passage mount further in that
direction, and bring me, if not to the gravesite into which I
had been pitched, but to some other point in the open air of
the world above?

I could see no other choice before me, or at least none which
I wished to contemplate. I stumbled forward, gladdened that
the slope of the path increased, indicating that I might sooner
reach the surface–

But at the same time, dismayed that both the light from
that immense factory, and the noises produced by its ceaseless
activity, also became greater as I proceeded, step after step. I
could not doubt that in my hasty flight, I had become turned
about – in such a sunken abode, all normal indicators of
direction were gone – and was now heading back toward
exactly that which had so horrified me, and had impelled my
attempt to escape.

Within a few more minutes of climbing, the gravelly soil
steep enough that I was forced to claw into it with my soon
bleeding fingertips in order to continue, I emerged onto a
more level place; but standing upright again, I was blinded by
the fierce glare before me, my ears assaulted by the pounding
clamour of iron, and the shrill hissing of the steam that impelled
it. Inching forward, I raised a hand to balance myself against
the rocks at the edge of the opening onto a greater space–

And one which I had witnessed before, though now I viewed it from a higher elevation. Below me lay those immense engines of production, no less appalling – or perhaps even more so, given that from this point I could better see how vast was their extent. And how inescapable; to have made such an arduous circuit, only to helplessly return and gaze upon them once more–

"Dower!" I heard a voice cry out, though barely audible through the din. "There!"

I brought my gaze up from the hellish factory, and saw another human figure, framed in the aperture of a passage opposite, some distance away from where I stood; it was Spivvem, his pursuit of me having brought him to that point. As I gazed upon him, I saw his hand point down toward something below both of us.

Yet another opening was there, which I had not perceived before, my vision having been fixed upon the furious machines, wrapped in the glare of their furnaces, and the rising smoke and steam. But now I saw that to which he wanted my awareness drawn; though I could discern but little, the upraised rifle I glimpsed was sufficient to indicate that at least one of those relentless assassins had survived and managed to track me here.

Despite my dazed exhaustion, I retained enough wits to flatten myself to the ground beneath me, just as that figure took aim and fired. The bullet struck above, passing through the exact space in which I had stood. Thus, rather than piercing my chest, it shattered the rock wall behind.

My endangering was scarcely ended, though; just as some reckless shout might trigger an Alpine avalanche, the impact of the bullet had consequences beyond its mere leaden weight. Rolling onto my side, I witnessed the rock wall continue to crumble apart, shards and larger stones separating from one another and clattering down.

Their sudden weight shivered the ground they struck, and it fractured as well. Before I had any chance of scrabbling onto my knees and lunging to whatever security was afforded by the passage through which I had climbed, everything collapsed beneath me, and I fell amidst the unmoored stones.

THIRTEEN

Conundrums & Conspiracies

HOW COMFORTING TO wake from bad dreams, and to know that all is right in one's world.

The downy pillow caresses the side of one's face; a lark trills from the blossomed branch outside the window; morning light pours like butter across the bedchamber's floor; all one's enemies are humiliated or dead, and one's friends are at least endurable…

So disturbed had been my sleep – so many nightmares had afflicted me! Dreams of falling, from rocky promontories both entombed in the bowels of the earth and elevated above the clouds; if all that had happened in the waking world, how could it be that I was still alive? Thankful that I was so, and that all my slumbering anxieties were illusions dispelled by the advent of a bright new day, I turned my head, expecting to see my wife nestled beside me, her eyes closed, still dreaming more happily than I had…

But I saw nothing like that – which puzzled me, I admit. I did not seem to be in a familiar room at all; this space was much bigger, and more luxuriously fitted, as I – still blinking in confusion – was quickly able to discern. The walls were covered with silken paper, set with a stylish *Japonisme* pattern, of an expense never glimpsed in a rude countryside

inn of Cornwall. Rather than candles and lanterns, ornate
sconces provided more congenial illumination; the hearth
was surrounded by gold-veined marble, carved in fluted half-
pillars.

"Mr Dower–" A low-pitched voice, of rumbling congeniality,
spoke my name. "You are awake – and rested, I trust."

By now, I was fully so, and somewhat alarmed. There was
no loving wife beside me – I remembered why there would
never be one again – and there would have been no space for
her, as I was not resting upon a bed, but rather a low divan
with a scalloped back; I lifted my head not from a pillow, but
the furnishing's upholstered arm.

I swung my legs down and set my feet upon the polished
floor, then turned toward the figure seated comfortably in
a morris chair nearby. Recognition seemed oddly possible,
but still evasive; his features evoked my furrowed brow as
I attempted to summon from memory any name, or what
place I might have encountered him. In a flash, a scene sprang
before my interior vision, of the gravesite in the cemetery
at Highgate, surrounded by all those jungle-like fronds and
looping vines – I could see myself standing there, gazing
down at the casket holding the late Miss McThane's lifeless
body, and listening to a similarly deep voice ranting about
various apocalyptic notions, light springing from the bowels
of the Earth and other demented twaddle. At the head of the
grave had been a wild-haired figure with furious expression,
clutching a ponderous tome to his chest, eyes displaying an
obvious degree of insanity as he had delivered an appalling
eulogy. The man here in this well-appointed chamber was
the same as the one I recalled – or at least some aspects of him
were identical to that earlier appearance. But now he was
not visibly disordered; his eyes were not staring wide beneath
thunderous brows, his snow-white hair was decorously
combed, and he displayed a smile of relaxed benevolence.

"Can I provide you with anything?" The Right Reverend Jamford – for it was he – gestured toward a tea trolley stationed beside his chair. "You have been asleep for some time, and you were – shall we say? – considerably occupied before your arrival here. So you must be famished."

Not waiting for my reply, he busied himself for a moment, lading a small plate with various morsels, then leaning forward and setting it on the small table before me. My hunger, accurately assessed by him, overwhelmed my continuing astonishment at my circumstances, and I devoured all but a few cake crumbs before I again leaned back on the divan.

"What... what is the meaning of all this?" I peered at him as I wiped my mouth with the back of my hand. "No, wait – tell me first where I am."

"Not far," spoke Jamford mildly, "from where last you found yourself. Weebsome – would you be so kind?" He turned and gestured toward the other side of the chamber. "Our guest might find the view... enlightening."

Following the direction of the other's hand, I saw that he and I were not alone. At a cupboarded secretarial chest sat the cleric I had first known from my obscure Cornish village. His semblance then had been an artfully deceiving masquerade – he was now garbed more finely, in an elegantly cut suit surmounted by a silken cravat, than I had ever seen him in his role as a rural priest. No explanation was required for this transformation; I realized now that he had likely been a spy all along, dispatched by one or more of these multiplying conspiracies to keep an eye on me; he had not died in the fire that had consumed the rural church, but had used the event as cover for his disappearance from the locale of his clandestine surveillance.

"By all means," answered Weebsome. Laying down his pen – he had been engaged with some papers strewn upon the desktop – he stood up from his chair, strode to the heavy curtains at the farthest wall, and drew them back. "There—"

I winced at what was revealed – literally so, for the fierce light that flooded into the chamber was of a blinding intensity. Shielding my face with an upraised hand, I managed to discern that what lay outside the shelter of this chamber was the same demonic, constantly churning factory that I had previously seen from an angle elevated above it – but now I saw it closer, and onto the floor of its operations and furious production.

Weebsome displayed some mercy toward me, no doubt perceiving how the unveiling of that vista struck me like a giant hammer blow, my torso and limbs contracting onto the divan like an insect crushed beneath a giant's boot-heel. He reversed the simple actions he had taken at the side of the window, allowing the heavy drapes to fall back into place and shielding us all from that oppressive light, and muffling the din from the machines beyond.

"It has taken so much effort to bring you here—"

With my eyes still dazed, I could not see the Right Reverend Jamford, but I could hear his low, unhurried voice.

"I am certain, Mr Dower, that you do not give yourself credit enough, for your skills of evasion, and determination to avoid capture," he went on, from the commodious chair nearby. "You are like that butterfly on a spring day, a prize specimen for a lepidopterist's collection, the seemingly erratic fluttering of which nevertheless frustrates every swoop of the net that would catch it. Granted, a good deal of that butterfly's performance might be attributable to sheer dumb luck – and the same for you as well. But the fact remains that it has taken a determined effort, on the part of a great many parties, to overcome all your ducking and dodging. Many plans, of tremendous import, would have been much further advanced by now, if it had been otherwise, and you had been of a more coöperative nature.

But be that as it may..." He paused, no doubt with a slight smile. "Here we are at last."

"So we are." Revivified by the food I had so voraciously consumed, my resentful spirits arose again. "That being the case – what are your intentions?" My vision had adjusted to a point where I could turn a slit-eyed gaze toward the man. "You can hardly blame me for being somewhat suspicious toward persons such as yourself, who are so prominently affiliated with that conspiracy who has dispatched so many of its agents with instructions to put a bullet through my head."

"Oh! By that, I take it you are referring to the More Loving Embrace–"

"Undoubtedly, he is." Weebsome spoke, as he stepped over to the trolley and poured a cup of tea for himself. "And understandably so – some charades are so successful, that many people never see past them to the truth."

"*Charade?*" My angered gaze swept across both of them. "What the devil do you mean by that? Are you implying that you are *not* associates of that organization? Or perhaps even its leaders?"

"Hmm..." Jamford nodded slowly, deep in some musing reverie. "Perhaps it is a function of advancing age; I have lived a long and – shall we say? – *complicated* life, and not always in the respectable guise of a man of the cloth. So devious have been the pathways I have traversed, and the pretences I have maintained, that truth to tell, I sometimes strain to recollect exactly which side I *am* on. Suffice it to say that there are a great many members of that collective known as the More Loving Embrace, who swear as much allegiance to me as they are certain that I bear toward their professed interests."

"And those others? The ones known as the Elohim – that is what I was told they are called, and that they are in deadly enmity toward the More Loving Embrace. Do you play a similarly deceptive game with them?"

"What is the point of making such enquiries?" One of Jamford's shaggy eyebrows rose as, seemingly amused, he studied me. "If I assured you one way or another, would you believe me? Or would you simply suspend all rational judgment and, like Buridan's overly thoughtful ass, find yourself uselessly stymied between one possibility and its opposite?"

Much as that butterfly to which he had previously compared me, I found myself pinned by the man's words; he had me there, as to what I would be able to accept as the truth. Thus exposure to Byzantine conspiracies, endlessly multiplying and overlapping, connecting and disconnecting, is like contact with those corrosive acids capable of dissolving the strongest metals; a man is left with nothing on which he can proceed, but much on which he can only doubt.

"Then why this bloody conversation?" My anger compelled me to speech again. "Is there any purpose other than to torment me?"

"I understand why you might think so," replied Jamford. "One of my chief regrets is that so many events have gone badly for you, and uncomfortably so, all the while that I and my associates have borne you no ill will at all, but only wished to have a friendly and mutually advantageous transaction between us. I know you have some skepticism in that regard, and justifiably so – but I will endeavour to overcome all such. Let me begin by assuring you that wherever my loyalties might ultimately lie, I am familiar enough with the inner councils of those who are not just known as the Elohim, but refer to themselves in that manner as well – so that I can inform you as to their intentions, in particular those which involve yourself. You would wish to hear that, I trust?"

"My sense is that you are going to tell me, whether I wish it or not. So continue, then."

"Very well." Jamford leaned back into the depths of his chair, placing his fingertips together before himself. "Briefly put, the Elohim are a purely benevolent league of high-minded individuals–"

"Pardon me, but I have heard that sort of thing before. If all conspirators were so lofty in their ideals, then the world would be largely populated by saints."

"In this case, Mr Dower, you might well give them the benefit of the doubt; they at least did not send out anyone to shoot you."

"There is that," I admitted. "I have reached the point where I am grateful for even those small considerations."

"Allow me to continue. As noble as might be the Elohim's intentions, I recognize that there might be some slight differences of opinion between themselves and the great mass of Humanity, yourself included. What you gazed upon just now–" Jamford parted the web of his hands, so he could gesture toward the curtained window. "Most people would regard that as an appalling sight, as I am sure you do; I could detect as much in your reaction to it. To the Elohim, however, it is otherwise; they regard it as the glorious future of Mankind."

"And you assure me they are *benevolent* and *high-minded*!" I shook my head in disdain. "How could any but monsters believe so?"

"Hear me out," said Jamford. "Allow me to amend my statement slightly: the Elohim do not see it as the glorious future of *all* Mankind, but of that considerable portion which must work for a living, and put food in their mouths by way of the sweat of their brows. The Elohim's benevolent agenda is funded by the more progressive captains of our nation's industry, who are concerned about the increasingly oppressive conditions of the *satanic mills*, as the poet Blake has termed the factories spreading across England."

"Wouldn't those soft-hearted industrialists be better employed in simply alleviating those conditions, rather

than financing some weird conspiracy regarding them? That
would seem to already be in their power, and which they
could easily accomplish by reining in their own greed. What I
have been shown here–" I pointed to the shrouded window.
"It differs only in scale and degree from what I have heard
about the factories that have already multiplied upon the
surface of the earth. If their proprietors are so grieved as to
what prevails there, why not shut them down, or make them
less cruelly hellish?"

"The problem with your suggestion is its impracticality.
These are businessmen of whom we are speaking, Mr Dower,
and they are motivated by a desire for wealth beyond your
comprehension – or mine, for that matter. To alleviate
these conditions, to dull even slightly the sharpness of their
impingement upon those who suffer thereby – let alone
do away with them entirely – would greatly cut into the
profits of these men, who are certain their own lives would
be miserable pits of despair unless their account books are
flooded with ever-expanding numbers written in the blackest
of inks."

"In other words, what you are saying is that these
benevolent industrialists are moved to tears by the plight of
those who labour for them, but not so moved as to actually
do anything about it. In this world, I suppose that is what
passes for saintly compassion toward one's fellow man."

"You are being overly harsh in your opinions." This time,
a frown accompanied Jamford's slow nod. "The persons you
disparage have not simply thrown their hands up in defeat,
and accepted the continuance of others' suffering; there is
another way forward, and this is where their support of those
known as the Elohim comes in to play. Let me see if I can
explain their intentions in a manner that makes sense to you.
Suppose a person were to prick his finger upon a needle;
one could say that the needle is the *condition* which causes

his pain, and the pain could be alleviated by removing that condition – that is, to remove the needle. But what if the person's finger were made of sterner stuff, that the needle could not injure? Or that the person's senses were altered in such a way that he felt no pain from the trifling injury? Then the condition – the needle – could remain where it was, and be unalleviated, so to speak – but his pain would be gone, and the person would be altogether more cheerful about his situation, needle and all. However awkwardly I might have formulated the analogy, it is essentially what the Elohim and their charitable backers wish to achieve."

"And how do they propose going about this?"

"Very simply, Mr Dower; it requires nothing more than a complete and total revolution in human nature, so that it might better accommodate itself to the demands of the modern world. The factories are fine the way they are – even such as the one you gazed upon just now. Any deficiency is not to be found in the working conditions that are produced within, no matter how oppressive you or I might consider them, but rather in those individuals – men, women, and yes, children as well – whose frailties as human beings leave them short of the necessary mark. That is the situation when regarded negatively – but there is indeed a brighter and more optimistic view. Consider the work of our remarkable scientific thinkers Wallace and Darwin – I trust you are familiar with them – which demonstrates that the kingdom of living creatures, Mankind included, has reached its current pinnacle of development, not by kicking against the physical world's conditions, but by evolving to happily adapt to them."

"I do not think you mean *happily*–" I could not refrain from a sour retort. "The word for which you are searching is *profitably*."

"However you wish; there is little essential difference between them."

"Accepting, for the sake of argument, the saintly motivations of these industrialists of whom you speak – how do the Elohim expect to adapt the suffering workers, so that they are more reconciled to their situation in the factories? *Evolve* them into mules, I suppose?"

"Hardly necessary–" Jamford dismissed my suggestion with a wave of his hand. "The Theory of Evolution – such a grand concept! – would suggest that the necessary adaptations would already have commenced taking place, but alas, that does not seem to be the case. Or else the change is occurring too slowly to soothe the concern of these industrialists; the workers are as miserable as ever, or perhaps even more so – especially the children pressed into service. How unhappy they seem, labouring away in those dark grimy mills! And worse, from their employers' view, how unprofitably, to use your word. Their output would undoubtedly be higher, and at considerably less expense, if they could be induced to smile as they went about their tasks. And of course, there is another concern about their predicament, which looms on the horizon – oppression breeds rebellion; it is a sad fact of human nature. The day might come when these unhappy toilers take up arms against those they unfortunately consider to be the authors of their misery, with violent consequences to all concerned."

"If that were to happen, my sympathies – to the extent that I had any – would lie with the mill-hands, rather than with their employers. One doesn't need to be much of a Jacobin, in order to feel that way."

"Many would agree with you, Mr Dower – which, of course, is exactly the problem. Social upheaval is a great affliction, especially when it joins with the popular sentiment, and should be avoided at all costs. Thus the support of certain wise industrialists for the Elohim and their remedy, as I shall explain. As the Elohim see it – and I have been convinced with them on this point – that underlying difficulty isn't that modern factory life is so bleakly different from the free, unconfined and sunlit existence that mankind used to enjoy, but that it isn't *completely* different from that previous world; there are still too many reminders of what used to be, such as the occasional sunny day that manages to break through the soot-laden clouds above even the darkest factories. Things like that only serve to delay labouring mankind's eventual evolution and adaptation to the unavoidable new world that has come upon them. Life in the factories would not seem so bleak and miserable if there were no longer traces of what used to be, by which the new world would be compared to the old one."

"This, sir, is a cruel and absurd notion." My tone was as much freighted with disgust as anger now. "People who would espouse such a thing are monsters – I do not wish to abuse the hospitality you have shown me, but you seem monstrous as well, for throwing your lot in with such. Do you really believe that you can so break human beings on this wheel of loathsome Progress, so that they would come to enjoy their own misery and suffering?"

"That," interjected Weebsome from across the room, "is exactly what remains to be seen."

"Oh, I assure you–" Jamford continued his exposition, unruffled by my bitter words. "Once I felt just as you do now; to say that one's fellow men are not the way they should be, and it would be better if they were some way more to your preference – that is arrogance bordering on the Satanic. But grand ideas have a seductive nature to them; *Like calls to like*, as the old maxim has it, and my soul – I confess it – is of a larger than usual variety, and thus the attraction to me of the Elohim's plans."

"And what exactly are those? You have spoken of what they wish to achieve; how do they expect to bring about such an alteration to Humanity?"

"The Elohim's great project for the betterment of Mankind..." Jamford's gaze drifted away from me, as though contemplating some more distant and nobler vista. "It is to eliminate the last vestiges of the world in which people used to live, so they will finally and completely adapt to the new one and have a chance of being happy – or at least not quite so miserable – in it. If people never saw the sun again – they would not miss it. They would adapt; they would evolve."

"Such is your grand scheme? To permanently immure the labouring classes into windowless factories, so that they would toil as best they could by flickering gas jets? This somehow would result in a more cheerful attitude on their parts? This is more than monstrous – it is insane."

"Did you see a dim and ill-lit environment when you looked out that window? No – for it was brighter there than under the radiance of any number of suns. That is, so to say, the brilliance of the Elohim's scheme. They consider themselves to be the ultimate bringers of light to a benighted humanity; soon, all of this subterranean factory world will be filled with an unending illumination, banishing night and shadow, and greatly assisting its working population to dedicate themselves to their appointed tasks, twenty-four hours a day. In fact–" Jamford now leaned toward me, his eyes glittering, "I can assure you that the whole concept of hours and minutes, and even Time itself, will be extinguished from Mankind's consciousness, as soon as the Elohim's plans come to fruition."

"What a dreadful possibility."

"No – it's *magnificent*. Do you not see? This will be something that is to the benefit of everyone involved. Those captains of industry who have financed the Elohim's humanitarian project will get more production from their workers, and the workers will joyously evolve to adapt to their new environment, just

as those savants Darwin and Wallace would predict, once it is
sufficiently different from the world which the workers had
previously known. Which it will be." Leaning back once again,
Jamford displayed a self-satisfied smile. "And that is why I have
joined my efforts to this cause – it would be heartless not to."

"So you have convinced yourself." Once more, I shook
my head. "And what you have convinced me of, is just how
much evil is accomplished by those who style themselves as
reformers. But at least I can take comfort in being certain that
the Elohim's plans will never come to fruition."

"Indeed–" Jamford's brow furrowed, as he took note of
the absolute confidence with which I had spoken. "And how,
pray tell, do you know that?"

"Simple. I might not be as well-versed in the writings of
those evolutionary theorists as you are, but I have followed
the controversy about them in the press, enough so that I
have knowledge regarding them – and thus I spy the flaw
in these cockamamie schemes. There is a limit to how far
the process of adaptation to conditions can be taken, unless
you are willing to undergo the passing of millennia before
seeing the results; some consideration must be taken of the
base material with which you begin. You might well be able
to impose circumstances upon a robin, that would force it
to eventually become an eagle – but you would have a hard
go of it, to achieve the same when starting with a turtle and
its subsequent progeny. I have read of naturalists discussing
what they term the *circadian rhythm* of the human species;
we are creatures accustomed to the alternation of night and
day, light and dark. For an alteration to occur, such as you
envision, unceasing daylight as bright as noon would need
to be imposed upon these poor, luckless factory workers." I
pointed to the curtains and what lay beyond them. "Do you
really think that qualifies as such, as hellishly bright and
glaring it might be? You might be able to blind the hapless

subjects of your ambition, but you would never be able to convince any part of them that they were living in perpetual, timeless day."

"Is that your only objection?" Jamford glanced over his shoulder and exchanged a smile with his associate, before bringing his gaze around to me again. "These are not the conditions which will bring the labouring classes to their happily evolved state; what you have seen is but temporary and will soon be supplanted by exactly that which you have deemed necessary – a brighter future indeed awaits the workers here, literally so, and soon all others. Have you never heard the patriotic expression, that the sun never sets on the British Empire? It is an accurate observation; so numerous and far-flung are our Queen's colonies, that at any moment sunlight is pouring down on some region of them. The Elohim seek to take advantage of that fortuitous geographical circumstance, and have already put in place the devices that will enable them to do so. What you have observed here is but the merest tip of the iceberg, so to speak. An elabourate system of mirror-lined tunnels have been constructed beneath the surface of the earth, by which sunlight is funnelled to this subterranean factory here in England – sunlight that is gathered by vast acres of focused lenses in distant locales such as India and Burma. Which of course is to the advantage of the inhabitants of those lands; in the Elohim's grand scheme, they will find no better employment than as tenders of these enormous light farms. So they would benefit as much as our own native Englishmen."

"The residents of those colonies might have other things they would prefer to do."

"Pooh." Jamford airily dismissed all such concerns. "Petty human desires are not to be allowed to stand in the way of the glorious and profitably evolved future that the Elohim have envisioned for mankind. There is such a thing as happiness, though you seem to have had little experience of it; if our present machines cannot grant it to us, then we must build even greater ones, that will be able to."

"Enough–" I raised my hand to forfend any further lunatical verbiage. "You have no need to attempt to convince me of the wonderfulness of these plans – for you cannot do so. What does it matter if I or anyone else cannot stop you, and these mad associates of yours, from driving such schemes upon the heads of those who most deserve to be simply left alone? All will come to ruin, as I have seen similar enterprises founder upon the rocks of an unforgiving reality. You think that your ambitions will overcome all difficulties; instead, they will be the engines of your utter defeat, as rigid in their operation as the mere iron machines you already believe that you command, but which order your thoughts about like the most imperious martinet."

"Bravo! Bravo, Mr Dower!" With evident delight, Jamford clapped his hands together. "It should not have been *I* who went about impersonating a fire-and-brimstone evangelical type, the better to conduct my surreptitious activities in the world above – you display a natural gift for such performance, that I could never match. You bring a genuine-seeming passion to your words – one might almost think that you believe them."

"Mock me if you wish; I am beyond caring. You have told me a great many things, all of which I would rather have not heard – but there is one thing you have not told me. There was some purpose in bringing me here; I would wish to know it."

"The boy!" From the other side of the room, Weebsome cried out in a surfeit of excitement. "Your son! Why else?"

"Calm yourself–" Jamford's injunction was directed toward the other man; he then turned back to me. "That is indeed the reason, Mr Dower; your son. Who was at one time thought to be an orphan, of indeterminate parentage – but who assumed a much greater significance, to both the Elohim and the More Loving Embrace, when it was determined that you were his father."

"To my shame," I said, "that child was abandoned, his parentage a blank anonymity – though to what defence I can make for myself, I was not even aware of his existence. If I knew nothing of any connection between him and myself, how were you and your associates able to discover it?"

"There are times when the workings of the Universe resemble those devices created by your own illustrious and clever father – we might not yet know their purpose, but those gears are precisely machined, to produce a definite effect. Perhaps, Mr Dower, there really is a divine Providence taking an interest in human affairs, and which gives a gentle nudge to move those affairs in a direction of which it approves. No one, either myself or the Elohim or the More Loving Embrace, would have known anything that would have indicated that your son was other than one more orphan, of no consequence – except that a person familiar to you came prying about, expending considerable effort to locate him. A certain Scape was that persistent individual; I presume you recognize his name."

"I knew him – though how well I knew him, I now wonder."

"What do we know of anyone, until after they're dead… and even then. Nevertheless, it was his activities on behalf of your late wife Miss McThane, that revealed the boy's importance. So much else might never have happened – and you would have grown old and undisturbed, safe in your bed – if a mother simply had foregone wondering what had happened to her lost child. Strange, is it not?"

"Such speculations, I feel, are best left to those who have

some interest in these matters, whether for good or ill – I have no such. I confess my hardheartedness about the fate of my son; I made no promise to anyone regarding him. It has already been demonstrated to my utter satisfaction that he possesses some importance to you and these Elohim people, with their fantastic agenda for what they profess to be the improvement of mankind; the significance of the boy is further indicated by the strenuous efforts of the More Loving Embrace, including the dispatching of their agents to murder me, all to prevent my being brought into contact with the child. All this striving back and forth baffles me. You have my son; I hold no wish to have anything to do with him – why not exploit the poor lad in whatever suits your purposes, and allow me to go my way? It is your seizing upon me that puts my life in danger; leave me be, and the More Loving Embrace's lethal concern about my affairs would likely cease – or at least I would hope so."

"If only we could!" Such was Weebsome's dark muttering.

"Let me assure you," spoke Jamford, "that my desire would be to act upon your suggestion with all alacrity – but unfortunately, I am unable to do so. The Elohim as well – if it were possible for them to forget all about you, and proceed unobstructed with their plans, they would do so immediately. But there is another – a single person – who wishes this meeting between yourself and your child to take place. And this is a desire to which we must acquiesce."

"I am astonished." In deepest perplexity, I stared back at the Right Reverend Jamford. "Enormous engines of conspiracy, set into motion and funded by what would seem to be the richest and most powerful forces in the land – and they are all frustrated by the desire of one person? Who on earth could it be?"

"The child himself; your son." Jamford's voice was tinged with the greatest import. "He calls the tune, to which we must dance."

"This is preposterous!" My gaze became even more wide-eyed. "How could such possibly be? He is an orphan, friendless and alone, with no more resources to call upon than a homeless dog attempting to shelter itself in a barn, from all the rain of miseries that lashes down upon him. *This* is the impediment to your grand schemes, that somehow requires my forced coöperation as well? You might as well say that an elephant of the Punjab is stymied by a pebble in the road, which he should be able to step over with no more effort than placing one colossal foot in front of another."

"Logically, it would seem so – and in a more logical world, such would be the case. But we live in this world, Mr Dower, and not in that other one. So we must proceed along the course into which we are compelled – and perhaps sooner rather than later. Are you sufficiently refreshed? I would have been delighted to give you more time for rest, as I am aware that you have endured quite a few incidents of an exhausting nature – but I fear that I must be a ruder host than I would otherwise have wished, and make some demands upon you."

"You are taking me to see my son? He is here?"

"Within a short distance," replied Jamford. "But yes, that is what needs to be done. I would hope you would have no objection – but in truth, it matters little if you do."

I was struck silent, gazing at the empty plate on the table before me, as if the crumbs there had been arranged into some decipherable omen. My feelings were as those of someone who had been snatched up by a tremendous whirlwind, spun across unreeling landscapes by energies beyond either his control or understanding, then deposited at last in a locale of unknown meaning – or worse, meaning that was soon to be revealed, whether I wished it to be or not. So much had happened to bring me to this point! To have set so much in motion, at the behest of a mere child – what could he want from me? I had forgotten about him, and been ready to force him from my mind forever – why couldn't he have the courtesy to do the same?

"No protest would suffice," I spoke aloud, "to forestall this meeting?"

"None. It is beyond your power to decide."

"Very well, then." I brushed off my hands, and stood up from where I had been sitting. My bones and flesh still ached – I was certain that every inch of skin was a map of purpling bruises – but I had recovered sufficient strength to perform the functions to which I was commanded. "*If it were done when 'tis done, then 'twere well it were done quickly,* as a Scottish lady is supposed to have said once." My literary references were an attempt to maintain a philosophical state of mind, one of stoic resignation. "Take me to him."

"This way, if you would be so kind…" Weebsome's words were delivered in a snide tone, as if he were taking some pleasure in seeing me compelled against my own wishes. He had stepped over from the desk at the side of the room, and to a position near the divan, so that with a slight bow of his head and a sweeping motion of one hand he could direct me toward the chamber's door. "This journey will only require a moment – much less tedious, I am sure, than your other recent excursions."

I ignored him as he continued in front of me, and drew open the door. Dismayingly, a flood of mechanical noise washed over us as he did so, made even more unpleasant by the roiling glow from the furnaces beyond; the dreadful prospect of having to make our way across the factory floor was one that I had not anticipated.

"Steel yourself, if you must." Jamford spoke from directly behind me. "As I previously indicated, it is but a short way to go."

Having no choice in the matter, I prepared to follow Weebsome out from the chamber, when he suddenly lurched back against me, with sufficient force to almost stagger me from my feet. With head thrown back, his body started to slide down across mine; I instinctively grasped hold of him, keeping him from dropping entirely at my feet. Thus I saw the cause of this collapse; looking over his shoulder, I spotted a hole in the centre of his chest, made more prominent by the blood leaking from it.

A shot had been fired, the industrial clamour masking its report – this much as well was immediately obvious to me. I took what evasion I could, to prevent myself from being the target of whatever assassin was there; throwing Weebsome's lifeless body from me, I dove to the floor, my shoulder striking the carved jamb beside me.

Taken by surprise, Jamford did not follow my example; my actions left him exposed just within the chamber. Looking up, I saw him stumble backward, a spatter of blood alongside his cravat. His uncomprehending eyes rolled upward, and then he dropped like a stone.

I could see no chance for escape; I drew back as a figure strode past, his torso darkly silhouetted by the glare behind him, the rifle dangling in his grip. Still dazed, I watched as the person used the weapon's muzzle to reach down and prod Weebsome's corpse; satisfied of the man's demise, the assailant stepped over me and did the same investigation on Jamford's unmoving remains.

"Fine, that is–" Spivvem glanced back over his shoulder at me, showing one of his characteristic lopsided smiles. "Double-crossers – do despise 'em."

FOURTEEN

Mr Dower is Further Appalled

EE THIS? BLUIDY HUGE, it is." Spivvem laid a hand on the riveted flank of the apparatus before us. "Do powerful amount damage, had mind to."

"Please – leave it be." I reinforced my plea by grasping his arm, and making what token attempt I could to drag him away. All about us, the din of this hellish subterranean factory continued to pound away, near deafening; either of us had to shout at the top of our lungs, to make ourselves heard at all. "We have other business to attend – you told me as much."

It was not just the urgency of those affairs that prompted my words; I could see him eyeing a bank of controls, a series of knobs and dials, and levers so big it would take both hands and all of a man's strength to shift them from one adjustment to another. With his propensity for tampering with disastrous effect, I feared his acting upon another such mischievous impulse.

"Know what is?" He glanced over his shoulder at me, the glint in his eye so demented as to increase my anxiety even further. "Do you?"

"For God's sake, man – I do not even wish to know." Clouds of steam cascaded by us, with an unnerving resemblance to those others through which we had passed with frightful velocity, when I had been marooned with him on that aerial cemetery, disintegrating even as it had shot across the sky toward London. "You were telling me…" I gasped for breath, stifled by the factory's heat. "Important things… concentrate on those instead…"

As best I could determine, we were in the centre of that industrial landscape, far beneath the earth's surface. Spivvem had led me to this point, once he had assured himself that there would be no further interference from Jamford or his associate Weebsome; he had tossed aside the rifle as being an impediment of no further use.

"Took off last of those bluidy assassins been following you about." That was how he described his acquisition of the weapon. "Won't have worry about any them, no more."

With those few clues, I had made my own surmise as to what had happened. Spivvem's shouted warning had saved me from a bullet launched by that final agent of the More Loving Embrace, though I might well have been killed in the subsequent collapse of the rocky tunnel opening in which I had stood. Unaware at that time of my fate, Spivvem had then confronted the assailant, and fatally bested him, likely with the rifle that he had snatched away from the other's hands. Making his way to the floor of the subterranean factory – a locale with which Spivvem was evidently familiar – he had then determined that I was in the hands of the Right Reverend Jamford, and had lain in wait for us to emerge from that chamber in which we had been conversing.

That Spivvem did not immediately take some vengeance upon me, after he had dispatched both Jamford and Weebsome, was not something I found entirely surprising. Much there was about him of a calculated and deliberate nature, however the degree he flaunted his disturbing eccentricities; he still had his own agenda to pursue, and I was of use to him in that regard. And – he indicated as much – he could not fault me for having tried to escape; he would have done as much if our situations had been somehow reversed.

"Damn me," he had said, after returning from inside the chamber. "Bastard's crawled away." Looking past him, I had seen that there was a smeared trail of blood across the floor, but otherwise no sign of Jamford. "Have to track down at my leisure – 'magine won't get far. Had agreement with him, but he welshed on – do hate being cheated, so will make sure good and dead. But no time for that now; we've urgencies, you and I, so let's be off."

Standing at the door of the chamber, with Weebsome's body lying halfway out, I had then inquired as to what exactly it was that Spivvem wished to do, and had received the answer that he meant to take me to my son, just as Jamford had wanted.

"I would rather not–"

"And rather not wring your bluidy neck," Spivvem had responded. "But will."

Thus our traversing the factory, through all its grinding clamour and wilting heat; wherever it was that my son was waiting, it was apparently at some point directly across from the luxurious chamber in which Jamford had received me. Passing the varied engines and machines, and the sooty human figures scurrying in attendance upon them, too intent upon their labours to even register notice of any intruders, we came to what I estimated to be the centre of the space. It was here that Spivvem had halted, expressing his admiration for the controls that were arrayed before us.

"What is–"

He ignored my protests, and continued eyeing the machinery with a keen avidity. "Regulates entire bluidy place, all its functions, from one end to other. Everything all interconnected, just way Jamford and his pals would like." He laid his hand upon the largest of the levers, protruding vertically from a wide slot in the floor, and caressed its steam-damp metal. "Want all sped up? Push *that* way–" He mimed shoving the lever forward, without actually altering its current position. "Slow down bit? Give all these poor bastards a break? Just ease back – like this." He peered down the row of controls, the various dials and only slightly smaller levers. "Know that much; what these others do – be lovely to find out."

"My son–" I shouted at Spivvem, hoping to distract him from the machinery. "You said you were taking me to him. Should we not be on our way?"

"Worried?" His smiling glance fastened upon me. "Needn't be – just cautious as always am."

I could have made an acerbic retort to that claim, but I refrained instead, not wishing to goad him into any demonstration; his history with such devices was not of the most reassuring.

"Onward, then…" To my relief, he drew his hand away from the prodigious lever, and strode into the factory's complicated depths again, looking over his shoulder as he went. "Haste, will you?"

At last, we came to the cavernous space's perimeter, the noise and heat from the engines and boilers diminishing behind us, though only slightly.

"Here we are," announced Spivvem, halting before a doorway distinguished only by the iron plate bolted across its surface, and a padlock the size of a man's doubled fists dangling from the hasp at its edge. "Soon enow, have your family reunion."

Extracting a small leather pouch from inside his jacket, he extracted a set of tools, rather similar to those a surgeon might employ. He bent down and commenced work upon the lock; within the span of a few moments, it dangled loose. Restoring the tools to their pouch, he pulled off the lock and tossed it aside; it landed with a heavy clunk on the grated metal floor, a yard or so away.

"After you–" With mock gentility, Spivvem waved me forward. "No fear; be right behind."

I hesitated a moment; I could see nothing but a lightless interior before me.

"Go on – after all's happened, 'fraid now?"

Thus prodded, I stepped inside. The darkness was alleviated by the snap of a safety match, which Spivvem applied to the wick of a lantern – he was as apparently familiar with this space, whatever it was, as with the close-set pathways of the factory through which we had just crossed.

An eerie sight met my eyes, in the pallid glow that had been produced. Rows of beds, of cheap and nasty construction, little more than buckling planks nailed to posts of raw and splintering lumber – they stretched out into the wavering shadows, to such a distance that I could not make out the farthest of them. There were two oddities about the beds; the first was that they were all of a size too diminished to accommodate the average adult body.

The second was – and it took some close study on my part, bending my head down low, to perceive this – that they were occupied by motionless figures, covered by ragged blankets.

Children; sad, small creatures, so thin and underfed as to resemble old men, so pale as to almost provide their own illumination in the darkened room. Some lay curled on their sides, others on their backs, fragile papyrus eyelids brushing their lashes against their hunger-sharpened cheekbones.

"Who…" I straightened from the side of the bed over which I had leaned. "Who are these?"

"Who d'you 'magine they are?" Spivvem was not smiling now. "Guess, if can."

"They must be the orphans – that the Elohim took." Appalled, I turned and gazed around myself; there were too many to count, if I wanted to. "Scape told me about what happened; that the Elohim scoured through all the orphanages and shelters of North England and Scotland, rounded up the children they found there, and went away with them... to someplace unknown. But now I see... that place was here."

"Done well, Dower; keen mind you have – and almost correct, too. Need look closer, though, and tell what find."

That Spivvem was hinting at some darker circumstance, I felt certain; it was with only the greatest reluctance that I again scrutinized the child in the bed I stood beside. A boy, perhaps ten years of age – though of course this was hard to determine, given the dim lighting provided by the lantern Spivvem held, and the underdevelopment of the child's physique, due to the scanty fare upon which he had been forced to subsist. I brought my fingertips down gently to the child's brow–

Which was icy cold.

I snatched back my hand, as though I had laid it on a hot stove instead. Startled, I peered closer at the boy.

"This child is dead!" My conclusion was affirmed by the absence of any breath from the boy's parted lips, or any motion of a pulse in his scrawny chest. A terrible surmise gripped me; I quickly went from that bedside to the next, and then the one beyond – and saw the same in them. "Why... they are all dead."

"So they are – in sort of way." Spivvem stepped next to me. "Look closer still, and see what meant."

Holding the lantern aloft, with his other hand Spivvem drew back the thin cover over one of the orphans, then parted the ragged shirt beneath. What was revealed there, to my widened stare, was the child's naked chest – or rather, what remained of it. Where pallid, unsunned skin should have been, was instead intricately crafted metal, the gears and springs of what had been implanted to replace the lungs and heart, and perhaps further portions of what had been the softer and more fragile organic nature of this diminutive form.

"What abomination is this?" I propelled myself back from what I had just glimpsed, so violently that I nearly dislodged the lantern from Spivvem's upraised hand. "What fiend would have so grotesquely murdered this unfortunate child?"

"Calm yourself. Not murdered – but sleeps. As they all do." Spivvem held the lantern out before himself, illuminating a greater portion of the room. "See yourself."

My initial horror had abated, so that I was able to confirm that the children, all of whom I had presumed lifeless, had had the same mechanical disfigurement performed upon them. I drew back the cover over the last of them that I inspected, and turned back toward my companion.

"But you say that they are *not* dead?" I frowned, as dreadful conjectures filled my thoughts. "What kind of sleep is this, then? Can they be woken?"

"'Course they could – if get machines in 'em running."

A memory rose to the surface of my thoughts, from long ago in my life; within myself I viewed again that moment when the construction known as the Paganinicon, one of my father's most artful achievements, had drawn back its elegant dress shirt and exposed the workings inside its chest, that propelled its every human-like motion. That had been a startling revelation, for which I had been ill-prepared, not yet knowing the extent of my progenitor's creativity. But to be sure, it had been a moment less horrifying than this – for it is one thing to see a machine become so much like a human being, and quite another to witness specimens of humanity such as these orphaned children become more like machines, if only in part.

"You say *if* – if these mechanical portions could be set into operation." I pressed the question upon Spivvem. "Is there some impediment to that happening?"

"Somewhat," he allowed. "Machines actually be working right now, to degree, even as palavering about 'em. If were to put ear down close, would hear a bit of whirring and ticking; that's enough to keep blood moving 'bout, and certain other bodily functions, so that general decay not set in. But more'n that, so as these sprats would open eyes, talk and jump like living children – really living ones – that'd be problem, all right."

"Why would that be? These are my father's devices, are they not, that have been surgically implanted in these unlucky orphans?" Another nightmarish recollection came to me, or rather a series of them – all the times when I had discovered that yet another machine, of malignant purpose, had come from the hand of that person, of whom I had so little knowledge other than through this unwanted legacy. "Surely if those responsible for this were able to determine these machines' operation, so as to set them functioning to this degree, then they should have been able to resolve any other mysteries about them."

"They have that, indeed." Spivvem tilted his head to one side, with a knowing expression. "But to know what be involved, not same being able to do. Set yourself; I'll explain."

He placed the lamp on the bare floor between us, as he sat down on the corner of one of the beds. Gingerly – though I knew I could not disturb its occupant – I did the same on the bed opposite.

"Take it," said Spivvem, "that old Jamford fed you line about *evolution* and *adaptation*, and lot other codswallop besides, and how that Elohim bunch just want make all the workers happy in future, *yadda yadda yadda*, as old friend Scape would've said. Am correct?"

"I did hear quite a bit about that. Frankly, it all seemed a bit far-fetched to me."

"Too right. As if those bluidy industrialists, folk with all the money, could care farthing's worth about what employees are feeling. Rather like imagining when wolf's feasting, it's wondering whether lamb's enjoying the process. Glad shot that bastard; can't bide hypocrites of sort – give decent thieves and swindlers such as self bad name, they do. All that claptrap – importing sunlight from fookin' Burma, for God's sake – nothing but front, bit of song-and-dance to make tender-hearted folk feel better, all while boots are planted on others' necks. See poor children here?" Spivvem gestured about the room, with its silent and motionless tenants. "Really what fookin' Elohim up to. Ripping out hearts, shoving in those devices your father invented – they've a whole workshop up by Hull, doing nothing but cranking out copies of ticking things, ready to go. Orphans nothing but ones come first, see if idea works at all – then can shove like into every mill-hand, work 'em to death, then work 'em some more *after* they're dead. What they feel, whether happy or rebellious or whatever, hardly matters when machine you've got in place of guts tells you what to do! Which it can, 'course, with flick of switch. So yes, come to think, maybe Jamford and his Elohim bunch aren't so much liars, after all – really *are* int'rested in evolving workers into something new; just that new thing is more like dependable, useful machines, and less like flesh-and-blood that's always moaning and complaining, and might come after bosses' throats someday."

"But if that is the Elohim's intention – and I do not doubt it; I put nothing past anyone's self-interested scheming – I fail to see its fruition here. If the devices created by my father have any fault, it is never that they fail in the function for which they were designed." I pointed to the form in the narrow cot on which I sat. "Why isn't this child up and about, and all the others here, set to work and performing useful labour, impelled by what now ticks and whirs in their tiny frames? It would seem that there is enough found for them to do, in the vast factory beyond the door. Instead, they just lie here, neither dead or sleeping, but just as immobile."

"There's rub, indeed." Spivvem gave a nod of his head. "Father's devices are as you boast, just fine – nae amiss with them, oh no! But like so many that came from hand, need be triggered, set into operation by proper kind of shove – otherwise, might tick away like mantel clock, but useless as one without hands to tell the time."

I knew whereof he spoke. This aspect of my father's creations had been amply demonstrated to me long ago, when I had first encountered that demonic Paganinicon. Without the necessary triggering impulse, it had been nothing but a dumb mannequin, stuffed with purposeless gears and springs. But when its machinery had been set into motion, it more than exceeded an imitation of human activity, being able to play upon the violin in the superlative manner of its namesake, and wreak seductive effect upon the fairer members of our species. Of course, it had been entirely to my chagrin and horror to have discovered that I myself was the trigger for the Paganinicon to spring fully into its artificial life, and begin its rampage through the elegant salons of the British elite; the device created by my father held subtle elements within it, that were so finely tuned as to receive etheric vibrations, otherwise imperceptible by even the most sensitive register, that were exactly those radiated by my nerves and brain. No more had been required than to bring me into close proximity with that human-like machine, and all its ticking and whirring had leapt to a higher pitch, fully animating the thing and setting it upon its course.

"Was this, then, the actual purpose in bringing me here?" I addressed this urgent question to Spivvem before me. "And the presence of my son nothing more than a lure to accomplish that? If the hideous devices residing in the chests of these orphans are of the same nature as others that my father invented and assembled, then my being so close among them should have already triggered the machines, and animated their bearers into whatever activity would be compelled upon them. But I see no such response on their part; where is their driven waking?"

"Know all of what talking about," said Spivvem. "No mystery for me there. But you've some confusion – *you* are not the trigger for what seen. Trigger there is, just as happened with other crafty devices, but someone other than yourself."

"If not me, then who?"

"Your son, 'course. He's the necessary element, key sets all chiming and whirring as should. The elder Dower, your father – his genius had no bounds, seems. Could not only build machines that set into motion by vibrations from his own son – that'd be you – but could do as well, with some sprat hadn't even been born yet. Dead clever, that is. As to why he did… well, perhaps thought these devices we've here were bit too awful for him to bide, and so set 'em to be inoperable until long after own death. Nice for him; too bad for rest Humanity."

As ever, conjectures about my father served only to annoy me. The man would always remain an enigma to me, best left unexplored.

"You perplex me still…" After a moment's thought, I spoke again. "I have been led to believe, by you and others, that my son is already in the custody of the Elohim; they came into possession of him when they were about their general scouring of orphanages, bringing them *en masse* to this dreadful locale. And then, as I was also informed, they were elated to discover his true identity, having been alerted to it by Scape's quest for the particular child. So here is something I do not understand: if my son is the trigger necessary to set into full motion the devices sutured into these other children, and if the Elohim have my son – then why has that triggering not been accomplished? What reason would there be for any hesitation on the part of the Elohim?"

"Again, Dower, lack bit knowledge – there's diff'rence between sort of trigger that you've been, setting off certain of your father's devices, and sort your son is. And that is, you've no say about being trigger; those fine, mysterious vibrations you give off, to which those devices were tuned – radiate 'em whether want to or not, and there's end of matter. But the Elohim found out something else with your son; little bugger can *choose* whether his vibrations set anything off. If decides suits him, then happens; if not, then not. Good joke on Elohim, eh? Thought just be able to snap their fingers like, and boy'd get all the other orphans up and running – but bit of surprise they had; he's apparently stubborn sort, with mind of own. Figured out what deal was, that all depended on him, and told those bastards where could put it, if he didn't get what wanted in exchange."

"I believe I understand now – at last." There was no need for my companion to link together the last pieces of the puzzle. "What he wants is me; his father. He wants to see me."

"Should be flattered," said Spivvem. "Boy's got whip hand, might've asked anything at all; maybe even own freedom, after doing Elohim's bidding. But 'stead, asked for just what you've said."

"But what does he want from such a meeting? What could I possibly do for him?"

"Who knows? Child's not same sort creature as men of the world, blokes like you and me. Still has some tender sensibilities, like – haven't been beaten out of him yet, as events of life tend to do. And 'course, knows nowt of you – such as stated pref'rence to leave him abandoned and friendless, rather than risk your own precious skin; very paternal and loving, that. Might think diff'rent, and harder, if knew – but as said, mere child, with great deal to learn way things are."

I lapsed into another bout of silent musing. That the

meeting between the two of us was inevitable, there seemed little doubt; Spivvem would effectively bar the door if I were to attempt to flee. And – I thought of this as well – why should I? What was being asked of me, that I should consider it onerous? A child – very well then, my own son – who, for his own foolish and childish reasons, wished to come face-to-face with he who had sired him, then as quickly abandoned him; would he fling some tearful accusation in my face? He well might, and be perfectly justified in doing so; at one time, my neglect at least had the excuse of ignorance, my having been unaware of his existence. But I had learned of him since then, and the knowledge had provoked no fatherly concern on my part, but only – as Spivvem had pointed out – a craven anxiety for keeping my own hide in one piece.

So, likely the confrontation would be an uncomfortable one, complete with recriminations and childish weeping, and no response but guilty silence on my part; did that matter? It had been a lengthy while since I had entertained anything but the lowest opinion of myself – would a child's words be able to send me farther into the pit of my own disdain?

And what about the child himself – was he any less self-absorbed than I? Did he put anyone's interests before his own? Once his selfish demand was met, and he had his meeting with his father, then what? The Elohim, having given him that for which he asked, would then insist upon having his side of their bargain completed – would he balk at having his fellow orphans, those poor creatures with whom he would seem to have the most in common, transformed into clacking, labouring automatons by his triggering of the devices planted in their chests, or would he comply? Granted, a child cannot be held to the same ethical standards as an adult, by which I judged myself a moral failure, but surely his sin would be of more grievous effect, and harm greater numbers, than any of which I was guilty.

"D'ye have more questions? Or know enow?"

I withdrew myself from these bleak musings, and gazed upon my tormentor Spivvem. His canted smile was a slight thing this time, but still evident, as though he were in some measure relishing my discomfort.

"And what," I asked, "is your recompense for bringing about this event? You indicated that Jamford had double-crossed you; am I correct in assuming that at one time the both of you, and that repulsive individual Weebsome as well, were acting on behalf of the Elohim? And that you were doing so in order to bring about that which would enable them to advance their loathsome designs upon the labouring classes? Not that appalling bright Future which Jamford rhapsodized to me about, but an even worse one, made possible by my own father's creations?"

"Don't get so worked up 'bout it. Let's just say, have my agenda – being on no one's side but own, that is."

"Trust me–" My voice turned even more bitter. "I never assumed otherwise. And which would make you no different from the general run of Mankind."

"Oh?" Spivvem raised an eyebrow. "And yourself?"

"I am among the worst of them, in that regard."

"What pity, then – feel bit sorry for your boy, having self-confessed wretch like you for father. Maybe if he'd been aware, would've asked meet somebody else, someone altogether more personable. Be as may – his lookout, sorry little bastard. Shall get on with it?"

"Do I have a choice?"

"Not really, no."

"And when I am done with this meeting..." I wanted to make my stipulations as clearly as possible. "When I have heard the child say whatever it is he wishes to impart to me, and I have made whatever reply of which I am capable; when he is surely sadder for having made his long-delayed acquaintance with his father, and I am no happier for having seen his face; when I have done my part to make the World and the Future an even more wretched place and time, enabling the conspirators known as the Elohim to advance their plans against Humanity, by granting my son's wish; when I have done all of that – then am I free to go?"

"But 'course – completely unmolested." Spivvem gave an emphatic nod. "Even the More Loving Embrace likely forget all 'bout you; they be more pragmatic than vengeful, and nothing to be gained by killing you now. So free crawl back into hole, as you like."

"Then let it be over." I stood up from the corner of the bed. "Is he here?"

"Close by." Spivvem pointed toward the darkness which the lamp's yellow glow did not penetrate. "Has own little room, befitting his status – nothing grand, 'course, but palatial compared to anything else he's likely known." Rising to his feet, he gestured for me to follow. "This way."

We walked far enough, past rows of other small beds with motionless and unbreathing figures beneath the thin blankets, until the clamour of the factory outside faded to a murmur.

"Here go–" Spivvem pushed open a bare wooden door. "Leave you be – 'magine it's a private moment for both."

I did not know, or care, if he was mocking me, as I stood in the narrow doorway. The spartan chamber beyond was illuminated by its own flickering lantern, dangling from a hook in the ceiling. I saw there was a bed, empty; a rickety table; a stool...

Upon that last sat a small figure, upon his knees a book almost wider than his shoulders. He looked up from the volume, and at me.

"I knew it..." A smile showed on his face. "I knew you'd come."

FIFTEEN

Mr Dower Meets His Fate

SITTING ON THE FLOOR, I was able to look the boy straight in the eye.

"Not quite sure..." Such was his answer, when I asked him what was his name. "There was something they called me, back a long time ago – before they brought us all here – but it was same as they called everyone... and it wasn't very nice. So no great loss, is it?"

"I suppose not."

Leaning forward from where I had sat myself on the room's small bed, I had been able to gain a closer study of the child. He appeared of indeterminate age – the way those starved of nourishment, both material and emotional, often do – with diminutive stature, bones frail as a bird's. His eyes seemed disturbingly large and perceptive, as though they alone were of the proper size, having seen sadder things than most, and more of them – sufficiently so, that they no longer wept but only watched.

By the simplest of reckoning, the mere counting up of years from his birth to this day, he should have been of larger and sturdier configuration – and he might well have seemed a lad about to enter upon those brief and rowdy years that precede the entry to manhood, had a due share of sunlight been allowed to fall upon him. But the lack of same had withered him like a potted houseplant left forgotten upon some unlit kitchen shelf, spindly and tenuous. So that now he was the very semblance of those ragged paupers glimpsed in London's darkest tenements, all vigour excised, caught in some frail state between infancy and senescence.

Even in this dim chamber, I could see that he had inherited his features from his mother. Fortunate for him, as he was rendered handsome, even beautiful, thereby – or would have been if his cheeks were not so pale and hollowed. Unfortunate for me, as this reminder of my lost Miss McThane stabbed me through the heart.

I am certain the boy did not realize how completely he tortured me, when he laid aside the book with which he had been idling time away – I saw that it was a battered old geographical atlas, half its pages torn or missing, and the remainder filled with vast blank areas labelled Terra Incognita – then got up from the stool and wrapped his thin arms about my shoulders. Seeing him upright, and measured against myself, I could only think that he should have been so much taller than he was now; but the cruel world's scorn, and my shameful ignorance of even his existence, had given the result which trembled against my chest for a moment.

"Are you... treated well here?" I could think of nothing else to say; this would have been an awkward situation for anyone more emotionally facile than myself – which is to say, for virtually all of Humanity; for one as stitched-up and inexpressive as myself, it was close to impossible. "Do you receive..." I made a pointless, wavering gesture with both my hands. "Enough to eat?"

"Ever so well, thank you." The child had an odd grace about him, no doubt inherited from his mother as well. I had been expecting bitter accusations to be flung in my face, all the language of loss and abandonment, but instead he had returned to the stool as before, but now with his legs drawn up and matchstick arms laid across his knees, peering avidly at me as though wishing to memorize every detail of the wretched father across from him. "And a lot more than when I was in that other place–" He flung a hand out, gesturing in no particular direction, but obviously meant to indicate whatever orphanage in Glasgow from which he had been taken. "So that be one of the good things here."

"And the bad?" I was unable to keep from torturing myself; with every word I spoke, I felt a sharpened pang against my heart. "Do they mistreat you?"

"Not of late," he replied with an impassionate frankness. "And even before – I mean, before they knew who I am, and that you be my father – they weren't so horrible. Not like the other place; they seemed very cruel, and most every day. No…" He looked up to a corner of the room, gathering his thoughts, then back to me. "The only thing… it's been lonely. All my friends – the other children – then at least I had someone to talk with. But now–" He pointed to the door, and all the silent spaces that lay beyond it. "They be just asleep, all the time. Not dead, I know – the old man, the one with the white hair, he told me that – but they might as well be, for all the playing that's in them now."

I supposed the man to whom the boy referred was the Right Reverend Jamford; no telling what other conversation might have gone on between the two of them. No doubt Jamford, with all his wiles and threats, had done everything he could to cajole the boy into doing his bidding, and by a simple act of will trigger the devices stitched into the orphans' chests, and set them about their labours, as the Elohim wished all mankind to be bound. But the stubborn child – that quality being one more thing he had inherited from his mother – had maintained his simple wish, like a storm-wracked sailor clinging to a spar, stolid as only children can be against all the grown world's fur...

And he had prevailed in that – such a deal of fuss he had, unknowing, caused! – and now here I was. Just as though that great teacher had spoken truly, when he had said that unalloyed faith could impel a mountain to rise up and throw itself into the sea, if one commanded it to.

"I am afraid..." I roused myself from the thoughts into which I had descended. "There is not much I can do for you, regarding companionship – though perhaps, when you have resurrected the other children as that old man wishes you to, one or more might be given an hour once in a while, to spend with you; it is worth asking him about. Though I do not know how much amusement you would derive from such an arrangement; I have encountered some very clever machines, who could act just like folk made of flesh and blood – I rather suspect the orphans sleeping here now, when awake would be more like things of iron and brass, ticking and whirring rather than breathing and... playing. For that is meant for them, by some powerful and determined people; and when it comes about, you should not blame yourself if the other children are no better company than a clock would be."

"I know." The boy nodded, unsmiling. "Seems very hard, though."

"Life is often so."

"Feel very sorry of them – it's not just hard, but so unfair!" He was still young enough to be outraged by Fate, despite his own experience of it. "Why be I so lucky, and go from this place, and be up in the sunlight and all – the real sunlight, not all that stuff brung here by the old man's mirrors and things – and they have to stay here? If life was fair, then they could come with us. But I didn't say that was what I wanted; I didn't make it part of the deal I struck. I was afraid – and I'm ashamed to say so – that it'd be miracle enough to get what I did; I mean, what with you coming for me, and all."

"Coming for you? I am not sure I understand what you mean by that."

"Well, it's what you've done, isn't it?" The boy brightened a bit, sitting straight upright on the stool. "You wouldn't have made your way here – must've been so dangerous for you! – if you weren't planning on taking me with you. But you are here, and I'm ready to leave now." Eyes gleaming, he leaned toward me. "Where is it we're going? I've wondered and wondered..." With his foot, he nudged the volume of maps that had slid onto the floor beside him. "There seem to be so many places it might be."

"Is this something you talked about with... the old man? The one with the white hair?" Within myself, I was cursing Jamford for having intimated nothing like this to me. "Did he tell you that you would be going from here, in my care?"

"Well... no..." Apprehension flickered in the boy's eyes. "But it's true, isn't it? It has to be! That's the way it was, back there." He flung his hand out again, as his words tumbled more rapidly in his high-pitched voice. "At the orphanage, where they found us all, and then they brought us here. But before that, there were times – not many, but often enough – when somebody else came for one of us – but just one, because they were his mother and father. Maybe they'd given him up because they couldn't take care of him, but maybe things changed, and there was luck and money, and they came for him and he went away with them – to be in their home, just the way things are supposed to be. And he'd be so happy, happy to be leaving that place, and we all tried to be happy for him, but mostly we just cried, because it was him and not us – it wasn't *me*."

What was I to tell him? He had imagined events, happy ones for himself and – no doubt he had thought so – for me as well. In his childish mind, he had built a castle of them, in which he had managed to live, no matter how dark the clouds mounting about him, no matter how securely riveted and bolted the iron machinery assembled outside this small chamber. Perhaps it is not only the abandoned who do so, but all of Mankind – awaiting one who will come and claim us, while every day we come that much closer to the final realization that no such saviour exists.

Which is what I had to inform this child now, that I was not such a one, either.

"Oh." His disappointment was evident, after I had informed him that when I left this place, it would be by myself. The self-constructed edifice within him had been swiftly laid to ruin. For a moment, his gaze travelled down to the book lying open on the floor, and to its map of lands beyond imagination; then he looked back up at me. "Are you sure?"

"It is not my choice to make," I spoke quietly. I am not wilfully cruel, though I would readily admit that my heart is calloused beyond redemption; I did not relish telling him of his fate. "It is nothing given to me, to be sure or doubtful of. There are people who would not let you leave here – not the old man; you do not need to be concerned about him now. But his associates; that is who I mean – they still remain. You are of considerable value to them, but only if you remain in this place, to do that which they desire you to do. The children there?" I pointed to the door, closed upon the narrow beds beyond. "When you wake them, as you alone are able to do – that is not the end of what shall be required. There will be a great many more, and not just children; grown men and women as well. All with the same mechanical innards, all clacking away, all labouring to their deaths and then even beyond. A day might come when you are not needed to set them on their courses, when another key to those devices will be found – but that day is a long way off; I cannot see it ahead." I nodded slowly, feeling exactly as that sort of wretch that any man feels like, when he must tell the truth to another. "If I were to try to leave here with you holding my hand, to mount up again to the sunlight with you – it would not be worth my life to try and do that. I have a bargain in place, which if honoured, allows me to remove myself; it does not include you."

He said nothing then. I would have preferred tears, a heart-struck wailing of grief – or better, scathing imprecations hurled at my face, a piping voice like a whiplash, the condemnation of the whole traitorous world, of which I was its chief representative. If nothing else, there would have been a certain functional economy of effect, his wrath and justified hatred sparing me the effort of loathing myself. For one might ask, *What is worse than a child's entreaty?* And the answer is – one knows it already – the silence that follows, when he has realized at last, as he inevitably must, that you are the same as all the others.

If a tear had fallen, as he looked away from me and down at the faded atlas pages, that might have allowed me an atom of pardon from my own damning regard, as it would have indicated that there was still something inside him that could hope and could be disappointed. But he remained dry-eyed; perhaps he had known all along, that my words would be the ones I had just spoken.

"My mother…"

Something he wanted to know, a question he wished to ask; I could imagine any number of them. Perhaps he was aware already, that it had been she who had sent someone looking for him – he could hardly imagine that it had been any initiative of mine.

What that enquiry was – the child might have wanted to know if she was alive or dead; who would have informed of that much?, or what she looked like, or what if anything she had ever said about him – I did not discover. Before he could say anything further, the little room's floor heaved and buckled beneath our feet, with enough sudden violence to toss the child's slight weight from the toppled stool, and send him sprawling against the wall beside him.

That upheaval was accompanied by a deep groaning sound from below, as of the earth's fundaments being torn apart; at the same time, from beyond the door and the chambers outside came the raucous clatter of metal striking metal, the immense factory's structural girders wrenched from their sockets and cast in all directions like jackstraws. The hissing of released steam advanced to a roaring bellow, as though all the furnaces and valves had cried out as one.

"Stay here–" Having managed to precariously regain my feet, the seismic motions continuing beneath, I had bent down and grasped the child's delicate wrist, lifted him up – his weight seemed virtually nil – and deposited him on the bed, that seeming to be the safest place at the moment. "Do not move–"

My immediate suspicions as to the cause of the tumult were confirmed by merely pulling open the room's door, and finding that Spivvem was not on the other side of it. When I had gone in to have this long-delayed meeting with my son, I had assumed that Spivvem would avail himself of the opportunity to eavesdrop upon whatever passed between the two of us – a person of his wiles is ever eager to obtain information that might be of future use. But his absence from that spot indicated that he had a different agenda, and one of greater urgency to him.

I ran past the rows of unmoving orphans, many of them tossed onto the floor, limbs sprawled and pale as those of glazed china dolls. Glaring light, brighter than I had witnessed before in this subterranean environment, struck my face with so much heat that I needed to shield myself with an upraised arm.

All was chaos when I stepped out onto the grated iron floor, and immediately perceptible as such, despite the blinding luminance. Entire sections of machinery, originally reaching far above the heads of its tending labourers, had fallen onto their sides; with supporting girders twisted and bent, the giant cogged wheels and gears had sprung from their axles, the sharp-edged teeth gouging out ragged trenches before tilting to a halt. Some of the human figures in the midst of the wreckage had managed to secure a measure of temporary safety for themselves, huddling beneath bent flanks of iron; others had not been so fortunate, lying crushed under vast weights of dislocated metal.

These ruined forces of industry were so close to me that I might easily have reached out and lain my hand on one of the heated pillars, its loosened rivets dropping like coins near my boots. I contemplated retreat, back into whatever security might have been afforded in the chambers from which I had just emerged–

"Moment, there." Another's hand apprehended me, grasping tight upon my arm. "Should talk a bit."

Startled, I turned and saw the figure that had stepped forward from the shadows cast by the mounded wreckage. Tips of fire were reflected at the centre of Spivvem's eyes, making his off-kilter smile appear even more darkly insinuating.

"This–" I pointed with my free hand. "This is your doing! You've brought all this about–"

"If have, all for better – that's what I'd say, and 'spect you to agree." He pulled me closer to himself, so that his every word could be better understood. "Int'mated as much yourself, no fondness for place, nor for what these bluidy Elohim want bring about – so if with nudge of few levers, twist of dial or two, can bring it all crashing down, would've thought you'd be all the happier for it."

"But… you are on their side!" I stared uncomprehendingly at him. "Working for them, in their pay – that was why you forced me here. The meeting between myself and my son has been completed, just as the boy had wished – and now he was to fulfil his side of the bargain that he had struck with the Elohim, to animate the orphans with those hideous devices struck into their chests. But now you thwart their ambitions – there will be nothing remaining here but steaming scrap metal. What reason do you have for turning on them in such a decisive manner?"

"Hard turn on anyone," said Spivvem, "if never on their side. Which never was, but wanted 'em to think so. How else would've gotten their trust, and free run of this place, if they hadn't thought I'd been bought well enow, and doing exactly what they wanted? 'Course, meant had to actually get hold of you, drag you here and all – but now that's taken care of, free to do what I wanted from beginning, which was to shut 'em down good and proper, once and for all."

"I can scarce believe this of you–" I eyed him with a considerable degree of doubt in my mind. "You have gone to great lengths to convince me of your essential rascality and criminal-mindedness – and I still believe those to be the case. Yet now you endanger yourself by bringing the Elohim's schemes to such a catastrophic end – what would have inspired such a worthwhile deed, so uncharacteristic of one such as yourself?"

"*Worthwhile deed*–" Spivvem scoffed at the mere suggestion. "As if ever would do such a thing. Had me dead to rights with first assessment – I've no more wish to do Humanity a good turn, or ability along such lines, than could flap arms and fly. But need take the long view – my tribe and I make our livings by way of others' foolishness, so as we can thieve and swindle of 'em. How would we be able to go on doing such like, if people be bluidy machines? Trouble with those, can't be fooled, can't run a fine confidence game on 'em – machines, and people with machines stuck in their guts, they just go clanking on like clockwork, doing what been wound up to do. Sure, fine for those Elohim bastards, have all Mankind working way they want 'em – but what's left afterward, for decent crooks such as myself? Damn Elohim might well be right, people'd be happier if they were less like people and more like clocks and other ticking gadgets – but my kind would be left out in the cold, were that great change to happen. Sure, a few coins in hand now, for having delivered goods they wanted, but that'd be just about the final brass I'd ever pocket."

Against the din of the factory's machinery, goaded by the maladjustment of their controls into an increasing fury of self-destruction, Spivvem had been forced to shout the explication of his devious motives, though my ear had been but a few inches from his mouth. Nevertheless, he had made his meaning clear to me, and in an impassioned manner; the Future that I had glimpsed to my dismay, seemed equally appalling to him, though for different reasons. He and his kind were predators upon their neighbours, and unabashedly so; in that sense, he was like a tiger faced with the prospect of the herbivores upon which he dined being transformed to inedible iron – thus, Samson-like, he had brought the pillars of this industrial temple crashing down.

Or perhaps there was a simpler reason for the destruction he had just accomplished, and one that I had already observed in the man. When he and I had been up above the earth, racing over the British landscape on the aerial cemetery, I had glimpsed the delight he had taken in those misguided actions on his part, that had set the construction disintegrating about us – as I had noted before, there are those among us who relish chaos, the more explosive the better for their apocalyptic taste, even if it threatens their own lives; they prefer the fiery crash to the dull placidity of an uneventful old age. How wrong I had forced myself to be about him, when afterwards we had traversed this immense factory floor, and I had seen him gazing covetously at those very same levers and controls that now were bringing about the end of this construction – his hands had seemed to twitch with a barely restrained desire to lay hold of those workings and thrust them into a final and fatal disarrangement. I had been convinced, or at least had pretended to myself that I was, that a normal wish for self-preservation would keep him away from them; now I saw that I had been correct before about his true nature. What other men most feared, he ran toward with abandon.

"This? This be *nothing*–" As though able to read my thoughts, Spivvem had perceived the course of my mounting agitation. "Soon enow, see bluidy lot more–"

The dire promise of his words was fulfilled, immediately upon his speaking them. As the factory's machines continued battering themselves and each other, the violence of the spinning gears and thrusting pistons tore away whatever elements had previously restrained their motions. With those governors eliminated, the only possible result ensued, that of the vast interconnected assemblage transmitting a *crescendo* of shocks into the underlying earth. A quake of such magnitude as to make earlier upheavals seem like mere teacup-rattling tremors, of no consequence, lifted the ground below us; I fell backwards, saved from landing upon my back only by Spivvem's grasp of my arm.

Worse, the effects of that event did not fade, but rather multiplied; holding onto the other to maintain my balance, I witnessed shuddering forces swarm up the stone walls of the subterranean chamber, launching cascades of shattered boulders tumbling down upon the factory below.

"There!" Swept into a frightening state of excitement, Spivvem pointed upward with his free hand. "You see?"

It would have been impossible for me not to have, as the vaulting dome above us, that had been only excavated rock before, lit orange by the glow of the furnaces and boilers, was entirely transformed as I watched. Jagged cracks shot through the stones, as though lightning had been inverted to pitch black. The apertures widened, boulders breaking free of their moorings, and plummeting to the racketing chaos below. For a moment, the broken dome held in place, though its surface seemed a crumbling web – then gravity asserted itself, and the remaining pieces rained down with a shouting roar loud enough to stagger backward both Spivvem and myself.

Dust churned upward, its obscuring cloud filling the chamber; some of the factory's machines were silenced, their girdered forms buried beneath the rubble, but others still pumped and thrashed with futile but relentless energy. If any of the human creatures attending the devices had survived, there was no sign of them; the only mercy that might have been granted was that their annihilation had been swift and final.

Spivvem and I had been forced to press ourselves as far back as possible, to avoid a similar fate; stones and shards of lesser dimensions rolled within less than a yard from us. As a few last fragments came free from above and fell upon the mountain that had assembled with such speed at the centre of the factory, a cold wind surged through the space, parting the gritty cloud choking our lungs. The gale swirled about in the manner of a tropical hurricane, the air itself rising from the battered iron floor and up to the heights above.

That motion drew my own gaze upward, and with head tilted back I perceived an even more astonishing sight. Through the thinning dust, stars were visible, studded in the night sky. So massive had been the destruction unleashed by Spivvem's manipulation of the factory's controlling levers, that the enclosing subterranean chamber had been completely broken open, exposing its contents to the outside world.

If that had been all his mischief had accomplished, there might have been a measure of safety afforded us – but I could see that while the greatest damage might already have taken place, the process was still ongoing. The surrounding earth had been so jolted by the impact of the factory's unleashed fury, it was still collapsing, sending more boulders down the chamber's sides. Indeed, even as I watched with widened eyes, a particularly large fragment struck the ground nearby, then bounced like a child's toy, its violent motion only stilled when it struck the wall a short distance from us.

"You bloody fool–" I flung away Spivvem's grasp on my arm, so that I could turn toward him and hurl my words directly into his face. "I hope you're satisfied – there will be no escape this time; you have engineered our burial!"

"Ever stop complaining?" He shook his head in disgust. "All's so serious with you."

"Are you insane? I allowed myself to be dragged here–"

"Didn't have much choice about that."

"Nevertheless–" Rage fuelled my persistence. "I would have been more obdurate, if I had known that you not only wanted to bring about your own demise, but mine as well."

"*Demise…*" There was still so much noise from the plummeting rocks and the factory's mechanical agonies, that his muttered response was almost inaudible. "Overly dramatic, a bit."

"Do you not comprehend our situation? There is no way out of this place."

"Bosh. Always way out, if not blind and feeble-witted. Look–" Spivvem pointed with an outstretched hand. "Right *there*."

I followed his direction, but it was some moments before I could discern, through the clouds of smoke and dust, that one side of the chamber – once totally underground, but now more like a giant well or the type of steep-sided canyon an explorer might find in the American deserts – had remained relatively clear of the stony debris that had buried the centre and other reaches of the space. Something like a narrow trail ascended diagonally along that farther wall; whether it had existed before, and to what purpose, or whether it had been exposed by the quake that had so shaken the surroundings, that could not be determined. Equally unknowable was whether the fragile path continued all the way to the surface above, or whether it was blocked at some point along its way, rendering any escape impossible.

"Very well–" A spark of hope, so slight as to make it easily extinguished, flickered in my breast. "Then lead the way; I have no other option but to put my trust in you, however discouraging my previous experiences have been."

"'Pologies, Dower – be on your own." His skewed smile appeared again as he punched a fist to my shoulder. "I've more business take care of – see you topside, maybe. Or…" He glanced back at me as he started away. "Maybe not."

I was struck speechless by both his words and his departure. The latter was quickly achieved, as he strode with what seemed to be unnerving *sang-froid* into the very thick of the tumult that had engulfed the factory grounds, his silhouette outlined by the flames before him, then masked by the roiling clouds of steam and smoke. What his intent was, I could only imagine; the levers and controls, the disarraying of which had initiated the engulfing catastrophe, might still be accessible somewhere in the rubble – if so, he was hardly likely to reset them to a position lessening the forces he had unleashed; if anything, he would prod them to allow even greater destruction, such being the personal inclination he had already displayed.

Which meant that I had no time to spare, if I wished to save myself; the irony was not lost on me, that at those sad and desperate moments when I had most wished to cease living, I had ample leisure to bring that about – but when my future prospects were constricted to mere minutes, then the desire for survival was keenest.

Philosophy such as that would have to wait; instead, I swiftly calculated what seemed to be my best course for reaching that section of the enclosing walls, at which I could mount upon the questionable but only apparent path upward. To plunge into the centre of the space, as the now-vanished Spivvem had, and hope to cross directly to that distant point, epitomized self-destruction to my mind; whatever evasive skills I might possess would be quickly overwhelmed by the fires and crashing machinery still in furious and erratic operation. Far safer, I decided, to take the longer way around, sticking close to the space's circumference and edging past the sparking and smouldering rubble toward my destination.

With no certainty of achieving that result, I turned about – and was immediately struck by a sight that halted me in my tracks.

The boy – my son – stood in the doorway from which I had exited a few minutes ago. He had disobeyed my order to stay where I had left him, and had come seeking to discover what events had so disrupted this world.

I stood frozen, my gaze locked upon his. At the centre of his eyes, so large in his pallid face, reflected as though in mirrors, were the mounting flames behind me, that would soon overwhelm this space where we stood, only a few feet apart from each other.

Madness to think that I could take him with me – the path that I hoped to climb was so threadlike and narrow, that it would require all of my agility and dwindling strength to clamber over the barriers it so obviously held. To take a child along, even one as starved skinny as this, would doom us both to our deaths in this inferno.

Those were the bleak calculations that shot through my mind...

Our better natures, or at least those parts of which we are least ashamed, are revealed not by what we decide, but by those impulses that flare up on their own, unbidden.

But even that thought was left unheard within me. I reached forward and grabbed the child's hand, pulling him along with me as I raced toward that distant spot.

The account of our arduous progress, mounting toward the open night sky, one clawing handhold after another – those events were scoured from my senses even as they happened. All that I had anticipated became true; the boy and I were forced to make our way along a trail no wider at times than my own boot soles, sidling with our back to the rock wall, fingertips bloodied as we barely kept ourselves from toppling into the smoke-filled air. At other points, we had to crawl on hands and knees over boulders wedged before us – I would go first, attaining some precarious footing beyond, then reaching back to draw the child above the blockage and on against my chest. I held him tight, arms wrapped around his slender frame – but only for long enough to catch our breath before continuing onward.

That we could not rest, even for a minute, was made evident by what I could see when I foolishly directed my sight to what lay below us. My surmise as to Spivvem's intentions was proven by the increasing wrath made visible from our elevated position; the workings of the machinery did not cease because of the boulders that had struck them with such force, but rather increased in their violent slashing, the pistons like battering rams smashing into every object before them, either iron or stone, the monstrous gears spinning from their axles, teeth scything through all they encountered. And through all leapt the fires unleashed from the furnaces, sparks swirling high enough to sting our faces. Whether or not the factory's saboteur still lived – a doubtful prospect – it little mattered; if his last desire had been to unleash forces beyond imagining, he had more than accomplished his goal.

But we persisted, the boy and I. We had little choice otherwise; to halt would be to die–

And we reached a place at last, where our safety seemed assured. A widened plateau on the trail, large and level enough that we could both collapse lengthwise upon it, face-down in dirt and ash, our chests heaving to draw in the fresher and cooler air that drafted down onto us. The fires continued to rage below, but their lessened heat indicated that we had escaped the worst of the leaping flames.

Still panting, I rolled onto my shoulder and looked upward; the stars were now a vast field of pin-pricked light, in which the coiling tendrils of smoke drifted and were lost. We were still some yards away from the surface, but only a sloping section of the path remained before us, clear of any obstruction. I could see what appeared to be the shadowed outlines of headstones, knocked askew by the eruptive shocks far beneath the graves they marked; we were evidently close to emerging within the confines of the cemetery at Highgate.

There were witnesses to our travails, or at least the simulation of such. I could see other silhouettes, and in erratic, jerking motion. Enough detail was revealed by the radiance below, that I realized our desired terminus was encircled by those mechanical beasts that I had encountered on the day of my wife's second burial; the chaos erupting from the depths had further disordered their inner workings, sufficiently that they now seemed intent on battering themselves to pieces. The machines did so while wreathed in fire, their ragged sheaths ignited by the bright sparks swarming up from the pit. So fierce was the subterranean heat, that the nearest foliage had enkindled as well, darkly smouldering.

I was jarred by the impact of an object on the path just beyond me. Once again, I gazed into the blank visage of a giraffe; one glass eye was missing from its socket, and the other shattered. We had but a moment to recognize each other, before the disconnected head toppled over the path's edge, and disappeared below.

I took this momentary spectre as a good omen; to emerge amongst these hapless constructs, however violent their actions, could hardly present greater dangers than those from which we were so close to escaping.

"We have arrived–" They were the first words I spoke to the boy, the rigors of our climb and the noise from the pit eliminating the possibility of any others. "Look: you can see."

He made no reply; his eyes were shut, as though he were sleeping, and remained that way even after I knelt beside him, took his arm and gently rolled him onto his back.

"Not much further; I promise you." I gave his small frame a shake. "Better that we should first get clear, and then rest."

His eyelids fluttered, then opened; a tenuous smile wavered on his lips.

"That's... very nice." Voice but a whisper. "It looks... lovely."

"Is there something wrong?" I gazed down at him with mounting concern. "Come – get to your feet. It is only a little ways."

"You go on," the boy said softly. "I can't."

"What do you mean? Of course you can – you have managed this far, and it was much harder."

"Yes..." A little nod. "But now I've run down."

A terrible suspicion struck me. Hurriedly, I undid the buttons and parted his thin shirt. Where I had hoped to see nothing but his pallid skin, I saw instead a clockwork assemblage in place of his heart, similar but for a few details to the ones I had glimpsed in the chests of the unmoving orphans left far below. Thus I realized how dreadfully I had misconstrued all that Spivvem had related to me; when he had described how the Elohim had discovered that the boy was unique among the orphans, that he was the one who could set all those hideous devices running, and therefore deserving of special treatment – I had thought that meant he was spared the same surgical monstrosity as the other children had received.

Or… that was simply what I had wanted to believe.

"It's all right–" He caught the look of dismay in my eyes. "Just the same as the others – didn't you know?"

"But…" I could hear a slow ticking, and the faint whir of an unwinding mainspring. "But you're… moving. And alive…"

"Because I could get this one started," the boy said simply. "I could do that." A feeble hand raised and touched the side of his head. "I could just… make it happen. But the other ones – I wouldn't do those. No matter how the old man – the one with the white hair – no matter how he cursed me. I wouldn't do it – not 'less I saw you." The hand lightly came to rest on mine. "Now I have."

"Then what is the matter? You started up this device–" I nodded toward the machinery visible in his chest. "I know how that is done; but now – what is wrong?"

"Nothing," he said. "It's just the way it is. They told me – that it wouldn't run forever. And it's a little different from the rest, the ones that all the others had put in them – they told me it's what they called the master device. So it's like a clock – it needs to be wound up again. But that's very hard; you have to know how to do it."

"But you know how, do you not? After all… it is there inside you."

"No–" A shake of the boy's head. "Nobody ever showed me how."

An unspoken question hung in the silence between us, like

a ghost that all knew was there, but which nobody wished to acknowledge–

But you know, don't you? That was what he wanted to ask me. *Your father made this thing – so you must know all about it.*

He feared to ask me, though – because what he was sure of, was what the answer would be. Just as I was sure of the same.

I gazed down at the slowing machinery in his chest; already, in just the little time we had been talking, the slight noises of its operation, the click of meshing gears and whir of uncoiling springs, had become even less perceptible to the ear. That the device was expending the last of its stored energy, even as I watched, was made apparent by the slowing of several intricately fitted pieces; a few had stopped entirely, that had been in motion when I first had parted the concealing shirt, and had glimpsed what was revealed there.

The folly of my life was similarly revealed. There is much I am rueful about, and little that I am not – but until this moment, I had not condemned myself for my lack of understanding about my father's creations. I had thought them abominable, and worse, incomprehensible – so I had made but the slightest effort to pierce the veil in which their operations were wrapped. That study I had at last left to wits cleverer and more persistent than mine, of which there had seemed to be quite a few – for what harm was there in my disdain of these machines? Nothing depended upon my knowing how they worked…

Or so I had thought.

Now I crouched on a rocky ledge beside my son, smoke rising from the inferno which we had escaped – and I would live, and he would not. For that was the price of my ignorance.

I brought a hand down, and lightly touched the topmost brass workings, with a vain hope that some sudden inspiration might spring into my mind, and guide my fingertips to the necessary spot, where they would move of themselves on their revivifying errand...

That did not happen.

The boy took pity on me; he even smiled, or as much as he was able, with what little strength remained within him.

"It's all right," he said. "You came for me. That's what... I wanted..."

His eyes closed. I stayed beside him, for what seemed a longer time than had been required to ascend here. And then for a while more, after every slightest ticking and whir had ceased.

I stood up; though I might as well have stayed where I was, for all that the world beyond offered by way of comfort. With leaden footstep, as though I were the machine now, I made my way up the sloping path; grasping the crater's ragged edge, I pushed myself stumbling out upon the surface–

And was met a blow that almost propelled me back the way I had climbed.

An object hard and weighty, and unexpected, struck me across the side of the head; I toppled to the ground, hands instinctively clawing at the damp soil to prevent a greater fall. Blood streaming from the corner of my brow, I looked up – standing above me was the Right Reverend Jamford, his gaze as maniacal as when I had watched him ranting at the edge of my late wife's grave.

Ranged about the man, in the blackened wastes of what had been the cemetery's overgrown foliage, were twitching figures, toppled onto their sides. The disjointed corpses of what had never been alive, the mechanical beasts that had roamed these grounds, had exhausted their false animation, and were even now decomposing to their unriveted elements. I had but a moment to glimpse what might have been the semblance of a lion or other fanged predator, writhing as the uncoiling mainspring burst from its guts, then shuddering to stillness. Close by careened the tottering form of the decapitated giraffe, engulfed in flame, stilt-like legs shearing apart at their knees.

"You meddling bastard, Dower!" One side of Jamford's garb was dark with crusted blood, and that arm hung uselessly – but with his other, he brandished what was evidently one of the rifles with which the More Loving Embrace's agents had pursued me. Its wooden stock was cracked, and its barrel bent useless, likely having been caught in the midst of the rocks and collapsing machinery far below. "Think you're so clever now?"

Surrounded by the dead and dying mechanisms closer by, he seemed the very image of some dark prophet of ruin, as he swung the improvised bludgeon at me again. The blow might well have rendered me senseless, but I evaded its impact by dodging onto my shoulder. Wiping the blood from my face with a forearm, I could discern him more clearly by the fiery glow of the pit only a few feet away. If his wild-eyed appearance, snowy hair disordered and expression twisted into a snarling grimace, had then been a mere pretence of madness, now it was without doubt genuine. He had still possessed enough cunning, however, to have lain in wait for me – in the process of making his own escape from the flame-engulfed factory, he must have spotted us labouring along the narrow path below him.

"And where's your son? Eh?" Grip tightened upon the rifle's twisted barrel, he raised the weapon above his head. "I had a bargain with that little bastard – and he turned out to be as much a conniver as his father."

I had recovered sufficiently from the blow that had so taken me by surprise, that I was capable of scrambling to my feet and launching myself at the shouting figure before he could attempt another – and more than self-defence prompted this action on my part; Jamford's sneering infamy about the dead child evoked my own angered fury. My hands seized about his throat, as the force of my charge staggered him backward.

Having brought my chest against his, any bludgeoning from the broken rifle was rendered ineffectual; he dropped the object at my back, electing to batter his fist against the side of my head and neck.

"But he's dead – isn't he?" Throttled by my grip, his face livid, he still managed to gasp out a few more words. "You never – could have saved him–" His face writhed even more demonic. "Or – anything else–"

A fragmented torso, the jointed spine and hindquarters of one of the mechanical beasts, dangling the flayed tatters of its pelt, still held enough spring-driven force to suddenly lurch upward from the ground. The angled shape struck hard against me, the impact partially breaking my hold upon Jamford – that reprieve allowed him to grapple as tightly onto me as I clenched him. Like wrestlers who had chosen to battle in a charnel house of smouldering iron, we swayed and stumbled, each intent on the other's demise.

Our entwined forms staggered toward the pit; I felt its welling heat at my back, the convulsive inferno turning the other's face into a reddened mask above me.

"You haven't – stopped – *anything*–" The strength of the demented surged within him, so that he was able to thrust me onto the crumbling edge. "The boy – he doesn't matter – there are other ways–" Jamford's voice was a strangled cry. "You'll see–"

In that, he was in error; I would not – nor would he.

From the man's whitened lips, I heard nothing more. Nor from anything else in this roaring, clattering world, from which for so great a time – perhaps from the beginning – I had longed to depart. With mingled shame and anger, I realized it had been but cowardice that had kept my hand from plunging a knife into the breast that most deserved it.

But where there is not courage, then desperate loss will suffice.

I ceased my straining resistance, that had kept the other from overwhelming me – but I tightened my hold, drawing him closer to myself. That small motion displaced his balance, and we fell together, into the pit and its leaping flames. To that certain death which had evaded me for so long, and which now – tumbling into the scouring fire and blinding light – I welcomed with all my silenced heart.